The Artfulness of Women

A Novel

Naomi Weiss

Published by Open Books

Interior design by Siva Ram Maganti

Cover image © Nejron Photo shutterstock.com/g/nejron

To

Rosie, Andrew, Bea and Mildred

Each generation will lift the fallen to their feet
and hold them as they learn to walk.
—*Gates of Prayer Hebrew Prayer Book*

Trouble in mind, I'm blue,
But I won't be blue always
Cause the sun's gonna' shine
In my back door someday.
—"Trouble in Mind" by Richard M. Jones

JANUARY 1941

Chapter One

Heir

Bayla Rothschild maneuvered herself to standing. With profound ignorance and a ferocious dread of childbirth, she aimed her body toward the bedroom door and waddled on bare swollen feet when a burst of warm liquid gushed down her legs causing an embarrassing flood on the Persian tree-of-life runner that covered the upstairs hallway. The past nine months had left her grotesque, misshapen, exposed, and stuffed. What consequences would her body inflict on her next? With the water drained out of her, she stood cemented in place. When her husband saw she was missing from their bed, she had already turned to stone.

She would never remember how he managed to get her dressed, coax her down the circular staircase, along the marble hallway, through the garage and into the roomy back seat of their blue Ford sedan.

Down the cobblestones of Beleaguered Hill's steep incline, past elegant homes lined up like picture postcards, their lawns silver-gray in dawn's winter frost, she dug her nails into the seat with one hand, and with the other, tried to steady herself.

"I don't know what to do," she shouted because no one had ever told her, and who could she ask when such things were rarely talked about? In wide-eyed panic she glanced back at the Victorian house at the top of the Hill, the maroon gables and dark blue tower.

"Grab hold," her husband yelled as they headed into the valley. He reached back with one arm, but the car swerved on to Main Street and she was thrown from his grasp as everyday places flew by: the Grocery, Five and Dime, Fletcher's Soda Parlour, Holiday's Music and on the last block, the Odeon Cinema.

Across the railroad tracks, past steel workers' row houses, beyond the Ohio and Chesapeake railcars loaded with newly-milled girders, early risers, who spotted the blue Ford sedan, plunged the town into such a flurry that phone lines were as pregnant with the news as the mother about to give birth.

"We saw them." "The Mister and Missus." "Flew down the hill." "The baby is about to be born." "An heir for Amory Lane!" "At last!"

The car screeched to a halt at the hospital's circular driveway where personnel in white uniforms were anxiously scurrying about. As the sky began to lighten, a squarely built matron elbowed her way through the crowd and opened the sedan's back door.

Sprawled across the backseat, her coat thrown open, her navy-blue maternity dress exposing a thigh, her hat flung elsewhere, Bayla extended one leg in a futile search for solid ground beneath her navy-blue oxford. Her success unlikely, two nurses reached into the car to pull her forward while a third rushed around the other side and pushed. An orderly raced over with a hospital bed and breathlessly cranked it upwards to meet the patient's buttocks. The moment she settled, an excruciating pain seared through her middle and she erupted with a three-octave roar.

Like infantry on the run, they whooshed her down a long corridor, into a harshly-lit room where she labored long and hard.

"Grab the bed posts," a nurse commanded. "Push. Push."

Bayla gripped the sides of the mattress. She tore at the sheets, clutched the white cotton blanket, and pounded the pillow behind her.

"Make believe you're a dive bomber like in the war," the nurse ordered. "Get those Germans. Push for France. For England. Push again."

"I can't. I can't."

"You must. You're having a baby."

Bayla drew in a slow, deep inhalation, and released a long rasping, "I'll get you for this, you bastard."

The nurse laughed. "Once the baby is in your arms, you'll forget."

Unaware if it was night or morning, or how many dawns had passed, on January 25, 1941, after some thirty-six hours, the doctor entered Bayla Rothchild's uterus with cranial forceps to deliver an eight-pound, five-ounce baby girl.

Her husband slept in the waiting room two nights in a row, praised her strength and courage and did his best to overlook how determined she was to ignore him. He knew the birth of their child had little to do with what she wanted most in the world.

She and her husband had never talked about a baby. They had talked about her career. She had a voice, not like a prize to be won, but a gift already given. Not measly or high-pitched, but a deep, soulful sound is what she had always imagined for herself. And luckily she had grown into a tall, heavyset young woman whose square jaw and wide cheekbones produced a singing voice that perfectly fit her expectations. Singing was her joy, her self-worth, her fatal flaw, her passion, her dream. Her promise to herself. And in its place—motherhood. As if that were the best she could do.

When Bayla opened her eyes she was lying on a steel-hard gurney in a dark, cold place that echoed its own silence. Her insides felt so stretched, she might as well have squeezed Pittsmill's public library building from between her legs. Suddenly a slab of light, and a voice.

"You're in recovery, dear. Time to tinkle." The nurse pushed an icy metal bed pan under her bottom. "Be a good girl now," she said then disappeared, taking the light with her.

Certain nothing would *ever again* go in or out of anyplace *down there*, Bayla tried to inch herself off the thing, but the shrill clang when it struck the floor startled her, like a fitful awakening. *What am I going to do with a child?* "Love it and care for it," her husband had said.

But maternal love, how and where would she find it? She was frightened to be a mother, frightened she might treat the child the way her mother had treated her. And what if in the future, who could predict it, this infant might one day do to her what she had done, what she had to do given her mother's rages, her mind here, then gone? Where were the guarantees for such things never happening?

"Childhood," she said aloud, as if she'd had one.

She could still picture men lining up at soup kitchens during the Depression, and hear her mother telling her she had to quit school, the one place she felt like somebody. She was fourteen years old, her second year at New York City's Hebrew Technical School for Girls. When she objected, "They should take a *meshugeneh* from the asylum and put you in his place," her mother yelled, called her a *dumbkopf*. Who else could support them in their two-room, third floor walk-up, on 236 East 89th Street, a toilet down the hall, shared with four other families? Didn't she realize an *einhoreh* was pestering their lives, jeering at what little they had?

Her mother's arthritic knees and stiff nubby fingers forced her to quit working at the millinery shop on Rivington Street. Now she sewed at home in a wheelchair donated by the Hebrew Immigration Aid Society; beautiful hats for fancy ladies, piecework, that barely paid enough to put food on the table.

And her father, who held her as no father ever held or loved a child, had kissed her good night, and walked out. She was seven years old.

I am looking for my husband, Yosef Yosefa Szabo, ironworker, 36 years old, small, dark mole on right brow. He left me with our young daughter. Whoever sees or knows of him take mercy on us. Words dictated by her mother, written in Bayla's childish hand on a scrap of paper, sat for weeks on the kitchen counter. But so shameful to admit, "You can't send it," her mother said. She meant to the column that reported runaway men in the *Forverts*, the Jewish daily newspaper. She cursed the fates instead, adding hours to her work pinning, cutting, and sewing under a dim bulb.

By the time Bayla was fifteen, with one year left to graduate, she knocked on doors after school in search of work: "I saw your ad.... I'm experienced in... I'll be the best...." When she returned home, she'd gather her dolls from the fire escape outside the kitchen window, where she had placed them each morning for fresh air and sunshine, dolls she'd fabricated from old socks, embroidered their faces, their outfits from her mother's remnants scattered on the floor. At bedtime, she'd place them on the cot where she slept too close to her mother, and sing them the song of Hungarian girl's names that her father had taught, names she gave her dolls: Arish, Bidi, Shari, Marishki, Rosalli, Ella, Bella, Utzi, Carolina.

When the day came to tell the principal that she'd found a job, she walked slow and begrudging along the gray corridors. At the large metal double doors that would never again welcome her each morning, the slightest push would not lead to her future, as her mother had promised, but to the end of her life. Never again would a teacher commend her smocking and embroidery, her grasp of a Willa Cather novel or an Edna St. Vincent Millay poem. Never again would she jump Double Dutch at recess, or have her music teacher praise her singing "Flow Gently Sweet Afton." Like someone packing a suitcase, Bayla stuffed inside herself everything she could about her years at school. She would become *not* a seamstress, the fancy word on the "wanted" sign outside Goldmacher's door, in the garment district, on Tenth Avenue and 33rd Street, but an operator who sewed outfits that turned people into what they did: assembly-line workers, prisoners, zookeepers, garbage men.

Et va zoh. This is how it must be, she heard her father say in Hungarian. Not wanting to disappoint him even then, she brushed away tears with her forearm, bit her lip, and walked into the harsh glare of city streets.

The time reserved for her growing up fizzled like chicken fat in a heated fry pan. It was winter, 1930. The worst of the Depression.

Bayla longed for her past to leave her in peace. Instead it bullied and tormented her, as if her life weren't made up of new events, but only old ones lining up for another turn. How could she care for and nourish a newborn when her own childhood was as alive as the baby she had not yet held in her arms?

Where *was* her child? Maybe she had delivered a baby with too many arms and legs, or not enough fingers and toes. One girl in her school wore a normal shoe on one foot and a monstrous, heavy black one on the other. Perhaps her daughter would end up with the same, or worse. Much worse.

"Nurse. Nurse." Bayla tried to raise herself up, but everything whirled around her. She eased back onto the gurney as years of hopes and expectations slipped from her grasp. Despite months of rehearsing for her debut, perfecting her songs, she would end up as colorless and ordinary as Pittsmill, Pennsylvania's forever-cloudy skies. Would being a mother help her forget everything that motherhood had forced her to give up?

When Bayla opened her eyes again it was to framed pictures, a private bathroom, spotless white towels. Those who ministered to the suffering of birthing mothers had moved her secretly at some mysterious hour.

"I prefer the ward," she had told her husband's family. "Remember who you are, living with us, in this town," they said. The problem was she couldn't forget. Didn't she precisely remember when she first arrived that winter's day, four years ago, when she still believed in her future, and carried few worldly possessions? Twenty-two years old, a newlywed, her husband at her side. No matter how often he had described it during their courtship, no matter how often her thoughts had lured her to it, she had never seen a Queen Anne Victorian mansion. Much less a house with its own name, *Amory Lane*, etched into a bronze plaque set into the ground under the broad limbs of an ancient maple tree.

If she were a different person, the right words to express her good fortune would have lined up in her mouth. Instead, from the place inside her head that spoke to her when she didn't want it to, she heard the townsfolk already gossiping. How clumsy and awkward she was, as she glanced with suspicion, or disdain at her new surroundings? They mistook her inexperience for shyness, her unworldliness for stupidity, equated her lack of education with not wanting to learn, this person who had captured Amory Lane's most eligible bachelor.

"Now you will become part of Amory Lane, and it will become part of you," her husband had said and lovingly took her hand, but she had no idea how to prove him right. How long until his family would realize she didn't belong, and throw her out? The thought was as damning then, but more so now when they would expect her to be a perfect parent.

Sounds of women in the wards *kvetching* and puking echoed from down the hall. Since she was a child, no one had to tell her the difference between, "Nobody Knows You When You're Down and Out," and "I'm Sitting on Top of The World," but wasn't she still one of them? Needy. Wanting. Fighting for what she wanted in life, battling the wretched circumstances that brought her into it?

Two nurses in starched white uniforms suddenly bounded into her room. "Here she is, dearie. Hold her close. Nice and steady. Her head up." They giggled and tiptoed out.

Bayla looked down at the pink package they had placed ever so delicately into her arms. A tiny hand freed itself and flailed fiercely. Legs, bound tightly, began to thump erratically. Crooked, open-mouthed yawns, high-pitched squeaks, and tight squints melded into broad, wide-eyed stares, frightening and strange. She reached for the bottle on the nightstand and eased the nipple between the newborn's lips, hoping not to douse or suffocate the creature. She observed the tightly-closed eyes, the automatic sucking, the fierce determination for nourishment, and she so woefully ignorant.

When the milk disappeared, she withdrew the bottle with quiet concentration, and caressed the soft, blond fuzz on the infant's head. Drawn by a bond she never knew existed, she inhaled the child's delicious scent, allowed the warmth of her little body to enter her own. "My daughter," she whispered.

"Hush little baby don't say a word, Mama's 'gonna buy you a mocking bird."

Why this dreadful tug of war? One moment overcome with unfamiliar emotions that pulled her toward the child with its sweet vulnerability. Seconds later, thoughts of forsaking the stage, the spotlight, the applause. What good were lullabies?

Maybe there was a way. Performing and motherhood. Why not? Endure the shame, fingers pointing, tongues wagging that she had a child only to neglect it. For her own selfish pursuits. That she had no respect for motherhood. For her husband and his family's reputation.

Bayla bent her body toward the newborn as if it were a refuge from the shame of her thoughts. Nurses on the floor deepened their vigil.

"Check on her again." "She's terribly silent." "Morose."

How could they know that inside her long silences and blank stares Bayla was weighing her destiny? How had she come so far off course? How tempted? How deceived? Led by what?

Back when she knew what she was about, and what she was after, all the talk was about her. And why shouldn't it be? Such raves she received when she performed.

"Bring 'dem melons ova' here!" "Sing it to me, hot mamma!" "Put your lovely body next to mine."

To hear them even now in her hospital bed. Men lined up on Manhattan's West Side streets back then. They packed the place to standing room only, and when she appeared in the spotlight, the ruckus and shouts, the yearning for her that night, and for each one after that, confirmed with the regularity of a downbeat in a four-beat bar how much she was loved and desired.

AUGUST 1924 – JANUARY 1937

Chapter Two

Blues Diva

Crazy for Tin Pan Alley songs, and Broadway musicals, blues were Bayla's favorite. Maybe their wail and whine penetrated flimsy walls in their tenement building on East 89th Street. Or during an Augusts' stifling heat the sounds oozed out of a radio from an open window as she sat on the front stoop. Blues came to her gentle and easy with a certainty in their lingering that left her yearning for more. Blues taught her about someone to love, and what no one talked about, and things she didn't understand. Despite all she never had, the smooth, easy rhythms of the blues comforted her. No one taught her to want, she just always did.

By the time she was nine years old, Bayla memorized blues songs from books at the Yorkville branch of the New York Public Library. Then she'd head to a dimly-lit record store tucked under the Second Avenue El where she'd place an Okeh, Decca, Black Swan, Paramount or Columbia label beneath the silver, horn-shaped arm from the wind-up Victrola, lean against the floor-to-ceiling shelves jammed with dusty 78 rpm records in brown paper covers, close her eyes and let the sounds—a trombone's groan; a clarinet's tears, a trumpet's woes—slip into her soul. She was born to it, this thing that had chosen her without thought, like a habit.

Victoria Spivey, Ida Cox, Ma Rainey, Mamie Smith, Bertha

"Chippie" Hill. Minus notes on a staff, or words of instruction, by the time she was twelve, she could imitate them all—their tones, their phrases, their styles. Like Bessie Smith, Empress of the Blues, one day she too would preside over a kingdom where people would pay money to hear her sing. She was building her stairway to the stars.

"Who sings such music?" her mother asked when Bayla practiced at home.

"Colored women, Mamma. From down South."

"Thanks be to God, to H'a Schem, who welcomes everyone to this country."

"Yes, Mamma. Strangers. Immigrants like us, all shapes and sizes and colors. A regular melting pot in New York City. A single Jewish girl, her mother would say, from Hungary to here without a word of English.

So much for her thoughts as she crouched over her sewing machine at Goldmacher's remembering her first day, standing on the sidewalk outside.

"*A loch in kop*. There's a hole in your head? What are you waiting for?" she heard her mother's Yiddish taunts. "It's a job. Go in already. Go!"

Up eight cement steps, through a short hallway, she stepped into a large hot room reeking of sweat. Girls, maybe a hundred, each at a sewing machine, flexing their feet on the broad, black iron pedal, causing ear piercing, sporadic monotones that displaced the air, and any chance to breathe.

A plump middle-aged woman, her dark hair pulled into a tight bun, beckoned Bayla into a tiny office. "I'm the Forelady, Mrs. Harmenschtein," she shouted above the drone. "You're due 8 a.m. sharp. Lunch twenty minutes. No gum chewing. If you're late, we dock your pay." Bayla signed her name, and followed the lady along the factory floor between two long aisles of jutting elbows. When a new girl arrived at her school, the teacher would introduce her, but here, no one moved. Not one eye in her direction. The discipline made her shiver.

At the last seat in the last row, Mrs. Harmenschtein pointed at an empty machine, the word "Singer" in peeling gold letters. "Your place," she said.

The next morning clutching a meager lunch wrested from meager means, two pieces of bread with jelly, or toast and hard cheese, Bayla tried not to count the steps. One, two, she would begin. Other times, fifteen or twenty, forty-nine or one hundred until she reached the end, or the beginning of her row, her seat, her destiny, her doom. What did it matter? In less than a month thoughts of school faded then disappeared entirely.

Bayla sewed along with the others until her feet began to burn each time she pressed the black iron pedal. She sewed when the flames grabbed her ankles, and the heat rose to her thighs. She sewed when newspapers proclaimed "Unemployment Passes 4 Million." Three years of her life she sewed while Mamie Smith and Ida Cox toured the South, Alberta Hunter appeared in *Show Boat*, Victoria Spivey was in movies, and Bessie Smith had bottom billing at the Apollo. Like them, she too started out poor, young, and alone. Like them, she knew her turn would come.

While the nation was singing "Keep Your Sunny Side Up," and "Who's Afraid of the Big Bad Wolf" to drive away the gloom of the Depression, Bayla eased her unfulfilled longings beyond the steps that led to Goldmacher's, by reliving memories of her father. Yosef Yosefa was a stocky ironworker with strong hands, who fashioned shiny brass mailboxes for fancy New York City apartment lobbies. Inside her head, she'd hear his words over and again: "When the wet nurse handed you to me, *a brucha fon himmel*, I said. My beautiful child. We'll call you Bayaleh." How he hugged and caressed her, his hands covering her body, and if she embellished what he said, people have done worse.

December 1933. Prohibition ended and liquor flowed from every spigot and open bottle in New York City's bars, restaurants, and cocktail lounges. Heading home one night on the cross-town bus, Bayla spotted a sign on the double doors of The Saloon, on Tenth Avenue and 48th Street. "Performer Wanted," it said. New Yorkers shielding themselves from the wind that blew off the river missed those words entirely, but for her they lit up like the lights on the Loews 96th Street marquee. *She was the performer they wanted.* And why not? She had prepared, a *bissel* here, a *bissel* there, her mother would say, if she knew.

On empty boarded-up lots on 57th Street, Bayla studied newsprint advertisements of Ma Raney bending over the stage messing about with the audience. Then Bessie Smith, hands on hips, legs apart, her head thrown back. At Harlem's Cotton Club billboards on 142nd Street, she practiced poses of sultry Lena Horne, seductive, lady-like Adelaide Hall, charming Ella Fitzgerald, enticing Dorothy Dandridge. And in Woolworths' Five and Dime, she thumbed through song sheets with sketches of how fancy ladies dressed.

Given her voice and choice of song, Bayla was certain she had everything she needed to be a success on stage, but where would she find the courage to walk into The Saloon, a God-forsaken place filled with men, in the part of town called Hell's Kitchen, and at her age, only 18? Her mother would say a prayer at Tikvah Shalom, the Orthodox synagogue on East 91st Street, for a daughter who would commit such a *shandeh*. A shame. A disgrace.

But each night, before sleep, Bayla pictured herself walking through the same doors as those dock workers, Irish gangs, laborers, mobsters, policemen. She imagined who she would approach, the questions to ask, what to say. Like stacks of newspapers tied together at corner newsstands, a day came when she had bundled enough courage inside herself. She was born in turbulent times, her mother told her. Risks had to be taken.

Without a turn of her head, or a sideways glance, on an early Saturday morning, she walked through The Saloon's double doors to the man behind the bar, who had few to serve at that time.

"Where's the owner?" she asked.

"Mr. Grady? He's over there." The bartender nodded toward the far end making a clicking sound with his tongue. "He's a powerful gadabout, that man. Watch yourself."

Mr. Grady was broad, his face red, a dark suit tight over his bulging middle. Of course. Irish. *Shikers.* Lovers of drink. Her mother had taught her plenty about people—Italian and Jewish girls were *zaftig*. Polish and Hungarians were best cooks. German women had strong arms. Jewish men made good husbands.

"With me on stage, you'll make money," she pushed herself to say, her eyes burning into his, and she broke into "St. Louis woman, with her diamond rings, stole that man of mine, by her apron strings."

"You wear something besides this?" Mr. Grady asked, easing his hand across her buttocks beneath her worn navy ankle-length skirt while she stood frozen in place.

"I have a beautiful costume," she managed to say. She had pieced it together at night while her mother slept, choosing remnants from her mother's work: a gold lamé band, a silk bow, a piece of black fringe, a feather. From pennies saved, she added a yard of black sateen. All of it hidden inside a dresser drawer, God forbid her mother should find out.

"And on stage, you know what you gotta do?"

"I've known since I was a child."

He ran his chubby index finger down the side of her face. "You're young and attractive, tall, not overblown, but meaty. A damn sight better than those middle-aged floozies with painted faces who show up."

The Saloon was a respectable drinking establishment, he said, not a dive like those other dirty, stinking, roach-and rat-infested Irish pubs on the East Side. He gestured to the mirrored wall that reflected the dark, highly polished wooden bar, the black and white floor tiles, the dome lamps that hung from the high ceiling casting 'a romantic glow,' he said. "Come back Friday and Saturday. Eight o'clock." He edged close to her ear, his eyes narrowing. "I'll give 'ya two twenty-minute sets both nights. See how ya' do."

Her first audition. A success.

Word spread. Having left the ranks of speakeasy, men pushed their way inside The Saloon, guzzling beer and whiskey, nervous and impatient, as they squeezed into tight spaces around the stage. When the piano man in rolled up shirt sleeves struck a few bluesy refrains on the upright, the stomping, whistling and clapping grew louder.

"Are you ready, gentlemen?" Mr. Grady shouted into the microphone. "Our blues diva." Bayla liked that he called her that.

"Bring her out, for Christ's sake."

"Where is she, 'ya bum?"

"Sing it for this!" a husky sailor shouted and grabbed his crotch.

A spotlight snapped on. With one foot on a chair, her arm resting on her thigh, Bayla stared over their heads. Aloof. Tantalizing. The men fell silent. As she eased her foot to the floor and stood, a short black skirt revealed lacy garters hooked to seamed stockings that exposed her fleshy thighs; a tight, navy, scoop-necked blouse held her copious breasts as a demitasse might hold an exuberant cappuccino; gold patent-leather pumps cradled her pudgy feet; a gold band around her head, a feather angled to one side, like Bessie Smith.

She sashayed to the edge of the stage in time to the moody piano rhythm, a sway, a dip, a hike in her hips. When she sensed the right moment, she inhaled slowly, flattened her stomach, expanded her bosom and allowed her thick, rich, soulful tones to drift across the room like cigarette smoke.

During the day, sewing in a sweatshop, life's burdens weighed Bayla down. Who did she have to share them with? But at night, in front of a live audience, as she clenched her deep auburn hair, swished it around her neck and shoulders, and eased her body to the blues, the stage with its restorative powers freed her from the grip that held her dreams and fantasies in check.

As she soothed the crowd's longings and caressed their desires, her heartaches and emotions ran rampant.

When I was young, nothing but a child, You men tried to drive me wild.
My Mama says I'm reckless, my Daddy says I'm wild.

She heated up the room provoking the audience to let loose spare change, a sailor's cap, carnal appetites.

Daaaaaaaaaaaaaady, Mamma wants some huggin.'
Hi 'ya, Pretty Papa, Mamma wants some lovin' right now.

She favored sexually-charged numbers: "Anybody Want To Eat My Cabbage?", "Call Me When Your Drawers Are Down," or "My Hard, Straight Handy Man." Though she had never been on a date with a man, much less had anyone offer himself as a suitor, it didn't matter that she didn't understand the inferences in the lyrics. On stage, in the spotlight, Bayla Szabo, the factory girl, became what every man in the audience wanted her to be.

No matter how little they had, or where they were born, or how hard they worked, she opened her audience up to possibilities. Dreams and desires were within their reach. That was her gift, and she gave it without knowing.

"Again you're going out? *Oi gotteniu*. Again by myself? My daughter, the runaround."

They had finished supper—sauerkraut soup with potatoes and caraway seeds, and a thick bean cholent. On the chipped, white metal table where they ate, the cigar box Bayla had plucked from a street-side garbage pail was in place. Filled with makeup paid for by pinching pennies, she withdrew a small, hand-held mirror, twirled an edge of tissue, and dabbed green powder on her lids to enhance her blue eyes. With her index finger she spread Princess Pat rouge on her high cheekbones. At the almost straight lines of her lips, she reworked Tangee's Strawberry lipstick, securing a delicate pout.

Her mother watched every move, her eyes darting, her face expressionless, as if Bayla didn't know her mother's thoughts that night were darker than usual.

"I go to sing, Mamma, in a club frequented by gentlemen. It helps pays the rent."

"Sing! You parade yourself. In the streets."

Whatever nonsense her mother dreamed up about her daughter's nighttime excursions, Bayla had taught herself to ignore. "My ambition will get us out of the tenements. You'll see." She powder-puffed her face from her forehead to her chin. "First chance I get."

At a speed Bayla never would have imagined, her mother swept her arms across the table, scattering her daughter's applied beauty to the worn linoleum floor. "Where you go these nights, someone could kill you, and I would be left here alone. And you talk of ambition. *Te, a gyerekeid, az unokaid, es minden leszarmazottad legyetek karhozottak az orokkevalosagig*. You and your children and your children's children will be doomed. *Dest liggin in bluter*. You'll lay in the mud. And I have said it so!"

Bayla rose from her chair, her body trembling. She gripped the edge of the kitchen table, and stared at her mother. Wisps of loose gray hair dangled from the bun her arthritic fingers still managed to arrange at the back of her head. Her blue-flowered housecoat, one of two Bayla dressed her in each morning, parts of it as threadbare as her mother's pleasant memories—the blue Danube, the Statue of Liberty, the Travelers' Aid lady who helped her through Ellis Island.

"I left school at fifteen to support us, working on a factory floor, and you curse me in Hungarian and Yiddish? You think a mother's curses are easy to forget? They ring in my ears, wake me at night. I'll get us out of here despite your curses."

"Do you know why they sent me from my home in Budapest to travel at fifteen alone, two weeks in steerage, sick to my stomach, to come to America?"

Bayla knew every word, able to imitate precisely her mother's accent and intonations about the watered-down milk that left her bones weak, the lack of oranges that rotted her teeth, the poverty, and no work, and terrible treatment of Jews. She knew her mother had come to find a husband whose money would provide tickets to bring her family from the Old Country.

"I came to marry a man who left us. Who ran off to who knows where?"

Bayla knew his leaving was her fault. Her childish disobedience. Her refusing to give in to his wishes, to let him undress her for bed, the two of them alone in the room, her strong will, displeasing him who loved her more than anything, had sent him away.

"I lived in a boarding house, slept in the same bed used by night workers. For that I came? And for a wheelchair? To be a burden to you?" Her mother began to whimper, the sounds that drew Bayla to her side.

"No need to cry. Who's here for you? Your daughter, Bayeleh. Your only child, and Mrs. Silverman, your friend from across the hall. She has the key. You won't be alone. Come. It's Friday night. Time for Shabbos." Bayla removed a white Shabbos candle from a small box on a kitchen shelf. Her mother heated the bottom of the candle with a match, melded it onto the top of an empty jelly jar. She covered her head with a small white cloth, closed her eyes and circled her hands three times over the flame. *"Baruch atah adonay, eloheynu meleh ha'olam. . ."*

"Good Shabbos, Mamma."

"God Shabbos, my *sheinah kindt*. You remember our Saturday mornings? The services at Tikvah Shalom?"

"Yes, Mamma, and at Rosh Hashanah, the challah we ate, and wishes for a *zissen yur*."

"To have such a synagogue. It's a *machiah*. Now go where you go. Maybe by a miracle *Hashem* will find you a rich man. A *choshever mensch*. And one day we'll have money to light two candles on Friday, as it should be. *Oi, gottenu* . I shouldn't say such things. *Isht forgessen*. The fates—"

"Again, the fates?" If you were too happy, you would attract an *einhoreh*. If you tried to better yourself, the fates would know, and bad luck would follow. There was so little left to speak about, or question. So little left to enjoy. Even thoughts had to be censored. The fates could divine those as well. Wherever she turned, the fates would be looking or threatening, ready to sabotage whatever she longed for, whatever little she was able to accomplish. She had to remain wary, be on the lookout, suspect them, bargain, and negotiate with them. Her mother had taught her plenty from the Old Country.

With her mother bedded for the night, Bayla searched on her

hands and knees among the dirt and grime on the kitchen floor for her scattered makeup. A final glimpse in her hand-held mirror showed her more striking than beautiful—less a Jean Harlow, more a Mae West.

"One day my mother will know what her daughter is made of," she said aloud inside the dank-smelling stairwell on her way out over the sound of an infant's cry.

Chapter Three
Free Dance

As if she would find riches or happiness there, Bayla stole seconds from her sewing machine to search among hastily scribbled notices, requests and announcements, pinned or pasted, for companions, live-in boarders, part-time jobs, items wanted or for sale that filled the wall in Goldmacher's entranceway:

> *Live Music. Free Dance. Friday night. October 10, 1935, 7:30 p.m. United Socialist Workers' Party. Lexington Avenue and 105th Street. Paderevski Hall.*

Though she didn't know a foxtrot from a waltz or a lindy hop, where was the harm? "Don't I deserve an adventure?" she asked herself as if it weren't a question, and with live music. From East 89th Street it was an easy walk, and not to spend for a bus was a good sign. If she took that night off from The Saloon, who was to say her big break wasn't waiting for her at Paderevski Hall? Maybe not a rich man or a *choshever mensch*, like her mother had said, but someone taken by her looks and stature would engage her in conversation, offer her a chance to sing in a nightclub, and in no time she would be famous.

One week later, she headed uptown, keeping close to the tenements. At that hour absent was the pretzel man twisting, salting and roasting dough; the knife grinder with razors and scissors hunched over his wheel; the junk dealer rattling tin pans; the old man selling used clothes shouting, "Buy! Cash! Buy!" the fruit seller juggling oranges and grapefruits; the elderly couple whose sugar-roasted peanuts, two cents a bag, wafted the scent of vanilla as far as 91st Street.

A glimpse in Rexall's Drugstore window made her ashamed for her two-dollar navy coat from Goodwill purchased eight winters ago. No better were the garments beneath it: a brown ankle-length skirt topped with a long-sleeved white cotton blouse buttoned in the back, a bit of lace trim on the collar clipped from her mother's dress. What use did her mother have for decoration? She pulled her brown felt cloche from Woolworth's tight to her face. "Best not to be accosted by a fan tonight," she told herself, as if such a thing had happened. Past German and Hungarian restaurants, Ruppert's Brewery and Loew's 96th Street featuring Garbo in *Grand Hotel,* commerce and crowds thinned beneath the roar of the El. When an October wind-gust bristled, she plodded into it, the broad, flat heels of her shoes sounding heavy on the empty side streets. Streetlamps at the beginning and end of each block draped her solitary figure in light. She barely noticed. She was picturing herself a Paulette Goddard, hand-in-hand with Charlie Chaplin, strolling into the rural sunset at the end of *Modern Times*.

Paderevski Hall. Known for wedding receptions, amateur entertainment, union meetings, and gatherings of Jewish immigrants, like her father, who would spend an evening there to talk freely among men friends about the new life that welcomed them. Beyond a short hall, she entered a large room where musicians, winds and drums, were setting up. On the walls were large posters in bold reds, blues, and blacks, their messages strange: *Press On for the Common Good. Join The Workers' Way. Sign Up For The Red Stars.* She wrested a folding chair from a stack against a wall, placed it near the stage, and draped her coat over the back. Crossing her right leg over her left, she fluffed her hair, and turned her body so her best side, the left side, faced members and friends of the United Socialist Worker's Party: Chatty girls dressed informally like her. Men in dark pea jackets.

Women in stylish form-fitting coats with fur-trimmed collars and cuffs accompanied by suitors in topcoats. She tried not to stare at them for wondering what it would be like: a man at her side.

While everyone gathered around a table of refreshments at the back of the large room, she remained poised up front and alone. Her navy coat, clumsily draped over the chair, was driving suitors away. She grabbed the coat, replaced the chair, and headed to the portable clothes rack she had overlooked in the vestibule. On her return, captivated by the lively um-pah-pah rhythm of "The Beer Barrel Polka" bellowed by an accordion, joined by a trumpet, clarinet and drums, she couldn't resist a skip and a dip, sashaying to the beat, as dancers took to the floor. She smiled at a man who caught her eye, and moved in his direction when something caught under her right foot. In trying to get free, she lurched forward, fell, then skidded through the crowd in a seated position, coming to a halt when her shoes broke through the purple crepe paper tacked around the bottom of the stage.

Everything stopped. No one breathed. All eyes were on her, a clumsy creature, her skirt rolled above her knees, a rip in the thigh of one stocking. How could she erase the shame? She wouldn't tolerate pity.

There was a rustle. A low murmur. Footsteps.

"May I help?" He extended his hand and a gentle voice. "Someone always falls when we wax the floor."

Bayla took a breath, afraid to face whoever had come to her aid. "I'm a performer," she said, uncertain why she did.

"Well, then, performers belong on their feet." They do, she thought. They do. She reached out with one arm and felt him take hold of her hand until she was on her feet.

He was handsome, somewhat taller than she, with dark brown wavy hair, a single curl about to drape on his forehead, a tweed sweater over broad shoulders, gray slacks. Her girlfriends at work might call him dapper, though she wasn't quite sure what that meant. The little she knew about how men and women interacted came from *Tess of the d'Urbervilles, The Heiress, Ethan Frome,* the library's romance novel section, or from a Garbo, Dietrich or Mae West movie at the Loews, when she had the money.

Bayla straightened her clothes, the buzz inside Paderevski Hall resumed, and as the band began to play, "that's 'Paper Moon,' Ella Fitzgerald's latest hit." Bayla raised her voice over the music while this stranger, this man, set up two chairs; a private corner of their own.

"Sit. Sit," he commanded, and leaned forward. Facing her. "So what do you perform?"

"I sing. Started when I was eighteen, two years already at The Saloon. 48th and Tenth. I'm quite popular." So many words out of her mouth. And him so close she could feel the warmth of his body.

"Well, besides being your hero, I'm a fabric salesman," he said with a laugh, "at the garment center."

She imagined him walking down Seventh Avenue on his way to clients, side – stepping men unloading trucks, past interns pushing racks of new fashions. They would have that in common, but why admit to working in a factory when he already pictured her a star?

He had a clean manly scent like her father, on the Sabbath, when he still lived with them, and wrapped himself in his white silk tallis from the Old Country.

"So tell me, what do you sing? 'Blue Moon.' 'Let Me Call You Sweetheart'?"

Bayla smiled, pleased that he knew pop music. "Tin Pan Alley songs. Gershwin, Cole Porter. Broadway musicals, but blues are my favorite."

"The stuff they sing in Harlem? You're trying to impress me? A white woman singing the blues? Well, in New York it is mostly acceptable, but elsewhere, outside of here, you couldn't do that."

"Anyone anywhere can sing the blues. If you don't have money, or someone to love, or you're sick and can't find work or—"

"You say that with such....*chutzpah*. But you're right. Our families, Jewish immigrants, left the Old Country, came here for a better life. In America, we're socially – minded. Public housing on the Lower East side. Mr. Astor providing tenements for the homeless. Underneath our skin we're all alike. White, black, yellow, or green. Right?"

"Yes," Bayla smiled, uncertain about what he wanted to hear. What she should say next.

"But singing the blues during the Depression?" he said as if it were a question. "Someone as striking as you should have hordes of men beating down your door."

"Men at my door? Oh, no. I live with my mother." She raised her voice as couples rushed to the floor for the Lindy Hop.

"Protected and cared for by a loving parent," he said leaning closer to her. "I've been known to date models, loose women, who share expensive two-bedroom apartments on the West Side, and lure men like me into their clutches."

Unaccustomed to such talk, Bayla shifted uncomfortably in her chair.

"You're a puzzle," he said. "I can't decide if your strength belies your innocence, which would make you an easy conquest, or if your innocence belies your strength, which appeals to me even more." He ran his fingers though his hair and studied her, as if she were something to buy, or own. Her Jewish immigrant friends at Goldmacher's would say he's deciding how far he can go with you. Where would he *go* with her? On a bus? A taxi? To where? The girls always laughed at the little she knew about what a man and woman do together.

"Maybe you've come here tonight to fool us," he said, moving closer still.

"What do you mean, 'fool'?"

"Some of us are....shhhh," he placed his finger on his lips, "Communists, because of, you know, how it was over there. Either rich or very poor. Communists believe everyone should rise together—like the tide."

Politics. Though she sometimes skimmed the headlines at newsstands on the way to work, Bayla wouldn't dare say a word about what she knew so little about.

"Maybe you're Austrian or Russian sent by enemies of the United States to spy on us."

Bayla threw back her head and laughed, momentarily forgetting where she lived and worked.

"I'm Hungarian, and not a spy," she said. What fun, flirting, she thought, as if she knew how.

"Our soccer team is The Red Stars." He reached down, and pulled up his trouser cuff, revealing a hairy, muscular leg, and punched his calf with a fist. "Maybe you'd like to come see me kick some goals next Sunday at Central Park." She felt her cheeks heating up. He lowered his cuff. "But before I get any hotter under the collar, do you want something to drink?"

"Dr. Brown's celery soda."

"Don't go away."

She casually brushed leftover dust from the back of her skirt, unconcerned by a couple who pointed her out for a quick laugh, too taken with this man who returned with a drink he paid for, like a gift. Unsure of what was happening, embarrassed, and uncertain what to do, "ask for a sign," she heard her mother say. So she did, and just like that, the lights dimmed, and the romance of Jerome Kern's "The Way You Look Tonight," captivated her.

His eyes entreating, the song already persuasive, "Would you like to dance?" he asked. Without knowing the steps, and never having been inside a man's arms, she backed away from him, but he reached out. His hand encircling hers was warm as he guided her slowly toward himself. His shoulder, when she touched it, so sturdy and broad. A slight pressure against her back tightened the space between them so that her breasts, those private parts of herself, gave way against his sturdy chest. Men gawking at her in The Saloon was no comparison. She felt disoriented, yet strangely exhilarated.

"You haven't told me your name."

"It's Bayla. Bayla Szabo."

"Ah yes, Hungarian. With what's going on over there, Hitler *der fuhrer. Deutschland uber alles*. And Germany's new air force. The Luftwaffe. Aren't you worried? But perhaps news reports aren't very interesting for women. How about I tell you my name?"

"Your name?" Bayla was so focused on coordinating her feet, trying not to say the wrong thing, and behaving in a way that was proper to a man whose arms were wrapped around her, she forgot he might have one.

"It's Mordechai Isadore. My mother, God bless her, named me." Her husky, robust laugh seemed to delight him. "Come closer and I'll tell you what my best friends call me. That's it. Closer still. Good. Now turn your head. Excellent." He placed his mouth on her ear, making that part of her body his own. "My friends call me Izzy."

His masculine whisper, his warm moist lips resonating on her earlobe sent titillating sensations down the back of her head to somewhere between her legs. She let the feeling linger until it compelled her to try the same with him. But in her eagerness to place her lips on his ear, she stepped on the little toe of his right foot, causing him to tip backwards in pain. She grabbed his lapels and pulled him to straight, whereupon he drew her into a spin tight enough for her to feel beneath the fabric of his trousers something hard between his legs.

"Bayla Szabo. My dear Bayla. You're an enormously wonderful woman, or should I say a wonderfully enormous one?"

Who had ever spoken to her using so many splendid words in a row?

Chapter Four

The First Time He Saw Her Perform

How often Bayla pressured him to tell her the story he fashioned, the words he chose to express his excitement, the way he described her on stage. "Tell me, again," she'd say, "tell me," and he did, reluctant though he was to reveal his true feelings until they knew one another better. He usually began with, "it was cold and damp by the river, when I got off the cross-town bus. I wore my new navy-blue slacks and a blue pin-striped shirt, but was I ready for a full-time girlfriend? To be tied down? Such serious thoughts after meeting you only once.

"On Broadway, the Alvin Theatre featured Gershwin's *Porgy and Bess*. Opening night. Crowds dressed to the nines. At Eleventh and 47th, I saw the sign over the double doors like you said. I pushed my way toward the stage, through the crowd, the cigar and cigarette smoke. When the piano man struck a few notes, the shouting and clapping, feet stamping and you, in the spotlight. So ravishing. So enticing. As a gentleman, I held back admitting certain things. I was careful not to push you away. But now, I can confess, when you began to move to the music, your fingers across your hips, your buttocks, your palms over your bosom, I wished those hands were mine. I imagined how you would move in bed, and when you sang, your voice, smooth and deep, your words so expressive. Those men who screamed lewd, crass things. I felt exactly the way they did. 'I know her,' I wanted to shout. For an ordinary salesman like me to attract someone like you. I couldn't believe my luck. What was behind me? A pillar? A wall? I was grateful to have something to lean on.

"After the show, I did what you said: I told Mr. Grady, the owner, that I was a friend who wanted to say hello to you. You appeared from the back, changed into in your street clothes. 'Can I walk you to the bus stop?' I asked. 'Why not?' you said. "So you liked it?' you asked.

I felt like a gawky teenager. I couldn't wait to see you again, to take you out, my beautiful, talented Bayla. After that they called me a regular, and I called you my prize."

As October turned to November, on Friday nights before her show, he treated her to dinner at Foltis Fisher on Lexington and 51st. Vegetable soup, a muffin, a lamb chop, one vegetable, and tea for thirty-five cents. What a splurge, him thinking she was worth that much!

On most Sunday afternoons, she met him in lower Manhattan to browse bargains on Orchard and Rivington Streets—clothes, shoes, household items. In Battery Park, he'd buy her a frankfurter on a bun, or buttered corn on the cob from a vendor. Amid cries of "hot peanuts, chestnuts," they'd relax on the wooden benches facing the Hudson River, and watch passengers board ferries for the Statue of Liberty while children ran wild. When the sun disappeared behind New Jersey, they boarded the Broadway bus uptown, a Hershey's chocolate bar in Bayla's coat pocket. "For your mother," Izzy told her. "I'll take a bite every night to make it last," her mother said, and called her daughter thrifty, to save for such an extravagance. Bayla never admitted who paid for it.

"You're treating me like a socialite," Bayla told him after their first movie, *David Copperfield,* starring Freddie Bartholomew at the Capital. Then it was vaudeville at the Paramount, Dolly Sisters, Eddie Cantor, Al Jolsen in black face singing "Swanee" by George

Gershwin, wrote it when he was 19. "Did you know that?" she asked. "It came to him when he was on a bus." On her birthday, December 22, he surprised her with balcony tickets to *Ziegfeld Follies of 1936-37*, starring Fannie Brice and Gypsy Rose Lee. Bayla sat at the edge of her seat, studying their moves, their words, every nuance.

"One day I'll be as famous," she whispered. "Nothing and no one will stop me."

"I don't doubt it. Tell me, who in your family has such *chutzpah?*"

"Me. Only me."

Though the girls at Goldmacher's were up to their ankles in uniforms for a New York State mental hospital, the black pedal beneath Bayla's feet ceased to be her enemy. The burning in her legs that used to reach her thighs disappeared so gradually she barely noticed. Inside her was a song she didn't have to sing. Through her waking and sleeping, the song sang itself. With Izzy in her life, her two-act melodrama, working and caring for her mother, was becoming a movie musical.

East 65th Street. Bayla had never been in that part of town where everything was quiet and orderly, not loose and overrun like on East 89th. A carpeted hallway led to an elevator, and on the fifth floor, a place where who knew what luxuries would be waiting.

"I've never invited a woman here but after three months dating." Izzy raised an eyebrow and winked. She smiled back, which seemed to please him. "You know how chatty garment center people are. Everyone into everyone else's business. I like my private life private. You understand."

He acted as if she knew a great deal more about life than she actually did, unlike her Jewish girlfriends at work. Whenever she told them about herself and Izzy during their 15-minute lunch break, they teased her about marriage, meeting each other's families, choosing fabric to sew her wedding dress. "Only hand-holding," they warned, "and an occasional peck on the cheek. Anything else is forbidden until they pronounce you man and wife." She minded them as she would a caring mother or father, too embarrassed to ask what more, specifically, she should expect.

Though he had described it as small, "It's a palace," she said about his apartment, a kitchen, living room, and bedroom. She ran her fingers over the furniture as he described it: a camel-back love seat covered in striped polished cotton; on the high-backed wing chair, tan and yellow tapestry; a matching ottoman; a hand-made maroon Turkish rug; and floor-to-ceiling rust-colored velvet drapes, to keep out the cold.

"The furnishings are from my parents' interior decorating business. My mother helped me. She put everything together. When I left home in Pennsylvania for New York, I ended up in the *schemata* business, like most Jews. Why not? Keep it in the family."

"Everything so beautiful from your mother." Such a person, who could put together such a room, she hoped to one day meet.

"My father did the upholstery. He passed, two years ago. But enough of that. Time to eat." She wanted to know more about this family who owned a business. How did that happen? Everyone she knew worked for someone else, but he drew out a chair from a small round wooden table at one end of the living room, and waited for her to sit.

"We'll start with a *forspize*."

"A what?"

"You don't know forspize, a nice Jewish girl like you? It's an appetizer. A Yiddish word."

"Me and my mother, we don't have appetizers. We're lucky to have food."

"Now all that's going to change."

"It will? How?"

"With you, I feel like a prince on a white horse," he laughed. "I'm going to show you more of life than beyond the cross town bus."

Was he saying she should move in with him? Such an invitation, and only her first time here? Maybe he was a little *meshuggah*. The girls at work would agree.

"Well, the flood gates have opened. Me, talking like this. Do you want to know what I've prepared?" He didn't wait for a reply. "Creamed herring, a green salad, and beef stew with fresh tomatoes, onions, garlic, and red potatoes. My specialty."

"You cooked?"

"Men cook, Bayla. My father did. You'll get used to it."

Again he was saying what she couldn't make heads or tails of. She pointed to what looked like dessert. "That too?"

"Cherry strudel from Ebinger's? That adventurous I'm not."

He waited on her hand and foot, clearing the table, putting dishes in the sink. She felt like a starlet in a Hollywood movie opposite Tyrone Power or Gary Cooper.

When he patted the camel-back loveseat for her to sit beside him, she obeyed, waiting for conversation. Instead, he inched closer. When he kissed her, nothing new about that, except, he pressed her lips more firmly. She returned his embrace, but when his fingers moved to her breast, she put her hand over his, the way Marlene Dietrich stopped Clive Brook, her lover in *Shanghai Express*. The girls at work had warned that going to his apartment, she was making herself available. For what they didn't say. Would Clive have withdrawn, backed away, and laughed the way Izzy did? She would never know. The scene in the movie went black.

"I should have known you're a tease," he said. "Don't forget I've seen you on stage, what you do to those men. I've dreamed about pleasuring you ever since. And you accepting my invitation, I assumed, well, I expected you'd want to do the same for me."

Bayla wasn't sure what would be required of her for that but she giggled coyly at his high praise.

"Well, I'm a patient man. If it's teasing you like, I can deal with it. I'll wait as long as you want."

"Wait for what?"

"For *all* the talents of The Saloon's star performer."

She thought he'd already seen all of what he suggested, but not wanting to be rude, she didn't correct him.

He kissed her, as usual, at the door that night, accompanied her outside, handed her the fare, hailed a cab, and watched until it drove away.

On occasion, after her Friday or Saturday performance, she'd returned to East 65th Street unannounced. She never considered she would find him with another woman. She never did.

"But your mother?" he asked. "You tell her you're here with me?"

"You know she's from the Old Country. Me, without a chaperone, alone with a man. It isn't proper. You understand."

If she wanted her relationship with him to continue, it had to be kept a secret. That was the only way she could avoid her mother's threats and outrageous accusations.

"It's important that I meet the mother who loves you. She should know I admire her for raising such an enticing daughter. How about one evening I bring her flowers and chocolates?" Bayla was so taken aback at what he described, she choked on her saliva, and coughed so furiously, he raced to the kitchen for a glass of water.

"I don't only sell fabrics, you know. The company's profits rest on my decisions," he explained one snowy Saturday night, the two of them cuddled on the love seat where they regularly settled. "Buyers hold off choosing material. Is Meyer cutting velvet? Will hemlines rise? And if the shipments are delayed, it's havoc, the models are waiting. The ups and downs can kill you."

"You think I don't know such things? Tonight I found the courage to ask Mr. Gadabout, Mr. Cheapskate, Mr. Big Shot Grady for more money than a small percentage of the house, which I fill to bursting, and what did I get?"

"You seem angry, my dear."

"That's what I got. Angry." She didn't say how each week that man paid her as if she were a washerwoman, a few bills crumpled into her hand which she straightened out, counted, then tucked into her bosom.

"But sewing is what pays the rent."

"You think sewing at a machine is my life's work?"

"Bayla, calm yourself. I didn't mean anything by it. Girls from immigrant families, they sew, and they fight for the American Ladies Garment Workers union. A union will raise your salary, pay you sick leave, vacation days. American Socialism at its finest."

"Singing is my dream, and nothing will keep me from it." Didn't he understand her even that much? What was wrong with him?

"You remind me of my sister, Roseamond. She wanted to be an auto mechanic but mother insisted on college."

"Mothers," Bayla said, "always telling you what to do, pointing out your faults. Tell your sister I said she should make up her own mind."

"Maybe you'll get the chance to tell her yourself. Maybe one day you'll come to Pennsylvania. We have plenty of room, even with mother and Roseamond and my brother living there."

He rarely spoke about his family. Not that she said much about hers. But now, she couldn't help herself.

"That house where they live, does it have a bathroom?"

"It has three."

As if such a thing were reasonable! He had said she could wander for days in that house and not bump into anyone. She could bathe in the tub with gold bear's feet, or were they lion's? She could put on makeup using mirrors that let her see her face and the back of her head at the same time. She could prepare a meal, choosing from their well-stocked pantry. And surely in that house there would be a room for her mother, God forbid the fates shouldn't disapprove, maybe even one with a window?

Chapter Five

As A Virgin

By the time snow and slush from the blizzard of '35 disappeared and New Yorkers sensed the possibility of warmer weather, Bayla found herself treading deeper into sexual waters. Beyond fondling in the kitchen, and necking or petting on the couch, one night during a particularly passionate kiss, Izzy eased his tongue inside her mouth. Another tongue besides her own inside her mouth she would have considered distasteful, not something people did. Yet she found it somewhat enticing followed, as it was, with him whispering, "There's so much more I want to teach you."

His words brought to mind Sunday mornings when her father, Yosef Yosefa, dressed in white boxer shorts and an undershirt, did a step hop, step hop around their tenement apartment. How she would laugh, her mother almost smiling, saying 'such foolishness,' returned her to childhood, and what her father called his 'special care' of her—gentle caresses and soothing words during their time alone. Was that the 'more' Izzy was referring to? Who could she ask?

She knew married women understood such things, though romance novels taught her exceptions: the daring Countess Olenska in *The Age of Innocence* who pursue a married man, or cold-hearted Mildred Rogers, who ruins her lover in *Of Human Bondage*. Of course Hollywood's starlets, the come-hither looks of Jean Harlow, the sultry tones of Greta Garbo, and Marlene Dietrich, a mistress, a tart. Women for whom men abandoned their families, destroyed their reputations, even married beneath them.

As she contemplated such things, sewing piles of brown cuffs onto gray cotton zookeepers' trousers, loose threads seemed to caress her thighs. Unfamiliar, yet pleasurable pulsations encouraged her to cross her legs. And though surrounded by the female operators and droning machines, she felt raised aloft, able to look upon her livelihood from somewhere enticing.

On one hand she wanted to be in control of whatever *more* was supposed to occur, but on the other hand, she felt an overwhelming desire to be led into the mystery of how being with a man would leave her transformed, more attractive, changed for the better. She would become a real woman like those she read about, and all who saw her would sense that she had been made anew. Her Jewish friends at work pooh-poohed such prophecies, called them *bobe-mayses*. Old Wives tales. Olga, from Russia, said a woman's duty was to do it with a man whenever he wanted. She didn't explain what 'it' was and since the others didn't ask, Bayla thought they understood, so she stayed silent. "Love happens when you and a man stand naked together," Esther, from Romania, said. Dora, a Hungarian like herself, disagreed. "No, no. You get naked only after the wedding."

Without a general consensus, and a lack of personal experience, after almost eight months of dating, Bayla decided she was ready to give herself to Izzy. What that involved and how it would occur, she had yet to figure out.

"I'd sacrifice anything come what might for the sake of having you near."

To heed or not to heed Cole Porter's words. Being naked with a man without the privilege of marriage seemed enticing whenever she compared it to what she could gain—a new life for herself and her mother in a house with three bathrooms. "When the fates provide, one must do what one must," her mother had taught.

Though she imagined endless variations of how it would occur, one was her favorite: Once her mother was asleep in her bed, she would walk to East 65th Street, follow Izzy into his bedroom, stretch out on the sheets, raise her arms above her head, and eye him with the sensual pout of Jeanette MacDonald adoring Clark Gable in *San Francisco*.

"You look radiant tonight, my dear," he would say.

"Undo my clothes," she'd say, an enticing Garbo to handsome Robert Taylor in *Camille*.

That part went as planned until he removed her blouse, skirt, corset, and stockings, and an unromantic, "I'm freezing," came out of her mouth.

He covered her with a blanket, and tucked the edges around her body.

"March 21st, the start of spring, the super turns off the heat but these apartments are like ice. Why should he care? It saves him pennies."

Under the blanket, her excitement mixed with fear regarding the mystery about to unfold, began with him removing his clothes, each item placed neatly, in turn, on a chair.

"Something's funny?"

"You. Sticking out that way." A naked man's private parts, forever buried, undercover, now fully visible, inches away, so unlike a woman's breasts, which are forever visible to assess.

"This," he grabbed himself with one hand, "is going to transport you."

"A change of scenery I could use," she joked to overcome her nervousness. He unearthed a small packet from his nightstand, turned his back and an instant later he was on top of her.

"Put your arms and legs around me," he commanded. She obeyed, surprised by the size and weight and feel of a man, his hands gliding to places no one but she had ever touched. With his hand between her legs, he inserted himself, moving slowly left and right, an experience so strange and overwhelming, followed by him surging forward with a grunt, his body arching upward.

"What?" He stopped abruptly when she cried out.

Was speaking allowed? "A pain, between my legs, when you…."

"You're not.... This isn't...Don't tell me I'm your first?"

She hesitated, embarrassed for him to think her a fool.

"You're a virgin. Oh my God. My own virgin. But you...on stage. How could it be?"

"Go. Do what you were doing. Don't stop." She was so abrupt, demanding, he eased back into her as the pain between her legs subsided, his movements slower, more deliberate but how much had he already damaged? As if his body had free will, he began to increase his pace. She tightened her legs around his middle hoping for a measure of containment, until an unnatural sound from some innermost part of him, frightening in its pitch. "I must, I must," ended when he came to a dead stop.

"You're magnificent," he said inching off her. "I'll make it up to you. I promise."

Make up what? she wanted to ask but why risk encouraging him to repeat what had just occurred?

"For how fast it was," he said as if he had heard. "And this being your first." With a long, breathy inhalation, he nuzzled her neck, closed his eyes and fell asleep.

Fifteen, thirty minutes, maybe an hour passed. She tried to wiggle free, but their bodies had congealed. "Wake up. Call me a cab. I have to get to my mother." But how could she approach him after what they had done? With what tone of voice? Pleading, coaxing, demanding? Everything was different now. She, naked and exposed. He, friend, companion, suitor—how many times had he, with whom?—had become a stranger.

Bathed in his sweat, fraught with alterations to her body, what would be so bad, she thought, not to venture out? He stirred, rolled onto his back and awoke.

"Bayla, your mother."

"I'll leave tomorrow early, care for her before she knows I was gone." She hoped Mrs. Silverman, from across the hall, had stopped by. And what would her mother say about a daughter who didn't come home to sleep? The entire building would know their shame.

The next morning Bayla dressed quickly. They said their

good-byes in an embrace, his hands sliding generously across her beasts, the gleam in his eyes from her unquestioning permission.

"You're like no other woman I've known," he said. "Such allure despite your innocence." His compliments were impossible for her to accept, much less to make sense of them.

When they stood, momentarily, on the street in front of his building, "Go to work," she said, pushing him away, pretending to joke. "Book your shows, service your clients, order fabric."

She was desperate to be alone, to understand what had happened, to discover in those gray, early hours what had changed in her; in everything.

Nothing was different. Not the dirty streets. Not men emptying trash bins into stinking garbage trucks. Not noisy children bumping into her on their way to school or crowds of people rushing up the subway stairs to catch the El. Did she feel more attractive, more womanly? What was that supposed to mean anyway? Was she more mature? She felt exactly as she did wearing the same clothes she had worn the day before. Being with a man hadn't transformed her like the *bobe-mayses* had promised. Absolutely nothing had changed. Everything was the same. Maybe worse.

Passersby glanced her way. Was there something in her attitude, her movements that signaled what she had done? The people next to her waiting at the bus stop, the elderly man, the pretty young woman, the disheveled housewife? Had they engaged so often in the same unnatural interchange of flesh that the signs, written all over her, were no longer visible on them? And what about the girls at work, her bosses, her favorite movie stars, her mother? Her angry, crippled mother, once a young woman. She had known the same contortions, grunting, sweating, painful invasion without preparing her only child. Never breathing a word of it. What mother would treat a daughter so?

After two or three stops, she grabbed an empty seat in the back of the bus. Those first few moments off her feet, facing a row of curious glances, she realized a transformation *had* occurred, but not what she had expected. Her body, once private and untouched, had been invaded by something foreign and unfamiliar, leaving her swollen and sore. Her mother would say it was a *shandeh* what she had done with a man who wasn't her husband. She was already buried in shame.

As the bus rode uptown, jostling its riders, in an attempt to reestablish who she used to be, she smoothed her skirt, closed the top button on her coat, straightened her hat. The intimacies she had allowed the night before had left her in a place she couldn't recognize or connect to. All of it her doing. Her fault. Her's alone. As always.

Sewing together precisely matched fabric that rendered a garment whole contrasted with fragments that had broken off from the pitiful framework of her life. When more than half the girls left at quitting time and the factory quieted down, she failed to notice. She sat with the skeleton shift, delving into a pile of waistbands, sewing each one to black trousers worn by state asylum workers. Her back was stiff, her neck ached, she could barely straighten her arms, and she was hungrier than she could ever remember. The wall clock showed she had worked past dinnertime. And what of her mother, alone since the previous morning without a bite of food, or help with her bodily needs? A change of clothes? Perhaps she had died. Things like that happened. She would find her slumped in her wheelchair. That would be easier than having to deal with accusations, hostilities, threats to her already diminished self. My mother is the enemy, she reminded herself before she turned the key in the lock. Enemies can be devious.

"What's that smell?" she said aloud.

"Now you come? Now? Now?" Her mother, upright in the wheelchair, at the kitchen table, screamed with a strength Bayla never dreamed she had. "Did you leave me here to die?"

"Don't talk nonsense. I'm here, like always, to care for you. I was—"

"*Zol zein sha*. I don't want to hear your stories. Bread and juice. That's all what I had to eat these two days. You forget you have a mother?"

Bayla followed the stench to the room where they slept. The *schissel*, her mother's bed pan, was overturned, its 24-hour contents overflowed on the floor.

"Why did you do this? To shame me?" Bayla shouted.

"What could I do? Ask Mrs. Silverman to empty this? To take me down the hall to the toilet? I have you for that." Her mother hung her head ready to cry.

Bayla gagged as she sopped up the liquid with old newspapers she collected from the basement, down and back up three flights of stairs. She gathered the mess, ran again down the stairs to dispose of her mother's shame into a garbage bin. Upon her return, she removed the iron hook from the wall peg, lifted the grate on the stove and placed into the opening a few pieces of coal from the tin pail on the floor. The orange flare from the match turned blue-gray, adhered to the coal then disappeared. Were her dreams to be a singer fated for such a destiny, to flare up then disappear?

"Now we'll sit and eat. Then I'll wash you, fresh and clean like always."

"Your *kugel* is like oatmeal. Your oatmeal is like stale meatloaf. Your chicken soup brings phlegm because you don't skim the fat."

"It's no use to fight, Mamma. To hear your complaints. Look what I've prepared." "Complaints are in my bones with the arthritis."

Sitting across the chipped metal table, avoiding each other's eyes, they ate scrambled eggs, thickly-sliced pumpernickel, and canned Del Monte pears. Sometimes it was the repetition, or frustration, or simply fatigue that brought them to silence, leaving provocations to drift unanswered. But eventually one of them would retrieve the incompletion, like a book off a shelf.

"Are you going to leave me tonight?"

"Tonight I'm here with you. Tomorrow, when I go to sing, Mrs. Silverman—"

"Tomorrow, she goes to a matinee at the Yiddish theatre, Second Avenue. The husband gives her money. She tells me about the show."

"Yes, Mamma. I know. Such a pleasure for you to hear about the theatre and Mrs. Silverman, such a good friend."

She left the dishes on the table to prepare her mother for sleep in her long flannel nightgown, tuck her into bed. Would a boarder make it easier? Provide company, a few extra dollars? Even if she could find someone, with her mother's *kvetching*, and the stink from the bedpan. Who would pay $2.50 a month for that?

Why think about such nonsense now? Her mother, an immigrant, was from the Old Country, her accent embarrassing to hear, her beliefs in the fates controlling their lives, keeping watch, while her world was a place where a man and woman exchanged themselves in a way she could never have imagined. What would it be like to face Izzy again? Had she made a terrible decision, allowing him? At Goldmacher's when a seamstress made an irreparable mistake, she'd tear the fabric, throw it in the "Not Usable" bin where it waited for the ragman's pushcart. Was that how Izzy would see her—ripped, undone, her body used, discarded?

"We came with bundles. From one cage to another." Memories of Ellis Island were escaping through her mother's dreams. "Soldiers grabbed my hair, looked in my mouth, shined lights down my throat. We slept on benches. Ate herring. Stale bread."

They were inspectors from the Health Department, and the food, sandwiches with cheese, or ham, pitchers of milk, bread and butter, more food than the immigrants ever saw. Americans took care of them. Only for her mother the food was bad, the people, soldiers.

"Women screamed. Left behind. Sick. Wandered like *dybbuks*, without a soul. . . ."

Even asleep her mother usurped whatever bit of privacy Bayla had, even tonight when she desperately needed to think. Those men in The Saloon who shout and yell, waiting to fill me like he did, use me for themselves, is that what they would make of me? A receptacle? Is that what I have become? Bayla lay down in the cot where she slept too close to her enemy, turned on her side and gazed into the darkness when out of the jumble inside her head one thing, one thing became clear: She could never be that way with anyone else ever again. Words that wrenched her insides and tested her resolve escaped her lips: *"Izzy must become as bound and attached to me as I am to him. Then I will be safe from the ragman."*

The talk at The Saloon was of a Blues Diva evermore beguiling, painfully seductive, who tantalized and taunted. No matter what those men yelled, or did, or wanted, Bayla decided it great fun to manipulate them by performing blues songs whose sexual inferences she now fully understood, then exiting the stage leaving them at the peak of their wanting. Such newfound powers brought her great satisfaction, even a tinge of revenge, though for what, or why, she wasn't sure.

After a performance, she would turn to Izzy, "Look how you can't keep your hands off me. How you dote on my every move." They would head to his apartment for what he called wild crazy sex, devouring her, pleasuring himself. But other times, without the slightest warning, the attention Izzy gave made her feel like prey, trapped by his hovering, his wanting to nuzzle and grope, his eagerness to pounce, his sole interest to satisfy his selfish needs. In this "dark place," she called it, his flesh became untouchable, his weight overbearing, his smell, his stink, all that she saw, and felt and heard made her want to escape. Quite accidentally, one night while they were making love, she did. She sensed she was in her body, yet also outside it, as if she could watch herself and Izzy from a distance. It frightened her at first, bearing witness to herself as two people—one viewing what she did; the other doing what she was viewing. But it was easier to see him touch her, than feel him do it, to scrutinize his performance, rather than give in to his desires. Her senses unplugged, sounds grew muffled, and though she bore witness to everything he was doing, the rest of her remained detached.

At some point, she returned to her body without understanding why, or how these episodes occurred. She merely accepted that she split in two, for some reason, then for another, became whole again. She called these her "shifts," and the more she experienced them, the more they seemed a common arrival leaving her without a sense of who she had become, or who she thought herself to be.

Chapter Six

You've Got to Have Friends

"My friend Manny's been hounding me for weeks, 'Bring her over for a meal already. I hear she's got you where she wants you.' 'She does,' I told him. 'In bed.'"

"You didn't say that. You didn't." Bayla covered her mouth with her hand unsure whether to laugh or hide her embarrassment. It was a late Friday night, after her performance. She and Izzy were in a booth at a coffee shop sharing apple pie and ice cream.

"Seems the entire garment center knows I've got a girlfriend who sings in a bar on the West Side. You know I promised not to say a word to anyone. So, you'll come? "

"A meal at your friend's house? Why not?" He was opening for her another door into his life. To be a guest at dinner with people her own age where eating served as entertainment, not as a somber ritual where she contrasted every mouthful with money earned for every hour of work.

"Good. He and I have been friends since elementary school on Philadelphia's South Side. We came here after high school, both eighteen, took jobs selling fabric in the garment district, dated long-legged models. Drinking, dancing, wild parties. Don't ask," he laughed. "Two months ago he married Annie. Her parents, Jewish Orthodox, emigrated from Brazil, rich from selling diamonds to the 'right people.' Impressed by that and Annie's ample bosom—over two handfuls each, he brags—Manny proposed. To impress his in-laws, he greases back his dark hair with petroleum jelly. A regular Jewish Valentino."

"It's a little *meshugah,*" is how Bayla would have described to her mother the loft where Manny and Annie welcomed her. A sink, a two-burner stove with utensils dangling from nails in the wall was their kitchen. Blankets draped over a couch and two chairs coming loose at the seams was a living room. A bedroom was a mattress on the floor, purple sheers tacked to the ceiling around it. A toilet with a shower curtain for a door was the bathroom. But to offer such an explanation, she already heard her mother's outburst. "He takes you where? To do what with you? To leave me here alone?" Some things were best left unspoken between them.

Leafy greens and freshly sliced red tomatoes filled a large dark wooden bowl beside an overflowing platter of black beans piled over white rice attractively laid out on a dark wood table with mismatched blue, white and brown dishes.

"Don't you dare," Annie warned Manny who had sidled up to Bayla and began wiggling his fingers over the platter of beans and rice.

"I want to see if your *fejouda* feels like your tits." He pulled Annie close, caressed her breasts, kissed her on the lips. Bayla looked away, pretending not to notice.

"No need to blush," Manny said. "They're just tits. When I met Annie she didn't know how to screw, but at least her mother taught her to cook."

Annie's deep full-throated laugh filled the room but Bayla searched Izzy's face for how she should react to his best friend who she already considered a *vilde chaya*. But he was at the table, motioning her to eat.

Bayla balanced her plate on her lap in the nearest chair. Izzy sat on the floor facing her, Manny on the couch, Annie on the bed. Bayla wanted to say "what a nice party," but having never been to one, why let Izzy's friends think she was a fool?

"Your girlfriend eats like a truck driver," Manny said.

Bayla considered it another of Manny's jokes, surprised at how hungry she was and how she had filled her plate, the food so tempting.

"Watch it," Izzy said.

"Watch what? We work in the rag trade and she sings in an Irish bar on the West side. Tut, tut. She's so refined? Wait till your high fallutin' mother hears about that."

"My mother worked her whole life. She's dealt with all sorts. Why should she care?"

"Oh she'll care all right. She became a grand old snob once the family business took off."

Bayla hoped to hear more about the woman she knew so little about but Izzy had stuffed a forkful of rice and beans into his mouth, and was trying to catch dark gravy oozing down his chin with a bunched up paper napkin. That he was as reluctant to speak about his mother as she was to speak about hers, she found comforting. Something they had in common.

The men discussed sales deals, bonuses, and how the fashion industry was rehiring with the Depression giving way to better days under FDR. Annie talked about rich clientele at the exclusive Madison Avenue dress shop where she did alterations.

"Hey Izz, ever tell Bayla how you rely on me for advice about women? When we should make a move. When we should hold back."

"Manny remembers everything he ever learned and experimented with and suffered through endless escapades with the opposite sex," Izzy said with a smile. "His advice is invaluable."

"Those summers," Manny said, "working at your parents' decorating shop on the South Side. Those were the days. Me and your brother hanging out on Main at night to meet girls, horny bastards that we were."

"All that's over now," Annie said.

"Working in the rag trade we learned the value of sampling. Can't make lasting decisions without sampling first. Right, Izz?" He winked at Bayla.

As Izzy's girlfriend was she nothing more than a sample to him? In this place where any and all topics were ripe for discussion, emotions, opinions, insults, fantasies played out among burps and curse words, and sexual affections freely displayed, was Bayla failing to convince Izzy and his best friends that she was in the know? Before she could figure out what to do, "How about congratulating them on their wedding?" Izzy suggested.

"Congratulations on your wedding," Bayla said.

"Oh yeah, our wedding.," Manny said, disparagingly. "Annie and I lived together a few months before we married, so my father refers to her as 'the whore.' My parents never showed for the ceremony. Neither did Annie's, who pleaded with God to separate her from me, a *paskudnik*, a *nochshlepper*! We were married by a judge in a Manhattan court house. Izzy, our witness."

Annie said she heard the story enough. Bayla said it was sad. Izzy said a father and a son should make peace.

"Screw you," Manny said. "Your family's so perfect?"

Bayla made a note to ask Izzy about that. Taking notes, she thought, as if spending time with Manny and Annie was like teaching her what went on between a married couple.

It was late when they crossed Fulton Street, walking quickly toward the uptown subway, Bayla bombarding Izzy with non-stop questions.

"What did Manny mean when he said some nights he thinks his tongue may fall off? And why don't you do to me whatever he does to Annie? And why did you give him the finger?"

"I gave him the finger and called him a lothario, a seducer of women, because he got himself a big-breasted Brazilian and can't satisfy her sexually, but he was making eyes at you."

"What eyes? I didn't see him making eyes."

"Feeling up his wife, and looking at you, to see your reaction. To somehow entice you."

"Entice me? That *schlepper*? How could you think such a thing? And what was that about a climax, and how come men have it before women?"

"A climax for a woman, it takes practice. Lots of sex. How about tonight we…."

"I can't leave my mother again." It seemed that men were a bit too practiced at finagling women for intimate pleasures she couldn't yet describe or imagine, while she and Annie, and how many other women were forever ready to follow, anxiously lining up behind one another waiting, waiting their turn for similar pleasures from their husbands or boyfriends who already had enough of their fill?

Before she closed her eyes that night in the dark, silent room where her mother was long asleep, something opened up inside her head; a realization that it wasn't her mother or her girlfriends, certainly not herself, a single working woman, but her relationship with a man that took her beyond the tenements, the garment center, The Saloon. Her boundaries.

Yet how different it was for men. Their lives overflowed with choice When the four made plans for the weekend, before or after her performance, she preferred Annie's suggestions—the Central Park Zoo, a stroll down Fifth Avenue, the Metropolitan Museum of Art—but Manny said her choices were boring. So the men decided. They got their way. That's what men did.

When they said their good-byes that night, with Izzy steps behind her offering thank you's to Annie, Manny grabbed her, one hand behind her head, the other on her breast. She wouldn't call it a kiss. It felt more like an assault, then he pushed her out the door.

She had enticed Manny without meaning to, disgraced herself in Izzy's world. She would never mention a word of it, such an abuse of herself, and Manny, that degenerate, that *bazzah*. Izzy knew, he suspected it all along. Bayla, his girlfriend, his one and only, flirting behind his back with his best friend. As if the fates had told him that what the four of them shared would become secrets and lies. And why? Because of Bayla.

Bayla, the destroyer.

Chapter Seven

Eternal Vows

The first heavy snowstorm had landed, bringing everything to a standstill. Subways shut down. Schools, businesses, The Saloon, even Goldmacher's closed.

Bayla served her mother breakfast, and after a late lunch, with the apartment colder than usual for early December, the woman only wanted to stay in bed. "Rest," Bayla whispered with a kiss to her forehead, then she wrapped herself in a blanket and settled on a chair in front of the radiator under the window, alternating her front and back towards the insufficient heat. Soothed by the warmth and glare from outside, she closed her eyes, surprised when she awoke to the sound of busses. She left a snack for her mother, put her father's galoshes over her shoes, and headed down the three flights of stairs.

"To come on such a treacherous day. And wouldn't you know, I have news."

After a kiss and an embrace, Izzy set out a light dinner—stuffed derma, potato salad, lettuce and tomatoes, rye bread and butter.

"What news?" Feeling her hunger, she didn't wait for him to eat.

"A friend of mine, Miklosh Brofman, a Hungarian, I might have mentioned him, he bought a warehouse, filled it with bolts of fabric. It could be bigger than my family's business. We'll use catalogs, requests for samples, mail orders, shipping. He'll sell yardage, but at less than garment center prices."

"Why less?"

"The business is in Pennsylvania, near my home. Costs are lower. More money to make."

"Your home is here," Bayla laughed.

"Bayla, he offered me Vice President of his company."

"I don't understand."

"You have your work, your singing, your mother. I can't presume. . . ." He paused abruptly as if he couldn't remember what came next.

"Can't presume?" She swallowed. Put her fork down. "You there? Me here? What are you saying?"

"I'm trying to tell you—"

"We're together over a year already. You were my first and only. What are you saying?" as if she didn't already know, but the way it hit her, like a finger in a socket. Izzy trying to distract her with food, fill her with nonsense before throwing her away like a useless cast-off. She had never mentioned a word, but he was bound to find out. Didn't her mother always say how undeserving she was?

"You don't want me to meet your family. You don't want me inside that fancy house of yours. You've been ashamed of me all along. I work in a factory. I sing to rowdy men. And my poor, sick mother. You don't think we're good enough."

"Bayla, don't say such things. Let me say my piece."

"Your piece!" She glanced at the food he had laid out, the bread *schmered* in butter, the lettuce and tomato. False prophets. Temptations to lure her. "Forget your piece. It's too late."

The apartment was stifling. Heat spewed from the radiator was tightening her throat. Desperate to inhale, her eyes filled with tears. She had to escape beyond that sound his apartment door made when she slammed it.

Under the naked ceiling light bulb in the silent hallway, the truth was impossible to ignore. She and Izzy were finished. Undone. The elevator that had led her so carelessly to her lover's fifth floor apartment would uproot her from him forever, and why not? He deserved someone clean and new. It wasn't because of a job. It was because of her. Who she was. Why else would he leave her behind like a dog, a bitter sickness and go to that place—Pennsylvania? Why else make such a decision?

"What I'm doing, it's because of you," her father had said in Hungarian. "Stay with me," he had begged. But she ran out of the bedroom, a disobedient child, and he left for good.

She pressed the elevator button once, twice, glanced over her shoulder. Izzy was standing in his doorway. His smile was gone. His hair was amiss for running his hands through it. His feet were bare for racing after her, forgetting his slippers. The food he had offered was still waiting.

Where would she find another Izzy? Her first and only. The attention he paid. His kindness and generosity. Another Izzy there wouldn't be. *The mistake she had made with her father, she was making again.*

Confused and uncertain, the elevator arrived, and her feet begin to move, goading her backward, retracing her steps. Gliding like a spirit, a wisp, a ghost, she floated inches above the ground, close enough to inhale his breath. She placed one hand on his lips. Was this a dream? A nightmare? A saving grace? He kissed her shivering fingers.

"I'll wait on you." Her voice was soft. "I'll keep a beautiful house. I'll cook fine meals. We'll be like your father and mother, so many years together."

"I never thought otherwise. Come inside."

Beside him on the loveseat, she felt the cushions give way.

"You have a temper, Bayla, and the way you jump to conclusions. You didn't give me a chance. I've never seen you like this, everything black or white but there are grays in between. The give and take of a sales deal I'll teach you so you won't pounce on me like that again."

"Can you forgive me?" She didn't want to ask what black and white had to do with it.

"Of course I forgive you. How could I not forgive you? I love you. But next time, maybe you'll listen before you decide what's what? Before you even know what I had left to say. You're calm now?

Good. Because I can't presume anything unless we talk about your mother. That's what I wanted to say."

"I can't leave her."

"Of course not. She'll live with us. We'll hire someone to care for her. There's a sunny room on the second floor, in a corner, with a window. It will be hers."

A beautiful bedroom for my mother, and someone to care for her. What was he saying? His words were too promising to imagine. In her mind's eye she saw a single bed, a window, that already would be enough.

"Why do you cry, Bayla?"

"To think my mother will have a better life and me, not her servant."

"You a servant? Never, Bayla. I'm asking, I'm saying we'll get married. If you'll have me. Will you have me as your husband?"

The snowfall had clouded her mind. She was dreaming, again. Or was it the fates toying with her future, the way her mother had instilled into her from childhood? Oh, those fates! They tempted you with wishes come true then withdrew them just when you were ready to accept.

"Bayla. Bayla, do you hear me? What are you thinking? I've just proposed."

"Yes. Yes, I'll marry you." He *had* asked. She was sure of it now. And she had said yes.

"I've thought of marrying you when we first met in Paderevski Hall."

"Even then?" Bayla said. She smoothed her skirt and rested her hands in her lap. "Where we're going, is there a place for me to perform?" It was her first clear thought.

"Of course. There's Cafe Genteel. A supper club just outside of town. You'll be a big hit. A star, like here, in Manhattan."

"A new audience, a different venue. I'll revise my repertoire."

"We'll have a wedding?"

Bayla had seen weddings in the movies, but her own? She smiled and lowered her gaze to keep her thoughts modest. "Our wedding. It will be lovely." Another word and the fates would be swooping.

In the cab on the way home, Bayla practiced words that would sweeten her mother's life. She threw open the door, let her hat and coat drop to the floor.

"Mamma, you won't believe, I have news."

"No news. No news. Feed me. Feed me." With each word her mother banged a knife into the wooden arm of her wheel chair, splintering the wood.

"Mamma, what's wrong? Give me the knife. How did you get it? I left it in the cabinet above the sink." Bayla reached out, but her mother held the knife as if to strike. "That's dangerous. Give it to me." She tried again to grab it.

"I know what you are. A whore. Rakel Silverman, across the hall, told me."

"Mrs. Silverman wouldn't say such a thing." What had gone wrong since she had left in the snow only hours before? She searched the apartment for a sign that someone had broken in. Nothing had changed, but inside her mother's head something had shifted.

"I've made myself strong without you."

Holding onto the kitchen counter with one hand, her mother trembled as she pushed herself to standing, reached the wall cabinet, and withdrew a can of Campbell's Cream of Mushroom Soup. She grabbed the can opener from off its hook, freed the rim and poured the contents into a waiting pot. From her housecoat pocket she unearthed a slice of bread, stuffed a piece into her mouth.

"I saw your father, how he embraced you," she said as morsels fell to the floor. "Embraced you!"

"Mamma, father loved you. And me, a child. For a father to love a child. Mamma, what have you done to yourself?"

"You think I forget? I saw him."

"Don't cry, Mamma, please don't cry."

Bayla guided her mother's quivering body into the wheelchair, their tears filling the silence. She sat beside her at the table, fed her each spoonful of the mushroom soup, and put her to bed. She saw the sunny room on the second floor in Izzy's Pennsylvania home, the woman who would bathe and feed her mother, the family together in the parlor, after dinner. All illusions that would remain in one, unforgiving place—her imagination.

How could she introduce her mother to strangers who would judge and stare? The shame and embarrassment would fall on her. She would be the one to pity, and she had long ago made up her mind she wasn't a charity case?

She left the knife on the kitchen table. What harm could a knife do compared to this woman who destroyed their future—a new wife, and her mother in her own room on the second floor?

For the next two days, Bayla kept her distance from Izzy. She left early for work and returned home promptly. On the evening of the third day, she knocked on his apartment door.

"I've been worried," he said. "What's going on?"

"It's my mother. She's my responsibility."

"I admire your independence, but if you don't want her with us—"

"I do want her with us. But it can't be. Don't you understand? She doesn't like visitors. She barely speaks English. She's a foreigner, embarrassing to listen to. She acts sometimes crazy. Not normal." If Izzy and his family never meet her, it will be as if her mother never existed. It was the only way she could marry him. Who in their right mind could accept into their home the person who raised her, who she supported, the one she called Mamma?

"Then let me at least pay for what she needs. Let me do something."

If she accepted, her obligation would never end. There weren't enough days in a lifetime for her to accumulate that kind of money.

"I'll manage. Please believe me. I know what's best. This is how it must be."

"Listen to me, Bayla. My grandparents came through Ellis Island in the middle 1800's without a word of English and no education. But a few lucky chips fell our way when my parents moved from South Philadelphia and opened the business in Pittsmill. My mother takes advantage of the Rothschild name as if we're upper class, but we never were. We're the working scion."

Bayla didn't know what he meant by all that but why create more distance between them, prove to the person who made her feel so special that she really wasn't?

"Bayla, please don't take on too much. I want you to have peace of mind when we marry."

Izzy had used that expression before, but how could she ever have peace in her mind when she had to figure out what to do with her mother?

Chapter Eight
Lansmanschaftn

Her mother was a lunatic. There was no doubting it. Something had broken or snapped like the sewing machines at Goldmacher's, but unlike them, her mother was beyond repair. It was no longer safe to leave her alone. She seemed capable of anything. There had to be papers somewhere, papers with important information. Her mother always said Jewish families planned for such things.

Lansmanshaften. A strange word from her childhood entered her mind. Her mother described it as something her father belonged to with others from the Hungarian town where he was born. Munkacs. "At the slopes of the Carpathian Mountains. *Di alte heym,*" he would say in Yiddish. How he loved spending those few hours with his lansmen sharing memories about the Old Country.

"Don't forget the payment," her mother made such a fuss once a month on Saturdays, when he left for Rivington Street. It was payment for when they got old, or if one of them fell ill. The *lansmanshaft* provided its members sick benefits, and a burial plot.

Bayla searched each night, while her mother slept, until under a loose floorboard in the bedroom closet, she came upon a worn brown leather purse tied with thin string. She undid the looped knot, and beneath the front flap, read *"Magyar Lansmanshaf."*

She unearthed a faded photograph of a well-dressed man and woman posed against a photographer's scenic backdrop; he, expressionless sitting on a chair, the woman standing behind him, her left hand on his shoulder. "Wedding day. Pest, Nov, 1887" it read in Hungarian. Her grandparents on her mother's side, from Budapest.

In caressing the photo of family she would never know, something jostled loose. It was an exquisite amethyst broach set in gold filigree surrounded by tiny pearls. No doubt it belonged to her great-grandmother, the one her mother had said cavorted with Hungarian nobility. "Take it," they would have told her mother. "Use it for tickets to bring us to the New World." She did as she was told because here it was, yet they were still there, waiting. The promise to secure for them rent and food and clothes in the land of milk and honey fit comfortably into Bayla's palm. Surely her mother had forgotten this hiding place, or even what had been hidden, forgotten even that she had neglected her loved ones, left them to suffer, or die during the Great War. Surely, that alone was reason enough for the fates to squander their lives on East 89th Street.

Bayla replaced the broach in the purse and withdrew a sheet of paper: *"The Magyar Lansmanshaft has joined the Workman's Circle. (Arbeiter Ring.)"* The next morning, before work, inside the telephone booth in front of Rexall's Drug Store, she looked up the Workman's Circle in the phone book, dropped a nickel in the slot, and made an appointment.

Days later she left work early, and let herself inside a musty-smelling brownstone on East Forty-Third Street. Mrs. Stein, dressed in a brown smock over a green skirt and a long-sleeved white blouse, introduced herself. She listened to Bayla's dilemma and set to work, searching in drawers, digging through papers, and extracting necessary files from shelves that covered the walls so high she had to climb a ladder that moved on wheels to reach them.

"It's a pity," she said, reading from pages spread across her cluttered desk. "It's been years since dues were paid. No funds available."

"But they paid...."

"They paid but they stopped. I'm sorry, my dear girl. It's not uncommon. Something happens, the money disappears."

"This was my last hope."

"You have one choice." Mrs. Stein turned her dark eyes downward. "The state mental institution."

The offer fell heavily upon the room's silence tightening Bayla's middle. "Perhaps if I took her to a good doctor, her health would improve."

"Who doesn't want a good doctor? You have money for such a thing?"

Bayla lowered her head.

"So now you have *tsuras* like everyone else. We had a lady client with the misfortune to give birth to a child not quite right. Unable to speak, or learn. They sent the child away. Years goes by. It's as if the child never was. Their children born healthy never knew they had a brother."

"It's a *shondeh* for people to behave like that. I have to do right by my mother. Why tell me such a thing?"

"I'm sorry. It's to show you there's always worse. I have stories like that up to here." Mrs. Stein raised her hand above her head. "If your mother is as dear as you say, the mental institution will give her three meals a day, and as her illness gets worse, she'll be looked after. There's no fee. Patients are wards of the state. Let me put it this way, when you mail this application, put in a money order, whatever you can scrape together. Your mother will be better cared for. This I know."

The state mental institution. At Goldmacher's, Bayla sewed their uniforms—beige with no trim or color. Were the patients' lives the same? Dull. Lifeless. Or was this a sign, her mother's connection to that place? Not something to ignore. Her mother might say it was meant to be.

A seamstress from Goldmacher's gave Bayla the name of a Jewish man who owned a pawnshop on Avenue A. He would understand her predicament, the value of the broach, give her a fair return. Bayla left his store with $300 in her pocket. Never had she seen, much less held, so much money, but she refused even a penny for herself. The money would guarantee her mother a life free from worry and concern, so Bayla could proceed without guilt in hers.

She wrote letters, made telephone calls in the booth by Rexall's, and returned several times to the Workman's Circle where she met 'necessary people,' Mrs. Stein called them.

"Giving your mother a good life takes time and coordination," she said. Did they think she didn't know about determination?

Two months after the papers were filed, the letter arrived. A bed for her mother. January 10, 1937, the date for her admittance.

Bayla prepared a breakfast feast—fresh grapefruit, two scrambled eggs, a cup of Nescafe from the smallest jar in the grocery store, and a blueberry muffin from Cushman's on Eighty-Ninth and Lexington.

"Of course I'll travel with you to a place that will give me a good life," her mother said. "Will they do a better job than my daughter?" she asked as if Bayla weren't there.

"Oh yes. It will be a big improvement. Plenty to eat. Caretakers at your beck and call."

Her mother responded with a glimmer of a smile. Her disappointment in America was giving way. "I'll tell Mrs. Silverman when she comes to visit."

"Yes, Mamma. Tell her your good news."

"But who could pay for such a place?" Her mother wrung her hands and buried her face in her palms. "I've tempted the fates with such a question. Some things must never be asked. Don't take me away," she pleaded. "This is where I belong. This home is what I know. Leave me here. I'll stay with you. Like always. The two of us. Let me be."

"Mamma." Bayla bent down on her knees and took her mother's hands in her own. "A bed. Food. Caretakers waiting."

"Such fine words, like a dream," her mother said, her voice softening. "Dreams," she repeated, as if she still had them. "Such a good daughter, my Bayeleh." She reached out with her arms and Bayla placed herself inside them. She couldn't remember the last time her mother had longed to hug her only child.

Bayla would never forget the thump and heft of the wheelchair as they descended the three flights of tenement stairs. Years already, since her mother could go out on her own. Then for the stoop, her mother managing to stand, clutching the wrought iron banister, her legs unsteady. On the cross-town bus to the Greyhound terminal, Bayla settled her mother first, and placed the shopping bag with her possessions in the overhead rack while a kind driver helped her lift the wheelchair, set it in the back which was unoccupied in that early hour.

She had selected her mother's best—a navy blue wool dress, cotton navy stockings, a black winter coat, and a red hat and matching scarf, her mother's beautifully crocheted handiwork over her black winter coat. Past the city limits, her mother stared out the window, awed by the beauty of an undisturbed landscape with evergreens on snowy fields in the country where she had become a citizen. It was a clear, crisp day, the cold air warmed by morning sun that stretched for some time into the bus row where they sat, side-by-side. To give her this much, wasn't that everything, Bayla thought? And within hours, a guarantee of being cared for the rest of her life.

The uphill climb was steady, requiring her to pause several times to adjust her mother's hat and scarf, pull her coat tighter around her legs. The sign was modest, black letters on an aged rectangular wooden board secured by a post in the earth—NEW YORK STATE INSTITUTION FOR THE MENTALLY DISABLED. Bayla pushed the wheelchair through insidious vines, winter weeds and tree branches, like live tentacles overtaking their path. What was so unkempt in winter would become, in summer, flowering grasses and shrubs. Bayla imagined her mother shaded from the sun by green trees. Benches along the way. A picnic with people serving food.

The grey stone building was two stories high, an imposing tower at each end. Bayla paused the wheelchair, walked several feet ahead, banged with her fist, once, twice, on a dark wooden door with a small window at the top, then quickly returned to her mother. Nothing stirred. No automobile or train sounds, no birds in flight, only occasional clicks caused by bare, frozen, branches snapping off or innocently reaching out to touch one another.

Suddenly the small window opened. Closed. The wooden door moved slowly inward. Three women in white uniforms and dark gray shawls wrapped around their shoulders, regimented and serious, marched in step toward them.

"This is my daughter, my only child." Bayla was surprised to hear her mother speaking up. "She's given every penny for me, Lillian Szabo, to stay here."

"How lucky you are, Missus," a tall, brawny woman replied. The other two held back.

"I'll go with her, inside," Bayla said.

"No guests. Those are the rules. We have received the necessary papers. A quick good-bye works best," the tall woman said.

Bayla's fingers around the bar that guided the wheelchair refused to release. How long she had looked forward to move beyond that place where she had spent most of her life.

"It's getting cold." The woman stepped beside Bayla, as if to dislodge her.

"You'll visit?" Bayla's mother asked. She reached behind her, a habit when she wanted her daughter's touch.

Bayla circled to the front of the wheelchair and took hold of her mother's hands. She bent down on her knees, ignoring the icy cold that seeped through her cotton stockings.

"Of course I'll come. I'm your only child."

"Say good-bye," the woman said.

"Good-bye, Mamma."

"I'm afraid," her mother said. "Should I be afraid?"

Bayla enclosed her mother's body in her outstretched arms. Could that tall stranger be trusted to keep her mother safe? To give her what she needed? To watch over her, day and night?

"No need to be afraid, Mamma. Look at the place. So many at your beck and call."

"Yes, yes, I understand. I will be peaceful here," she said with a sigh confirming that her daughter's promise would come true.

"It's time," the woman said, her fingers tight around the wheelchair handle.

In this *fahbissener* setting where time stopped and her stomach turned inside out, Bayla placed her hands on both side of her mother's face, the face of a 48-year-old woman, her cheeks soft, rosy and warm despite the cold. She kissed her mother's forehead, her eyes, slowly, gracefully, consciously ripping herself from the person who had given her life, knowing if she had prepared for a thousand days and nights, it wouldn't have been enough to forsake this woman who appeared more sane and calm than she had been in years.

"You couldn't have done better by me than this," her mother said in Hungarian.

Feeling her knees buckling, Bayla managed to stand while the woman who never introduced herself gave the wheelchair a push. Two matrons took their places on each side, then amidst the thump and squeak that had permeated Bayla's years of her life, the three of them walked toward the grey stone building. Her mother was being taken by strangers to a foreign place, something she had done once before, and now again, because of her daughter.

"Mamma," she called out, but the wooden door slammed shut sealing her mother behind it.

She waited until the air eased back into her lungs and the dizziness in her head subsided. After one more glance, she turned away to face down the crooked, pitted, pavement, with its insidious tentacles that grabbed at each of her foot falls, slowing her pace, threatening her determination .

Amid nature unkempt and tears like ice stinging her face, she hoped a time would come when she would no longer be haunted by the peeling paint, broken windowpanes and barred entrance of where she had promised her mother a decent life. And God forbid one day she should end up in such a place, sent there by a daughter like herself.

Her mother would have insisted that the marriage ceremony be overseen by a Rabbi. One week later, at the Jewish Theological Seminary on West 114th Street, Bayla and Izzy stood ceremoniously, side-by-side, inhaling the cloying scent of aged and worn religious books, housed in floor to ceiling shelves inside the Rabbi's study. She heard her mother praise her simple round collared white dress that fell to the floor, a white satin bow in her hair, in her arms four long-stemmed red roses from Izzy. She promised her mother she wouldn't look *ungepatchked*.

Anxious to win the favor of the mother he would never meet, Izzy made it a point to tell Bayla that her wedding trousseau would be a gift from his family. She modestly accepted.

With Manny and Annie as witnesses, when the Rabbi asked, Manny handed the ring to Izzy who slipped it on to Bayla's finger. Then Izzy stepped hard, breaking the wine glass the Rabbi had blessed after the bride and groom had sipped from it. Everyone shouted *maazel tov*. Bayla heard her mother crying from joy.

The four of them celebrated at Schrafts on Central Park South: hot fudge ice cream sundaes and white petit fours. It was January 20th, 1937.

In England, there was talk of Edward VIII abdicating as King to marry Wallis Simpson, a commoner. Izzy told Bayla it was a good sign for lovebirds like themselves.

JANUARY 1937 – MAY 1940

Chapter Nine

Pittsmill, Pennsylvania

Bayla smoothed her red wool coat that fell above her ankles, tightened the black leather belt around her middle, indented the brim of her red felt hat so the imitation purple mums sat directly over her right eye, and walked hesitantly beside her new husband into January's chill. Beyond the train station's sloping, red-shingled roof, along a wooden platform, and down a short stairway, she suddenly stopped short, let go of Izzy's hand, and grimaced.

The vista before her was a stir with metal contraptions wedged between monstrously high smoke stacks spewing red, yellow and orange flames into whatever breathable air existed beneath a sky unashamedly gray and thick, devoid of the slightest patch of blue, deep blue, partial blue, sky blue. The roar of engines, high-pitched clangs, and thunderous blasts, discordant, atonal sounds accosted her ears. She had allowed her husband's explanation about the Shenandoah Steel Company, worked in twelve-hour shifts, twenty-four hours a day, to sit inside her, forgetting this was the heart of the town. Not traffic flow, bird songs, or train whistles set the tone, but glowing girders melted, hardened, reshaped by blast furnaces, alongside cranes built to lift thundering weights assaulting one's sights, and obstructing moonlit evenings.

Spongy soot blanketed roofs, and lawns, patio umbrellas in

summer and freshly-made snowmen in winter. School children at outdoor recess, and men playing chess in the park had to remove their outer clothing in a basement or a hallway and bathe with Coltsfoot soap before going to bed to get rid of the gritty coating that had settled on them. And beyond the scent of fumes and burning gases, steel workers living in company-owned row houses found it impossible to dream otherwise. This is where marriage had taken her. But her husband had promised that at the top of Beleaguered Hill, the highest point for miles around, she wouldn't be so bothered, as if she hadn't endured the stink of tenement alleys, illness raging behind doors, cries of birthing mothers and hungry, ill-dressed children.

The taxi drove them out of the valley where the air felt lighter, easier to breathe, where winter's shimmering white-capped mountains surrounded them. Along the steep incline of cobblestones, elegant homes lined up like picture post cards appeared on both sides of the road. At the top, the cul-de-sac, with the engine still sputtering, Bayla bounded out of the car. No matter how often he had described it during their courtship, she stood there gaping at the house that peered down at her as if it were alive with feeling and breath like any living person.

A Queen-Anne Victorian mansion. A gray wraparound porch, with dark blue columns every few feet, was edged with fanciful lemon-yellow latticework beneath a gray roof with an imposing maroon gable at each end. At the roof's center, a white spire, rising from a dark blue tower, disappeared into the town's low-lying clouds as if it were connected to something beyond anything Bayla could ever know or imagine. On the front lawn, beneath the broad ancient limbs of a large maple tree, a bronze plaque read: *Amory Lane*.

Izzy led her along the orange brick curlicue walkway to the main entrance, and up dark blue porch steps, so distinct from New York City's cracked cement stoops. The taxi driver set down their suitcases. "Welcome home," he said, bowing as if they were royalty.

Izzy pressed a small white button on the side of the front door whose center was a glass oval etched with flowers and tall, flowing grasses.

"For a door to have this," Bayla said. "And music?" as chimes rang out. "How does it....?" In seconds, the door flew open.

"My son." She was tall, her voice strong, similar to Bayla's except it had a lilt, like a twinkle. With her hands on each side of his head, the woman kissed each of his cheeks.

"Mother, I'd like you to meet the new Mrs. Rothschild." He stood straighter than usual, his words without hesitation, as if he had practiced. "My wife."

There was a second of lost composure as Izzy's mother faced her new daughter-in-law, the long red coat cinched with a wide black belt, the felt hat, fake mums.

"I'm so pleased to finally meet you," his mother said, her words free of any accent of where she was born or what country she had left behind. Her bobbed white hair, brushed forward in a mannish style Bayla had never seen on a woman. It highlighted her blue eyes, her angular nose, her deep pink lipstick. Her gray silk jacket gracefully draped over an ivory blouse above a slightly flared ivory wool skirt, high-heeled gray pumps to match.

"Hello." Bayla hesitated before meeting the woman's hand with her own. She thought she should have said something more.

"Come in, children. Come in," his mother invited.

A backward glance at her son's new wife convinced Bayla that her winter outfit had made the perfect impression.

"Let me take your coats."

"We'll do it, Mother. I'd like to take my bride upstairs to freshen up."

"Of course, after such a long journey. Go ahead, you two. We'll have refreshments in the parlor. It's warm and cozy in there. My son Solomon tends to the hearth."

"Where is he?" Izzy asked.

"He and the men are hanging Austrian shades for a Philadelphia hotel. He'll return in a few days."

"Soon enough," he mumbled.

"Don't be long," she smiled, her high heels aimed toward a pair of double doors which caught Bayla's attention for their glass panels draped in fine white lace.

"I'll get our suitcases, my dear. The coats go there." He pointed to a large oval mirror with large white hooks set into a dark wood frame. "It's a Victorian coat rack. Mother chose it on one of my parents' trips to England." Bayla stood there, fixated by what surrounded her. "Go on," he almost laughed, gave her a gentle push, and left her alone.

The white marble floor was the same as the entrance to the Metropolitan Museum of Art on New York's Fifth Avenue. And like there, large paintings of country scenes in fancy gold frames hung on walls draped in maroon velvet. Three graceful palm trees, in separate planters, stood in a far corner and a grand circular staircase covered in a dark green rug with bright red roses led to an upper floor.

Bayla approached the mirrored coat rack, and fell dumbstruck at what stared back: a red-hatted, black-belted monstrosity, a touch of purple dripping down the right side of her face. The towns people already calling her a joke, a laughing stock who'd managed to snare Pittsmill's most eligible bachelor. Something faint and wispy seemed to glide behind her. Something hazy. A shadow perhaps. Someone in a wheelchair?

"So you made it. Your *fahvor finna vinkle.*"

"Yes, Mamma. My Never Never Land. What are you doing here?"

"These people. You think they won't see you don't belong? They'll throw you out. Fast. Then what?"

"I'll make myself belong. You'll see," Bayla said in a loud whisper. "I won't give up. Now leave me alone. Go. Your curses are no good here."

"Who are you fighting out there?" Izzy asked at seeing Bayla's fist in the air.

"I'm not fighting. I'm just...." She quickly placed their coats on a hook, making sure each was centered, hanging just so.

Up the grand staircase, walking slowly beside her husband, she stepped ever so carefully on the fine Persian runner with a tree-of-life design in shades of coral, maroon, and gray that covered the second floor hallway.

"Come here, wife," he commanded in a deep voice. He flexed his knees, and lifted her over the threshold of an open door, the first of several others along the hallway.

"Our very own bedroom, my dearest."

"My hero," she giggled, and momentarily glanced at the full extent of her failed expectations. "A bed, two night stands, and a dresser? It's so small."

He set her down, leaned over the bed and snapped open the locks from a suitcase. Bayla reached over him to slam it shut, but her hips got caught between the bed's high dark wood carved footboard and a knob on the dresser drawer.

"There's not even enough room in here for me to turn around. We've travelled so far for this? And me leaving my mother in that place? Where were you going to put her?"

"A room at the end of the hallway has a single bed. Bayla, we're paying such little rent."

"Rent, like immigrants? Like we're boarders in this grand house?"

"Since father died six years ago, the business doesn't bring in what it used to. Mother lives on his insurance. This was my room. Small, but it's an old house."

"Your brother and sister, do they pay rent?"

"Solomon does, but not Roseamond."

"If Solomon pays and we pay, why doesn't she?"

"Roseamond . . . can't."

"What are those other rooms on this floor?"

"There's mother's boudoir and Roseamond's room and...."

But she was already in the hallway having opened the door to his brother's room.

"So elegant. So lived-in," she said in a whisper at the mahogany four-poster bed, two upholstered chairs, a desk, armoire, and footstool.

"If Solomon finds out we've barged in...."

"Afraid of your brother? A little brother in a family, my mother would say is *maazel*. What's that that smell?"

"Solomon smokes cigarettes. Camels. Nonstop."

"There's no air in here." Bayla pushed apart a pair of floor-to-ceiling velvet draperies and opened one of the double windows. "There," she said, inhaling cold winter air.

"No. I'm not afraid of him, and I'm not lucky to have him. I've barely spoken to him since I moved to New York nine years ago and I know what I'm saying when I tell you to put everything back the way it was."

"Who's going to get upset over fresh air? He'll want to make a good impression on me."

"Solomon doesn't care about impressing anyone. Bayla, my dear wonderful wife, every family has rough edges. You'll get to know all of ours but for now, how about putting your best foot forward? Try to fit in."

"Once we're settled, I'm going to audition at Cafe Genteel. People in this town should know you married a star. If I tried to fit in, I couldn't do that, could I?"

"You'll always be a star no matter what."

The bathroom was larger than the tenement apartment where she and her mother lived. Filled with exquisite light from two large windows, an off-white velvet swag across the top of each, the room glowed from opaque pink glass tiles that covered the floor and walls. The sink was cream with gold faucets, a porcelain cream tub rested on gold lion's claws.

"You admire, my dear. I'll head downstairs. Mother doesn't like to be kept waiting."

Bayla removed her shoes, pulled her skirt to her thighs, reached one leg at a time over the tub's side, and stretched full length along its smooth bottom. She placed behind her head a thick cream-colored towel precisely folded on a rack near the tub, and closed her eyes. Imagining hot water, frothy bubbles up to her chin, she sang softly, "Oh my man I love him so, he'll never know. Oh my life is just despair, but I don't care."

How long had she dozed? She awoke to loud voices, rose quickly, put on her shoes, straightened her clothes and tread carefully down the grand staircase, pausing several feet from the open kitchen door. Don't keep Mother waiting, he had said.

"A white, Jewish girl, she thinks she's Billy Holiday? This isn't Harlem. You need a wife, my son, not a blues singer." It was her mother-in-law spouting accusations. "Pittsmill is no different from any other small town. There are unwritten rules for behavior, from mill workers to the wealthy few, like us. Not even a 'Hello? How are you?'"

Bayla felt her jaw tighten. What had she missed that this mother-in-law had already said about her? And she *did* say hello. She even shook the woman's hand.

"You know me. If I see something, I speak out. And no offer to help? Put these napkins on the tray. No. Smooth. Like this. They're linen."

"Bayla doesn't care about a wrinkled napkin, linen or otherwise."

"You're starting a new job, it should be a success. What kind of wife will she make? You think she'll cook and clean like I did when the three of you were small? And how could you let her walk into town dressed that way? So brash. So bold. Perfect fodder for the townsfolk."

"I didn't bring my wife here to make a fashion statement. We fell in love. Your hard-working reliable son, in love. Imagine that. You're the one who taught us to ignore the gossip."

Bayla held back from barging in. She had always assumed that Izzy rarely spoke about his mother because she didn't want to talk about hers. Now she understood.

"You want to know what this is about? You call one week ago, one week to tell me you got married. Not a word that you're dating, no plans to marry in Amory Lane, to invite family, friends? No Jewish wedding? It's unlike you. Hurtful to me…and to your brother."

What would her new husband say to that? Bayla was rooting for him.

"My wife had to put her mother in a state facility. The woman's mind was gone. It wasn't easy for her. We weren't about to arrange festivities."

"Why didn't you bring the mother here? We could have found her a proper place. A refugee from Hungary. For God's sake. She came at the turn of the century with the largest number of Jewish immigrants. She deserves better than an institution."

Bayla was pleased to hear her compassion, the kindness to her dear mother.

"I offered. Bayla refused. You want the whole story, Mother? My wife's a deprived child whose strongest instinct is her will to survive. She had to leave school at fifteen to help support the two of them. She's worked ever since. She's talented and she loves me and for all she's been through, she deserves a break. And she's going to get one here, in this house. With us. She's the wife I want and I know you'll do your best to accept her."

Not wanting to hear any more, Bayla took a few steps forward.

"Ah, Bayla, come in. We were discussing refreshments," her mother-in-law said. "Izzy dear, the tray please. I'll take the platter. Come, children." The lilt in her voice had returned.

She felt she was on a Hollywood movie set. The parlor walls were dark green, green velvet draperies were drawn from the window with peach-colored tassels, the rug had purple vines and fluffy white flowers. In front of a large brick hearth was a pair of settees, a glass coffee table between them, an ottoman in front of an upholstered bench and two armchairs. Floor lamps, with multi-colored cut-glass shades, reflected the room's warm colors.

Such a place, and she in her beige wool sweater, too tight around her chest, and her plain, calf-length brown skirt. She stood in the center of the room with no idea where to sit or where to place her hands. Izzy had offered to buy her a new outfit, but she took offense. The wedding dress, and outdoor winter clothing, were obligations piling up. The clothes she wore living with her mother were good enough. No point to spend when those would do.

"Make yourself comfortable. Sit. Sit." His mother chose one of the settees facing the hearth, Izzy opposite her. Bayla stepped toward a low chair with wooden arms, but as she sat, there was a distinctive snap.

"Ya' broke it already?" her mother-in-law said over a throaty laugh.

"Mother's working-class persona escapes now and then."

"I'm not ashamed of where I've come from, my son. The years I worked with my dear husband, Sam, putting every penny into our business."

While smiling at the bemused faces pretending not to notice,

Bayla tried to fit between the chair's open arms by wiggling unobtrusively from side-to-side. In a final frustrated gesture, she thrust herself back causing a loud smack against the wall. Izzy's expression of sadness and humor contrasted with his mother who seemed to want her new daughter-in-law, incapable of sitting properly on a chair, to disappear.

Bayla rubbed a pain in her neck and sensing cold air under her thighs suspended beyond the edge of her seat, she rose. Feeling more exposed than when she was performing on stage, she settled near her husband in a chair whose bottom more perfectly matched her own.

Her mother-in-law broke the silence. "First things first. You don't mind me calling you Bayla, do you?"

How could she answer such a question? "It's my name." The conversation she had overheard while standing outside the kitchen was still roiling inside her head.

"Yes. Well, my name is Charlotte, Szarlotka, in Polish, S-z-a-r-1 – o-t-k-a. It means apple pie, can you imagine? After my parents arrived, they Americanized it. My friends call me Lotzky. I wasn't sure you'd be comfortable calling me 'Mother,' so why don't you call me by my first name? Charlotte."

"I'll call you whatever you want." Such a fuss over names when all she wanted was to make her husband proud.

"Is that a Victrola?" She pointed to a cabinet with a circular speaker in its middle.

"It's a radio phonograph, dear, a Stromberg Carlson. We take our after dinner drinks listening to the masters—Mozart, Beethoven, Chopin, Liszt."

"Do you listen to anything popular?"

"Of course. Franz Lehar, Romberg. Gilbert and Sullivan."

Bayla didn't recognize one of those names and she wanted to get a word in about her performing, but Charlotte Lotzky, who probably never heard a blues song, cut her off.

"Time for refreshments. What would you like, dear?"

Bayla turned to the silver tray service Izzy had placed on the glass coffee table beside the platter of chocolate brownies.

"Hot tea with lots of sugar."

Charlotte reached toward her with the tea, but in Bayla's eagerness for something warm and sweet, as she brought the china cup and saucer to her lips, the nervous flick of her hand caused a gush of liquid to splash onto her sweater.

"Oh my, I'm so sorry. This should help." Charlotte handed over a folded white linen napkin fringed in lace, but, hesitant to soil something so delicate, Bayla let it fall into her lap and with her hand, she nonchalantly whisked the liquid off her sweater as if she were at a Goldmacher's lunch break. Charlotte turned to her son who lowered his head.

"Bayla, why didn't you just—"

"It's fine, Mother," Izzy interrupted. "Leave it alone."

Such *meshagas*. So much to deal with. A family's exchanges, and where to sit and how to sip tea from a cup. Bayla was glad for the silence that followed, but it was short-lived.

"Tell me about your family, Bayla, so we can get to know each other. What does your father do?"

"He was a metal worker in a factory that built brass mailboxes for fancy New York City apartment buildings."

"Metal work is a respectable trade," Charlotte said. "Izzy always wanted to be an entrepreneur. He never cared for college like his younger brother Solomon. Solomon received his Bachelor of Science degree from the University of Pittsburgh. He runs our business. And what about you? Your work?"

What kind of welcome was this? His mother pushing her to reveal the shame of her past with questions and judgments? What had Izzy told her? Bayla waited for him, her safety net, her stand-by, hoping for a clue, but not one word out of him. Is this what he meant when he said the world would open for her if she married him?

"I didn't have a chance for. . . ." Bayla rummaged for words, "much education." She selected one of the brownies perfectly aligned on the large platter designed in colored florals.

"She had to work, Mother."

"You told her, didn't you?" Bayla said ready to accept the

inevitable. "We lived in the tenements, barely survived, my father left us. I had to—"

"Not quite as bad as growing up on the South Side of Philly," Izzy interrupted. "A little something for you to remember, Mother?"

Charlotte drummed the fingers of one hand on the coffee table for the briefest second. "Of course, what I served in those days wasn't off Limoges."

"We know, Mother. We've all been through the Depression."

"Me and my husband Sam, we worked, we sweated, built a business—"

"Mother's *schpiel*," Izzy interrupted, and rolled his eyes, jokingly, at Bayla.

"The owner was anxious to sell Amory Lane," Charlotte said, ignoring him. "His family had lived here for generations. He sold the mill to U.S. Steel for quite a sum. No one had an interior decorating business for miles, so we left the old neighborhood. Bought this house at a damn good price. I've been grateful ever since. Roseamond was only ten. Solomon—"

"He was fourteen. I was seventeen."

"But one also has to give back. I volunteer with the Red Cross, run the *Tikkun Olam* in our Pittsburgh synagogue, collect food for those in need." Charlotte was content to go on indefinitely. More tea and coffee were poured, conversation eased. Tempers cooled. Familiar as she was with cues, Bayla sensed the timing was right.

"Izzy, did you mention—?"

"Mention what?" Charlotte asked sweetly.

"Bayla, it's not important. Mother and I will talk later."

"We have no secrets here," Charlotte said. "What is it?"

Bayla brushed some crumbs from her lap onto the rug. "It's just that, well, our room—"

"Yes?" Charlotte leaned forward and smiled.

"Not now, Bayla. Please," Izzy entreated.

"I can barely move in there. You must have something more," she paused again, searching for the right words, "more, more roomier in this grand house?"

Izzy dropped his china teacup into its saucer with a loud clunk.

Charlotte rose from the settee, her voice biting. "You have been invited to live at Amory Lane. Do not forget your place."

Who was this stranger to remind her of her place? If she tried for the rest of her life she could never forget her place as her mother's servant, a factory worker, the primary support of her family. She had left New York, quit her job, given her farewell performance at The Saloon to cries of 'Encore.' And now this woman whose fancy style and manners deepened the hole in her heart that came from having to leave her mother where she did.

Bayla rose from her chair, her heart pounding inside her ears. To have believed Izzy that in her new home everything would be better: comfort, protection, acceptance, a singing career.

"You have no idea what my place has been, or what I've been through or what I had to leave behind to come here. To live."

"Mother, don't!" Izzy shouted as his mother stepped towards his new wife.

"This is my house and no one speaks to me that way or tells me what to do, and don't think you're going to rule me through my son. You would be wise to ensure his happiness. If you don't, you'll end up with zilch. Nada. Nothing, not even him."

Bayla held steady for a moment, desperate for a safe place to set her sights. They fell on the Limoges platter. Charlotte lifted it to her face.

"Why don't you finish them? You've eaten all the rest."

Bayla reached out, something in her hand, an empty platter, the sound of high heels thumping out of the room. Dazed and wounded, she sank back down into her chair.

"I know you don't believe me, but give her time. She starts out tough, but she'll come around. That's how she raised us."

"You must be crazy," Bayla said, her mouth full. "One wrong move and I'm done for."

"Solomon has always been mother's favorite son. Roseamond, her favorite child. I'm the only one standing on my own feet. But the way she just defended me was a first. And why? Because she recognizes in you the take-charge, no-nonsense part of herself. I found it terribly arousing."

Clinks and hisses from Amory Lane's hearth warmed the chilly atmosphere while the hot tea banished Bayla's shivers from their long journey. She had to think fast. Stay alert. Her life with her husband's people in this house where she had willingly come lay in the balance.

"Close your eyes. You're as exhausted as I am." He stretched full length on the settee. "Take a nap. Live dangerously. Tonight, when I make love to you, I'll transport you to uncharted territories. The size of our room will be meaningless."

She didn't want this terrible mounting up. Perhaps Charlotte would be the last to add to her enemy's list. Behind her head, a soft red velvet pillow. She leaned back and closed her eyes, forgetting she hadn't met the rest of the family.

Chapter Ten

Roseamond

A bell, the faintest jingle sounded.

"It's Roseamond," Izzy said. "Come. We'll pay her a visit."

Bayla remembered the red velvet pillow but that sound? Had she dreamed it?

"Why doesn't your sister come downstairs? Meet us here? She's not sick, is she? If I'm going to audition—"

"It's nothing you can catch." The way he said it, she felt like a fool. Best to meet her another time. Maybe not at all.

Her room was more like an apartment: a pedestal table and chairs, a four-poster bed with an exquisite lace canopy, and on the far side, a door with 'Bath' on a decorative tile.

"This is Roseamond," Izzy said by way of introduction, "my sister."

The white skin, delicately sculptured profile, blondish hair waved to her shoulders resembled the cameo her mother had brought from the old country, pinned to a piece of tattered lace that sat on their dresser. But while the cameo was dull and flat, his sister had a translucence that shimmered from her slight frame, as if she were enchanted.

Dressed in peach bedclothes, Roseamond reached out from under the tassels of the canopy that framed her private atmosphere. "I'm so glad you're both here." It sounded as if she were welcoming treasured gifts. "And Bayla, a friend my own age. Come. Let me hug you."

As Bayla's sights were lavished by the wistful beauty of linens and lace—spreads, coverlets, pillowcases, and throws—everything peach and beige, and a rug of soft mauves on the pine floor, her sense of smell was also entertained. Rose, lavender, and lemon scents lingered from all shapes and sizes of cut-glass and crystal dishes, atomizers and perfume bottles waiting on an antique tray, atop a dresser, on a chair seat, a bookcase, and night tables on each side of the bed. At the same time, subtle patterns of light, reflected from the outside world through three large windows, roamed freely on walls, furniture, and fabrics.

As if she were delivered into an undiscovered kingdom of beauty and grace, Bayla was afraid to move, the way you might be charmed by a dream that one misstep could destroy.

Izzy bent beneath the canopy and kissed his sister's cheek, then settled in one of the chairs around the claw-footed pedestal table at the foot of the bed. Bayla remained near the door.

"Give her a hug. Go on."

In the tenements, if someone had an illness it was talked about in whispers, if at all. "I haven't seen your Sadie." "She's resting." People understood. To mention specifics might attract an *eine horah*. So what kind of introduction was this, as if the episode in the parlor with Izzy's mother wasn't enough? And hug her? Bayla hugged her mother, and at Goldmachers her Jewish girlfriends offering good-byes after work. But someone sick in bed, so young, and fragile? Izzy's family might all live in this house, but to Bayla they were strangers.

"Yes, Bayla, come closer," the cameo said.

Rather than risk being taken for a fool in this place where reality seemed to elude her, the request, asked in such a soft voice, Bayla chose to ignore. She pointed instead to what looked like a small vase with colored baubles that sat on a dresser. "What's that?"

"Lentheric Bouquet," Rosamond said, "for daytime wear, from Paris. You can try it whenever you wish. The jewels are embedded in the glass."

"No thank you," Bayla said. She remembered the pretty lady at the Five and Dime on 96th Street who offered a spray of D'Amour, but such a rich gift for this Roseamond. In bed?

"I'm crazy for perfume," Roseamond said. "When I could go downtown to Delia's Variety with my friends, I knew every essence, eyes closed: citrus, rose, oriental." She waved her delicate hand around the room. "You're smelling the potpourris. Dried herbs and flowers. Lavender for love, chamomile and lily of the valley for peace, peach, apple, citronella and cinnamon sprinkled with ginseng for strength and energy."

"What's that?" Bayla stepped toward a large square boxy thing on the night table.

"It's a radio."

"Your own radio?" Bayla couldn't hide her astonishment at the impossibility of one person in a room larger than the apartment where she lived with her mother, having a radio.

"Tell her your favorites," Izzy said.

"Soap operas. And big bands. Garland, Sinatra, Billie Holiday."

Izzy smiled broadly as if he had for some time looked forward to his new wife meeting his bed-ridden sister.

"How long do you have to stay in bed, and when do you think you can to go outside?" Bayla took a few more steps into such a room she could never have imagined.

"I go outside, around the garden, but I'm required bed rest. It has to do with...." She tapped her chest indicating where the trouble was. "My friends visit, and now I have you."

"Don't tie her down, dear sister. Bayla is her own person."

"We're alike then," Roseamond said. "I know about your plan to audition and I know about The Saloon and those men who adored you. I can't wait to hear more, but don't mention any of that to Mother. She'll give Izzy a hard time. With her, Solomon, can do no wrong. He's such a spoiled brat, only thinks about himself. Anyway, I handle mother the best."

"I know how to protect myself," Bayla said.

"That's my job as your husband. It's not for you or Roseamond to take on."

"Bayla's a stranger in a strange land," Roseamond said.

"So biblical," Izzy laughed. "Leading my wife out of the desert?"

"We need to guide her, make her feel like she belongs. Here. With us. In this house. In this town."

Still standing at the far end of the room, Bayla wanted to say thank you for thinking of her in that way, this person she barely knew.

"You can come closer," Roseamond said, her hand drifting to her lips as if to cover her disappointment in case Bayla refused. "I don't usually bite."

Bayla stepped toward Roseamond's bed, paused, then plopped down, jostling the canopy's tassels.

Roseamond laughed. "What a refreshing change. Someone who doesn't tiptoe around me. You can practice your singing whenever you like. I'll be your biggest fan. And I'm excellent at keeping secrets. Tell her, Izzy."

"My sister is excellent at keeping secrets, but she's best at playing hooky. Sneaking into the movies in Pittsburgh, swiping perfume off the counters in our department store when naughty girls like her should be in school." He spoke with a touch of nostalgia, as if the person in bed wasn't destined for more of the same.

"I called them field trips," Roseamond laughed. "It was more fun than sitting in school all day on hard, wooden seats, though I liked flirting with boys, and holiday dances."

"I loved school," Bayla blurted out. "Mine was all-girls but I couldn't finish. I had to work. My mother and I, we…."

"I didn't know." A sadness descended over Roseamond, as if she was the one who had to leave the one place she loved more than anything. This person who Bayla had just met, able to understand how she felt back then.

"I'll tell mother you'll both have dinner here tonight," Izzy said, indicating they had visited long enough.

"We can't eat here," Bayla said, shocked. "Your mother's so strict."

"Not with me," Roseamond perked up. "We're going to do whatever we want. Someone my own age in Amory Lane. The times we'll have."

Bayla wanted to ask, like what?

Izzy explained that his mother still enjoyed her place in the kitchen but for that evening Mrs. Diedero, Amory Lane's housekeeper for over ten years, who mostly cleaned house and did grocery shopping, cooked the food. There was roasted chicken, mashed potatoes and creamed coleslaw served on rose-colored Wedgewood china, apple cider sipped from purple goblets set on a large tray which he carried up the grand staircase and placed on the pedestal table. But Bayla barely noticed. Everything was Roseamond. How she ate—dabbing the ends of her mouth with the napkin. How she laughed—soft, at first, then full and sweet. How she moved—lifting her arms, shifting her body with a dancer's grace.

"Our first night in Amory Lane," Izzy said when they were cuddling in bed. "This will be our private time. Without family. We'll make it a tradition."

"After sex?"

"Of course after sex."

"Twice, like tonight?"

"Tonight we're celebrating."

Bayla replaced her nightgown below her knees. His exuberant lovemaking left her chafed and swollen. Always twice? Once was already enough.

She inhaled deeply, and eased beneath the heavy woolen blankets that shielded her and her husband from icy winds that asserted themselves beyond Amory Lane's age-old window frames. Her talent. What would happen to it in this place where she was untethered to anything familiar—streetlamps, car horns, neighbors' voices, a child's cry, the scent of a coal stove after a meal? Perhaps the fates would offer a sign, but there was only silence, not the kind she was used to, the kind she lived for when everything stopped after one of her songs, then a burst of applause.

How astonishing. The wall opposite their bed had turned startling white because of moonlight from the back garden. Moonlight where she slept. To believe such a thing was possible. Never again would she awaken in a tenement. For the rest of her life, her mornings and evenings would begin and end here.

Bayla turned toward her husband, rested her head on his

shoulder, and closed her eyes, anxious for morning and Roseamond, her soft, childlike laugh, her graceful movements, her warm welcome, like a lasting embrace.

Early one afternoon, seated at the pedestal table, Bayla was reading *Gone With the Wind* aloud to Roseamond, propped up in her bed.

"Is anybody home?" It was a man's voice shouting up to them.

"It's Solomon," Roseamond said. "He knows I'm here. He does that to get a chuckle out of me. Mother will be worried that he didn't get the job done because he's two days early, but she won't reprimand him. She never does. Hurry up. He'll be here in a minute."

For two weeks Roseamond had been filling Bayla's head about Solomon's good looks, his charm, his way with women; the gifts he brings her after an out-of-town job: a handkerchief with her initials, a chenille throw for her bed, a Guerlain lipstick; how their mother refers to him as King Solomon, like in the Bible, though he's only king inside this house.

Bayla adjusted her clothes and perfected her posture. Roseamond smoothed the bed covers over her feet and puffed her pillows. In a tweed blazer, a light green shirt, and khaki slacks, his head cocked to one side, his blue eyes sparkling, his smile was broad as his outstretched arms which he wrapped around his sister in a hug held slightly too long.

"This is Bayla," Roseamond said. "She's more than a sister-in-law. We're best friends."

"Well, let me see." He took hold of Bayla's hands and pulled her to standing. She didn't know whether to feel flattered, or embarrassed, Solomon assessing her as if she were a chicken roasting in the oven. "And where did my hardworking, New York City brother find you, the lucky sap?"

"He picked me up when I skidded across the floor at a free dance." Some admission to a man who entered the room expecting everyone in it to stand at attention?

"Was it a fix up? A bar? A chance meeting?"

He reminded her of new fabric from Goldmacher's, uncut silk that slipped through your hands as you worked it, no matter how hard you tried to keep it steady.

"You'll have to ask him," Bayla said demurely.

She was certain he could read her thoughts, see her sorrows and inadequacies beneath the weave of her blouse, the shape of her undergarments. She wanted to gain his approval for reasons she couldn't understand, much less explain.

"Sadly, I confess, my brother isn't inclined to tell me much. Anyway, it doesn't matter where he first cast his eyes on you. You're an official member of the family now. Come downstairs. We'll get to know each other over coffee." His voice was smooth as the vanilla ice cream on the wafer cones Izzy bought her from vendors on Saturdays in Battery Park.

"Don't take her away," Roseamond wailed, "and she's not going to make you coffee."

"I don't need Bayla to make me coffee. And I would never deprive you of anything, my dear sister." He reached beneath the canopy and ran his index finger across Roseamond's cheek. "I'm broadening her horizons. Come, Bayla, come with me."

Bayla followed him out of the room as if he embodied all the light in the world.

"Don't forget to bring her back," Rosamond yelled after them.

They sat face to face at the small French bistro table in the kitchen sipping Perrier which he had poured. He mentioned her singing, told her he knew an agent who booked acts at Café Genteel. He said he would arrange a meeting, proving Izzy wrong. He *did* want to make a good impression.

"What kind of talent does he book?" Bayla asked.

"What kind of talent does he book?" Solomon repeated in a way that confirmed him the expert, she the protégé. "You've got the lingo down pat, I see."

"You flatter me, Solomon." One agent, one audition. That was all she needed. Her career would take off, here, in Pennsylvania.

"Ah, yes. Flattery gets you anywhere, doesn't it?"

She laughed. Is that what he was doing? Was that it?

He gulped the last drop and gently set the glass down. "Well, I must get back to work now. We'll continue our discussion later. It never ends when you're a business owner. Go back to my sister. It pleases me greatly how well you're both getting on."

The evening meal celebrated the newlyweds and Solomon's return: Honey-roasted turkey with chestnut stuffing, creamed string beans, roasted potatoes, radicchio salad with greens, pineapple upside down cake with vanilla ice cream for dessert, and champagne toasts. With everyone joyous around the dining room table, Bayla felt like Jean Harlow celebrating her winning a horse race and a marriage proposal from Clark Gable at the end of *Saratoga*. Then she remembered Harlow died tragically before filming was completed.

At the end of the meal Solomon announced he was off to a client. Izzy and Charlotte meandered into the parlor for after-dinner cordials. Bayla walked Roseamond upstairs. "Baby Snooks," starring Fanny Brice, was interrupted by a knock on her door.

"It's Cary Grant."

"It's your husband," Roseamond giggled. "Come in."

Izzy settled into the empty seat at the pedestal table.

"Mother and I had a tiff," he said, somewhat amused. "Go sit with your wife and Roseamond," she said. "I don't enjoy being insulted by my firstborn."

"You insulted your mother?" Bayla asked astonished.

"I merely asked her how our dear brother was managing. 'Your brother's an exemplary businessman.' That's a new one. So I asked who paid for his white Buick sitting in the garage."

"Mother did. Who else? You think they shield me but I know what's going on." Roseamond was oh so smarmy. Bayla was almost gleeful. Family secrets. Izzy never told her much about such things. Now she would hear everything, she from the tenements.

"Solomon cleaned out a ten-thousand-dollar-bank account in three months."

"Roseamond, how could you say that?" To Bayla it might as well have been millions.

"It's true," Izzy said." When I left this house I never asked for a penny. All I got was a ride to the train station. Mother forgets. Solomon goes too far. Bets at the track. Expensive trinkets for girlfriends. Money for cards. Custom-made clothes. Investments that go nowhere."

"If father only knew, in the six years since he's been gone, debts piled up."

"Father knew. He always knew: Solomon would ask mother for money. Mother would threaten father. Father would give it to her to pass on to Solomon then complain to me. Father couldn't confront mother, Mother can't say no to Solomon, and Solomon will never stop asking. The famous Rothschild secret. Shhhh." Izzy placed his index finger to his lips. "Never say a word, then it won't exist. I'm no longer a child Mother can manipulate. I'm back, on my own with a wife. The status quo inside Amory Lane has shifted. Solomon won't take that lying down. Anyone for a game of Hearts?"

"Teach me," Bayla said. It was all too much for her to absorb; money problems in a family that had so much of it.

After a morning-lavender-scented soak in the tub with the gold lion's feet, Bayla tied her robe around her middle and headed down the silent hallway to her room.

"Good morning."

She was certain Solomon had left for work, but there he was closing the door to his room, so handsome in a suit and tie, ready to meet customers.

"Prepared to audition?"

"Not like this," she laughed.

"My friend, the agent, is anxious to meet you. I considered telling you last evening at dinner but didn't feel right talking freely about your career in front of family."

"I'm happy to audition for your friend." Bayla nonchalantly tugged her robe where the nape of her neck was too exposed. She wanted to dress quickly for him, shed her pink bunny slippers, a gift from Izzy, but he moved toward her with a curious urgency.

"There's something you should know."

"Yes?" she said, curiosity and admiration in her smile.

"It has to do with a friend of mine, something he told me about you."

How strange. They knew no one in common. He looked pointedly into her face as if to find something he believed was there, then moved his gaze to the nape of her neck, the place she had taken care to cover. She turned somewhat away from him, but he closed the space between them, as if he would touch her? Kiss her? Hadn't Roseamond mentioned his way with women?

"What is it?"

"It's about Manny."

That name in this house? She had to remain calm, find out what this was about.

"He told me there was an incident. You throwing yourself at him in their loft, after dinner, when you were leaving."

"Hush. You'll wake your sister."

He lowered his voice, baited her with pauses, his voice rising at the end. Questioning.

"You kissed him. The way you did it. So my brother, your husband, couldn't notice?"

"Never. I never did."

"I have no reason to doubt him, but you. Performing where you did, biding your time for a repeat performance here, in this town? My mother won't have it, and neither will I. A floozy blues singer living in this house, that's quite enough. You'll never fit into this family."

"You can't stop me from singing."

"The thing is, I can. And if you ever again enter my private domain, touch my drapes, open my windows, move a chair, a piece of paper, your stay here will be more temporary than you might have anticipated. One dirty little secret. That's all it takes. And now I have one, about you. Do you understand, Miss Singing Star?"

"All this because I went into your room? What a tough guy. A regular Jimmy Cagney."

"How dare you compare me to a two-bit actor."

"He's a Hollywood star."

Solomon grabbed her wrist with one hand. She wrangled free and stepped away. Solomon, the dashing man about town, believing Manny's lies, the two of them scheming behind her back, to do what?

"You mind your place, or I'll tell my brother about you and—"

Again, her place. First from Charlotte, now from him.

"Tell whatever you want to my husband. To your family. Tell the whole town."

"Don't threaten me, Missy."

"You're a joke compared to what I've been through. You have no idea who I am."

As if she were nothing, a nobody, he shoved her out of his way and disappeared down the grand staircase. She wanted to go after him, Mr. King Solomon, hit him with some choice words, or God forbid, give one quick push to the person who slept barely ten steps from her and her husband.

"Bayla? Bayla. Is that you?"

Roseamond had come out of her room. What had she heard?

"Oh, my. What a sight. Flushed at the gills in your robe. What have you been doing?"

"Relaxing in the tub, enjoying myself at Amory Lane, exactly like you suggested."

During the past few weeks Bayla had become used to acting civil towards Charlotte. Now she would have to do the same with Solomon. Another enemy in this house she didn't need.

Chapter Eleven

Soap Operas and Other Tales

The story soon fell into place: How the beautiful, mischievous teenager spent more days ill at home than in high school. How handsomely paid doctors concurred when the Rothschilds lived in the old neighborhood, Roseamond's sore throats, residual aching muscles and swollen joints indicated rheumatic fever. The bed rest she required had to do with a weakening heart that had little chance of strengthening. How long she would last, the doctors couldn't specify. Periodic checkups, drawing blood, and medication were provided by the family physician, Dr. Javitts. And a modicum of her energy was preserved by Mrs. Verplanken, who assisted Roseamond with dressing and bathing several days a week.

During Pennsylvania's frigid winter, while bare tree limbs in the back garden tapped unfamiliar rhythms against fragile glass panes and ferocious wind gusts rattled Amory Lane's ancient window frames, and very little bloomed during those long bleak months, the friendship between Bayla and Rosamond blossomed.

Inside Amory Lane, Bayla's days were occupied by the rhythm of its inhabitants, a rhythm, tone and mood that encouraged her to spend her days primarily with the unpredictable, deliberate, amusing, occasionally threatening Roseamond.

"Why don't you ever talk about your father?"

"No one asks me such things. Why do you?"

"I'm curious."

"My father left when I was seven. Why don't you talk about being a garage mechanic?"

"My brother told you? I would have loved to work with my hands, figure what was wrong, then fix it. Mother hated the idea. And the townsfolk. Imagine the gossip. Someone from Amory Lane, working in a garage! No. It was cruel to think I could."

"Your mother was cruel for not letting you."

"If anyone knows about cruelty, it's you, tormenting your sick mother!"

"I had to be cruel to be kind. You can't possibly understand."

"Sweet, cruel girl." Roseamond giggled. "Your life back then, compared to mine? You're probably right, but never be afraid to tell me about it."

"I had to work. You stayed in school. And what you say. No one I know says what you do."

"What do I say?"

"Meaningful things."

"I'm sure my brother, your husband, says meaningful things."

"No. When a man converses, his ardor plays into it."

"Ardor. That's a sex word."

"What do you know about ... that?"

"You and I are only eleven months apart. I'm not the child you think I am. When I was sixteen Danny Ridell tried to put his thinger in me, but it only went part way. His parents came home early from the movies, so we had to stop."

"I was supporting my mother when I was fourteen, and it's called a penis and part way in isn't sex. Who talks about such things?"

"Close friends."

"I never had a close friend. Till you."

"If I impress you with my words, you impress me with your voice. Singing your head off all day. In this house. Blues songs. Pop songs. Stuff I never heard."

"Only when we're alone so your mother and brother would be bothered."

"They're not bothered now that they know you better. How do you feel when you sing?"

"I don't know. Wait." Bayla broke into "Am I blue." "I feel like I go somewhere," she said when the song ended, "and don't ask where because I don't know. I disappear."

"One day I'm going to have intercourse," Roseamond said, a dreamy look in her eyes. "I'm determined to know what it's like."

"Where did that come from?"

"Your song. I'm not going to be 'a sad and lonely one.' I'll find someone. You'll see. It's almost time. 12:30. We almost forgot. Hurry up!" Roseamond shouted.

When she first met Roseamond, Bayla considered it extravagant, one person in all that space with her own radio. Now she understood. Now it made sense. Bayla leaped off Roseamond's bed and turned on the radio.

And now for Our Gal Sunday, the story that asks, can an orphan girl from a mining town in the West find happiness as the wife of a wealthy titled Englishman? Then it was *Backstage Wife, a stenographer in New York who married matinee idol Larry Noble, only to find herself in the wings.* And then, *The Romance of Helen Trent determined to prove romance can begin at 35.*

When their shows ended, Bayla and Roseamond revisited each nuance, action and sentiment of their radio characters as if they lived in the same towns, interacted with their troubles, shared their secrets. They groaned at romances betrayed, suffered dramatic disagreements, and laughed at made up "what if's." Throughout winter's snow, sleet and plunging temperatures, from under the canopy on Roseamond's bed, or walking around the room when her legs needed to stretch, with the men out at work, and Charlotte with her lady friends or volunteering at the Red Cross, Jewish or various charities, Bayla, marked by deprivation, and Roseamond, restrained by illness, each instinctively sensed the other's unwanted realities.

Roseamond's innate ability nurtured the hurting child inside Bayla, and Bayla, in turn, become pervious to Roseamond's goodness.

As weeks passed and Bayla's wounds from her early life began to ease, such validation brought Roseamond newfound strength. The more each one gave, and accepted from the other, the stronger the bond grew between them. Bayla secretly hoped the time she spent with Roseamond would never end.

Inside Amory Lane, Roseamond was becoming less the invalid, more like healthy girls her own age, relieving the family of the burden to prolong her breath. *I did this without knowing I could,* Bayla told herself. She believed the fates wanted her to discover what she was capable of outside of her life in the tenements. Besides learning to placate Charlotte, fulfill her wifely duties, and serve as Roseamond's confident, she imagined ways to maneuver Solomon so he would agree to introduce her to a theatrical agent.

As she approached her first spring at Amory Lane, Izzy grew more determined to inform the family at breakfast or after dinner about worldwide events from his beloved newspapers.

"Germany, Italy and Japan joined in an alliance. Fascists bombing Spain, innocent people dead. All of it for what? War in Europe was inevitable," he predicted. On top of that, the coal miners and autoworkers had unionized. "John L. Lewis, President of the Congress of Industrial Organizations, warned on NBC that the steel industry would be next. Pittsmill is already gearing up. Secret meetings, emergency measures behind the scenes. It's all the townsfolk are talking about."

"You mean our Shenandoah mill?" Bayla didn't think she heard correctly.

"Yes. They must have a union," Charlotte added, "and decent living wages, and regulations to protect our workers from carbon monoxide poisoning, pneumonia, lung disease." A woman who kept up with politics was a marvel to Bayla.

"Don't forget, Mother," Solomon chimed in, "the men work double shifts with no extra pay, no vacations—"

"Thank you for reminding us, dear. The decorating business that your father and I started was a union shop. We put workers' safety first. The steel industry should do no less."

"Everyone knows swing is the rage, and I want to learn."

"Learn what?"

"The dance steps. All my girlfriends know them. We don't have to go anywhere. Just a small gathering in the parlor. When no one's home. If you promise not to tell, I promise I won't overdo it."

"Benny Goodman just gave a concert at New York City's Paramount Theatre. Gene Krupa on drums. Harry James, trumpet, Twenty-one thousand, mostly teenage girls and young women lined up for a ticket. With "Sing Sing Sing" Goodman has become the King of Swing, but no. Absolutely not. You haven't the stamina. And how long have you been planning this? Your mother would kill me if she found out."

"I do have the stamina. You just don't know it. You haven't been here long enough."

"Three months is long enough." It was risky, even dangerous, yet why displease Roseamond if it was in her power not to?

"Call my girlfriends. They'll tell you. I get spurts of energy. I get to be my old self again. That's how this goes. I've decided to call it a 'A Swinging Afternoon.' Anyway, I've already written the invitations."

Two days later Bayla drove to Holiday's Music and Records on Main Street.

"Swing is boosting sales through the roof," Harry Hirshorn, the owner, led Bayla around the store. "During the Depression, we hit rock bottom. Only 5.5 million records sold across the country. Thank God, that's over."

She was tempted to ask, but there would be talk. It would get back to Charlotte who wouldn't be pleased. Don't ask for trouble, she heard her mother say. "Do you have any blues?"

"Blues? Of course. Singers, guitarists, bands from the Delta to Harlem. Original label recordings. Some of my best patrons are collectors. What are you looking for?"

"Swing. Today I'm after swing." She brought home a stellar selection beginning with "George White's Scandals of 1927" to the "King

Porter Stomp" arranged by Fletcher Henderson, the version Goodman was performing in concert, but one day she would return, flesh through the choices he offered like a child, anticipating rewards.

Mid-afternoon, one week later, with the family out of the house and Duke Ellington's "It don't mean a thing if it ain't got that swing" blasting from the Stromberg Carlson, Roseamond's girlfriends moved the furniture to one end of the parlor, and rolled up the rug.

"Bayla's the D.J.," Roseamond announced, "and Betty's calling. She knows the steps."

"We're gonna start with Tommy Dorsey's 'The Big Apple,'" Betty commanded. "Have you got it, Miss D.J?"

"I've got it," Bayla shouted, and changed the record.

"First truck to the left, shoulders down, step, step, wiggle those hips. Now to the right. Work in the stomps. Now Praise be Allah. Arms high. Higher. Improvise with the Suzi Q, or Shag. Keep the beat, girls. Roseamond, what's wrong?"

"I can't keep up."

"It's not as easy as the Lindy Hop," Alice and Jane piped up.

"Bayla, you've got to learn this with us."

"I can't. I'm the D.J."

But Roseamond insisted, so Bayla took off her shoes, forgot which foot went where, laughed through mistakes until everyone's steps were synchronized from Count Basie's "Blue Room," to Artie Shaw's "Non-Stop Flight." She was so focused on getting it right, she didn't notice that Roseamond had eased into one of the chairs. Her face colorless.

"She'll be fine," Betty shouted. "We've seen her like this. Give her a minute."

Bayla knelt beside her. "I'm calling the doctor."

"It's only momentary," Roseamond said, breathless.

Bayla ran into the kitchen for water certain it was her fault, knowing she'd do anything. Roseamond took a few sips. Her color improved.

"We told you." "She always perks up." "She's okay now."

"No one's to blame, Bayla. Don't take away our fun."

When the grandfather clock in the hall chimed three o'clock, the girls restored the parlor to its original condition. Roseamond watched. Bayla would never again forget how fragile Roseamond was or how she had manipulated her and how much worse it could have been.

"Your mother would have said no, and Roseamond wanted it so badly," she told Izzy in bed that night. "Those girls. Nothing to worry about but learning dance steps. Can you imagine?"

"It was wonderful what you did. I won't say a word to Mother, and my brother will never know. And forgive me, my dear, but I had to help with fabric deliveries. Tonight I'm too exhausted for—"

"I forgive you." She covered Izzy's face with kisses. Was sex necessary every night? All that huffing and sweating? "We need to laugh more, like those girls," she said. Izzy turned on his side, his back facing her, as usual.

Bayla smoothed the covers over his shoulders, inhaled his dusky, manly scent. It was still something of a surprise, him in bed beside her every night. Yet other things, things that she hadn't thought about, were changing. The temptations that drew her to his apartment on 65th Street were drifting away, and wasn't his desire that made him yearn for the Blues Diva also fading? Five months married and pondering alterations in their relationship seemed unreasonable. Was marriage to blame or moving to Pennsylvania, their time together limited with his family always there? Surrounding them. Doing this or that. Awake. Or asleep.

Saturday was their escape. Izzy would open *Pennsylvania Highways and Byways*, close his eyes, ruffle the pages, plunk down his finger. "Today's outing." They would see the sights, eat lunch in a local joint, dine in a restaurant after dusk. Sometimes it seemed as if their time together was a promise Izzy felt pressured to keep. She had no answers for what to do, as if anything needed to be done. Her relationship with her husband felt so different from what she had with Roseamond. The ease, the camaraderie of two women. Their disagreements and arguments, deeply-held feelings honestly exchanged. Their spontaneity. Their relationship, like a game, was so different from what she had with Izzy, which she would have described, if anyone had asked, as two separate worlds, never to meet.

With the town's steel workers planning to strike, a possible war in Europe, and Roseamond's precarious health, Bayla could no longer use 'all these goings on,' as excuses to avoid telephoning her mother. After months of being put off or turned down or rudely dismissed, she was determined to get through to the institution where she sent her mother to live. She had to hear her mother's voice. When Roseamond was napping, Charlotte was out, the house quiet, her voice on the telephone in the kitchen on the wall above the bistro table wouldn't echo. "Insist they bring the phone to your mother," Izzy had urged.

"State Institution." The voice was flat, dull, almost dead.

"This is Bayla Rothschild. I need to speak to Mrs. Lillian Szabo, my mother."

"I believe she's asleep."

"That's what they always say. I've paid extra so they would wheel her to the telephone."

"We can't disturb them when they're asleep. You have to call back when she's awake."

"If she's not asleep, she's eating or someone else is on the line. Wake her up. Wheel her to the phone. I give you permission. She's waiting to hear from me. I've been through this week after week. I'm calling long distance, from another state. Please get her."

"Why don't you write to her? Our patients can receive letters."

"I do write, and how dare you tell me what to do. It's bad enough I put her in your care. Now put her on the phone."

"I already told you. We're not allowed if they're asleep. Those are the rules."

"Put her on," Bayla shouted. "I want to hear her voice. I want to ask how she feels."

"I can tell you that. She's fine. She's doing very well."

"I want to hear it from her. I'll call the police, you hear me? The magistrate. The mayor."

The woman laughed. "This is a state institution. People don't care about that. Try later when she's awake." She hung up.

"Mamma. Mamma, I'm here. Your Bayeleh is here," she cried out. She pictured those women in white, that dilapidated building, her mother's body sloped forward in her wheelchair. Even if she did get through, "You are who? Who is Bayeleh? Why are you speaking to me?" her mother would ask. Even if she drove the hours-long trip, that wouldn't mask the truth. Her mother wouldn't recognize her from a tree stump or a rock, much less remember she was her only child.

"I have an announcement," Roseamond said. "I haven't felt so good in ages. Your being here has made me strong. Will you be my best friend—forever?"

"Whatever you want," Bayla said, trying to sound nonchalant. Roseamond's need of her had instilled in Bayla a sense of worth and purpose unlike anything she had ever known. Her wanting to protect the delicate creature, to take her in her arms, embrace her for safekeeping, had deepened during the almost six months they were together.

"Be careful what you say, Missy." Roseamond straightened up, suddenly playful and threatening from under her covers. "I steal your strength when you're not looking."

"Take it. I have plenty," Bayla laughed from her place on the bed, ignoring a sudden flutter somewhere in her middle, thankful that Roseamond didn't notice because if she did Bayla wouldn't be able to explain what it was or why it happened. "I'm going to make everything all right. I'm going to make you better."

"You're spooky, Bayla Rothschild. No one has that power. Believing in the fates. It's scary and you're ridiculous."

"And you're rude. My mother taught me about the fates. All she has is me and her old wives' tales. *Bubbe mayses.* They bring meaning to her life from the Old Country. "

"Do one thing wrong, a bad deed, an ill thought, and the fates will get you. Really! Believing in unseen powers and superstitions." Roseamond reached out and gently pushed Bayla back onto the bed, her head on the pillow scented by Roseamond's lavender bath oil.

"I'm not spooky. Now help me up."

"Got magic up your sleeve, or inside your dress? There or there or there?"

"Don't poke. It tickles. Stop. I can't breathe."

Among gales of laughter and periodic screams, Roseamond didn't stop.

Bayla spotted the open dish of sweet-smelling potpourri on the dresser beside the bed. She grabbed a handful and threw it at Rosamond. Roseamond scooped up two handfuls of dried flowers from her nightstand and tossed them at Bayla who had already rearmed herself with more of the same. By the time buds, leaves, vines and flowers decorated their hair, hung on their clothes, clung to curtains, furniture, lampshades, and covered the floor, their laughter slowing, their bodies close beneath the lace canopy of the four-poster bed. They smiled, or glared at one another, turned away or explored what each sought in the other's expression. For some minutes they didn't move. With their faces inches apart, minus the slightest provocation, word or warning, Roseamond inched toward Bayla and kissed her lovingly on the lips. Bayla jolted straight up, her face bright red.

"What was that?"

"A friendly kiss," Rosemond said as if what she had done was commonplace.

"I sewed uniforms in a sweat shop when I was 15 because I had to work and you, you, reckless child, you...." Words that weren't at all what she wanted to say leaped out of Bayla's mouth as fast as thread spinning on a bobbin.

"What are you talking about?"

"I don't know what I'm talking about. How can I know what I'm talking about after what you just did? For two women to.... My mother would call it a shame. A disgrace. A *shandeh*. I have a husband."

"I wanted to see what it feels like. To kiss someone I love before I leave."

Someone I love. Someone I love. What was she saying? Potent words. One woman to another. An onslaught of feelings deluged Bayla, like a sudden rainstorm, threatening her with something she couldn't say or name. She felt a surge of heat. A loss of breath. Her face turned bright scarlet. The realization that *someone I love* meant her.

Bayla slid her feet to the floor and backed away from Roseamond's bed.

"You're not going anywhere, and I'm a married woman, for God's sake."

"I am leaving. I don't know when but I am. What I did was a first. I don't have many firsts left. You should know that by now."

"Expecting me to bend to your will like everyone else in this house?" Bayla raised her arms to her sides them suddenly brought them down. " Oh," she shouted.

They retreated to separate corners: Bayla reclining in a chair, Roseamond draped down one side of her bed.

"Are you still mad?" Roseamond asked.

"Sometimes I don't know who you are. What you did was unnatural."

"What are you so afraid of? Doctors say I'm going to die, and I'm not afraid."

"You don't know your destiny. Unsuspecting things happen, sneak into your life. I came here wanting to audition and...."

"And you've been dilly-dallying and I don't know why. Do you know why?"

Now she'd done it. She said the worst thing anyone ever could. Like a knife in her chest. Bayla pushed herself to standing, walked from one end of Roseamond's room to the other.

"I'll tell you what I know. Time is a thief, a *gonif.* Time tried to stop me when I lived with my mother and sewed on a factory floor, but I got up on stage and performed. Then I married your brother and moved here. He tells me that here, time is on my side. I can audition whenever I want. So I spend time with you. I can practice for hours. Audition with a band. I'll never forsake my music. Should I forsake you? Is that what you want?"

"No."

Everything stopped in the silence of the room. Bayla took a breath.

"Sometimes when I wake up, I don't think I can let another day go by without choosing the one thing that I love more than anything. But other times, it's so much a part of me, I have to let go of it. I have to know that I can."

"Ridiculous. Go to Café Genteel. Go inside it. See yourself there."

"I will go. When I'm ready, but no more of—" Bayla brought her hand to her mouth.

"Okay. I'll never soil your pristine reputation again."

"It isn't funny. You have no respect for what's right between people."

"Ok, I won't, not ever. Happy now? And you promise to audition?"

"I promise to audition."

With peace restored, Bayla remained with Roseamond for the rest of the day until Izzy returned from work as eager to greet his wife as she was to smother her feelings especially after that kiss. The delicate touch. The perfect frame of her lips. The taste of her mouth, like warm, sweet tea.

Chapter Twelve

She Could Never Tell Anyone

"Mrs. Verplanken is leaving town," Charlotte raised her voice. "She's leaving the state. I can't bear to talk about it. She's moving to Oregon, to family. I've pleaded with her. Offered more money. Tried everything. She's taken care of Roseamond for years."

On a morning of Bayla's favorite breakfast—pancakes and hash browned potatoes—Charlotte, at the head of the table, looked as dreary as all outdoors. Bayla gulped her mouthful.

"I know what Mrs. Verplanken does for Roseamond. I've watched her."

From across the table, Izzy beamed at his wife. "It's a generous offer but—"

"Hold it right there." Solomon held up his hand like the crossing guard on Second Avenue, Bayla thought. He drew the cloth napkin across his mouth and plunked it down beside his plate. "She's my sister, so I have a say." He took a breath which deepened his voice. "Hire a professional. Listen to me, mother. My sister deserves nothing less."

"You aren't trained. Bayla," Charlotte said. "Roseamond may feel strong, but then—"

"And when Roseamond has one of her attacks, what's my brother's wife going to do? Sing her the blues?"

"Why not?" Izzy said and winked at Bayla, who grinned.

"Listen to me, Mother." Solomon rose from the table, the last bite of his cheese omelet in his mouth before heading to the garage, "Roseamond's got years ahead of her. She needs a professional," he yelled back. "With experience."

"I can do it," Bayla yelled after Solomon but the garage door slammed. "Let me try, Charlotte."

"Think about it, Mother. *Steel Strikes of 1937. Over eighty thousand steelworkers are being locked out of plants from Ohio to Pennsylvania,*" Izzy read the day's headlines. "John L. Lewis said U.S. Steel just signed on. Their workers will have the right to organize but our Shenandoah Mill is against it. If they call for a strike, all hell is going to break loose. Strike breakers, threats, rallies, protests, arrests."

"You're not telling me anything I don't know," Charlotte said. "At our synagogue the Ladies Auxiliary is already collecting money, clothes, food, everything our striking families will need. How can a man raise his family on less than $5.00 a day working 50 hours a week? Starvation wages, FDR calls it. As for your sister…." Her voice trailed off.

"We could ask Roseamond?" Bayla pleaded.

Charlotte turned to face Bayla. There was a remarkable kindness in her expression. Bayla didn't dare say another word. Charlotte liked to make up her own mind. So let her.

At the buffet table, Bayla selected Roseamond's breakfast, placed each item artfully on the tray, and without another word, headed upstairs.

"But your brother said hire a professional."

"Listen to me for a change. Give Bayla a chance," Izzy said so Bayla could hear. "You've got two weeks before Verplanken leaves. Let's at least keep Rosemond's life running smoothly."

Bayla dared to imagine it! From the moment Roseamond opened her eyes, Bayla would help her bathe and dress, oversee her meals, launder her clothes, suggest activities, fashion her hair into curls, or an upsweep, a French braid, maybe pig tails. Compared to the burden and obligation of assisting her mother, with Roseamond each day would offer the bounty of the day before, a guarantee of acceptance, newfound purpose. Rather than consider the chores as a sacrifice or I wish she didn't have to, she would see and hear and taste life from a place that had been eaten away, petrified like aged wood. Caring for Roseamond would feel like a reward, something earned. Officially granted.

That night, in bed, Izzy congratulated Bayla. "My mother has given you permission to take on Mrs. Verplanken's job, but it isn't going to be easy."

What she heard was, *here, in this house, in this new life, I could care for Roseamond and sing any time I choose.*

"Who has such an amazing wife as me?" he added with such a sense of pride when, to Bayla, it seemed that all she had done was to casually raise her hand like when she was in school. "Choose me." That's all she wanted. By volunteering for Mrs. Verplanken's job, she wasn't inching toward the one thing she never would have thought possible—forsaking her career. Her dream was still viable, available, as always. This raising of her hand was merely a one-time distraction, a renegade idea that wouldn't lead to anything more, or separate her from her true destiny.

By Memorial Day, Bayla had grown accustomed to picket lines at the mill, and Steel Workers Organizing Committee (SWOC) placards displayed throughout the town. Strike breakers, called 'scabs' in uniforms, each shouldering a rifle, were hired to keep the mill running. Additional cops were recruited and stationed around town prepared for trouble. The worst took place over one day in the Midwest and Northeast. Strikers beaten with billy clubs, some shot or killed. Pittsmill got lucky. Shenandoah Steel readily agreed to become a subsidiary of U.S. Steel which had already unionized. Everyone in town could relax.

"Our steel workers will have a shorter work week, a salary increase, a week of vacation, and improved working conditions," Izzy announced.

But for Bayla the significance of what the steel workers had achieved was personal. With everyone in the family breathing a sigh of relief, the pressure from Solomon, regarding her role with Roseamond, had dissipated. She felt a kind of freedom in her relationship with Roseamond, something like ownership, and rather than question what that meant, she simply let it be.

Among the grace of Augusts' sunny skies, early one morning Bayla found Roseamond in her nightgown leaning out of her bedroom window.

"What are you doing? Are you crazy? Get away from there."

"It's a perfect summer day. Today I can do anything. We're going to town."

Bayla slammed the window shut. "You don't need a cold, and put on a robe. I'll be right back." She ran down the stairs, darted across the hallway, opened Amory Lane's front door, sniffed the air, and quickly returned. "We'll leave after lunch."

They made their way beyond the brick walkway, down the cobblestones, across quiet back streets. As they crossed the intersection of Main and Oak, Bayla took Roseamond's hand, surprised by how warm and welcoming it felt, their fingers easily intertwined. Each was stylishly dressed in a long skirt, and summer blouse, Roseamond with a fine off-white cotton shawl draped over her shoulders, a wide-brimmed hat shading her face. Bayla wondered would two young women holding hands be viewed by townsfolk as something unreasonable, or peculiar?

At Fletcher's Ice Cream Parlour they sat on chairs with red vinyl-cushioned heart-shaped backs. They ordered melted cheese sandwiches and vanilla ice cream frappes with hot fudge.

"We're miles away, in a foreign city where no one knows us," Roseamond fantasized despite the stares and whispers of customers who belied that notion.

During the walk home Bayla felt a sense of excitement. The

two of them together, as if they were on a date. Dating, like with a man, and where did such an idea come from? And where would she take that idea next, she wondered, and after that and after that? She barely recognized such thoughts as her own. Had the fates intervened in this private escapade with Roseamond amid prying eyes, a swirling in her stomach, her heart racing? It almost felt, dare she use the word? Romantic. Weeks ago, after that kiss with Roseamond, the feelings she had, the ones she admitted to, would never return. Yet here they were. Again. If Roseamond knew, she would joke about it, say something silly and tempting and lewd. But no matter how certain she was about willing them away, Bayla was unable to stop an unnatural piling up of whatever it was drawing her toward Roseamond, as if the two of them were in love. As if she were in love with her, ignoring the role the fates played, how much they had intervened, what they had to do with this.

These last four months, serving as Roseamond's caretaker, and despite how close they were, Solomon's words remained. Be professional. She had already the guarantee of Roseamond's promise: *I'll never again soil your reputation*. Anyway real love only ever occurs between a man and a woman.

It was nearly five o'clock when they walked up Amory Lane's front porch.

"You'll have to get me washed before you dress me for dinner," Roseamond said. Even on clear days, there was no escaping the mill's grime. But Bayla knew there wasn't enough time to bathe separately. Impossible for one to appear at dinner shiningly clean, the other covered in soot. They would question her. Reprimands would follow.

"We'll have to bathe together."

"Lah de dah," Rosamond curtsied her willingness to obey.

"Stop it. No fooling around. If your mother finds out that I've kept you downtown all afternoon, and all that walking, she'll fire me for sure."

"We'll rendez-vous in my bathroom," Roseamond giggled.

Was it only weeks before when Bayla offered her mother's

lecture about the fates and their retribution, which convinced Bayla she would never again have to consider the deviancy of that kiss, or feel guilty for any lingering memories?

The day was so forthcoming and remarkable, the generous flourishes of shimmering light as the sun began its descent, transferred the pattern of roses in trellised arches from the lace curtains to the walls surrounding the oval tub in Roseamond's bathroom. Shangra-la, Bayla thought, as a gentle shiver flew through her body. Textures firm and delicate, a range of soft earth tones and the scent of lavender bath oil she drizzled into the hot water set the scene as they undressed, averting their eyes from one another as if something other than Bayla bathing Roseamond, as usual, was in the offing.

As Bayla tenderly folded their clothing, placing each item on a low, round ottoman, the feelings that made her so ill at ease during their walk home grew more intense. When it came time to step into the tub, she believed she could ignore what was churning inside her. She could do that. She could. Then inside that wet, warm, silent giving place where possibilities forbidden and unknown waited, she met Roseamond, face-to-face.

As she had done so many times before, Bayla worked up a lather with soap, using the Swedish loofah Charlotte had requested from a London apothecary, and handed it to Roseamond. Except this time she was no longer on her knees, dressed and outside the tub. She was inches away, the two of them buoyed by the water's gentle swish and flow.

Stealthy glances between them confirmed for Bayla the startling contrast between Roseamond's lithe, smooth curves and her own generous flesh, a difference too tempting for Roseamond, who was never one to let the obvious pass.

"Heading for the mountain range. Get ready." She floated toward Bayla who instinctively extended her arms, palms facing Roseamond, to prevent her from coming closer.

"Am I a mountain range now?"

"From where I sit you are." Roseamond took the loofah with an, "Allow me."

Rather than feeling soothed by the lather on her skin, Roseamond's touch felt like flames, heated currents that consumed her insides with pulsating temptations. Before rinsing her off, Roseamond paused, and with a graceful tilt of her head, a childlike innocence, "Please," she said, waiting for Bayla's expression to inform her. Bayla slid far back into the tub, her final attempt to forgo what she knew she had no chance of forbidding.

"Yes?" Roseamond said, as if it were a question. As if she were asking permission.

Though it threatened who she knew herself to be, Bayla chose to stare down her mother's philosophy about retribution fully aware that to disobey would be nothing less than provoking the fates, but in the face of an intoxication that nudged her to consent, all possibilities were barred except one—to feel Roseamond's arms around her. And when she did, Roseamond's gentle caresses followed, then her mouth, first soft, then urgent, lips that Bayla kissed in return, a kiss that made her moan as if it were something she longed for before she knew this was something women did. The kiss complete, their faces inches apart, Bayla inhaled unfamiliar longings, and in the second it took for her breath to return and waft across Roseamond's naked breasts, she allowed what would follow as if it were planned ages ago. She rested her head on the wall behind her allowing Roseamond to find her way into the folds between her legs. Willingly accepting how Roseamond fashioned her movements, wanting her to stop, wanting her never to stop, when it happened, moments later, Bayla's whispered "Oh, oh, oh" saturated the air with the hushed tones of young womens' private ecstasies delivered into a world of their own.

With fractured light rendering images hazy, they remained captive to that giving place even as the sun dipped below the window sills. No longer shy of the other's nakedness, the thrill of possibilities replaced hesitation. Life inside Amory Lane would become, for them, one of secrets and anticipation.

Bayla reluctantly stepped out of the tub. In forsaking the water's warmth for the bathroom's chill, like a camera lens realigning its focus, what felt like a hypnotic trance became suddenly sharp and clear exposing what Bayla had allowed herself to become.

"I'm Izzy's wife. That's who I am. Who I must be," she said, her voice breaking.

"Nothing can prevent us from being friends, and loving me doesn't make you unfaithful," Roseamond said as if this wasn't the first time she'd thought about uttering such words.

Bessie Smith had a girlfriend. She called her a travelling companion. So did Ma Rainey. They both dated men, slept with them, but they loved women. Did that make Bayla more like them? A blues singer in that way too?

"How can you look them in the eye after this?"

"I just can. See." Roseamond opened her eyes wide.

"What happens now?"

"Whatever we want."

"We just did whatever we want."

"No one needs to know."

Even if no one in the family found out, the fates always made themselves known.

Bayla settled Roseamond in bed for a rest before dinner. Then she scrubbed the bathroom to thoroughly ensure it was free of a devastating deed. As she worked, her mother's Yiddish curses filled her ears: "Your stomach will turn upside down, leeches will attack you, your teeth will fall out, the earth will reject you when you're buried."

Inside Amory Lane, Bayla had discovered a lifeline tethered at one end by Izzy: her escape from the tenements, her entrée into the world, her protection. At the other end there was Roseamond: her awakening, her fulfillment, guiding her to love and serve, filling her with the treachery of romantic love.

Evenings in the parlor, Charlotte listened to classical music. Solomon sipped sherry and smoked his Camels. Izzy read his newspaper. Bayla, beside him, discovered F. Scott Fitzgerald's *Tender is the Night*. When Roseamond joined them, choosing a chair across the room, Bayla rose to cover her legs with a cotton throw to prevent a chill. She remained acutely aware of the rustle of Roseamond's clothes, her altered breath when she shifted position, her nimble fingers working the crocheted stitches she had taught her. The slightest knowing glance between them set off a rush that made Bayla blush or lower her head at what they had become—partners in illicit pleasures. Remembering her initial objections to Roseamond's advances, she now marveled at how her heart could hold so much love without it ripping at the seams, or suffering imperceptible punctures interrupting its flow, curtailing breath.

For Bayla, this was an uneasy heaven. "These games," she told herself, "I don't know how to play. These games, I don't know how to win." Because of her impoverished past, like a starving child handed food, she was incapable of denying herself. But as she basked in the bounty of Roseamond, unfamiliar pangs began to gnaw.

Shame and a sense of wrongdoing made her feel like Hester Pryne, Nathanial Hawthorne's heroine destined to wear a scarlet A, for "adulteress." At night, a dreadful all-encompassing fear might jolt her awake. If a single suspicious thread arose, or the slightest mishap that God forbid might occur at any moment, she would lose them both, Izzy and Roseamond. And even if no one in the family discerned the truth, her mother, in some uncanny way, in the State Mental Institution, would figure it out. What consequences was that woman conjuring up to strike down her daughter during an unsuspecting moment in this, her life, where she enjoyed each day as she pleased? Eventually, such things make themselves known, her mother had taught. Guilt surrounded her like the ebb and flow of ocean tide, stubborn in its refusal to dissipate.

To banish such unthinkable possibilities, Bayla behaved more affectionately toward Izzy in front of the family, more amorously toward him in bed. While he welcomed her renewed attention to his sexual longings, she was grateful for his bedtime excuses, which he attributed to long hours spent at Miklosh Brofman's fabric house.

Roseamond spent more days dressed and on her feet. Her improved health and newfound strength, signs of Bayla's superb caretaking, was surely reason enough to outweigh the unspeakable part. Even Charlotte was admiring of the relationship. "The townsfolk are enamored of you two, 'real sisters,' they're saying. I'm so pleased. Thank you, Bayla. You're doing a world of good for our girl." But how charitable would she be if she suspected that inside Amory Lane, the forbidden interchange between her daughter and her married son's wife; the ecstasies besotting the air, the rugs they walked on, the chairs they sat in, secrets infiltrating the walls, roof, and attic were witnesses to their desires? Bayla worried if performing on stage had the power to sufficiently forestall or entirely extinguish whatever punishments were her due for harboring such an all-consuming love that could never face the light of day or be whispered into the darkest night. If she could pull the wool over Charlotte's eyes, she wondered how difficult would it be to continue indefinitely at Amory Lane as Izzy's wife, and Roseamond's lover?

Chapter Thirteen

Medical Practices

On that late fall morning, the sky was grayer than usual. Men from the mills were still out of work and strike breakers, strangers, were being trucked into town from who knew where?

"Everything feels disjointed. Out of tune. I don't even want to go to town anymore."

"I can take your mind off all of that," Roseamond said.

"Another of your games?"

"No, I'm serious." The way Roseamond said it, her voice free of innuendo.

They were lingering over breakfast at the claw-footed table bedside the canopy bed.

"Go on. What is it?"

"I'm in love with Dr. Javitts."

"He's married and he's too old."

"He's not old. He's devastatingly mature and experienced in ways of the world."

"You mean he's had sex."

"I want to know what it's like. *You* know. Why can't I? And don't think this is about us We're fine. It has nothing to do with my loving you. He's separate from that."

"You can't separate that from us."

"You do, with Izzy. You consider yourself a faithful wife."

"Because I am. You're the one who said loving you doesn't make me unfaithful to him."

"You see? That's exactly what I'm talking about. Now you've put your foot in it."

Bayla's argument had fizzled, but the prospect of Roseamond with Dr. Javitts felt like an arrow to her heart. "You think it's such a big deal. Sex with a man. It isn't."

Bayla rose from the table. At the window, she parted the lace curtains and stared into the back garden. Through a foggy mist that would bring a dark afternoon, the reflection in the glass showed a waif-like Roseamond still in bed clothes, looking more angelic than usual.

"What do you think he and I do in my room once a week?" Roseamond asked. "It's not all medicinal. We indulge in romantic fantasies, Edward and I."

"He's Edward to you?"

"I want to do it, the sex thing, to find out for myself, to take the memory with me."

"You'll have plenty of memories when we go to the New York World's Fair in Flushing Meadows when it opens in April. We'll see all the exhibits, and I'm going to take you to 89th Street, where I used to live, and to The Saloon, where I was a singing sensation."

"I don't care if he's married. It's not like I'm going to run into his wife. Can I at least tell you how it's going to happen?"

"You've already planned it? Please, don't play around with this." Bayla paused a moment. With her as a confidant, perhaps any chance of Roseamond and Dr. Javitts becoming a reality would diminish, even disappear. "How about you get dressed first?"

Bayla eased the nightgown over Roseamond's head unable to resist a kiss to each of her bare breasts, a soft moist tap of her tongue on each nipple tip. "Will you sigh like that for Dr. Javitts?"

"Probably."

Bayla selected a pink alpaca sweater, warm cotton stockings, a long blue plaid woolen skirt, and coral earrings. Upon returning to their seats at the table, Roseamond began her fantasy.

"He'll enter my room on his Thursday afternoon visit dressed in his light green Oxford shirt, navy slacks, and tweed blazer. I'll be reclining suggestively on the chaise lounge dressed in my gold tweed ankle-length skirt, and white scoop-neck cashmere sweater. A touch of face makeup, peach lipstick, small coral earrings."

"And I'll be the one to help you look like a tart?"

"Yes. Don't interrupt. He'd open his black leather doctor bag, place the stethoscope on my chest. I'd whoosh it away with my hand. 'Roseamond, let me do my doctor chores.'

"'Consider it an act of charity,' I'd say.

"'Making love to you would be no act of charity.' His expression would be serious, his eyes penetrating. Time for my mother to stick her head in. 'Need any help, doctor?'

"'Your daughter is being difficult.' 'Do as you're told, Roseamond,' my mother would scold and disappear. I'd laugh.

"'You can't always play with people like they're toys,' he'd say.

"'I love them first.'

"'For God's sakes, Roseamond, I have a wife and children. All I think about is how can I heal you? What more can I do?'

"'Let me know what it's like. Just once."

"You're being pushy and pathetic," Bayla said. Was she actually giving her advice?

"He likes when I'm bossy."

"Good luck toying with your old man doctor. I've heard enough, and don't tell me if it happens because I don't want to know."

The following Thursday afternoon, Bayla listened to the doctor's good-bye. Perfunctory and friendly, it offered no clue. What did it matter? Roseamond had insisted on her gold tweed ankle-length skirt, white cashmere sweater, coral earrings. A touch of makeup.

Several days later, Rosamond professed a change in plans: "I've made up my mind. I'm not going to die. Despite what the experts say, my mind and body want to stay. I have to live. There's so much to discover. I can't die when so much of life is at my fingertips."

The arrow that Bayla believed was meant to pierce her heart was, she realized, much more delicately aimed. Rather than a betrayal, or a game, Roseamond had raised the subject out of the love they had for one another. That, in turn, made Roseamond's determination to have sex with a man more bearable for Bayla. If it had never been mentioned, once the truth was known, because Bayla would eventually discover, or learn or instinctively sense it, the damage would have made it impossible to forgive Roseamond for what she had accomplished with Dr. Javitts.

Like sand through an hourglass, what had passed between Roseamond and Dr. Javitts filtered through Bayla's imagination, encouraging her, in the middle of one night, to rouse her husband. Awakened in such a manner, he was instantly ready.

She drew him deeply onto her, arched her back, squeezed and released, whispered commands: "Wait. Not yet. Hold it. Longer. Faster. More. Now. Now." With her forearms rigid, her legs wrapped around him, sensations, thick and heavy, pounded through her reaching, stretching, finding wherever was left of her from the place where he had been. Her body wasted, her energy drained, enveloped in sweat, a heavy deed had been done.

Bayla collapsed onto the bed and stared at the ceiling as the sensations gradually lessened, allowing her to catch her breath from an occurrence she had never known.

"What only a man can give to a woman," Izzy whispered. "Your first vaginal orgasm."

It sounded like an ailment.

Chapter Fourteen

World's Fair

It began quietly enough. A few coughs before dawn, then more consistent. Bayla awoke and ran down the hall, Izzy after her. "She gets these episodes. They take their course. You don't have to go in," he implored.

"I do. I do."

Dr. Javitts was beside the bed. Charlotte and Solomon already there, expectant, alert.

Roseamond was lying on her back, her head tilted upward, her neck extended, her throat facing the ceiling. Her hands gripped the vertical wood posts on the sides of her bed as she struggled for air. With each gasp for breath, a struggle so vigorous, she pulled the bed inches along the bare wooden floor.

"The oxygen tube in her nose helps," Izzy said softly. "Dr. Javitts comes and goes. She'll recoup, Bayla. You can stay, but there's not much anyone can do."

The cough, the gasps, the bed's jog on the floor—cough, gasp, jog, cough, gasp, jog—made her flee. Izzy found her on her knees on the bathroom floor, sobbing into towels no longer folded into thirds, the way she always left them, but mashed between her grip. He knelt down, encircled her in his arms.

"It's not me you should worry about," she whispered.

By early morning the attacks were wider apart, by midday they had slowed considerably, and when Bayla could no longer bear being useless, she rested one hand over Roseamond's forehead. Her touch, brief and unstudied, produced an unquestionable calm on the patient. The family, even Solomon, noticed.

"Stay with her, Bayla," Charlotte said. "She knows it's you. And you boys, go to work. She's on the mend."

"She'll now sleep," Dr. Javitts said and tiptoed out.

At noon, as the sun began to alight on Roseamond's perfume bottles, lighting up her room, the attacks had ceased. Her tasseled canopied bed, that otherwise inanimate object, had moved, with Roseamond in it, several feet from its usual place against the wall into the middle of the floor. At seeing how the bed's new position disrupted the room's symmetry, Bayla felt momentarily ill, but comforted by Roseamond's steady breathing, she tiptoed slowly toward her. Reaching out with one arm, she smoothed the tautness under Roseamond's eyes, around her mouth, along her throat. She moved the chair from the claw-footed table near Roseamond's head and sat there the remainder of the day while Roseamond slept.

The next morning, the bed moved back into place by Izzy and Solomon seemed to signal Amory Lane's return to normal. When Bayla brought in her breakfast tray, Roseamond was already sitting up.

"What is a day to you?" she asked biting into lavishly buttered toast and cherry jam.

"A day is. . . ." Bayla couldn't imagine why Roseamond asked such a question. "There's breakfast, lunch and dinner. There's the two of us. Then it's time for bed."

"That simple?" Roseamond laughed. Her color was good, her voice strong, her eyes bright. All of her—alive. "It's different for me. When I'm confined to my room, the day moves according to sounds and light. When a whitish-gray enters the windowpane just there, strikes the wall, reaches my dresser and lands in that corner, it's morning. I hear the water running, Izzy getting ready for work, mother's quick steps, your gentle knock on my door. What will breakfast be? How will you arrange it on my plate? How will it taste? Suddenly I've so much to do. When everyone leaves and you're busy with Amory Lane, I rest or think, sleep or read. From the color of the trees or how the clouds darken the sky, I guess the time throughout the day. Each moment passes. Neighbor's children come home from school. Mother returns, Izzy arrives. Dinner, night, and sleep. Everything drops away leaving us with less. Want to know why I'm telling you?".

"No. Yes. Why?"

"I make less lead to more. Less leads to more. Say it."

"Less leads to more," Bayla repeated, detached. "What are you talking about?"

"I turn unwanted realities into happy endings. Fantasies. You can do the same."

"I know about your fantasies, Missy. Sometimes I wonder how anybody knows anything. I was born in New York, but what brought me here, to you? The fates. Destiny, like my mother always said."

"It's not like your mother said. I've told you before. You married my brother. He fell in love with you and you with him. Those are the facts. He wanted to come here to work and you came with him. That's reality. You came here to sing and to be with him."

"Sorry but how all of that happened is *not* simple. Destiny is a powerful force. It tests us, plays with us. We make plans, then the plans change, everything changes. Why? It's the fates. Like my mother taught me. You don't have all the answers, neither do I. What about us in this house?" Bayla lowered her voice. "What we do under their noses. What does your own flesh and blood know about that?"

"They know nothing," Roseamond said, her hand at her mouth to smother giggles.

That Saturday, Charlotte entered the parlor holding a letter in one hand, her other hand over her heart. "It's from cousin, Natie," she said which made Bayla wonder why Charlotte retrieved the mail from the box at the front lawn when that was reserved for her? "Natie writes from his home in Germany, a few days ago, November ninth, 1938. He calls it *Kristallnacht*. Night of Broken Glass. Synagogues destroyed, Jewish shops looted, hospitals, homes, schools, cemeteries vandalized. And Jewish people, men, women, children, pulled from their homes for deportation, supposedly headed to work camps."

"What does it mean?" Bayla asked, seated on the settee beside Izzy.

Charlotte took a breath. "It means they're going to kill the Jews like they did to my grandparents in the pogroms in Poland. No excuses needed." She walked back and forth, then up and down the room as if her feet didn't know where to take her. "Natie will need money. I'll send some immediately to bring them over—Natie and his wife Esther and their two children, a boy six and a girl eight. And there's not a word of this in our newspapers or on the radio? They're being set up for slaughter and only the Jews know."

"People know, Mother," Izzy said. "It's Hitler and his armies. The signs have been there for what, three, four years now? Appeasement. Give him what he wants, then he'll go away. But he won't. He'll take and take until he controls all of Europe."

"We'll get them out," Charlotte said. "They'll live with us."

"Immigrants in this house?" Bayla spoke if she were having one of her mother's nightmares. "They scream strange things in the dark, frightening to hear. They come hungry, without money, in steerage, sick to their stomachs."

Solomon rose from his chair across the room. "They're our family, you selfish ingrate. If Mother wants to help, who are you to contradict her?"

"Shut up, Solomon and leave her alone," Izzy said. He placed Bayla's hand in his as if he would rouse her from a dream. "Natie and his family aren't going to hurt you. They're cousins."

"Do you still have people there?" Charlotte asked, as if she knew the answer. "I've heard heartbreaking stories from synagogue members. I'm so sorry."

"My mother's father and mother. My grandparents. In Hungary," Bayla whispered, her body stooped as if it were collapsing from within. She remembered an old photograph with brown edges unearthed from a worn leather purse under tenement floorboards on 236 East 89th Street.

Charlotte rose from her chair. "I didn't mean to revive all that for you. I understand how terrible... " She stood over Bayla and embraced her. "I'm sorry, my dear. Now that you've told us, brought it out of yourself, you'll feel better."

"Uncles, aunts, cousins. All of them. Waiting," Bayla said. How could she feel better harboring the secret of an amethyst brooch that held the hopes and dreams of her mother's people in the Old Country. A brooch sold not for tickets to bring those still waiting to America, but to give her mother a good life in that place where she brought her. She drew her lips together, forbidding another word.

Weeks later the letter Charlotte had sent to Natie was returned. The envelope stamped "Verboten." The money for the tickets gone.

"What can I do? What can I do?" Charlotte pleaded. "There must be something."

"Hitler's army is already in Czechoslovakia, Mother," Izzy explained. "It's going to get worse."

Bayla felt helpless at Charlotte's despair. Politics was an unfamiliar world, and the part it played in the lives of her family was unreachable. The letter's return and its implications and the war in Europe constantly discussed over meals, on dull weather weekends, over chores, on walks around the neighborhood. It was too much of a burden for Roseamond to hear, or contemplate. She couldn't expect to guide the others, but she never spoke of it to her.

"I'll write to Roosevelt. Better yet, I'll write to his wife," Charlotte said. "Eleanor is a humanitarian, a true liberal. She must know what's going on. And I'll write to the Hebrew Immigration Aid Society. I'm sure they're making plans to get the Jews out of Europe. They'll influence our President to put a stop to those camps. Doesn't it ever end?" she asked.

Bayla reminded herself to ask Izzy what Charlotte meant by "it."

With the start of April turning Pittsmill's skies bluer and for March winds having cleared some of the mill's gray residue, Bayla looked forward to days of occasional sunshine. She and Roseamond discussed late into the evening their plans for a trip, April 30, to the World's Fair in Queens, New York. Flushing Meadows park. Close to sleep herself, Bayla helped Roseamond into a long-sleeved, floor-length cotton nightgown rather than a heavy flannel, the only difference in their routine was the lighter weight bedclothes.

The next morning, Bayla prepared Roseamond's favorite breakfast: one blackberry pancake, two poached eggs, and a cup of hot chocolate mixed with warmed milk. She arranged the tray with her usual care and carried it upstairs. It was already 9 a.m. when Bayla knocked lightly and then opened the door.

"Roseamond." She was still asleep, her eyes closed, so restful, the coverlet up to her middle without one wrinkle, the way Bayla had left it the night before. "Roseamond, wake up."

Bayla looked at the tempting choices, the care she had taken with the garnish. A sprig of parsley on the eggs. A dollop of marmalade and raspberry jam on a tiny plate.

"Roseamond, it's time for breakfast. Your favorite jams. Don't play games. Everything is hot, waiting to be eaten. Roseamond, come on. This is heavy." She glanced at Rosemond, then the food; at Roseamond, the food, back and forth, several times. Pinioned by the tray, she didn't move. Not moving meant denying what she knew. "Maybe for a change, I'll eat first," she said. "Where's the harm? By then you'll be awake. Breakfast time is breakfast time."

Bayla slid the tray onto the pedestal table that she cleared each night in preparation for breakfast, but instead of moving towards the food, with slow silent steps, she walked toward Roseamond, bent slightly beneath the tasseled canopy, and sat on the bed beside her.

"Hush," she said petting Roseamond's brow. "No need to be afraid. I won't leave you." She intertwined her fingers ever so gently into Roseamond's hand, allowing it to rest comfortably in her own. With her other hand she ran her index finger over Roseamond's eyelids, certain to remember what light had always shined beneath them. She kissed the silent, stilled lips devoid of blood recalling the pink cheeks, moist and dewy, after they had made love. She stared at the face that would stay in her mind's eye, and after a long while, she sank slowly upon a wave of agony until, leaning forward under the bed's canopy, without pressing too hard or weighing too heavily, she laid down beside Rosemond.

Hours later someone drew her away with soft loving words, arms that held her upright because her legs refused to work, and removed her to a forsaken place that had no name, or shape or sound.

Two days later, April 30, the World's Fair opened in Flushing Meadows, Queens. Bayla and Roseamond would never see the 200-foot round crystal Perisphere, or the magnificent 700-foot tall needlelike Trylon, golden as the sun. They would never walk arm-in-arm through the Hall of Nations or down Constitution Mall. Their scrapbook, filled with press clippings and photographs, which they had taken turns cutting and pasting, would remain Bayla's most cherished possession. Its frontispiece, inscribed: *January 31, 1937 – April 28, 1939.* Their time together.

For hearts that are torn, we perform this act of keri-a.

The Rabbi spoke the words as he tore the black strip of fabric he had pinned to the lapel of Bayla's dress, the same that he had torn and pinned upon the clothes worn by Charlotte, Izzy, and Solomon. Traditional for the immediate family.

Bayla barely remembered the funeral. The chapel packed with family, friends and townsfolk. The Rabbi's words: *"Let God remember the soul of Roseamond Rothschild who went to her place of eternal rest. Let her soul be bound up with the living in the continuum of life, and may her rest be peaceful."* Or the plain pine coffin draped in dark blue velvet with a white Star of David embroidered in its center, how it was lowered into the ground, or when she released a paltry shovel of earth scooped from an unruly pile beside the gravesite, signifying the finality, the impossibility, of Roseamond returning.

She knew little about the Jewish custom of sitting *shivah* that honored the passing of a loved one and enabled the living to grieve.

Every mirror inside Amory Lane was covered in cloth. Friends and neighbors brought food and returned each night to clean up. Plain wooden boxes from the synagogue arrived for the family to sit on. She wore the same outfit, slippers on her feet, forgetting to wash, unaware, until Charlotte told her, that these, too, were *shiva* rituals.

When the Rabbi came with 10 men, a *minyan,* to recite the Hebrew *kaddish,* the prayer for the dead, every morning for a week, Bayla barely acknowledged them.

Yitgadal veyitkadash shemey raba be'alma divra hirutey veyamlih malhutey.

At the end of that week when the *shiva* was concluded, the *schloscheim* followed for the next 30 days, which prohibited the family from parties and festive occasions, but otherwise allowed them to return to normal life. So soon? Forsake Roseamond so easily? Bayla interpreted the tradition as the family's failing. She deepened her grief, ate alone in the kitchen before they did and cried herself to sleep. She lost weight, acknowledged neither daylight nor darkness. Gray filled her insides and shackled her will.

Izzy told her that the most difficult part for him was passing Roseamond's suite to get to their bedroom. He would keep his gaze straight, stifle the truth that his sister was gone, then grab his handkerchief.

Solomon's grief took him into the kitchen, the place he had never taken an interest in except for the food that came out of it. "Leave me all the dirty dishes," he commanded. "The repetition of washing plates, it soothes me."

Charlotte attended a weekly grief session at the synagogue in Pittsburgh. She couldn't bear to say the words: *Loss of a child.*

One morning, Bayla heard Charlotte speaking to the framed photograph she kept of Roseamond on her dressing table, in her boudoir. "I didn't do enough to keep you alive. There wasn't enough time, I was too busy. Please forgive me"

Bayla tiptoed in, and gently placed her hand on Charlotte's shoulder.

"She was here, wasn't she?"

"How do you know?" Charlotte's eyes were tearful.

"The curtains flutter when she passes. She turns the boiler on at odd times. It has nothing to do with the thermostat. I've checked. She comes to comfort me."

"You must let her go, Bayla. Do you understand? You must let her rest in peace. I'm concerned about you."

Bayla said she understood except for the fog. "It's gray and smoky. It separates me from you, from everything." She heard Charlotte instruct her boys, "Keep an eye on her. Let me know anything out-of-the ordinary."

They tried to comfort Bayla with choices. Take a rest. A bath. A walk. A drive. Cook a meal. Listen to your radio shows. Shop for new clothes, food, record albums. They talked endlessly about Roseamond. They avoided saying her name. They offered her books from the library, her favorite movie magazines, a chance to confer with Dr. Javitts. All of it purposeless.

Grief and lamentation kept Bayla sequestered. With Roseamond gone, there was no reason to do anything. She found it incomprehensible, the family behaving like *her* wellbeing was more important than respecting Roseamond's death. Whenever that was. Days, weeks, months ago? So much had occurred around or between or because of Roseamond, time had become an illusion. Unrelated to her. Once known, now forgotten.

The only disruption to the sameness of each day involved events in the outside world. And her husband so increasingly troubled by all of them.

"Germany, Italy and Japan joined in an alliance. Fascists bombing Spain, innocent people dead. And for what? War in Europe is inevitable," Izzy said.

Though there was little she could do about any of it, much less follow what was being said, on certain days she faced a growing awareness that the gray smoky fog which had so thoroughly engulfed her, began, now and then, to resemble misty patches similar to Pittsmill's skies after a spring rain. In the open spaces between the fragments, town life wandered in.

"Dr. Javitts has taken a sabbatical." "Closed his office." "The poor man." "Did what he could to save her." "Drove to the mountains." "A spiritual retreat."

Bayla found that an almost welcomed distraction. The doctor's efforts to mend Roseamond's ailing heart had led him to lose sight of what was taking place in his own. He had fallen completely in love with her. And Roseamond, no doubt, implored him to succumb to what doctors are trained to avoid—personal involvement, the pull of sentimentality, the temptation to go beyond what medicine requires. Their secret would remain Bayla's gift from both of them.

There was the day she walked out of Amory Lane beside Charlotte to help her deliver food and supplies to the striking families. "There weren't enough beds for all who needed them," she told Izzy, "the children cared for one another, windows had curtains and a cloth on the kitchen table, though they didn't have a penny more than my mother and I had back then."

"Such an excursion after five months without Roseamond. You must be feeling better."

"I loved Roseamond as a friend. I love you as a husband. She helped me sort it out."

"You were going to audition when we came here? Do you remember?"

"Singing is my life. I used to say that, didn't I?"

"It's something you were born to do."

When only a few manageable strains of darkness surrounded her, Bayla came to understand there was no end to mourning someone who was deeply loved. As if a hand reached into her ribs and tugged outward, she would be seized by a sudden longing to see Roseamond, to talk to her, touch her. Tears would follow. She'd dry her face, and minutes later continue with whatever she was doing without a thought as to when, or if, a similar episode would reoccur. It always did.

Chapter Fifteen

Muddy Blues Society

When she entered the parlor that morning, everyone was hunkered around the Stromberg Carlson. Charlotte, her brows furrowed. Izzy and Solomon eyeing one another. Everyone tight lipped. Talking about her? Something she had said, or done? Her deep attachment to mourning Roseamond? There would be a lecture. Comments. New suggestions.

"Sit beside me," Izzy reached out his hand and patted the settee. "CBS just announced it. Hitler's army has invaded Poland. Britain and France have declared war on Germany." He ran his fingers through his hair. "September 7, 1939. The start of World War II. A date for the history books."

Charlotte glanced at her sons. World War II, Bayla thought. Nothing about me.

All the talk in town was about the war in Europe, that America wouldn't get involved. But news reporters and war correspondents predicted the fighting would escalate. At the dinner table that was all they talked about. Fuzzy read news reports about able-bodied men called up, drafted. Solomon repeated gossip about young men preparing to be sent far from home and Charlotte, dear Charlotte, worried constantly about her boys, their lives upended.

Worrying sentiments continued to fill the air and surround the family inside Amory Lane, but once fall's leaves were raked and burned and winter's freezing temperatures arrived, it seemed no one in the household except Bayla knew that the most heralded, talked about movie of all time, *Gone With The Wind*, was to have its grand opening in Atlanta, Georgia, December 15th.

"When it arrives at Pittsmill's Odeon, we must all go," she insisted "to erase the talk of war, for at least for four hours plus intermission. It has Hollywood's biggest stars: Clark Gable. Vivien Leigh. Leslie Howard. Imagine, bringing Margaret Mitchell's thousand-plus-page drama to the screen." The book, she had already read.

The family capitulated, but once seated in the darkened theatre, Izzy beside her, Charlotte and Solomon next, unexpectedly preceding the feature was the patriotic strains of the "Star-Spangled Banner" and Movietone News. Flashing across the screen, to everyone's wide-eyed silence, was black and white footage of Germans shelling U.S. ships, and allied soldiers firing on Nazi armies bringing home the very real possibility of wretched events that no one and nothing seemed to have any control over. FDR promised that their boys wouldn't be sent into a foreign war, but Charlotte reminded the family that the President had said that at one of his third term election speeches. What did they expect? He was a brilliant politician.

"The war isn't here. It's there and that's where it will stay. It has to," Bayla said. "I can't think beyond that and neither should any of you. We're here, safe and sound. That cannot change. I refuse to think otherwise."

"Open your eyes and your ears. Read a newspaper, for God's sakes," Solomon demanded. "Britain needs our help. The Germans are bombing the heck out of them."

"My brother's right. Britain's our greatest ally. They can't do it alone. We have to stop that maniac Hitler."

But Bayla continued to deny the possibility that her husband would be drafted, and that she would be left on her own to face fear and destruction same as Scarlett O' Hara.

On a typically cold Pennsylvania morning in late February,

bundled in her winter coat and hat, thick cotton stockings beneath her long wool skirt and sweater, Bayla stood on Amory Lane's front porch surveying the world, her fourth winter at Amory Lane. Ten months after Roseamond's death. Pines were draped in snow. Houses on Beleaguered Hill blasted chimney smoke. Ice hardened along the rutted edges of cobblestones. The air was sharp, the skies whitish-gray. Dare she venture from Amory Lane's cloistered setting? With Roseamond gone nothing felt as it should be.

The crunch of snow with each tentative footfall along quiet back streets led her to Strobe Library. She waited at the information desk for the head librarian, the one with the sensible shoes.

"Mrs. Rothschild. It's been a while since …." She spoke in a muted whisper. "I was so sorry to hear about your loss. The two of you, such devoted friends."

"Thank you," Bayla managed to say, her eyes already glassy.

"How can I help you?"

"Do you have a section, I mean, do you have anything on blues?" Bayla was surprised at her request.

"Blues? In my twenty years as head librarian, I've never had that question. How fascinating. Our music section isn't bad, mind you, but blues?"

Bayla turned to leave, uncertain whether it was the right thing to do.

"I could check the Pittsburgh Branch or Inter Library Loan. Or you might be interested in…." She paused, barely a moment, "The Muddy Blues."

"The what?"

"The Muddy Blues Society. They're aficionados, on the outskirts of town." She glanced around pleased at the slow morning. "They're a fount for blues material. Original works. Song sheets. Recordings. Each summer they sponsor a down-home blues fest. Hundreds come from across the country."

"I never heard of them. No one in my family ever mentioned it."

"As a librarian, I know these things. Performers are mostly Negroes, some whites. Singers. Musicians. Their talent gives them good reason to be there."

I have good reason to be there, Bayla thought. *Don't I?* What was it? Her good reason? Childhood dreams? Her fine singing voice? Being a devoted daughter? Mourning Roseamond all these months, or were they years? Was that reason enough? How could she be certain? There was no way to know. What if she was imagining all of this? The library? Her mind speaking to her when she didn't want it to. Sometimes it made her believe her thinking was real. Or maybe it wasn't. Even if her life depended on choosing the correct words to say to the person standing in front of her, maybe she wasn't real either. It was too much to figure out. Too much, really. If only the fog that had clouded her mind would disappear. But the jumble of shelves surrounding her, packed with endless spines, authored by people she would never know or meet. How many already dead, their ghosts parading the floor? She'd had enough with death. She'd had all she could take. She turned and took a few heavy steps toward the entrance.

"Wait. Muddy Blues isn't an easy place to find. I'll mail you directions," the librarian raised her voice to a loud whisper. "I know your address."

Bayla nodded to the person so willing to reach out, so different from the townsfolk. She wasn't a gossip. Books—loyal, steadfast, unfailingly available—were her life. She had sent a condolence card, very tasteful, a single rose below the word, "Sympathy." A person like that would never tell how a mysterious loss of reality had overtaken one of her patrons, momentarily overwhelming her. Best to forget what had just happened, she decided as she walked home. To never mention how her mind had run away with itself. How foolish she was to believe she could attempt such an adventure so soon after Roseamond.

Three weeks later, with Fuzzy and Solomon at work, and Charlotte escorted by her lady friends to some cultural event, Bayla ignored her morning chores and drove off in the blue Ford sedan, directions to the Muddy Blues, written in the librarian's exquisite cursive hand, on the seat beside her.

The partly sunny day was unusual for early March, though no Pittsmudlian counted on the sun to hold for long. Down a silent dirt road she never knew existed, only a few miles from Amory Lane, uneven ruts and crannies, rocks and mud holes jolted her mercilessly up, down and sideways. As strains of gray began to darken the sky, they snuck up on her, first one, then clusters of wooden shacks and lean-to's along one craggy mile after the other. Not on proper streets, or paved sidewalks, but plunked randomly, set back from the road, or partly obstructing it. Feeling like a trespasser in a hidden universe, she tried to fathom the negligence of this strange hideaway, more disheartening than where the steelworkers lived. Worse, maybe, than the tenements.

Over her right shoulder, on a small, horizontal board, aged and weathered, dangling from a rusted wire tied to a branch were two barely readable words: "Nutmeg Quarter." Expecting to find herself within reach of her future, how foolhardy, dangerous, even, to have set off alone without knowing where her path would lead.

For the next quarter mile or so, past barren fields, as if by sleight-of-hand, a group of children appeared huddled around a large puddle, poking sticks into floating ice patches, giggling and dodging what splashed onto clothes that didn't seem warm enough. She rolled down the window to smile at them, but they never turned from their amusement as a rush of icy air, stinging her eyes, forced them momentarily closed.

Around a narrow bend, refusing to give in to what appeared a wanderer's folly, several Negro men carrying foodstuff walked out of a withered two-story house taking no notice of her as she continued into what seemed at once frightening yet strangely titillating, as if something never before discovered was about to unfold.

"Clothes Washed." "Milk N Eggs." "Fresh Catch Fish." "Cures," scribbled large and uneven across doors and ram shackled shanties, while smoke from their chimneys filled the air with pungent, sweet, or savory scents.

Beyond another barren stretch was a driveway littered with broken-down cars, a rusted flatbed truck, and a mini-mountain of tires. Was this her destination? She sat for a moment, staring at a small cottage that slouched to the right as if the ground beneath it had given up. Peeling white paint exposed splotches of bare wood. A few trees with broken limbs surrounded it. She turned off the motor, drew her winter coat tighter to her middle and trudged through slush that rose onto the black fur of her boots. Finding no knocker, she pushed at the door, and stepped cautiously into a semi-lit room, warmed by an old fashioned coal-fired stove. The low tones of Baby Natchez Baldwin singing "Ain't Got No Home" was playing. Few would be familiar with the song, much less have the recording. This had to be the place.

A rectangular wooden table, the kind used for generations in a kitchen to cut, chop, and eat on was in the center of the room. Four old ladder-back pine chairs were fitted around it. Wooden file cabinets, like in Strobe Library, stood against a wall. A silver school bell waited on something resembling a counter.

Ting. Nothing. *Ting. Ting.* A pair of flowery curtains parted and an elderly, white-haired Negro man appeared.

"Yes, ma'am?"

"I'm looking for the Muddy Blues Society."

"You've found it."

"Is this where....? I was told that......What do you do here?"

"If you don't know. . . ." He turned to walk away.

"Wait, please. What's wrong?"

"Nothing wrong, ma'am, but you seem a bit confused."

"I'm a performer. A singer. I need new songs. Original numbers."

"You in the best place." He seemed more interested in returning to where he came.

"But how do I....?"

"Look through those drawers. Pull out one that begins with the first letter of the subject you're looking for. Or a performer's name if you know it." His voice trailed.

"What if I need help?"

"If you're a performer, you won't be needing any. If you do, maybe you're one of those busy bodies from down South coming up here to spy on us."

"I need to audition at Café Genteel."

"You want to sing blues, you come by the Old Songhouse. Wait here." He turned and was gone.

At the file cabinet, she pulled out a drawer marked, "L—M" and searched for "love," wondering if anyone ever wrote a song about one woman loving another.

"Hello in there."

Bayla slammed the drawer shut, startling herself.

She was a large woman, light-skinned, dressed in a loose sweater, a skirt to her ankles, soft gray hair waved around her face. She was considerably older than Bayla, her smile gentle, her teeth perfectly shaped.

"How can I help?"

"I need to audition. Where's the Old Songhouse? That man, the one just here, he said—"

"No need to audition. You just get up and sing. If you're good, they let you know it."

"What about an accompanist? The music? Rehearsals?" There was so much she had to know. The words leaped out faster than they settled in her head.

"Seems you're all about questions, and I need to sit down. Have a seat."

Bayla followed the woman to the wooden table where they sat across from one another.

"That's better, a chance to rest my feet. What's your name, child? I wasn't sure I caught it."

"Bayla. My name is Bayla." She decided not to reveal her married name. Surely even here, in these back roads, townsfolk gossip about Amory Lane was within reach.

"Nice name. Different, like mine. M-I-L-H-A-D-Y." She spelled it out. "The 'H' is silent, it's my patois influence, and there's no need for an accompanist. Those musicians can play anything you throw at them. Men, women, even children perform, mostly colored. There's been white lady singers, good ones, some swooped up by the big bands. Thank the Lord for Benny Goodman, what he's done for our musicians and singers."

"Who does the announcing? And lighting? Where do the

spotlights go? What's your stage like?"

"We have a wooden stage out back, but performers prefer to sing standing on the ground. It's the singing that counts. The singing's got to be right."

"Are you a blues singer?" Bayla felt somewhat agitated because the woman's responses were out of sync with her own urgent needs, but her question was more curious than critical.

"I suppose I should say yes to that. I especially enjoyed 'Fevered Brow,' and 'Bottom Edge of My Soul.'"

"What did you say your name was?"

"Milhady. Didn't I already tell you?"

"Milhady Brown?" The unfamiliar road, the mysterious surroundings, this strange out-of-the-way setting. Could it be? "And that man I met? Is he the saxophonist, your brother, Candy Sugar Brown? 'Plays as sweet as candy?'"

"That's us," Milhady said seemly satisfied as if Bayla knew at least that much.

"Two blues legends. New York, Chicago, L.A., Boston. You performed everywhere. The best clubs. I followed your careers. Read everything I could find. Broadsheets, newspapers, magazines. What do I have to do to make it?" Bayla leaned across the table, as if some of who Milhady was would rub off on her. "Tell me. You must know."

"It don't quite work that way," Milhady said and laughed. "Benny Goodman, he hired my people without blinking an eye, pianists Mary Lou Williams, and Teddy Wilson. Charlie Christian, swing guitarist. He got Dizzie G and Charlie Parker to teach his band. Lady Day recorded her first two vocals with him. East and West Coast. Radio shows. I performed with them all. I was older than most, but I got there."

"I want to sing. To be heard, like you. I got slowed down for a while with terrible, unexpected.... life brings such...." Bayla took a breath. "But I'm back. Nothing to stop me now."

"That so?" Milhady turned to face her as if she were penetrating her mind. Bayla wasn't fearful or bothered. It was more like a connection which she couldn't for the life of her understand, yet trusted.

"How did you find us out here in the Nutmeg?"

"Town librarian."

"And does anyone else know you've come here?"

What was this woman talking about? And so suspicious. "Why? What do you mean?"

"Trekking to the Nutmeg, to colored folk, a young white woman by yourself? If I had to guess, I'd say you snuck out of wherever you live with no one in your family knowing where you was headed. You coming here and no one knowing, a lot of trouble could come to you and your family, and me and mine. It's better here in Pennsylvania than down South but it's not the same as up North. You can't be color blind here. Black men work at the mills and black women clean houses and they both come into town but we keep with our own."

"I don't care about people's skin color. Negroes and whites walk on the same street in New York City, ride the same subway cars. They even live together." Milhady had touched on what required more thought than Bayla had given it, which was very little. "I know it's different here, but like you said, it's not like we're down South. Can you teach me?" Bayla asked.

"Teach you what?"

"I'm sure you do, teach, I mean. I'm not wrong, am I? I want to sing blues like black women singers from the South. I can imitate the voices of the best of them. I practiced to their records as a child, but with a teacher I can perfect what you already know. I can sing for you right now if you—"

"It's lunch time," Milhady interrupted. "I'm hungry and wondering what's in my cupboard and what my brother Candy needs to pick up in town. And if you know anything at all, you know the folly of off-the-cuff performances. A voice needs to be warmed up."

"I don't warm up. I just sing."

"I figured as much. Blues are part of a culture. I'm not saying it's not your culture, mind you. White women, white men musicians, talented people, they all—"

"Me and my Momma, we lived poor and needy in the tenements."

"Tell you what, though my heart might soften to a stranger's needful demeanor, a protégé, when I choose to take one, has to be tested. At my age, whatever knowledge my career has brought isn't to be wasted. If you know what you want to sing, come back when you're ready, and I'll give you a listen. Success is in the wanting."

"That's what I want," Bayla practically shouted. "That's all I want."

"Then you better tell someone you trust, and have a damn good excuse if you decide to keep coming here. I don't want trouble and neither do your people.

"And before you head back to wherever your home is, there's one other thing, something very different, that you need to know. They say those who find the Muddy Blues end up touched by magic."

Chapter Sixteen

Fledgling Prodigy

When Bayla arrived one week later, Milhady led her beyond the public's view, past the flowery curtains into the kitchen-dining-bedroom where everything was worn: the linoleum floor made to resemble bricks, a sink and two-burner stove, a yellowing cloth over a table, three pine chairs, their legs slightly crooked, two single beds each covered with a hand-me-down quilt, torn in spots. On the walls were theatre bills, advertisements, notices, and reviews from Milhady's and Candy's performances, some beautifully illustrated, others newspaper clippings. In a corner, a coal-fired stove similar to the one in the library room, its pipe vented to the roof.

"What's that sweet smell?" Bayla said.

"Orange and lemon shavings. I boil them down." Milhady pointed to a pot on the stove.

"Your own potpourris," Bayla said with a smile.

"A connection to some memory?"

"Someone in my family." An off-handed mention of her loss was still a long way in coming.

"You need to take a slow inhale," Milhady advised. "That's it. Now exhale. Again. Clear your mind as best you can from sorrows and obligation."

Had this stranger recognized something of what she had recently suffered?

"You sure you're ready to take this on? By that I mean singing lessons?"

Bayla nodded. "Where do we—?"

"I sit at the table. You over there by that wooden music stand. For the voice to soar, your feet need to be grounded to the earth. That stand was carved out of maple by a slave, my great uncle, made for his master in Pittsboro, North Carolina. Got passed to me. That stand exudes the blues. That's what you got to do when you sing."

Bayla ran her hand across the wood, admiring the work. Glancing around the ramshackle home of people who were once famous somebodies, she felt almost welcomed by the simplicity of having lived with what could not be spared, the way she and her mother did.

Two days a week, two hours each time for the next few months, the teaching Bayla asked for took on the shape of serious lessons. There were exercises for breathing: deep and long, quick and teasing. Exercises for intonation: surprised, devastated; for phrasing: "easy now," or "dig deeper." For the music—twelve bars with three chord changes—Milhady would crank up the Victrola that sat on a crate filled with 78 RPM records, lean over and choose one.

"That's Victoria Spiney doing "I Ain't Gonna Play No Second Fiddle." Did you catch how she drops the octave? How she releases those last notes? Now do it like she does. Now vary the emphasis. Now change the tempo. Now make it your own. Blues requires invention but it's got to seem like it comes to you natural."

"I always thought my singing was natural," Bayla said.

"You've got a rich, smooth contralto, and there's a nice blousy flow to the voice. Your height, your lungs, your square jaw. They all work together. You've been given a gift."

"Good enough to appear at the Old Songhouse?"

"Now don't get all dreamy. I need to understand what you're capable of so I can get you from your down-and-out blues to your break-your-heart blues, all sounding authentic. You've got to have that if you want them to return."

When Bayla suggested she wanted to pay for the lessons, "Stop right there," Milhady balked. "You see how Candy and I live. There's not much we need. Whoever your people are, and I'm not asking because it's not my business, but for sure they're a sight better off than what we have here. If you can do something for me, I'll ask. For now, you pay me by learning what I'm teaching."

"To make my dreams come true?"

"If that's a question, the answer is I lead the way. You make that happen. Not me! You're in charge of your dreams."

Bayla wanted to ask just exactly how was she supposed to do that.

At the start of another day's lesson as they sat in their places at the table, "I don't aim to intrude," Milhady said. "Much of my teaching is based on a student's revelation, but every now and then I do have a personal question."

"Yes?" Bayla tensed up. Did Milhady know that her mother had come to her two nights before in a dream? *Do est? Vus mockster?* Her mother had undoubtedly told the fates about her errant, heartless daughter who instead of visiting was spending time with a stranger teaching her to sing.

"Why is it you never agree to a lesson except on Tuesdays and Thursdays?"

That was it? That was all Mlhady wanted to know? Bayla almost laughed from relief.

"Tuesdays and Thursdays are when my mother-in-law goes out with her lady friends to charity events, social affairs. On those days, I'm free."

"You mean you head for the Nutmeg without having to make up excuses?"

"Yes."

"Then I need to tell you, you best come up with some damn good reasons why a white woman in a big blue car keeps coming back here. To the Nutmeg."

"Why are you bringing this up again? I come here for lessons, for you to coach me."

"Prejudice is something we cannot ignore." Milhady banged her fist on the table. "I can teach you what you want to learn but there are risks. Nutmeg people don't care who I teach. The folks out there do. Your mother-in-law can tell you plenty about black and white mixing in this town that you won't like hearing."

"If someone in my family asks where I've been, I say I went to the market."

"How about you want to visit someone, or go into Pittsburgh for a new outfit? Get your excuses ready before you need them or your family will find out about you're coming to a Negro woman. Living in that big fancy house and everyone in town knowing your family, you got to take good care coming here if you want you and your family safe, cause I want the same for me and mine. A Negro woman teaching you. It's 1940 and we got FDR's New Deal and Mrs. Eleanor fighting to get my people working with whites in the mill. But still."

Feeling adventurous from unfettered freedom inside Amory Lane, Bayla began to sing even more than when Roseamond was there: spontaneous phrases, scales, obbligato's.

"You're your old self. Vibrant. Alive. Better than ever. What's going on?" Izzy asked.

"I'd like to.... but I can't say."

"I suspect a surprise."

"The best ever. But not a word to anyone." She turned toward the kitchen then whirled around. "Is anyone asking? Because I have to know. You must tell me so I can do what's necessary to calm things down."

"No, my dear. No one's said a word. You just keep playing your LP's, singing along with Garland, and Dinah Shore, and Billie Holiday and Ella. I find it delightful. I'm sure they do too."

Bayla did as Izzy suggested, using her full voice cognizant, now, of subtleties in technique and interpretation. How grateful she was to have at her disposal the record player and Harry Hirshhorn's music store. Yet each time she headed for the Nutmeg, Milhady's warnings accompanied her though she would have much preferred to ignore them. Why couldn't people be accepted for who they were regardless of the color of their skin?

At the start of April, her second month of lessons, Bayla was in the kitchen sipping tea, thinking about her current lesson: Sing from the story. After years of being together, your honey walks out on you, leaving a note on your pillow. Or you're a widow with a rash of children and no job in the poorest of the Mississippi Delta.

"Well, well, well. Miss Busy Bee taking a break." Solomon, late to breakfast as usual.

"What are you implying?"

Bayla dried her hands on a dish towel and placed the last of the breakfast dishes in the cabinet above the sink, hoping to short-circuit what she sensed was coming.

"You are aware that Mother and I have friends in high places."

"Solomon, you and I have been at peace for months, can't we keep it that way?"

"I only want to mention my friend Jimmy Jacks who has been seeing you pass his Shell station in our sedan a little too often. He thinks—him, not me—maybe you've got a little something going on the side? Seeing someone special?"

"Jimmy Jacks is right. I've been performing in the Copacabana, driving to New York City twice a week. They love me there and I didn't even need an agent to get in."

"People in this town are watching you, Missy. If you've got a boyfriend—"

"I do. I sleep with him every night upstairs in the bedroom. Tell that to your friend Jimmy And also tell him he sees me on my way to buy groceries so our family has enough to eat."

"Bring me a corned beef and pastrami from the Carnegie Deli on 57th Street the next time you're in New York, or I'll tell my brother what I know."

"Was there any other incident?" Milhady asked before the next day's lesson began.

Bayla knew she couldn't hide it from her, so she told when she and Charlotte were leaving Variety's Dry Goods last Friday afternoon with ready-made floor-to-ceiling curtains for her and Izzy's bedroom, Candy Sugar Brown was walking towards them, about to raise his hand to his hat.

"Lord God help us," Milhady said. "What did you do?"

"I tried to signal him with my eyes. 'Don't do it, look who I'm with.' He caught on, walked by but not soon enough. 'Do you know that Negro man?' my mother-in-law asked. 'I'm sure I don't,' I told her. 'There was something about the way he looked at you.' Later that night, she brought it up again. 'I've been thinking about you and that man. If you're up to something, and I can't imagine what, you can be sure it will get back to me,'" she said.

"Is that it?" Milhady asked, still concerned, which bothered Bayla.

"Days ago, I was about to turn down the Nutmeg Road but a car was behind me, following, I thought. So I drove toward town, waited, then drove back. The coast was clear so—"

"You think it's time to confide in your husband? You said he's your best ally. Maybe he has some suggestions so you can keep coming here without worry."

"My debut has to be a surprise. I can't say a word, not even to him. I want to see their faces when they find out who married into their family."

Bayla listened intently as Mihady counted on her fingers. "You've done your down and out blues, your weeping willow blues, your St. Louis blues, now it's workhouse blues. Beside the work, the fields, cooking and cleaning, birthing children, caring for them and family, truth be told, a woman singing workhouse can break your heart."

"Don't worry about me giving birth. I told my husband long ago that's out."

"I'm not about to change your mind, I'm offering background. Let me hear what you been practicing. Breathe. Put yourself into it. Plant your feet. That's right. Now go."

Say, I wished I had me a heaven of my own.
I'd give all those poor girls a long old happy home.

After five stanzas mingled with sounds of children playing outside, "A touching rendition," Milhady said. "Feelings so strong, I could touch them."

"I knew about a workhouse from the time I was a child," Bayla spoke haltingly.

Milhady leaned back in her chair. "Bringing out the bad in life is needed for singing the blues, but maybe I'm pushing you too hard. Your face has lost its color."

"Don't worry about pushing me. Push me harder than you ever pushed anyone, harder than you pushed yourself. My color will return." And Bayla talked about her mother, an immigrant, her father walking out, having to leave school, Goldmacher's ....

When it was time for her to choose her own blues song, "Blues audiences love the naughty," Milhady commented, "but it isn't as easy as you think, putting that over to an audience." She folded her hands in her lap, and leaned forward, smiling. "Let's hear it. Four stanzas."

"Lyrics by Bessie."

"I know, child."

Bayla inhaled.

> I've had a man for fifteen years, gave him room and board.
>
> Once he was like a Cadillac, now he's like an old Ford. From now on, according to my plan, some things have got to change: He's got to get it, bring it, and put it right here or else he's got to keep it out there.

"Well?" Bayla asked tentatively.

"I don't think I would have done it much different."

"And the walk?"

"You mean your hips on top of the shuffle? Truth be told, I loved it."

"You loved it!" Bayla repeated, her hands over her heart. "Words from a master."

"A teacher," Milhady reminded. "A teacher. And no tears. There's no tears for accomplishing what you're capable of doing."

"That's what my mamma always tells me."

He was a tall, young handsome man with broad, muscular shoulders and a beautiful smile.

"Well, well," Milady said. "This is Travis, my baby. He comes to eat, calls it 'visiting.' My first child, Eulayla, I delivered her when I was quite young. She wanted to be a secretary so we sent her to my sister's in Chicago for schooling. She has her own babies now. But this one, he came late, just before his daddy passed. This is the young Mrs. Rothschild."

"Hello, Miss Rothschild." Travis extended his hand. "Mamma's told me about you. She must think highly of your talent. She hasn't taken on teaching in some time."

"Is that so? Your mother is very spare with compliments."

"Travis has been working at the mill over five years," Milhady said with pride, "a clean job, in the stock yard, and 23."

"You have one good-looking son, Milhady. Nice to meet you, Travis."

"Girls don't hardly leave him alone. Do they, hon?"

"No, Mamma," Travis said, somewhat embarrassed. "Not hardly."

"But he's taking his time finding the right one. Right, Travis?" Her voice had an edge.

"My mamma bosses me around 'cause I'm her favorite." He winked but she frowned.

"He's looking for a wife who will fit in. I want some grandchildren pulling on my apron."

After three months of lessons, a wife and children for Milhady's son had little interest for Bayla. Milhady was her teacher. That's who Bayla needed her to be. Motherhood was something she could never grasp, anyway.

After three months of lessons edged closer to July 14th's Muddy Blues Festival, Bayla considered wearing something sexy because that's what performing the blues required. Milhady leaned back in her chair, and laughed as if that was the most outrageous thing she had ever heard.

"You once asked about my life," Milhady said as she caught her breath. "I wanted to sing blues much as you, but in Beaufort, South Carolina, where I grew up, my mamma had twelve kids. We had schooling to fourth grade, walked miles to get there, most times with no shoes. When Daddy died, we had to work the fields. I prayed, cause that's what Mamma taught us, and I sang whenever 'cause I knew once they heard me, they wouldn't let me go. I left the drink that ran like weevils through every family. I left the poverty that anyone 100 miles around could smell on me. I ended up singing about the pain and struggle of our people. Did I bother about titty-tight costumes, or what others thought about how I looked? No. I sang the truth. And you so intent on singing about people not your own. Every word, every sentiment has to come from something you've seen or felt. Nothing to do with clothes."

"And where am I supposed to get what you're talking about?" Bayla asked with a smugness Milhady did not care for.

"You already got more than enough. What do you think drives your talent? The other day when you did workhouse blues, that time came alive. I heard how it was for you. You need to dig that up from where you hid it."

Some assignment, Bayla heard inside her head, *uncovering what wounded and tore at my insides.* "Those parts are going to stay wherever I put them so they can't get to me again."

"It's not scary as you think," Milhady softened her voice so that Bayla had to lean into it. "If you don't bury the bad and the ugly, or deny it altogether, it will be there when you perform. Up and out, that's what you tell yourself. You'll hear the difference in the lyric. That's how you keep an audience. Up and out. Remember."

As the afternoon turned to dusk, a hint of spring wafted through the car window. It reminded Bayla of Roseamond. A good sign, she thought. Or perhaps it was Roseamond telling her so.

"Up and out," she said aloud. "Up and out."

Chapter Seventeen

Debut

"Hitler's armies are unstoppable. Germany vanquishing country after country. Italy fighting France and Britain. Paris under Nazi control. Edward R. Murrow referred to it as a Blitzkrieg, and God knows what's happening to the Jews."

"Mother, you're so well informed," Solomon complimented.

The family had gathered for a Sunday buffet brunch around the dining room table, Solomon's occasional treat of deli, whitefish salad and lox and cream cheese from Brustein's Bagels in McKeesport.

"A member of the state legislature spoke to the women's group in our synagogue, and thank you, dear, for this lovely spread. Such a generous surprise."

Bayla turned to Izzy who rolled his eyes at his mother's obligatory compliment to his brother, then read from the *Herald Tribune*.

"The U.S. is involved in the largest peacetime military draft in history. Men 21 to 35 have to register."

"No need to worry, Mother," Solomon said. "They're not taking married men. Anyway, my dear brother is too old to fight those Nazi bastards. Right, Izz? As for me, I have my own plan."

"A prescription for world peace, dear?"

"No, nothing like that. When I get called for my physical, I'm going to polish my nails, wear a dress, long earrings, face makeup, curlers in my hair."

"That new muumuu my wife just bought, you know the one,

Bayla," Izzy said, "the one with the green and purple roses, you must loan it to my brother."

"I bet you twenty to one I'll look better in it than she does."

"Doing that is unpatriotic," Charlotte said, "and anyway the muumuu might be too tight around your rear."

"Maybe not, Mother. Maybe not," Solomon said. Everyone turned to Bayla who laughed rather than fault her brother-in-law for his sense of humor.

With all the talk about war and conscription, Bayla knew she had to focus on Milhady's advice: "Think about nothing but your debut. Your performance."

During her time in the Nutmeg, something extraordinary happened to Bayla. She had discovered a haven where she could entrust her talent, experiment, learn from her mistakes, and, most of all, sing her heart out to someone who understood, who validated the person she was desperate to be.

Surely it was the poverty that connected them: Bayla's tenement days to Milhady being brought down from having known better times, "'cause that was what life did to some folks," Milhady explained, meaning Negroes. Among their easy give and take, and the commonplace of exchanging family tales, their relationship was sealed through their bond born from sharing the most precious part of themselves: their music.

Her songs were perfected. She had a new dress made from leftover blue silk which Izzy brought from work, sewn by a seamstress in the Nutmeg, hidden at the back of their closet. Each morning, she marked off the days to her debut on a small calendar she kept in her purse. Most nights, before she fell asleep, she reviewed how she would announce her debut to the family. The day, the time, each word decided and practiced.

To mark the start of June's warmer weather, Izzy and Solomon dredged up the white wicker furniture from the basement, and lined up each piece in the back garden to be washed by hired hands then left to dry in the sun. Mid-afternoon, the family settled in the parlor. Bayla on the upholstered bench facing into the room felt more confident than she could ever remember. The timing, she decided, couldn't be more perfect. Almost obligingly, the entire family was somehow facing her. Izzy in his wing chair in front of the hearth, swept clean of winter's cinders by the town dustman. Solomon, his glass of Cabernet Sauvignon on the coffee table between himself and Charlotte, and she stretched out on one of the settees. The garden doors at Bayla's back, left slightly ajar as if by design, allowing the lace curtains to decorate her frame with each gentle puff of a summer breeze.

"You're going to perform where?" Izzy asked, as if he had misunderstood.

"The Old Songhouse. I just told you. July 14th. In two weeks. You're all invited."

"And what is the Old Songhouse? Is it around here?" After more than three years at Amory Lane, Solomon's fake sing-song voice convinced Bayla he knew the answer.

"It's a famous blues place a few miles away," she said rather nonchalantly.

"Do you mean…" Solomon paused, "could it be… in the Nutmeg?"

She hoped he wouldn't find some way to turn the news against her, but there it was. His laughter made her wince.

"You hear that, Mother? She's been going to that part of town." Solomon raised his wine glass and downed the liquid in one gulp. "Someone must investigate. This is as a job for the Green Hornet." Though he didn't dress in a cape and mask, or drive Black Beauty, the fastest car around, Solomon would imitate the sum and substance of radio's latest craze whenever it suited him. Bayla found it maddening. Charlotte thought it charming.

"The Green Hornet will *not* investigate," Izzy said, "and leave my wife alone. Bayla, how did you find this Schoolhouse place?"

"Songhouse. Songhouse. The librarian at Strobe told me about. Only aficionados know it's there."

"And where did you learn that word?" Solomon asked. "Not in

the Nutmeg. Those people barely speak English."

"They speak English as good as you."

"How many of 'them' do you know?"

"Shut up, Solomon!" Izzy said. "I'll ask the questions."

Charlotte suddenly sat up and moved to the edge of the settee. "When we went to town for curtains that day, I asked if you knew that Negro man who passed us by. You said you didn't, but you did. You knew him. Didn't you?" She grew more accusatory. "Have you been going down the Nutmeg Road, associating with someone there?"

"Musical legends," Bayla blurted out. "A well-known blues singer who took me on as her protégé. For free."

"You went there unescorted? For God's sake. How often? I send those people food, clothes. I care about them, I do, but social visits? Don't you realize—"

"Realize what?" Bayla shouted, ready to defend Milhady.

"You listen to me. When Dick Arnheim's wife passed, they invited the Negro janitor from Dick's garage to their home for a meal. Arnheim lost half his customers after that. And when the Flaherty girls were seen around town with Hattie Brown, neighbors told their parents and that ended the friendship. I'm not saying I agree. I don't. Maybe one day things will be different but ..." She took a moment to catch her breath. "The position you've put us in. Once word gets out, the neighbors, town officials, the Ladies Auxiliary, they'll all question—"

"Mother, that's enough?" Izzy said. "Nothing's happened."

Bayla looked across the room at her husband, the person who protected her from her enemies, the ones on her list, the list she hadn't thought about in ages, the list she had somehow misplaced.

"And what do you think your wife's being there could do to them?" Charlotte said. "They could be arrested. Driven out of town. Last April the Daughters of the American Revolution refused to rent Constitution Hall in Washington D.C. to Marian Anderson for her concert, and you traipsing to the Nutmeg to sing? Who do you think you are?" Charlotte raised her palm to her forehead and slumped back into her chair.

"Hang on, Mother. No time to be weak-hearted." Solomon rushed to her aid knocking over a chair in his haste. "You need to be strong with this, this...." he struggling for the perfect word, pointing to Bayla, "this ignoramus."

"I should have stopped her, followed my instincts," Charlotte berated herself.

"Enough!" Izzy shouted. "You're both behaving like lunatics."

The fortitude it took for Bayla to relinquish her deepest longings from a journey begun in childhood to a warning suitable for her enemies left her trembling.

A breeze from the garden stirring the lace curtains caressed her hair, her neck, tempting her into a world free of judgment and hurt and disdain. She rose slowly, as if awakening to a nightmare.

"I will sing in public in the Muddy Blues Festival at the Old Songhouse, in a new blue silk dress, from Izzy's remnants, sewn by one of *those* people *for...my...debut* and not one of you will stop me."

Bayla's face burned, her blouse was drenched with sweat. She began to circle the room pacing among chairs, tables, the settee, her hands turned into fists, her arms stiff at her sides, determined that justice would be done despite these ungrateful people, enemies thwarting her will, her best intentions. She felt unstoppable, a wild creature unleased from the cage they kept her in inside this house, as if she didn't know all along they planned for her undoing from the moment she arrived. She paused at one of the end tables, seemingly fascinated by her reflection in the table's glass top. In this grand house, filled with luxuries she never could have imagined, they had no right, forcing her to abandon what she wanted most in the world, and for what reason? Why forbid her this? Her voice sounded unusually deep and onerous.

"I can wash your floors, bleach sweat stains out of your clothes and clean your toilets, but none of you wants me to succeed."

She raised her right arm slowly, held it in the air, then brought her fist down hard. There was a loud snap. Charlotte's scream. Solomon's, "Look what she's done."

Fuzzy wrapped his handkerchief around his wife's bleeding hand.

"Such gall," Solomon said.

Bayla ran past him out of the room and up the stairs, thankful her tears held.

"You will not take this from her," Fuzzy shouted. "You hear me? No matter what you both think, or do, I shall be in the front row to watch my wife perform, in her new blue dress!"

Bayla slammed the bedroom door, grateful for what she longed to hear.

"They were terrible to me," she told Izzy later that evening when he brought her a dinner tray to their bedroom, though she had no appetite.

"I'll handle it. You know I'm good at fixing things. This will never again—"

"No use speaking to them. Nothing will change. I will not give up my debut, no matter what your family says. Or what they think of me. Or what townsfolk's might say. I know how terrible I was. I was out of my mind. Wasn't I?"

Convinced that people from miles around would hear her sing and cheer and applaud, and she would make a name for herself, Bayla continued to mark off the days to her debut until one morning she was too weak in her knees with an on-again off-again nausea to get out of bed.

"Sleep in the other room," she told Izzy that night, "so you don't catch what I have. I feel awful. I may not last till morning."

"If you only have hours to live, I want to be as close to you as I can."

"This isn't a joke. I'm exhausted and dizzy and I haven't had a mouthful all day."

"You're seeing Dr. Javitts tomorrow. I'll take you there."

Bayla refused, demanding only a bit of rest. But the next morning, given her pallor, her exhaustion, Izzy managed to get her out of bed, and on his way to work, paused to walk her into Dr. Javitts' office. Charlotte would pick her up.

Sitting across from the doctor, she described her symptoms.

"Humor me," Dr. Javitts said. "Remove your clothes from the waist down. Put on this robe, then lie down on the examining table. I'll return shortly."

Bayla eased onto her back, placed each foot into an icy stainless steel stirrup, legs apart, bent at the knees. Her gaze rose to the ceiling, its corners, and edges darkened by years of women's embarrassment for having to display themselves in this way. Why did a woman's bodily openings necessitate a man's invasion to promote good health? Just because he treated the family for years was no reason to be so available.

Humor him? Bayla couldn't help but wonder if her presence brought back thoughts of him and Roseamond. Or perhaps an inkling of what he might have suspected between her and Roseamond, something Roseamond haphazardly, or brazenly, dared to mention. To think of such possibilities after a year and another summer had passed since the doctor and Roseamond had been intimate.

She turned her head sideways, away from him as he entered the room.

"Relax," he said, as if anyone in that position could. He switched on a small light in the middle of his forehead that was attached to an elastic band, squeezed something from a tube onto his gloved hands and moved toward her, as if he were about to descend. "Relax." Still that word, muffled this time, his head between her fleshy thighs. A man's voice instructing her. She trusting and obedient, something opening her up, inching inside her. A torrent of rage and nausea rose upward from her middle, prompting her to stuff her fist into her mouth.

"Hum," Dr. Javitts mused in low tones.

At feeling the weight of a man holding her down, she squirmed. "I have to throw up. Let me go," she screamed. "Stop."

Dr. Javitts ripped off his rubber gloves, dribbling cold jelly on her abdomen.

"Leave me alone."

"Bayla. Open your eyes."

"No more. Please."

"Wake up. Mrs. Rothschild, snap out of it. Mrs. Rothschild, where are you?"

She glimpsed a pristine glass cabinet across the room, non-descript walls, a man peering down at her.

"I don't know," she whispered. "In a doctor's office." But it was only a guess.

"You're with me. Dr. Javitts. Are you sure? Breathe in. Out. Again."

"Yes, I'm with you."

"Where were you?" he asked softly. "Where did you go?"

"A terrible place." She searched for answers, though she barely understood what he was asking. She swallowed hard. A lengthy pause. Her breathing steady.

"Are you still nauseous?"

"What makes you think….?" What was he talking about? She didn't feel well that day so she went, at her husband's insistence, to the great doctor who was inferring what? Had Dr Javitts lost his wits? "I'm fine. Perfectly fine."

"You said this was your first pelvic exam."

"Yes. It was."

"You're calm now? You're yourself again?"

"Of course I'm myself. Who else should I be?" *Was he suddenly thinking I was someone else?* Forgetting who she was after all these years She would tell Charlotte not to recommend this man to anyone. He was most likely out of his mind.

"Good. Well then I have something important to tell you."

"What is it?" She felt suddenly drained, exceedingly tired, and the doctor's behavior, so strange. Uncomfortably solicitous.

"It's as I suspected. You're pregnant."

As his words fell upon the part of Bayla's brain that unexpectedly translated it into meaning, her right arm, the one closest to him, smacked the hand that had so masterly probed her insides. Dr. Javitts stepped away.

"Okay. Call me a monkey's uncle, but there's a softening at the tip of your uterus. You're about six to eight weeks. Due late January.

You'll need to see Dr. Frommer, the obstetrician I recommend. Congratulations, Bayla. You're going to have a baby."

"I can't have a baby. I'm having my debut. Help me up." He extended his hand and she grabbed hold. "The date's set. I'm a singer. That's the plan. My husband and I agreed. I've been rehearsing for months. I'm ready to perform. I've got a new dress. Made to order."

Rather than converse, much less reason, with so agitated a patient, Dr. Javitts lowered his voice. "You speak of a career, Bayla." When was he given permission to use her first name? I'm Mrs. Rothschild, she wanted to say. "What's a career compared to being a mother? Motherhood is what a woman is about. You're gestating the next generation of Rothschilds. Think of your family's position. Performing pregnant, here, in this town would be too embarrassing. Even if you're not showing. Once the child is born, people will count. It would be difficult for your family, their position in this town," his voice momentarily trailed off. "There will be plenty of time when the child is older for you to have a career. You're bringing a new person into this world. That's a blessing. You get dressed now. I'll meet you in reception and we can talk a bit more."

When she reappeared, she said she was being picked up. He placed his hand at her elbow as if to guide her to the door. "I don't need help," she said and stormed out. She would shun the doctor's advice, bury his words in a place where neither she nor anyone would ever find them. To predict something like that. Pregnant! That's all it was. A prediction. Maybe even a guess. A wrong one.

That evening Bayla told the family she had a flu. "There's nothing to do but drink liquids. Rest." After all, a child. Who would have thought it? Who would have expected it? Who would have wanted it? She and Izzy were always so careful.

Pray for a miscarriage. Ask Charlotte to raise it. Keep it a secret. Give it up for adoption. Have my debut anyway, no matter what.

She lay there that night, unable to sleep, her body listless, surrounded by a suspicious calm while something strange was clamoring for recognition, a familiar presence practiced in ruthless accomplishments. It subjugated her will, siphoned her strength, made sawdust of her motivation, demolished what she wanted most, forcing her to face what she had tried so long to deny—who and what she was.

Beholding. Small. Powerless. Unworthy. The shadow side of herself.

Her worst enemy ever.

Chapter Eighteen

Full Circle

At 8 a.m. the following morning, Bayla stepped cautiously beyond the flowery curtains that separated the Muddy Blues from the public.

"Lovely morning. A bit early for you." Milhady was filling the teakettle at the sink when she saw who had entered without a word, or an appointment.

"I've something to say."

"I can see that." Milhady scooped cooked grits into a bowl, added a splash of milk from a pitcher, a pinch of sugar from a jar.

"I'm pregnant."

"I did that when I was sixteen. Two young married people. It's only natural." Milhady set a place for herself at the table, and sat in her chair.

"My life is over."

"Why's that?"

"Who's going to come to see my pregnant body on stage?"

"Who's going to know you're pregnant?"

Bayla fell to her knees, her head in Milhady's lap. Emotions held in for the past 48 hours splintered into sobs dampening Milhady's apron. "I can't be a mother….and perform…. in public. Don't you see? It's impossible. They took me in. Let me live at Amory Lane. It's a disgrace. For all of them."

"Most every woman blues singer I know had at least one child and a career. I've heard a lot worse than a baby being born." Milhady withdrew a handkerchief from her apron pocket. "Here. Take it and come sit beside me."

Bayla took the handkerchief and dried her face. "I told them about my debut. They acted like I had committed murdered."

"And I'm saying you can get through this."

"I'll be almost two months pregnant at my debut. People can count. My mother never wanted me to sing. I can't escape her curses. I thought I could inside Amory Lane but the fates watch your every move. Listen to every thought. You can't show you're too happy."

"No one's cursing you except yourself by giving up," Milhady scolded. "Your whole life is ahead of you. Did you ever ask your mother what *her* life was like? You think she wanted to end up in a wheelchair with no husband? She blamed it on the fates, but you don't have to."

"Damn these men. Izzy fixed me good, didn't he? I got pregnant the last day of my menstrual. He said it was safe."

"You think what's been done to you is any different from what's been done to millions of other women? Don't blame spreading your legs on him. You're going to do what we all do. Bear this alone. He knows how you feel. Let him be. You're behaving like this is the worst thing ever happened to you."

"Losing my sister-in-law was the worst," Bayla mumbled, and took a breath.

"She's gone, but your debut don't have to be now. Have your child and sing. That's the best I got. Maybe one day you'll return the favor."

Momentarily distracted by the quiver in her voice, Bayla turned to face Milhady. "Do you need help with something?"

"Why don't you just keep talking about you? We can spend the whole day—"

"What is it? You won't take money for lessons. You said we could barter, so?"

"Don't insult me talking about money. I spoke without thinking. You don't need to get involved." Milhady shifted in her chair. "It's my Travis."

"What about him?"

"He's still seeing his boss's daughter on the sly. When her people find out, they'll kill him for sure, and you talking about family wanting to throw you out for singing."

"No one's going to kill Travis for keeping company with that girl. That's crazy."

"She's white, foolish child, and a black man does not date a white woman in this town. The mill bosses are probably up to something awful for him this minute." She buried her face in her hands. "My boy. My baby."

"I'm sorry, Milhady, for what you have to consider because of ....who you and Travis are, but—"

"Travis says they're in love, and nothing's going to change that. The only place for him is dead 'cause that's where he'll be if they don't end it. 'Strange Fruit.' You know about 'Strange Fruit'?"

Milhady's voice resonated with a vibrato that paused the few tears she allowed herself.

"'Strange Fruit.' Billie Holiday protesting racism. It was number 16 on the charts," Bayla said, sensing the song's devastation. Lynching in the southern U.S. during Jim Crow.

"You live with rich and white, but my Travis is in the worst trouble a black boy can have." Milhady sighed deeply, an attempt to release whatever horrors she imagined the situation would bring.

"My husband knows someone who owns a rooming house downtown Manhattan. Houston Street. If Billie Holiday can sing 'Strange Fruit' at Café Society in Sheridan Square, and white people can line up outside the Apollo in Harlem, Travis and his girl can live on Houston Street."

"You need to see her perform. Lady Day," Milhady said, sounding like Bayla's teacher again. "It will do you a great good watching her live. Take a trip in your blue car with your husband, the one who did the evil deed." Milhady smiled, then turned downcast again. "I'll take care of my own."

"See Lady Day! You know who hangs out in the Apollo? Rockefeller, Chaplin, Paul Robeson, Lena Horne. Famous people. Movie stars. Who am I—?"

"You're a Rothschild, from Amory Lane. You're entitled to go. You can afford the cover charge."

"Travis and his girl, they'll need money for train tickets," Bayla said. "I'll give that to you, but I need something." She paused. "I've heard it gets harder if too much time goes by. You must know how I can—"

"I'm a blues singer, not some voodoo woman. You have a family who can pay—"

"You're the only one I can trust. You know that."

Milhady gave Bayla a woman's name in the Nutmeg. For the next two weeks, Bayla took pills, powders and teas; jumped rope, soaked in hot baths; took long walks, trudged up and down Beleaguered Hill; dusted, vacuumed and mopped floors.

"Nothing worked. Useless, all of it." She banged Milhady's table with her fist.

"I don't know if my Travis and his girl will stay together, but I know you're supposed to have this child."

Was it only three years ago when she volunteered for Mrs. Verplanken's job to care for Roseamond, thinking it was the only thing that would take her from singing the blues?

"A child, of all things, and what do you mean, 'supposed to?' There is no supposed to and I didn't ask for your damn opinion."

"You talk to me like that—in my house!" Milhady glared at her protégée.

Bayla lowered her head. To have spoken that way to the only person who believed in her, in her dream. At the sink, she filled the iron kettle with water, sprinkled a handful of chamomile flowers from an open tin into a cup, waited until the tea steeped, then poured.

"My, my, you've never fixed me tea." Milhady took a sip of the warm sweet liquid. "There's no reason why you can't perform any time after the child is born."

At twenty-five she was old to be a first-time mother, but as a singer wasn't Milhady right? "I can do that, can't I? Make a comeback. A spectacular one. Put my career on hold until all this is over."

"It's never over. A child is forever. Don't ignore what you got inside you, or that child will come out strange, not at all to your liking."

Emboldened by desperation, and having withheld what tempted her for so long, Bayla felt the courage to ask: "People say you're a seer."

"It don't work how you think," Milhady sounded brusque and put upon. She took another sip of tea, rested her hands on the table. When she spoke, it was with a reticence. "Sometimes people just got to get through things."

"What things?"

"Something dark, slow and, I believe, unsuspecting, is going to rob you of what you want most. It will last for a time, arrive in a while, but you'll get through it. You'll be led by someone not yet in this world." She paused a moment, as if she were listening for something. "That's all I got. If there's more, I'd tell you. Just remember. There's no giving up. When I first set eyes on you, I knew I'd come to respect....even love you. I knew you had it in you, that wanting to sing the blues."

"I'm so grateful. Thankful for all, you're the only one who—"

"I know, child, I know." Milhady stood and reached out with her arms. Bayla walked around the table and they embraced for what seemed like a long while, their eyes telling what each needed to know about the pain of an unwanted good-bye.

"Don't misplace your dreams, that's what keeps you together," Milhady spoke softly into the top of Bayla's head, as if reciting a prayer. "Keep singing," she shouted and waved from the open door of the Muddy Blues, as sweat dripped down her face from the morning heat.

Bayla drove the Ford along the Nutmeg Road, determined to never forget how the bumps and crannies jolted her every which way, certain this would be the last time she would venture over them. She hoped one day to learn that Travis and his girlfriend, whose skin was a different color from his, found happiness. And she hoped an LP with her on the cover featured in a record store, or her singing over the radio, would inform Milhady that her student of three months was a sensation.

The next day, after he came home from work, Bayla told Izzy he was the one who had made her sick. When he asked her how, she told him she was pregnant.

"A child. Our very own. Maazol tov, Bayla. Your debut," he said, practically whispering, searching her eyes, "you'll have to put it on hold."

He took her hand, and let it rest gently in his. To soothe her? Bayla wondered. To show he understood the loss of her future, the gaping emptiness that seared her insides like a carefully planned recipe overcooked, forgotten, dried out and inedible?

"What am I going to do with a child?"

"You'll love it and care for it, like you did with Roseamond,"he said joyously.

"Roseamond is dead as dead can be."

Bayla forbade the purchase of gifts. Not so much as a rattle, bib or booties, stuffed animal, cradle or high chair. "Nothing until after the birth or the fates will do who knows what to the unborn child?" her mother had long ago warned, and Jewish families in the tenements abided.

With a gain of thirty pounds, she was forced to wrap herself in Izzy's red plaid flannel robe that barely closed around her middle. For her constipation, her husband offered prune juice. Charlotte suggested apple cider vinegar in water for her runs. Solomon offered boiled green cabbage as a poultice for hemorrhoids. When her breasts became so engorged, causing her back to round, Solomon suggested that she try out for Lon Chaney's double in *The Hunchback of Notre Dame.* He tattled to Charlotte about Bayla's late-night binges: an entire apple pie, a strawberry cheesecake; three Nathan's Kosher frankfurters, several Hershey's Milk Chocolate bars. But Bayla knew she held the winning hand: her child, Charlotte's grandchild, the first, and undoubtedly, only one she would ever have, the heir to Amory Lane, would permanently dethrone King Solomon.

Bayla gave birth to an eight-pound, five ounce baby girl, one minute after midnight, January 25, 1941. Ethel Waters was performing on Broadway, Alberta Hunter was touring Europe's nightclubs,

Ida Cox was at Café Society Downtown, Bertha "Chippie" Hill was performing with Louis Armstrong, and Bessie Smith's biggest hit, "Down Hearted Blues," recorded when she was 29, barely three years older than Bayla, was selling like hot cakes.

JANUARY 1941 – JUNE 1954

Chapter Nineteen

Baby Naming

As if parts of her were missing, left somewhere, or forgotten, Bayla felt a stranger to herself. She would lie for hours on the cushioned bay window seat in the dining room, staring at nothing in particular.

"Are you in pain?" Charlotte would ask periodically.

"It's nothing like that. I want to hold my baby and care for her, but I don't know who is thinking these things." How could a person who didn't know who she was offer a reply when she had no idea who was doing the listening? She was someone she never was or ever wanted to be.

Despite handmade baby blankets, hats and matching sweaters, congratulatory cards, and well wishes from townsfolk, the fates had taken her life in a direction she could have done without. After all, a child. What she drank. What she did in her diapers. When she slept or didn't. If she sucked her thumb or not. If she wanted to be picked up or left alone. Nothing prepared her for such lavish attention, so out of proportion to what the child offered in return. She couldn't blame the child for its inability to show appreciation so integral to her own life for having a place to sleep, food on the table, a toilet down the hall, and a father, when he stayed. She struggled to accept the imbalance of the situation, along with her inability to find her place within it.

"You're Bayla Rothschild from Amory Lane, and you've got a beautiful baby daughter sleeping peacefully upstairs beside her parents' bed in the white Victorian bassinet used by my children, passed on to her—the next generation. She will be the pride of our family, dress in the finest, mingle with the most influential, be educated in top universities. She will have what no one in this town ever will, life exactly as she wants it. Your daughter has been born into a world of superlatives, I promise you."

Bayla enjoyed when Charlotte promised, but until she knew how to regain her rightful path, the path she had set for her future, the one where she was a singer, she had no idea what to do except to allow the story that was already running to play out, like a movie that had already begun. "It's only for the time being," she told herself usually at dusk when there was nothing she could do to prevent what had already occurred or night from encroaching, except to close her eyes and wait for come what may.

Bayla was resigned to enter the world of motherhood—a place that held little or no meaning except for the inadequacies she brought to it. And the child's crying, pitiful sounds that broke her heart and weakened her spirit already burdened with frustration, and irrelevance. Charlotte called the baby fussy, but Bayla knew she was at fault. How could she produce a child greater than the sum of her own inadequacies? From the moment she had smacked Dr. Javitts' hand for claiming she was pregnant, she wondered, with her as a mother, would her child turn out normal?

Two weeks had passed and they still hadn't given the child a name. The Department of Health had called three times. Izzy insisted they choose something.

Since she was seven years old, if she were to ever become a mother, her child would have one special name. Izzy showed her great compassion as he guided her into the parlor where the family waited in silence for her to confess what she had never told anyone. The fireplace added extra warmth, lending an orange glow to the settee and the high-backed chairs that faced the hearth. The dark green papered walls flocked with white peonies, and the exquisite

French and English antique furnishings that once made Bayla so ill at ease were a comfort now. Even the green velvet draperies that shut out most of the light from the tall windows encircling the parlor made her feel protected.

Immigrants, like her parents, who arrived in the early 1900s, thought nothing could be as bad as a *schtetel,* but tenement life, they didn't expect. In summer, apartments were hot like an oven. In winter, the only warmth came from a coal stove in the kitchen. Walls were so damp, your hands came away soaked. One cold led to another, bronchitis, pneumonia, then to what no one dared mention—TB, the same that struck her baby sister, Caroleena. Bayla was her father's favorite, Caroleena was her mother's. At first, a runny nose, then spikes of fever. Then her appetite slowed and her cough so terrible Bayla would cover her ears. The terrible worst, as Bayla called it, that brought her nightmares when she slept, and made her sick in her heart when she was awake, was how her sister's pink cheeks, which she loved to cover with kisses, despite her mother's *luzzen alaine, mitcha her nicht* turned white, then gray; her plump arms and *zoftig pulkas* became thin and lifeless like a rag doll. Her mother held the child over the kitchen sink creating with a towel a tent of steam, and filled her bottle with warm tea, honey and lemon. After blood appeared in the child's mucus, without a cry or a complaint, she died, barely a year old.

Her mother sat at the kitchen table for two days, clutching the lifeless child to her chest, her sobs deep and low, as she soothed the body inside a blanket she had crocheted to keep her sister safe and warm, refusing to let the women prepare her for burial. Why did He take her? Despite how often she asked, Bayla's mother never received an answer.

"It's a sin what you're doing." In Yiddish, German or Polish, women from the building spoke to her as they came and went through the open door. "The child must be washed and blessed. Rabbis are waiting in the Bronx at the Jewish cemetery." The frenzy attracted a street policeman who had seen such things from the Kochinskis on 2A, and the Glodeks on the ground floor. He bowed his head and walked away, but not before catching a glimpse of a child, maybe six years old, under the kitchen table, her hand grasping her mother's skirt for safety from the world.

"The child will be called Leena, after my sister," Bayla told the family, relieved that the story was out of her. But whatever joy would come to her for thinking that some part of her sister would live again, for Bayla this was a sacrificial offering. The name carried within it the guilt she would forever bury inside herself: Caroleena had gotten sick from a cold she had brought home from second grade. If not for her, Caroleena would still be alive, and she wouldn't have to live the rest of her life knowing she had caused her sister's death.

Charlotte insisted on a baby naming. "It's tradition. A *mitzvah*," she said. "How a Jewish child begins life. Family and friends will come to the synagogue in Pittsburgh and afterwards a party at home. You'll enjoy, Bayla. You'll see. It's a celebration of the child and the mother."

Bayla couldn't for a single moment imagine it. The crowds. Strangers in her face. The child surrounded.

"Tell you what," Izzy leaped to her aid that night. "I'll say you don't have the strength. I'll be very convincing. You and I will take Leena to the synagogue. I'll invite Mother. Solomon won't want any part of it. And no party at home. How does that sound? I'm not mother's *boichick* anymore. I'm a father, with a child of his own."

The Rabbi Solomon Minsk welcomed the new parents and grandmother into his study, a small room filled with floor to ceiling books. From a wooden chair behind an ancient desk, he smoothed a sheet of translucent paper with Hebrew writing in front of him, dipped a quill pen into an ink bottle, held it ready and asked, "The child's Hebrew name?"

"Leah," Izzy said, "Leah after Caroleena, my wife's sister. And Raizel, after my dear sister, Roseamond." He smiled at Bayla. "Leah Raizel is our daughter's Hebrew name."

"And the child's father and mother?" The Rabbi asked.

"Mordechai Isadore," Izzy said, "after my maternal grandfather. Bayla, what's your Hebrew name?"

"Me?" Had her mother forgotten, or didn't she care enough to have picked a Hebrew name for her daughter, her first born child, her only one?

"Your husband called you 'Bayla,'" the Rabbi said. "In Hebrew it means 'goodness.' That's what I'll write for your Hebrew name." Bayla smiled.

Facing the congregation, the Rabbi called Mordechai Isadore to the *bemah* to receive an *aliyah*, the honor of saying a blessing before and after the Torah reading. Then the Rabbi blessed the baby and everyone, at least a hundred people, applauded, chanting *simintov and mazeltov*.

"When Jews get together, they eat. Did you know that, my dear?" Izzy asked.

Of course, she knew. When her mother took her to Tikvah Shalom, the Orthodox synagogue on East 91st Street on Shabbos morning, they had a sip of wine in a little paper cup. But here, in the social hall, on long tables draped in fine white cloths, pound cakes and danish, chocolate bobkah and cookies from the finest Kosher bakery in Pittsburgh, beside a collection of long stemmed glasses half filled with red Kosher wine. Charlotte's bounty.

On the drive home Bayla sat in the back of the car whimpering, a sleeping Leena wrapped in a blanket in her arms. When Charlotte or Izzy offered to help, Bayla was unable or unwilling to explain. How could she admit that for those few precious moments in the synagogue, the child's birth had returned her to the spotlight? What mother was so shameful?

Weeks later, after dinner, Bayla walked into the parlor exhausted from nights of trying to get the infant to sleep. With unusually cold temperatures for late March, everyone was positioned around the hearth, Charlotte and Solomon playing gin rummy at the bridge table, Izzy in his chair with his newspaper. Bayla, cross-legged on the rug, closest to the warmth.

"A new mother, I realize the difficulties." Charlotte said as she set down a card. "There's no end to it."

Solomon rolled his eyes. "Now you're on her side because she made a baby? You didn't feel like that when she first arrived. That kid has turned the idea of sleeping through the night into a nightmare. Shouldn't the mother know what to do?"

"Our daughter upsetting the family's status quo?" Izzy said without looking up from his newspaper.

Bayla braced herself. At the first signs of a family feud, she tried to imagine how each of them would respond, how they would act towards one another, but she never got it right. Whatever she expected always got turned around or completely fell apart. And now, still not fully herself after the burden of childbirth, she was at such a loss.

"Listen to me, big brother," Solomon threatened, "by marrying that woman," he pointed to Bayla, who lowered her head, "and moving her into our home, did you think she would become one of us? God knows what genes she's passed on to that child with our last name."

Izzy closed his newspaper. "Between boozing and screwing women, now you're an expert on new mothers?"

Bayla wanted to applaud. Maybe Izzy would slug the SOB like he recently promised.

"We've been blessed with a child, for God's sakes," Charlotte said, "and you two, accusing one another for what? That's not how I raised you. The money I've donated. The people I've cared for. The food and clothing I've collected for the poor. I know about a new mother. I was one. Three times."

She does know, Bayla thought. She understands. Now that she was a mother, Charlotte had become her protector, someone she could count on, both of them united by motherhood.

"There's something I want everyone to hear," Charlotte continued. "I've been thinking about this for quite a while. The spare room at the end of the upstairs hall, I've hired a crew to turn it into a nursery for Leena. And I'm ashamed for not offering sooner, the child sleeping in the same bedroom with the new parents. You've been through so much, Bayla. Pregnancy, childbirth, forsaking your debut. You both deserve better. We've treated Roseamond's room like a shrine. It's such a large, beautiful space. It's yours. Both of you. What do you say?"

Hearing her name Bayla stiffened in her seat and clasped her hands together.

"Who are they to occupy Roseamond's room?" Solomon bellowed. "It should remain a shrine. Don't forget, Mother, my brother moved to New York. Broke your heart."

"Now you're starting this?" Izzy said. "Dad worked like a dog to build the business, and you'd show up, make a few phone calls, then disappear again until pay day."

"It's called a salary. When God offered manna to the Jews wandering in the desert, they took it. I did the same with our parents," Solomon said.

Izzy laughed. "Is that the best you've got? You're much better going after my wife." He winked at Bayla.

"Have either of you heard one word I said?" Charlotte tried to intercede. "You enjoyed the decorating business, Izzy. Your brother wanted college. So your father and I sent him."

"And he messed that up, too. Gambling in the Freshman dorm? Selling drugs? Pimping out co-eds? It was all so hush, hush. How did you cover it up, Mother? Friends in high places?"

For all the years she sewed at Goldmacher's, what did Bayla know of such things? Those words. How even to understand them? Not that she wanted to. They made her stomach churn.

"Rumors," Solomon shouted. "Nasty rumors. I'm running a successful enterprise. Isn't that right, Mother?"

"That's who you ask! Ask me!" Izzy demanded. "I bet a day doesn't go by where something doesn't cost us. Mistakes in measurements. Wrong fabric ordered. Late deliveries. How long until you run our family's business into the ground?"

Bayla would wait for a lull, escape their anger, their threats, their attempts to make her believe she was one of them. If she was good at anything, it was her sense of timing. She knew when to withdraw, dissolve into whatever was going on inside her head.

Solomon rose slowly. His nostrils flaring, his breathing audible.

Bayla swallowed hard. Her jaw tightened. Her teeth meshing, clenched together, crushing uneven surfaces.

"The only thing that's going to run us into the ground is you and your wife. No one asked you to come back here. Mother and I don't need either of you."

Is this what her life had become, bearing witness for three years to endless, ugly displays she had married into? Her own choice. Her own decision. No one forcing her.

"Enough," Charlotte shouted. "People are worried to death that their men will be sent overseas to fight in a war, and you two, so mindless and uncaring. Cities are being bombed, innocent people killed while here in Amory Lane….."

Bayla rose unobtrusively, and without a sound, sidled out of the parlor. She opened the front door with such stealth, pleased how the mechanism of the door lock obeyed her will. Bending her legs, she sat on the top porch step, drew her knees into her chest, and encircled them with her arms. No one would notice she was missing. Why should they? She had endured losing Roseamond. Now she would endure succumbing to an ordinary life of motherhood and wifely duties. How much more could she be than this?

The icy cold stinging her flesh felt enlivening. She was nothing to herself. Less to them. And if they found her frozen in place they would realize the offenses that she had committed were instigated not only by her, but by each of them. Sooner or later the guilt they bore for keeping her from performing would consume them. Even Izzy. Maybe him too.

She remembered feeling something like a covering over her body moments before she closed her eyes and fell asleep. By the time she felt his warm fingers coaxing her forward, she was too stiff to stand.

"Oh my God, Bayla, what have you done? You weren't in bed, in the kitchen, the garage. Thank God I opened the front door. Don't speak. Don't even try. I'm so sorry. You've been out here over an hour. Mother and Solomon went to bed. We thought you were upstairs."

He carried her inside, placed her on the settee, close to the hearth, brought two blankets from the linen cupboard upstairs, wrapped them around her, massaged her legs, her arms, her hands. He filled the hot water bottle, placed it on her stomach, fed her sips of hot tea, told her she'd be fine. "Sometimes families are terrible. I'm so sorry." When she was able to stand, he helped her upstairs, into their bed, held her hand until she fell asleep. Leena slept all that night.

She needed to come to a decision. Protesting might bring a return of grief, the weight of sin, suspicions about the two of them, shameful in their secrets. After more than two years, the pain of losing Roseamond had settled; scars that had formed over deep wounds were smoothed over. Unlike the embers in winter's hearth, her love for Roseamond would never die, and though occupying that room felt sacrilegious, a violation of Roseamond's memory, "I've been thinking about your mother's offer," she told Izzy one night in bed. Everything would have to be dusted, vacuumed. The perfume bottles shined and packed in tissue-papered boxes with the antique china and porcelain dishes except for a few which she would refill with fresh herbs. The two open arm chairs, the claw-footed table moved to one corner, the canopy stored, impossible to sleep under what had sheltered "our reckless youth," as Roseamond called it.

Bayla told Charlotte she agreed to the move, hoping all the while and long afterwards that Izzy would never divine that each night three people would be sleeping in the bed where she and Rosemond "sinned in the safety of our home." And she hoped that in a dream she would never whisper Roseamond's name with such longing that her husband would suspect the truth.

By the end of July, the nursery was complete. A border of playful rabbits ran the length of the room. A mobile of circus animals under a yellow umbrella was attached to a Swedish crib with no moving parts except the mattress, highest for newborns, lowest for a bed. An Amish daisy quilt in pastel colors for warmth. A child's table and chairs. A dresser for clothes and diaper changes. The child Bayla had given birth to had infused Charlotte with such zeal the woman seemed reborn.

"Such an effort, and money for what?" Bayla's mother would say. "When people are starving and cold. What a waste, and for an infant who can't show appreciation." That was the crux. Bayla grew up understanding appreciation. She appreciated a place to sleep, food on the table, a toilet down the hall.

"What's that?" she asked, pointing.

"A white enameled day bed when you need to spend the night if Leena is up late, or needs you to care for her when she's not well."

A bed of her own. Her first, ever. Not a flimsy cot beside her mother in the tenements, or one shared with her husband.

"Thank you, Charlotte." Bayla longed to lie down on its untouched surface, inhale its fresh scent, but what a fool, they would think. If they knew how much it meant, they might use the information to goad or threaten. "Do this, or we'll take the bed away," was too precious a ploy to place in enemy hands.

Late that night Bayla tiptoed into the nursery. With the child asleep in her crib, she eased onto the day bed, stretched her fingers to the top, her toes to its end, and closed her eyes. She dreamed about a little girl who had a room of her own with a door she could lock that prevented her father from entering though he knocked and tore at the knob, feverish to be with her, asking, begging her to allow him to do what she knew he loved best.

It was still dark when she awoke. She tiptoed out of the nursery, determined to forbid any part of herself from ever again being enticed by the bed's ruinous temptations.

August with its unbearable heat left Bayla drenched and restless. It was close to 1 a.m. when she threw on her silk robe, and in the kitchen, poured a cool glass of lemonade. Strange that over the racket of crickets and katydids it sounded as if a tree branch fell on the roof. Or was it a knock at the door? She peeked from behind the parlor's heavy green velvet drapes. A familiar figure, tall, heavy-set, was visible in the dim light over the front door. It couldn't be. Here, at this hour? She eased the door open.

"Milhady. What is it? Why—"

Beads of sweat ran down her face and neck into the bodice of her cotton dress.

"It's Travis, my boy." She was breathing deeply, her shoulders heaving. "I walked here. He's hurt bad. They beat him up. I'm sorry. I need you to...."

Bayla glanced left and right before shutting the door. She hadn't seen Milhady since she was pregnant and Leena already eight months old.

"What's going on?" Charlotte at the bottom of the stairs was brazen in her stance. A stranger, this hour, in her house? She peered at them through sleep-filled eyes.

"She's a friend," Bayla explained. "She needs help. I'll get her a glass of water."

"I'll do that. You do what's necessary."

Charlotte, coming to her aid without a disapproving word, a sideways glance? Bayla had seconds to figure it out. She ran upstairs, changed into clothes, and the three walked through the back door into the garage.

"Take good care and God forbid that you two should be spotted," Charlotte said, the empty glass still in her hand. "I'm here if you need anything."

She believes like I do, Bayla thought. People are people no matter the color of their skin. She wondered why she never realized it before. She drove speeding then braking over familiar bumps and turns, without a word exchanged.

At the Muddy Blues in the room behind the flowery curtains, a soft cone of light from a kerosene lamp revealed Travis on the bed, his eyes beaten bloody. He moaned softly. His Uncle Candy held a blood-soaked cloth to the boy's forehead.

"Who did this?" Bayla asked.

"My dad's people at the mill." A blond-haired white girl stepped from the shadows. "They planned it. Stalked him down," her voice fevered by anger.

"Look at her, young, beautiful, and my handsome son. How many times did I tell them? This world ain't big enough for the two of them."

"We've got to get him to the hospital," Bayla said.

Half carrying, half dragging him, Travis hissed through clenched teeth so as not to cry out from the pain. Candy and the three women managed to lay him flat in the back seat of the sedan. Milhady kneeled down beside him.

"They won't let me in," she spoke softly. "Mrs. Rothschild will make sure they do everything right. We'll be praying."

Through a private hospital entrance, Bayla spotted a colleague of Dr. Javitts, whom she could trust. He buzzed for a nurse and together they maneuvered Travis onto a gurney, avoiding reception. The doctor cleaned and stitched the gash across his forehead, straightened the cartilage in his nose. After a few x-rays, he put a cast on his broken arm, taped his chest to anchor his broken ribs and handed him pain killers. Bayla had to get him out before word reached the men who beat him up, before anyone from the hospital caught on.

It was still dark when they returned to the Muddy Blues. "He's stable," Bayla told Milhady. "If the two of them insist on being together…."

"We do," Travis said, his voice shallow as he eased into bed.

Christine took his hand. The black and white of their skin Bayla would never forget.

"You'll settle in a rooming house in New York City. I'll cover the rent until you find work." When the private car drove up, Bayla handed the man a slip of paper, told him to drive all night, stop for nothing.

"Bless you," Milhady said and hugged Bayla. "Now you get home. It's getting light. I'll never forget what you've done."

In bed beside Izzy it was impossible to sleep. If anyone had spotted Milhady at the front door, or the two of them in the car, or at the white people's hospital, word would spread. The entire family would be in danger, violence could, potentially, break out because of her.

Renowned entertainers who performed in clubs or hotels, Bessie Smith, Ethel Waters, Billie Holiday, Lena Horne, big bands from Louis Armstrong to Duke Ellington were routinely led to back or side entrances past garbage cans and refuse. Such an unforgiveable way to treat people had to end. She was pleased she had it in her to do what she did.

With the arrival of fall, whenever Bayla went into town all the talk was that the last of the steel strikes were coming to an end.

"September 25, 1941. Over 10,000 workers at Bethlehem Steel, the last of the smaller companies to hold out, had voted to unionize. FDR has won. Four years of struggle ended," Izzy confirmed the news to all of them that night from *The Herald Tribune*. "What are you going to do with your free time, Mother?"

"Don't worry about my free time, dear. With German troops advancing, Europe's facing a war. There will be plenty of need to go around."

Chapter Twenty

War Games

Recruiting Station signs around town frightened Bayla the most. While townsfolk saluted, or shook their heads as they passed, school classrooms were being commandeered for recruiting eligible men. Charlotte had already sent a letter to Dr. Javitts requesting that he document Solomon's damaged heart to the local draft board, but what would happen to Izzy?

"I already told you you're too old. Anyway, you're a father. The army doesn't want fathers," Solomon advised. "You can forget about fighting the Nazis. Right, Mother?"

"We don't know for sure, but you may be right."

"They're taking men up to thirty-five, dear brother. I'm only thirty-one. Still eligible. Didn't know you cared."

"The government doesn't expect a man with an infant to go to war. Risk his life," Bayla said. "It's not right, and for what?"

"To protect our country from a Nazi invasion. Thumbs up for ignorance," Solomon smirked.

Izzy stared momentarily at the food on his plate, then he glanced at his family seated around the table. "History has proven all of you wrong. Wars drag on and married men, with or without children, sooner or later get called up. Don't kid yourselves. That's how it is."

Pittsmill's first snowfall of the season landed eighteen days before Christmas. Charlotte was still in her robe, her ear close to the Stromberg Carlson console, Solomon and Izzy standing beside her when Bayla walked past the parlor hungry for breakfast. Leena had fallen back to sleep after her morning bottle.

"The U.S. is at war," Charlotte said, her voice flat. "December 7, 1941. The Japanese bombed the U.S. Pacific fleet in Pearl Harbor. A surprise pre-dawn attack." She repeated what would be broadcast on every radio station, and headlined in every newspaper: "Our troops are going in."

Bayla encircled Izzy in her arms, draped her head on his broad chest. "Don't leave me here alone with a child. She's barely a year old. I can't manage without you. Please, you can't go."

"Bayla, I need you to stay calm, and you're not alone. Don't ever say that. It isn't up to me," Izzy said as he embraced her. "I haven't even been called for a physical. Nothing's happened. I'm here, safe and sound with you and Leena. With family."

What could she do? What did she know of war, or world events, which she rarely followed or cared about? Pray. She could pray. If she prayed occasionally, or even every day, that might keep him home, prevent him from going to war. After all, war.

Now, before she fell asleep each night, she repeated the sounds she heard as a child recited by her mother over the Sabbath candle on Fridays before sundown. *Baruch atoi adonoi* Bayla would say, unaware the Hebrew words were translated as "Blessed art thou our Lord." Sometimes she would add, "I'll do anything," or "whatever you say," or "please keep him home." It reminded her of when she adlibbed a blues song, adding personal or amusing or sexy asides to entertain her audience.

As a backdrop during the war years, the family at Amory Lane enjoyed the child who was growing up among them. Leena inherited her father's long, dark eyelashes, her mother's blue eyes, and as the pudginess of her first and second years gave way, it was clear she would have her grandmother's aristocratic looks. From the moment she arrived in Amory Lane, the family took charge of her waking moments according to their whims. They selected her clothes and dressed her each morning, chose her games, and guided her play. They supervised what she ate, applauded when she cleaned her plate. Izzy bought her a new toy every Friday on the way home from work. Charlotte tucked ribbons and bows in her hair, small purses in her hands. Solomon taught her to wave good-bye, say no, and throw a ball. Each of them saw in Leena what they wanted to see, which allowed for an innocence of child rearing to persist in the household.

The excitement and joy each of them expressed when they interacted with Leena left Bayla dazed. When she held the child, or fed her, or put her to sleep, if she concentrated more, focused harder, or extended their time together, she supposed the warm, positive, loving feelings she observed from the rest of the family would occur for her. But neither patience, time or concentration brought the change she hoped for. Izzy was, by far, the better parent.

Each night when he came home from work, she watched when he lifted Leena in the air, covered her with kisses, played with her in the nursery. How captivated he was when she unearthed a day's treasures from her pockets—crumbled paper, a colored pebble, a bird's feather. He disciplined her so she obeyed. He understood her babble, her moods, her expressions. Everything the child needed, Izzy could give while Bayla didn't know what to give when, and if she did offer love or patience or understanding, each always seemed in short supply.

As the child moved through infancy with each family member constantly doting, Bayla thought their constant hovering, telling her what to do, showing her *their* ways, proved frustrating. She tried to intercede.

"Leave her alone for a change. Let her be so she can think on her own, learn to make decisions. How else will she be prepared for life?"

"Oh my. She's too young for that," Charlotte insisted with a pathos that shamed Bayla. What mother wouldn't know at least that much? What she had to offer regarding Leena added up to little more than ignorance. It was futile to convince the family otherwise. The best way forward, she decided, was to keep a tight lip, even if she had another opinion, which she rarely did, on the subject of child rearing. Once or twice when the child threw herself on the floor and screamed, Solomon called it a tantrum, Bayla carried her into the nursery and sang lullabies which calmed Leena and left Bayla feeling secretly justified.

The flood of new songs fresh and poignant, uproariously upbeat or deeply romantic that expressed the longings of those on the home front and those already fighting was Bayla's greatest indulgence. "Don't Sit Under the Apple Tree," she sang cute and chic. With "Boogie Woogie Bugle Boy" she stayed close to the Andrew Sisters' version. "I'll Be Seeing You," she kept soft and dreamy, like Crosby. She sang around the house no matter who was home. Sometimes even Solomon joined in.

In keeping with the hairstyles adopted by women who worked in plants across the country, Bayla switched her Veronica Lake peek-a-boo for an upsweep. With the beauty business booming and women earning their own money filling in for men's job, a new cache of makeup flooded the market which she took full use of especially for a Saturday night with Izzy at the Odeon Cinema.

"Perhaps we should only see musicals. Judy Garland, and Gene Kelly," he said as they walked home after seeing *Watch on the Rhine*.

"No. It's just that war movies seem.... so real."

"They are real. Our neighbors, losing a husband, brother or son. We have many reasons to count our blessings, my dear."

With gas and tire rations, evenings to Bayla seemed longer. Staying inside felt safe. Izzy lit the hearth early so the parlor would be warm when the family retired there after dinner. She on the Victorian rug, leafed through movie magazines, and kept up with the latest novels. Hemmingway's *For Whom the Bell Tolls*. In his high-backed wing chair, Izzy devoured the newspaper. Solomon and Charlotte, playing gin rummy at the bridge table, bet pocket change.

Like millions of families, radio was the primary entertainment. Between eyewitness accounts of the fighting, and dramatic stories portrayed by movie stars, Izzy liked Jack Benny. Solomon preferred *For Double or Nothing*. Charlotte waited for *Molly Goldberg*, and Bayla's best was Hedda Hopper's Hollywood gossip. Those without a radio gathered in bars and saloons to find out what Hitler was up to next.

With Izzy at work scrambling to produce berets, like the British soldiers wore, and the Eisenhower jacket, and Charlotte volunteering at the Women's Army Auxiliary Corps as a clerk-typist, when War Ration Books arrived, Bayla determined that her family would not go without despite severe restrictions. Solomon was the ally she needed.

"Thirty percent of U.S. cigarettes are going to be shipped to our boys overseas leaving fewer here, and as the war continues, you might not have a choice unless—"

"Unless what?"

"Volunteer for the Rations Board. You would know who supplies cigarettes when, and what foods would be rationed before anyone in town."

Policing cheaters while providing his family with confidential bans on butter or sugar, coffee, meat, and canned goods, combined with a steady flow of cigarettes, was too intriguing for Solomon to resist. He applied to the board the following day and was accepted. Like other mothers, with go-carts, wagons, anything on wheels, Bayla lined up hours before the supermarket opened to stockpile as much as would fill Leena's baby carriage. With Solomon's help, she became a master at fulfilling the family's needs under a complex system involving blue or red stamps assigned to different products, always keeping one eye on the price of goods. Once or twice when Charlotte caught Bayla carrying cans of food or a pound of sugar up from the basement, "I don't want GIs to go hungry because of someone in my family," she scolded. But Solomon came to Bayla's rescue. "She washes labels off every can, removes both ends, and flattens them for the Metals for Victory salvage."

In her evenly-paced but oddly unexpected lifestyle, characteristic of those on the home front, Bayla felt productive, well-cared for and loved. She was able to please everyone, and everything she did came out right. Most evenings, having finished in the kitchen after a day of securing what everyone needed despite severe shortages, she felt capable, effective and accomplished. She allowed herself to bask in an overwhelming feeling of herself as worthwhile. This newly rewarding sense of herself added a measure of confidence to her mothering. How she enjoyed reading from Mother Goose nursery rhymes, purchased by Charlotte, the child easily repeating "Little Miss Muffet," "Jack and Jill," and "Little Bo-Peep." Soon she would teach her songs, Bayla thought and smiled to herself.

When she walked along the Monongahela, passed the government-built Quonset huts, long, gray tunnel-looking houses resembling cylinders, occupied by families on soldier's pay, she felt especially grateful living at Amory Lane, a recipient of the family's thanks and praise. Secretly she hoped the war would never end.

It was a familiar morning when she headed to the mailbox at the front lawn. Not until she had set the mail on the hall table did she notice, "State Institution." Where had the time gone? She had written about Leena's birth to give her mother a reason to be proud, and the child was already two years old. She set aside the envelope, anointed by her mother's touch. Something to look forward to. Just the two of them. Together.

That night after everyone was asleep, she tiptoed down the staircase, into the library, reached for the silver letter opener initialed A.L , made herself comfortable in the soft brown leather chair, and read: *We regret to inform you that Lillian Szabo passed away suddenly of an illness, May 3, 1943, at 54 years of age. She was buried at the Guardian Saints of Heaven Cemetery at.... We are sorry for your loss....*

The breaking, bending, crushing sound of paper between her hands returned Bayla to how exquisitely she had feigned honesty to cover her deceit. The delicacies at breakfast, dressing her mother in finery, the fine-weather bus trip promising it would be the start of a new life, as if she didn't know all along her mother would never return. Facing her mother's death was merely the beginning.

In the past, when Izzy suggested a visit to the institution, Bayla would say she had things to do, she wasn't feeling well, bad weather made it unsafe to drive. Now she would have to be more precise. Her mother didn't like her schedule of walks and baths and activities interrupted. Ignorance of the truth was the only way she could protect him. Solomon, who never asked about her mother, wouldn't give a damn if the woman was alive or dead. When Leena was older, curious about her Hungarian grandmother, Bayla would tell her about the woman's courageous journey across the ocean to America. And each year they would write a birthday card signed, *Szereto lanyod es unokad*, Your loving daughter and granddaughter, in Hungarian. Charlotte was the problem. She couldn't stand for her mother-in-law to discover how neglectful she was toward her own mother. When she first arrived, embarrassing creature that she was, she had worked hard to prove herself, held her own these past six years, delivered an heir to Amory Lane, cared for the house and everything in it. But God forbid a questionable mood or expression, one misplaced word should escape. Charlotte would fix on that. No matter how close they had become, or how much Bayla trusted her, Charlotte, her protector, would do what she thought was right. People from the institution would arrive. At seeing the front door with its flowers and flowing grasses, "The daughter couldn't wait to live here. She chose this life at the expense of her own mother."

Bayla tore into the letter, ripping every particle as if the faster, the more urgently she tore into it, the less damage it would inflict. With evidence of her guilt suitably destroyed, she stuffed the incriminating handful into the mostly empty paper trash bag under the sink, secured the top, and brought it into the garage. Removing the lid from the large silver metal trash bin, using both hands, she went to work thrusting the bag into the weekly refuse among chewed leftovers, lamb ribs, potatoes skins, egg shells, apple cores, rags soaked in turpentine Izzy used to clean tar off the Ford's bumpers, old newspapers, empty Pinot Blanc, Pinot Rouge, Dewars, Tanqueray, crushed beer cans, Solomon's habit. As her handiwork disappeared, slimy wet refuse oozed through her fingers past her wrist, crawled up her arms, reaching her elbows then beyond her shoulders.

Confident that no evidence would escape, she stepped back, replaced the lid, lifted the bin, carried it out the back door, and set it down at the top of the walkway that ran along the side of the house. The cement turned the soles of her feet to ice, and a cold March wind struck full force at her legs, naked beneath her white night gown.

Amory Lane's maroon gables and dark blue tower witnessed her retreat into the shadows, and watched as she glanced up at the moon whose silver glow reflected off the metal bin, that would wait, stationary, culpable and alone until morning, and the arrival of the garbage men.

Chapter Twenty-One

New Clothes

After the second year of entering the war, U.S. factories had broken every record for war supplies from guns and planes to cargo ships and munitions. Like most small towns, Pittsmill was swept clean of healthy young men. Due to gas rationing, most everyone was on foot, the streets resounding with older folks, widows, young girls, newly married women, and wives managing a home and children, or living with family. A regulated number of steelworkers kept the mills going, but with so many vacancies, housewives took jobs driving taxicabs and buses, fixing cars and bartending, supervising work at the mills, monitoring work schedules, and overseeing steel shipments. But for the Rothschilds at Amory Lane, gossip had taken on a threatening tone.

"Both boys are still at home." " Missus bribed government officials?" " High falutin connections." "Our lives in turmoil, but not theirs." "It's not right!" "At a time like this."

"We've never experienced anything like it," Charlotte said. "Suspicion and envy at every turn." She had spread the word that her youngest son was a health risk. His heart could never make it through basic training, or keeping up with a platoon. But on his way to work or in town, it was Izzy who told of sideways stares and whispers.

For months, Bayla counted on Charlotte's remark that with truckloads of paperwork filed and coordinated by the U.S. Army, things got lost, misplaced, maybe forever. That was why he hadn't heard from the draft board but then a letter arrived. If anyone knew about cues, it was she.

"It came two days ago," she said, practically whispering. "I didn't want to open it. I wanted to hide it. Or rip it up. Here. take it." She thrust it hastily, haphazardly, into Izzy's hand. "Department of the Army. Official Business."

It was after dinner. The family were in their usual places in the parlor.

"Now, now, Bayla." Izzy embraced his wife. "No tears. We don't know what it says."

"Dear God." Charlotte placed her hand over her mouth. "When did you go for your physical?"

"A month ago. I didn't want to worry anyone."

"You should have told me. I would have loaned you my earrings," Solomon said, expecting a laugh.

"Not now," Charlotte said, almost scolding.

Izzy looked from one to the other, as if this would be his last glimpse at them for some time. Then he tore open the envelope and read as silence reigned.

"Physical Examination Report."

Bayla reached for the top of the settee to steady herself.

"*Weakness in heart most likely resulting from a childhood illness. Permanent arrhythmia—irregular heartbeat. 4F.*" He glanced again from one to the other. "Four F. *Not suited for military service.*"

They stared at the full-bodied married man, the father of a two-year-old child, each of them trying to absorb the significance of what he had just read.

"You won't be able to fight," Charlotte said, as if she weren't convinced that what she had said was true.

"I'll be at my job. At home. With family."

Bayla propelled herself towards him, pushing him backwards a few steps.

"You're going to be here. With us. All those nights, I did so much worrying."

Izzy freed himself from Bayla's embrace and ran his fingers through his hair. What had she done? What had she said? She sidled away from his annoyance at what? Her love? Her concern? Wasn't she allowed to feel relieved?

"I wanted to get out of it, I did," he said. "Maybe most men do, but it's not right. Rejected by the U.S. Army. I should be out there fighting with the rest of them."

"You're not the only one," Charlotte said. "Bob McKenny at the garage, and Ed Grobscheid, the high school principal, they weren't taken either. Who knows why? At least now the gossip will stop."

"And your health is a concern," Bayla said.

"Now you can spend your days cooking all the right foods for me," he said, "so I'll have the healthiest heart in Pittsmill."

"We're not unpatriotic, only grateful," Charlotte said as she turned the key in the liquor cabinet and withdrew a bottle of Dom Perignon. Solomon snapped it up.

"1927. A wonderful year for red grapes in Provence."

"My brother, the sommelier."

With the war entering its second year, Charlotte continued to process paperwork for the Women's Army Corps. Solomon remained at the Rations Board, and Izzy's career turned inside out with a new emphasis on accessories: gloves, turbans, handbags. With everyone so occupied with patriotism, there were days when Bayla faced hours alone with Leena. She taught her songs with stage directions to *Red, Red Robin*, *Mairzy Dotes*, and *Yankee Doodle*; dressed her in purple tulle, a white and pink ballet tutu, outfits from Grandma, for early evening performances. The child stepped forward all smiles and endless curtsies, proof of a mother's care. But it was when she had Leena alone, in bed beside her, or in her stroller on a neighborhood walk, or singing her a lullaby before sleep, that she felt this was the child she'd given birth to. *She is mine. I can give her what little I know about being a mother.*

It was only occasionally, in the midst of those bright moments, that darkness closed around her leaving her doubtful of whatever she had once considered worthwhile about herself: If not for Leena she would have been who she had set out to be. If not for Leena, she wouldn't have cast aside her singing. If not for Leena, there would be auditions, performances and a spotlight. If not for Leena, those tiny fingers that gripped her pinky when she held her for the very first time would not have become unrelenting, like her life.

Though they couldn't wait for the boys to come home and they had enough of doing without, people on the home front had become accustomed to wartime living. When the Japanese surrendered after the shock of the atomic bombs that devastated Hiroshima and Nagasaki, followed by the hoopla of V-J Day on August 14, 1945, the war's end seemed strangely abrupt.

As the country faced a period of adjustment, an eerie uncertainty descended upon Pittsmill. The foundation everyone had worked so hard to maintain for almost four years had to be altered, revamped, dismantled. With the war over, Bayla's place as guarantor of the family's needs was coming to an end.

Her food shopping was done. Leena, almost four, was napping. Everything was in place. Her day was on schedule, like all the other days, one after the other, day after day sliding into weeks, months, time upended by trivialities, and useless repetition.

Time, that *gonif*, that thief, once so available, had absconded with her will, led her in meaningless directions, blinded her vision until she let go of what would have taken her onstage into the spotlight. To withstand such a loss, she had to do something. But what?

She began to pace, endless turns into every room, first floor to the attic, top to bottom, bottom to top. At the full-length antique mirror visible from Charlotte's boudoir, she paused. Hadn't Izzy said it would one day stand in their bedroom, yet there it was, an affront to what he had promised. What more had she given up?

"If you get a job, you take it," her mother always said. "When there is food, you eat. When someone asks you to marry, you say yes." But her mother left out what women never talked about: how they succumb to the day-to-day doing and the day-to-day living until what a woman really wants becomes so out of reach she can barely grasp, or worse, remember what it was she wanted to begin with. Like singing. That was it, for her, wasn't it? Singing.

Bayla knew about suffragettes who went on hunger strikes so women could gain the vote. And seamstresses who fought for their union. And movie stars who rose from the gutter to fame. But her accomplishments during the war years, running a household, scheming for food, herself in charge, were all illusions forcing her to believe she was somebody when she was the same as women in the tenements, women like her mother. What chances did they have, if hers were so short-lived, despite marriage into wealth? Who among them got the life they wanted, as if any of them were allowed to choose?

In Roseamond's suite, the bedroom she and Izzy had occupied for years, she tore open closet doors, pulled out dresser drawers, and flung in frenzied abandon housecoats, blouses, skirts, underwear, shoes, stay-at-home uniforms that turned her into who she had become. She gathered what she could in her arms, and climbed the narrow staircase inside the dark blue tower that rose from the center of the house. It took four more trips to collect what remained and what had fallen along the way, but on the fifth, sweating and out of breath, she opened the octagonal-shaped window that looked onto the front lawn and heaved every bit of it out. All shapes and sizes and colors floated silently, gracefully downward freed from the confines of Amory Lane.

Standing on her toes, Bayla peered down at a woman's wardrobe scattered over the gray stucco roof, impaled on the maroon gables, overlapping the dark gray porch, wrapped around the dark blue porticos, stuck to the lemon yellow latticework, crumpled on winter's cold ground. So unsettling in the prestigious calm of the neighborhood. Pondering Charlotte's embarrassment, neighbors on the Hill peering from windows, fresh gossip filling the townsfolk, she began to giggle. Giggles that turned to laughter, pig snorts and machine-gun inhalations that forced her onto the floor, her knees into her chest, her body rolling from side to side.

"Not to worry, dear," Charlotte said calmly when she returned that afternoon. " It's nothing new. I know about this. Women's uncontrollable urges. There are reasons for them happening. I've gathered and folded what I could for the Salvation Army, hired a man for the rest. We'll buy new clothes, if these don't suit you."

As if clothes mattered, Bayla thought. As if the empty drawers and hollowed-out closets didn't resonate with whatever deadened her insides and left her wanting. As if her entire being didn't long to be soothed and caressed, liberated and completed by the darkness that filled her so thoroughly, she smiled, happy to embrace it.

Chapter Twenty-Two

Descent

Weeks passed. Bayla slept late into the morning, then past lunch. A day came when she was unwilling to leave her bed. The words of an old Tin Pan Alley song played inside her head.

> I'm forever blowing bubbles, pretty bubbles in the air.
>
> They fly so high, nearly reach the sky, then like my dreams, they fade and die.

She never performed the song fearing its message about dying dreams. Now that no longer mattered. Voices told her she was a sorry bed-ridden creature, fated to prove her mother's expectations: this is who she was, who she would always be. She believed she would be safe if she stared at the ceiling.

Dr. Javitts diagnosed her with a deep depression, and suggested electroshock treatments. She would be issued a different name, a private hospital room, a quick in and out. Charlotte anguished if word got out; her strong, capable daughter-in-law, her whole life ahead of her, a grown woman silent as a mute, vulnerable as an infant. Someone from Amory Lane.

"I want to keep her with us," she told her sons. "Service is something I know." With home care and bed rest, whatever had driven Bayla to such a low place would, in months, perhaps, be resolved.

The doctor was agreeable.

In the morning she served Bayla tea and toast in bed. Afternoons were for naps, her radio soaps in the background. Occasionally Charlotte coaxed her downstairs into the parlor, sat her in front of the hearth, her legs on the ottoman, a blanket to withstand winter's chill. She read to her: *Little Women*, *Pride and Prejudice*, *Jane Eyre*, *The Foxes of Harrow*. On a sunny day, they strolled around the garden. Indoors, she taught her to plant narcissus and tulip bulbs in clay pots. She ate dinner with her at the kitchen bistro table, served her grandchild, Leena, her boys last.

At night, in bed beside her husband, Bayla believed he was someone with whom she needed to reacquaint herself. He would give her a kiss on the cheek, then "Good night, my dear," pull the blanket up to his neck, and turn on his side, away from her.

"Fallen" seemed a clue to what had happened to her, as if she had once occupied a finer place in life but had somehow descended from wherever that place was.

Charlotte brought Leena to her mother's bedside every day after her kindergarten class.

"Your mother's recuperating," Charlotte would explain before Bayla found the right words to express to the child. "Are you okay, Mommy? Can you sing me a lullaby?"

"How do you learn to care for a child?" Bayla asked one afternoon.

"It takes time, dear. Soon you'll be well enough to care for Leena."

"I can't care for my daughter just like my mother couldn't care for me."

"You're a fine mother to Leena. She's quite capable for a five-year-old."

"Yes. You're all doing a good job. Remind me to say thank you."

At times, Bayla was inclined to say whatever words reached her lips. She might begin when she opened her eyes after a nap, or while she was relaxing in the tub.

"'Fathers leave children who don't obey them. Lift your dress,' he used to say. When I refused, he left us to starve."

"Did your mother know what he said to you?"

"When he closed the bedroom door to be with me, it frightened my mother's muscles to death. She needed a wheelchair."

"I loved Roseamond more than anything," Bayla began another day. "She was my nature, my nurture, how do you say it, Charlotte?"

"I wouldn't put words in your mouth, dear. Say it however you want. Whatever comes out is probably what you want to say. I promise."

"I like when you promise. It makes me feel safe, but I can't remember where I came from, or who I decided I was supposed to be."

"As you get better, it will all sort itself out. You'll see."

One afternoon Bayla said she had a secret to tell. Charlotte moved close, took a breath, and folded her hands in her lap.

"Roseamond tried to kiss me, but I had a husband. 'It's only a kiss,' Roseamond said. 'I don't have many left.'"

"That girl of mine. Your attachment to each other, your time together, your devotion, the love you shared. Sisterly love."

"More than sisters. You were there. You saw us. You understand, don't you, Charlotte?"

"What was between the two of you, kept her going. I was grateful for that. I've always considered myself a modern-thinking woman."

"I never seem to be good enough. Tell me the truth, Charlotte. Am I worthy? She doesn't speak to me anymore. Aren't I good enough for her now?"

"Of course you're worthy. The whole family thinks so. Roseamond did too."

"Roseamond liked when I sang."

"Yes, dear. We all enjoy your singing. Perhaps one day soon you'll—"

"Yes, one day. But not to her. Not anymore."

After four months, when March had passed, Charlotte carried into the parlor a tray with two champagne glasses filled with homemade cinnamon rice pudding topped with a large dollop of freshly whipped cream.

"Who cooks the food?" Bayla's voice was unusually clear. Her question distinct, easily expressed. Charlotte steadied herself, expectant, and wide-eyed.

"I do. I prepare the food," she said cautiously.

Distinct ripples of understanding, previously torn and mangled, seemed to reconnect after being at loose ends for what seemed like ages ago. As if a slowly brightening morning was leading her beyond that undefined place where darkness emerges into clarity, Bayla glanced around.

"I'm in the parlor, aren't I? No need to answer. I already know. You brought me back, Charlotte. You brought me back from wherever I went, didn't you?" The light had returned to her eyes, and as she spoke, she reached out with her hands.

Charlotte placed the tray on the coffee table, and instead of laying out the contents in her usual exacting manner, she sat on the settee beside Bayla and took into her upturned palms Bayla's hands, no longer stiff and cold, but warm and welcoming.

"You brought yourself back," Charlotte said with quiet certainty.

"Thank you for taking care of me." Bayla removed the white lace handkerchief from her housecoat pocket where Charlotte placed one each morning, and dabbed Charlotte's tears.

Moored to neither time nor demands, they faced one another, sensing the distance one travels after returning from a long ago, far away destination.

Bayla began to spend more days out of bed. She dressed in street, not sleeping clothes. In the garden, she cleared boughs twisted and broken by winter's storms to make space for healthy regrowth. And she returned to the kitchen, a place where she felt accomplished.

During the day Izzy called from work: "What are you doing? Can I get you anything? I'll be home in twenty minutes." At mealtimes, to avoid her family's worried glances from across the table, Bayla would lower her eyes as if she were admiring, or critiquing the meal she had prepared. Solomon tried so hard not to speak offensively to her, he developed an on-again, off-again stutter, particularly when he was about to choose an off-color word. Charlotte laughed, finding his stutter utterly delightful but Bayla appreciated that her brother-in-law was controlling himself, giving her time to recover. Townsfolk gossip complied.

"Seems the girl had influenza." "A mother with a young child." "And such a sturdy woman." "Took a toll on the misses." "Seems have recovered." "Took quite a while."

At 31, the start of her ninth spring at Amory Lane, during four months of illness, Bayla shed the fifty pounds she had gained with her pregnancy. Some mornings when she awoke the truth ran as clear as when she remembered what she was about and what she was after. Milhady's words beckoned: "If you want to be a performer, make a plan and follow it till you get on stage." But Charlotte said she had to get back on her feet, live up to the family's name, join the world around her. More challenges, and for what? Time misspent. Time lost. Time forgotten. Her life had stealthily whittled itself away through detours, camouflaged waylays hidden to lure her off course. Perhaps her illness was a marker. A message. Had she been given a second chance, Bayla the show-stopper?

Choices had to be made. Brutal ones. She would have to put herself first. Allow nothing and no one to diminish her determination to prevent whatever would distance her from what she wanted most. *Do I still have it in me to devote myself to my dreams, or will I give in to the forces that make life ordinary?* Bayla dared ask herself. For as far back as she could remember there were only two choices: Life without singing would be the end of her. And who could she blame for the consequences?

Of course, over time, certain evidence could no longer be ignored. Attention had to be paid.

Strange how it began, everything so relaxed and easy that night when Leena, already 13 years old, returned from having dinner at her best friend Margie McGlochlin's house.

"What's wrong?" Izzy asked as soon as he opened Amory Lane's front door

"You don't look well." Charlotte stretched out her arms to embrace her tearful granddaughter.

"What's going on?" Bayla joined in.

"Mrs. McGlouchlin says I'm sick," Leena said.

"Did you puke in their house?" Solomon smirked. "Must be that Irish cooking. Corned beef and cabbage You won't find that in this house."

"Margie and her family are moving to another state because her father got a better job, and it's all my fault," Leena shouted over her uncle then burst into tears.

"It's terrible to lose your best friend. I understand perfectly. Come here," Charlotte said. Leena walked into her grandmother's open her arms.

"Let her cry," Solomon blurted out. "She'll get over it."

"I won't get over it. I'll never get over it because I'll never see Margie again."

"Every father wants a good life for his family, Leena That's not your fault," Izzy said.

"They didn't even give me a chance to say good-bye to her."

"Maybe they didn't want to catch whatever it is they think you have," Charlotte said. "What *do* you have?"

"I don't know," Leena sobbed. "Mrs. McGlochlin didn't tell me."

"You're not sick and there's nothing wrong with you," Bayla insisted after hearing everyone else. "Who do they think they are saying such things? You'll find a new friend. It's good they're moving. Nasty people."

"Not one of you understand. I need Margie. She's mine. You have to help me get her back." She stamped her foot, pushed them away, dashed up the stairs, and slammed the door to her room. She swiped books off shelves, kicked her closet door, and threw something against a wall made in the after-school arts and crafts class she had taken with Margie, smashing it to bits.

"I'll go up," Bayla said.

"Wait till she's calm," Charlotte said.

Hours later, with family settled down for the night, Bayla tiptoed up the staircase in the silent house and entered Leena's room. A single night light in the prevailing dimness drew her to the words that filled the blackboard which Charlotte had arranged to install on one wall for Leena to practicing math and spelling. The same words, over and again, repeated endlessly, filling every space, their weight, their significance, their *fabissener* message made her jaw tighten, her eyes cloud over, her heart thump unmercifully.

> LEENA LOVES MARGIE LEENA LOVES MARGIE LEENA LOVES MARGIE LEENA LOVES MARGIE LEENA LOVES MARGIE LEENA LOVES MARGIE.

How vigilant the fates were. How threatening. To think she could salvage her career, prepare for an audition, perform again, with *them* interpreting her decision as a move in the wrong direction. Redemption for her prodigal youth, her blatant indiscretions was the path the fates had decreed for her. Redemption and atoning for the guilt which she had so carefully hidden she no longer remembered where she had buried it.

Beautiful, gentle Roseamond who held her, nurtured her, soothed her childhood wounds. Believing the love she had for her was safely stored only to discover she had passed down to her child unnatural, unspeakable passions, unnamed secrets never to be revealed. For her only child to be in love with .... Is this why she became a mother, to deliver such a legacy? For her child to be singled out, regarded with prejudice and disgust, her life a sham, our family disgraced, and she, a failed mother, exposed. The gossip, the shame, the ridicule would be unbearable. But it was unthinkable to have lived without what Roseamond offered, denied what they had, believing for all those years that she had escaped her mother's warnings, her Old Country superstitions. side-stepped the fates. And God forbid her husband should question where his wife had learned about women loving women.

She had lost her mind once. "Not again," Bayla whispered as she tiptoed back down the stairs. "Not again."

In the library, from under the desk lamp, on a sheet of stationary, the family name embossed in gold, as if that would do her any good, she wrote, and crossed out and agonized, until, sinking into the cushion of the brown leather desk chair, she perused her work:

"*I vow to make Leena as normal as they come.* I swear it upon the fates," she said aloud.

Though she and Leena appeared to be enemies, on opposite sides, they had more in common than they or anyone else could surmise. Just as she would forever hide that Roseamond was her true love, Leena would forever deny her true self. Simultaneously, or apart they would share what was as integral to their lives as breathing: abiding their shame and suffering in a silence as vast as their vulnerabilities.

Chapter Twenty-Three

No one Is As Strange As I Am

In sixth grade, like so many about to about to break through the floodgates of puberty, Leena fell in love. Margie McGlochlin was a petite, soft-spoken, curly blond-haired Irish beauty, who attracted all the boys in their class. Leena loved how Margie looked and what she wore, how she walked and how she sounded. She loved what she said, and how sweetly she smelled, and how it felt to hold her hand when they walked in two lines to the cafeteria.

Leena helped Margie with her homework, protected her from boys' teasing, and treated her to the Odeon Cinema on Saturdays. Cartoon day. She never mentioned how hard she had worked to get Margie to be her friend. She never told her how she didn't fit in, how she always felt alone. She never mentioned to her, or anyone, that she wasn't like other girls. She didn't think like them, or want to dress like them, and most of the time she didn't act like them, especially in front of boys. All that jittery and giggly and flirty stuff.

And there was the secret part of her life that she tried to hide even from herself. She never confessed how in second grade, instead of practicing reading at the book nook, Mrs. Stein, the teacher, discovered her and Jennifer Sorrenson peering into one another's underpants. Her mother was called into school, and that night, instead of her father's bedtime story, he informed her that some things are private, like parts of our bodies. Because her mother had told her father what the teacher had said about her and Jennifer, she was so embarrassed it outweighed any lesson her parents had hoped to teach.

In fourth grade, instead of shooting basketballs underhanded from the foul line in gym class, the girls' PT coach discovered Leena and Melissa Erico in the locker room kissing. That night her father talked to her about proper locker room behavior. Leena wished her teachers and her mother would stop tattle-tailing and her father would quit getting involved.

When Margie became her friend, the pain of being an outsider disappeared. Her life was perfect. And now that they were headed for Junior High School, Margie was moving away for forever, relegating Leena to the same horrible place before they were friends: excluded by the whole school. The entire world. A total weirdo.

Leena stayed in her room that entire weekend hurting from her insides to her outer edges. She thought about Margie so much she grabbed a piece of chalk from the ledge of her blackboard and frantically wrote the same three words, covering every inch, pressing so hard her fingers turned white and the chalk broke twice. When she was done, she stared at what she had written and language that never before existed spoke to her saying that she was not, and never would be attracted to a boy, or to a man, but only to someone female. To a girl like Margie. A girl like herself.

Students and teachers didn't pay much attention to the two girls who always hung out together. Neither were they aware of what Margie told Leena about dreams that frightened her at night; dreams where she was led to a secret place by someone who kissed her on the lips and played touching games. Margie told Leena that her parents called those nightmares which would disappear by morning, but they didn't because the person behaving this way was Leena, and Leena made Margie swear on her crucifix, the one Margie always wore around her neck, to keep what they did a secret until the day they died.

Her relationship with Margie was special and exciting because it was about wanting Margie to love her as she loved Margie. She thought Margie felt the same, but Margie had told her mother everything that she had promised to keep secret and that got Mrs. McGlochlin telling Leena at dinner that night, when the others were excused after the meal, that she was sick, and what she did with Margie was indecent, and evil. "And if you want God to forgive you," Mrs. McGlochlin said, "you had better tell your mother, so she can take you to a hospital where they care for those with a sickness such as yours. The sooner she takes you, the better, so no other good girls like our Margery will be hurt. Here's your coat. Take it and please leave."

Mrs. McGlouchlin had a dishtowel in her hands which she had been twisting into a rope. *She's going to strangle me,* Leena thought, so she quickly buttoned her coat and Mrs. McGlochlin slammed the door behind her with such a thwack Leena nearly fell down.

Leena was anxious to fix whatever part of her was broken but she didn't know what IT was or if IT had a name. Even if a doctor could help her get better, that meant telling, and she could never do that. She would be expelled from school, called a freak, a disgrace. All of Pittsmill would point and giggle when she passed. Girls were supposed to love boys, if loving a girl was a mistake, her mother had given birth to a mistake. *She* was a mistake and that's who she would be for the rest of her life. An out-in-the-open weirdo mistake.

"She's a teenager, going through puberty. It's her hormones," she heard her grandmother consoling her mother.

"When I was her age, we didn't know from teenagers," her mother said. "I worked in a sweatshop, the sole support for rent and food." She went on about how lucky Leena was to live in Amory Lane with a family who loved her, who gave her whatever she wanted when all she ever really wanted was to be like the other girls. And her mother saying there was nothing wrong with her which Leena couldn't believe because she knew anything and everything that could be wrong was, and weren't mothers supposed to know stuff like that?

Her mother, who forever criticized her for not having posters of Bill Haley, Elvis, Chuck Berry, or The Everly Brothers, or a single 45 record or anything to play it on, for not conversing with the family, or helping around the house, or cleaning her room even though she was raised to be a decent human being, meaning that she wasn't, and probably never would be. Her mother who seemed to know everything about everything, had no idea what was going on with her only child. What if her heart, or liver or kidneys had problems, like she had learned in biology, and she did need to be taken to a hospital like Mrs. McGlochlin had said so she could be made right, if that were possible, because she wasn't, as Mrs. McGlochlin said, not normal. The only thing she knew to do was to keep the not normal part of who she was hidden inside herself. Forever.

In September 1956, the start of High School, the idea came to her in Algebra class.

"If Tom is X, and Jack is Y, and Tom is twice as old as Jack, how would we show that as an equation?" Miss Melasky called on Stephen Mellman, the mathematical genius from Leena's elementary school, who always waved his hand like a lunatic desperate to be called on.

"X = Tom, Y = Jack, Tom's age = 2Y." Stephen Mellman, right again.

Leena slumped in her seat and tried to apply the algebraic minutia she had just learned to herself. By the time the change of class bell sounded, she had reached an astounding conclusion.

If X = eliminating the weird part of me, and Y = denial, then X = 10Y or 20Y or 200Y or 2,000,000Y. Here was mathematical proof: if she combined that with the hypothetical method, taught by her science teacher and added the work of Sigmund Freud, father of psychoanalysis, to explain why people did what they did before they themselves knew why, imagine having that ability! By using her algebraic theory to deny who she was, then apply Freud's methods of behavior, perhaps she could find ways to appear more normal.

At Strobe Library she read sections of Freud's *Interpretation of Dreams* concerning how the unconscious mind resolves conflicts. In the *Ego and the Id*, she read that the mind can take charge of emotions, or confuse us, or promote hysteria, guilt and dishonesty. Once she got home, she unearthed her secret diary from the bottom desk drawer in her room. Keeping her bedroom door locked, she postulated, as Freud did. To disguise who I really am, I must—

1. Present a tough exterior so others wouldn't pry into her true feelings.
2. Act self-assured.
3. Be alert to people's reactions.
4. Be daring so as not to seem too controlling.

By following this four-point program, Leena would appear to be in charge of her life. At school, everyone would be impressed with her self-confidence. Girls would want to be her best friend, invite her to their homes for parties and sleepovers. It all sounded perfect except for one thing: What Leena had vowed to deny for the rest of her life was her SELF—the stuff that made her who she was. *Would there ever be a time when she would feel free to love someone like Margie?* She decided to join the Boosters.

"Wonderful!" Her father, as usual, was immediately supportive at the dinner table that night when she made her announcement. "What's a 'Booster'?"

"It's what you do before becoming a cheerleader," Leena said. "As a junior, I'm eligible. Boosters are the most popular girls in school and I want to be popular to them."

"What do you mean 'to them'? You want to be popular to boys, boys who chase after *you,*" Bayla said, correcting her.

"Ah, a cheerleader, rooting for all those handsome young men," Charlotte said.

"Let her be popular with girls," Izzy said. "She'll have plenty of time for boys when she's older. Stop pushing her."

"She needs to be pushed," Bayla said. "She lacks motivation."

"Why do you always pick on your daughter?" Solomon asked. "Leave her alone for a change. High School is a tough grind for any kid."

Leena smiled and threw her uncle a kiss from across the dinner table.

"To be a Booster, you'll need to learn routines. Dance steps. Timing. You want to blend in, not stick out. You'll need my help," Bayla said. "

"If I need your help, I'll ask."

"What about your singing, Bayla?" Charlotte asked. "Now that you're doing so well?"

"Hearing you singing around the house again will be a *machia,* my dear," Izzy said.

"I was telling you about joining the Boosters.," Leena interrupted. "Mom has all the time in the world to do what she wants. If she wants to sing, no one's stopping her. Anyway, she does sing. Blues in the morning, Gershwin, and Broadway shows in the afternoon."

"*Gypsy, Sound of Music, Camelot,* I thought I'd learn some new lyrics. I've taken out my old music stand. Today's Broadway shows, they are magnificent."

"Speaking about motivation, Leena," Solomon interrupted Bayla, "with that beautiful face of yours, you're never going to turn a boy's head the way you dress. A black shapeless winter coat, a book bag draped down your back, a woolen cap pulled over your ears. You look like a boy."

"So what? I don't care how I look."

"You and I will go shopping this weekend for some feminine outfits," Charlotte said.

Leena remembered walking home from school the other day wearing exactly as Solomon described, trailed by some girls, jabbering about getting "that boy" to carry their books. But when they caught up, "It's a girl," one of them shouted. They giggled and ran off. Mistaken for a boy. She was cursed, like her grandmother Lillian, who her mother told her came to America from Hungary on a ship filled with immigrants at the turn of the century, and died of old age in a nursing home.

By the time dinner was over, Solomon had passed out at the table, his head in his slice of lemon cheesecake Bayla had baked.

"It was the red wine," Izzy said. "He drank most of the bottle. I'll get him upstairs." He placed his arms around his brother's middle and coaxed him into the hallway.

Moments later they heard a frantic cry. Bayla bolted from her chair. Izzy was on the floor gripping his chest, a drunk Solomon sprawled on top of him.

"Leena, call an ambulance. Quick," she screamed.

The way her mother described the scene at her father's hospital bed was impossible for Leena to imagine: intravenous leads in his wrists hooked up to bags filled with clear liquids, wires on his chest registering numbers on a screen, an oxygen tube in his nose. It was a heart attack, not massive, not mild. Charlotte, Solomon, and her father's friends took turns visiting. Doctors predicted a good prognosis, but Leena found it difficult to bear his illness. She had never been inside a hospital. Sick people frightened her. She didn't want to be exposed to germs. And if she did visit him, what if she saw him take his last breaths?

Her mother drove to the hospital every day over the next four weeks. Her metal stand with her sheet music waited in her parents' bedroom. Leena would listen outside the closed door. Her mother practiced "You've Gotta Have Heart" from Broadway's *Damn Yankees*. She stylized the upbeat, robust song into something slow and easy, making the message her own.

Leena liked to hear her mother sing. When she sang, the hardened, demanding, controlling part of her mother's personality became gentle, softer as if it was released.

With her father home from the hospital, her mother administered small white pills each morning, large blue ones three times a day. There were regular check-ups, healthy meals, mild exercise, no work for a month. As he convalesced, Leena couldn't abide seeing him barely able to walk around the neighborhood, her mother at his side, holding him up, watching his every breath.

If she hadn't been so miserable to the family, if she hadn't excluded them from her life, if she had been more helpful around the house, if she was less concerned about herself, her father wouldn't have become ill, and her mother's audition might be taking shape.

As she watched her father slowly recover from his heart attack, Leena gradually let go of her idea about becoming a Booster, which had excited her father and her mother had turned into a threat. She would have had to wear a short skirt, a tight polo and cheer for bunches of idiot guys. Why make friends with girls like that when she still didn't know how to reestablish her relationship with her father. It was hard to know what to say to a person who had been so ill, and she was too ashamed, or embarrassed to ask advice from anyone in the family who didn't seem to notice, or care. Though she had removed the STAY OUT!!! sign taped outside the door to her room, crumbled it up and threw it in the trash when Margie moved away over four years earlier, it might just as well still be there. She had remained that same person, distanced from her family, removed from herself.

As the fall of 1959 approached, when Leena compared going to college with preparing a resume, filling out job applications, and appearing at interviews when she had no idea what to apply for, or what she longed to do, or even what was she was best at. After high school graduation she would find a menial job for a while where her days would pass without too much disagreeableness, but like tyrants wreaking chaos over her meagre plans, there was her family.

"President Eisenhower sent federal troop to Arkansas so nine Black students could enter a white classroom in Little Rock Central High," her father explained, "and you can choose any college you want."

"Buddy Holly, Richie Valens, and the Big Bopper gone in a plane crash, and Billie Holiday, dead at forty-four from drink and drugs," Bayla moaned. "I've had enough grief. Do what's right. Go to college, and while you're there find a nice boyfriend, Jewish for your grandmother's sake."

"She wants to stay an idiot. Let her be one," Solomon shouted.

"The heir to Amory Lane must be educated," Bayla admonished him.

"I'll pay your tuition wherever you want," Charlotte said. "Your mother had to leave school..."

"Please, Grandma, I've heard the story a million times."

Without announcing her decision, she filled out an application to Pennsylvania's State Teacher's College, the go-to place for the few Pittsmill students who chose higher education. If she were accepted, she would be free of her mother. Her new home, an hour's drive away, would be a dormitory filled with women her age. As if it had a will of its own, Leena's sexuality was growing more demanding. When her fantasies turned too inviting, prompting her to satisfy herself before sleep at night under the bed covers, her thoughts reverted to possibilities.

What if she met a woman whose romantic preferences matched her own? How would they recognize one another? What would they say? What would they do? Two women like that?

THE SIXTIES

Chapter Twenty-Four

Nice Girls Don't Go All the Way

The town of Showharie, settled by American Indians, was home to Pennsylvania's State Teacher's College founded in the mid-1800s. Of course, when colleges allowed only male students, and names chosen for streets, parks, highways and housing developments were based on the areas original inhabitants, no one dreamed that Comanche Hall, christened after the most powerful American Indian tribe, would, years later, be occupied solely by females, five of whom had gained a reputation as the Third Floor Clique.

Amid cushioned couches and chairs, Formica tables, a TV, and a vending machine that offered Three Musketeers candy bars, the dorm's basement level filled with girls in lounging attire for the Sunday celebration of some 20 dorm coeds whose birthdays fell in that month proved to be the slumber party of Leena's dreams. No males were allowed beyond the main floor reception area. On a bleak evening, early winter, when the party ended, the Third Floor Clique was up for mischief.

Joanie, from Queens, was a bosomy Italian beauty with long black wavy hair, political science major; Mitzy, her roommate from Manhattan, also Italian, a peroxide-dyed blonde, Italian major; "Sia," short for Athenasia, an exchange student from Greece, literature major; Susan, from the Bronx, an overweight Jewish girl ready with a joke, English major, and Leena, her roommate, psychology major. Rather than question how she fell into a mix of big city females, Leena deemed it was meant-to-be.

"Sia was bad," Joanie said.

"What did I do?" Sia asked, unfamiliar with coed tomfoolery.

"She snored last night," Susan said, "and picked her nose.

"She didn't wait for us for breakfast," Mitzy proclaimed.

"I saw her smoke," Leena added.

"You lie," Sia said appalled. "I never did."

"Get her," Joanie commanded.

Sia flew out of the room. She raced along the hallway's waxed linoleum floor and disappeared into the double-sided bathroom somewhere among the toilet stalls, showers, and mirrored walls of sinks.

"Here she is," Leena yelled, but Sia slipped from her grasp, ran into the hallway, skidded then landed face down. Body parts slammed against body parts, slippers flew off, and robes flew open exposing thighs, shoulders, and buttocks as the girls pounced, bumped, and rolled on top of their felled victim.

"Mitzy, grab her hands," Joanie ordered over screams and laughter. "Leena, Susan, get her legs. Hurry. It's almost seven o'clock. Quiet Time. Go. Go. Go."

"Now!" Joanie shouted. Susan released a blast of icy water into the shower stall savaging Sia's body. At her ear-piercing screams, the vigilantes doubled over in laughter.

"Hello, ladies. I brought dessert."

"Mrs. Rothschild, what a surprise," Joanie said.

"Look what they did to me," Sia shouted to Bayla who held a large platter covered in aluminum foil. "They're savages."

"Maybe you should call before you come," Leena said. It was all she could do to avoid staring through Sia's soaked nightgown at her robust breasts, dark nipples, and plump stomach.

"I always call before I come. Didn't they give you the message?" Bayla said aware of her daughter fixating on the drenched girl.

Fred, the Dorm Monitor, a tall, slim, mannish-looking Norwegian, her blond hair pulled tightly back from her high forehead, appeared from around a corner.

"Ah, the police," Bayla said. The clique snapped to attention as Fred, savvy to what had transpired, placed a comforting arm around Sia.

"Very funny, girls. You're all going in the Dorm Book. Ten demerits each. A few more and you'll be docked for a weekend. Sia, get into some dry things and keep away from these brats. Hello, Mother," she said over her shoulder to Bayla, and dropped the pink message slip on the platter. "For you."

"Thanks," Leena said. She snapped up the message and headed toward her room as Fred slowly caressed Sia's back before the girl walked away leaving a trail of puddles. Was Fred trying to determine if Sia wanted more, or was she offering a signal to Leena? An affair with the Dorm Monitor was unquestionably too risky.

"You don't write. You don't answer my calls. I'd rather sit with you on a Sunday than be with your Uncle Solomon while your father reads the paper and your grandmother naps. I come here to know what's going on with your life."

"I don't want you to know what's going on with my life."

"Don't be ridiculous, I'm your mother, and listen to me a minute. Girls going after girls, it's not normal. It's a *shandeh*. A disgrace. That Fred, I don't like her. She looks like a man. You should know better. I thought you had more sense."

"What we did to Sia was a joke. And don't lecture me on what you know nothing about."

"I may be from another generation, but don't think I don't know what's what. Girls going after girls? They hide who they really are, you know. It's the only way they can live with themselves. Joanie and Mitzy, they both have boyfriends. I'm sure that's all they talk about. That's what you need. A boyfriend."

"There's eight women to one male on this campus. Even if we cut each of the guys in half there still wouldn't be enough to go around."

"Now you're cutting up men? Very nice. Keep your eyes open,

Leena. I'm sure some handsome young man is out there, waiting for you. All you need is one. Listen to me for a change."

Leena dismissed her mother's advice as quickly as the clique devoured the lemon marshmallow squares Bayla left in her wake. Later that night, in her private notebook, Leena entered churning thoughts. *If only my father would rescue me from my mother's controlling-invasive-narcissistic-self-centeredness. She has no clue what I endure. Exposure. Ridicule tempered by hopes of meeting a female who wants to love a woman like me!*

Out of the five in the clique, Joanie's sexual savvy, which always stopped short of actual intercourse, or "going all the way," impressed Leena. Each of them had been raised to believe that sex before marriage was taboo if they wanted to marry a "respectable" boy. Joanie called this an arbitrary societal prohibition which dared her to go further sexually than anyone else in the clique but without crossing into what she called "slut territory." A slut, she explained, was someone who *had* gone all the way and bragged about it.

Joanie had applied to State Teacher's College because Ritchie, her boyfriend since high school, was accepted at Bracknell University of Science and Technology, less than a mile away. Throughout the next four years, Joanie transformed the dorm room she shared with Mitzy into a salon of sexual intrigue. The language she used to describe her adventures was foreign, yet intriguing to Leena. How she and Ritchie had "gotten into it" in the grassy area behind his dorm. How she was "so wet" one night behind the football stands. How he had "eaten her out" during the drive-in move, and how she gave him "blue balls." Joanie espoused sex as natural, exciting, and wonderful. Without question she trusted each of the girls to safeguard her confessions as eagerly as they anticipated hearing them. If not for Joanie, where else would Leena be exposed to such intimacies?

One night when Ritchie's mom and dad went out for the evening, Joanie and Richie returned to their house after seeing *Breakfast at Tiffany's*. "Richie couldn't control himself," Joanie had restarted one of her sex tales. "He's on my neck, my middle, my legs, my back, feeling me up everywhere. He pulls off my sweater, kisses my stomach, heads for my boobies, licks the top of them with my bra still on. I can't stand it anymore. I had to touch his—"

"No." "Don't tell me." "Really?" "How could you?" "Why?"

"I just had to. I eased my hand into his pants, felt this hard pole, maybe eight, maybe nine inches long and the circumference was, look, bigger than my wrist! So I tried to move it. Left. Right. It doesn't budge but he's loving it."

"How can they walk like that?" Susan asked.

Joanie looked at her incredulously. "When we're not around, it goes soft, back to its normal size."

"What's normal? You think Greek men are bigger? Or Americans?"

"I never saw a Greek penis, Sia." Joanie said.

"What's wrong with you? You think Joanie goes around comparing Greek ones to American ones?" Mitzy said. Everyone laughed but Leena thought Sia and Susan's questions were warranted.

"Okay, okay, enough!" Joanie shouted. "So Ritchie tells me how he can't take this anymore. I'd better let go of him or he's gonna come. So I did."

Everyone, including Leena, recited Joanie's last line in unison: "But one of these days I'm going to grab hold of his pole again, and I Won't Let Go." Their screams and laughter echoed down the hallway.

It wasn't that she disliked males, or rejected them out of hand. Generally speaking, Leena believed she could compete with the rest of the girls if she applied makeup, and wore more feminine-looking clothes instead of loose corduroys and oversized tops. Yet, that flash of desire she felt at seeing a woman from behind, the shape of her legs, the fullness of her buttocks, her look when she smiled, turned her on. But dorm life, filled with women on the brink of sexual discovery—and a few who allegedly had sex and admitted it—gradually convinced her to leave room for what she labelled "The Male Thing." Her reasoning was simple: As a child, she knew she was weird because she loved Margie. In college, her total ignorance and lack of experience with men enabled the same assessment of herself. If she ever did have sex with a man, she might be more accepting of herself for loving a woman, less desperate to rid herself of feeling abnormal. Having sex with a man as an experiment might guarantee, or at least point the way, to her true sexuality.

"My room. Hurry," Mitzy commanded as she ran down the corridor. They filed in like religious devotees. She had just returned from a weekend at home, in Brooklyn.

"Tony, my boyfriend showed me eight-millimeter silent films. Dirty movies. Black and white. Two people doing it."

"No way." "What was it like?" "You joke." "Really?"

"Well, they were acting but it looked real."

"Can you get those films for Homecoming Weekend?" Joanie asked.

"Sure, and you can all stay overnight in Brooklyn. We'll sleep in my parents' bedroom, they'll sleep in my room, but if they find out, I'll have to confess to Father Donahue."

"They won't find out. Leave it to me," Joanie said. "Are you all up for it?"

"If it wasn't real, what's the point?" Leena asked.

"It's the Sixties," Mitzy said. "Women are burning their bras in garbage pails labeled Freedom Trash, baring their breasts, marching for women's rights. Hippie flower power is everywhere. It's sexual freedom with a capital S-E-X, and you…."

Leena felt her face turning red. She had crossed the line between defending herself and making them suspicious. How careless and stupid. "What I mean is, why don't we see the real thing? Can't your boyfriend get films like that?"

"How come every semester goes by and you never had a date?" Mitzy asked. "Do you have something against men? Huh?"

"That is sort of…. not normal," Susan mused. "Are you scared of guys?"

"Not even a little smooching….?" Sia giggled.

"I date. I do. There was this tall, lanky guy from art class. We had an ice cream soda at the counter at Merril's Drug Store. And I had lunch in the diner with an A student from my Abnormal Psych class. He's dying to be an elementary school teacher. One of those. Anyway with eight females to one guy, I'm not going to meet Prince Charming here. So quit picking on me."

"The University-State Mixer!" Joanie interrupted. "It's after Homecoming, when we get back from Mitzy's dirty movies. I'll ask my Ritchie to fix you up with his roommate. I'll do your hair and makeup, a sexy outfit and with that gorgeous face of yours, you'll be fabulous."

They looked her up and down as if she was some kind of freak that needed to be renovated, which of course, Leena knew she was.

"She won't let us," Mitzy said. "Look at her. Beet red. If she's this embarrassed with us.... Sorry, Joanie, your idea won't fly. Not with this one."

"Yes, it will," Joanie insisted. "We're all going to make it happen. Right, Leena?"

She had to play this right. "Are any of you going?" she asked, more relaxed.

"All of us have been to a Mixer except you," Mitzy said. "Joanie, call Ritchie now before she changes her mind. Here's a dime."

"What do you know about this guy?" Leena asked.

"He's a brain. Cute. Nicely built, dark, curly hair. Lives in Manhattan. His name is Teddy Goldman. It's one date, for Christ's sake!"

Joanie returned all smiles. "Richie said his roommate will go, on one condition: After this he goes out with who he wants, or he stays in and studies. His head is always in his books. An A student. You won't have a problem with this guy. I promise."

Despite their reassurances, whatever hormonal or mysterious forces regulated her sexual desires, Leena was certain that her escapade at the University-State Mixer would not lead anywhere except to confirm who she wasn't—a college coed desperate to date a man.

Chapter Twenty-Five

Homecoming

The prelude to Leena's expectations regarding the sexual discoveries that awaited her began at Mitzy's family dining room table that groaned with platters of meatballs, lasagna, mozzarella, a green salad, a loaf of Italian bread and pasta with gravy.

"Go ahead. Eat! My mother didn't want us to go hungry."

The comfortable familiarity Leena had gained over the four years of their being together, the groundswell of understanding among them because they were women, contrasted sharply with the pressure Leena felt to maintain her place in the clique by proving she was no different from the rest of them.

Close to midnight, with Mitzy's parents asleep, Joanie eased the movie projector from the bottom of the hall closet onto the night table. Leena closed the bedroom door, Sia turned on the flashlight, Joanie flipped the projector to "on," and Susan turned off the ceiling light.

Grainy black and white images flashed on the wall above Mitzy's parents' headboard where Gaugin's *Tahiti* framed in brown plastic previously resided. A skinny janitor in a t-shirt and jeans, mop and pail in hand, entered a room where a fully dressed woman lying on a bed beckoned with her index finger.

"Stop," Mitzy whispered. Joanie switched the projector off.

"Why?" What?" "Shush." "Quiet."

"The motor's too loud. My parents will wake up."

"What should we do?" Susan asked.

"Music. They're used to me playing my records late at night," Mitzy said.

"Leena," Sia whispered, "hand me an album."

Leena glanced behind her at the bookcase. "Rock or folk?"

"For Christ's sake," Joanie said. "Grab anything!"

Minutes later, Perry Como crooned "Have Yourself a Merry Little Christmas" to five college girls captivated by a woman who proceeded to undress, while the wide-eyed janitor ogled her nakedness, and removed his clothes to reveal an erect penis. After several minutes of rolling around on the bed, he eased on top of her, and thrust his mid-section into her, pushing in and out for several seconds. Then he collapsed on her. She stared at the ceiling. They rose, dressed, and walked out of the room arm in arm.

"He forgot his mop and pail," Leena said. No one responded.

The following morning, over juice and doughnuts, the grainy black and whites of the night before seemed to have turned the unknown into the unforeseen, perhaps even the unwanted. Joanie spoke pensively about all the times she came close to having real sex because Richie coerced her and she didn't want to. Mitzy reiterated her mother's teaching that sex is a woman's duty. Sia was frightened by the possibly of being manhandled like that woman. Susan said she was glad she was overweight because no man would be sufficiently attracted to her to do *that*. Afraid to implicate herself because it was the woman's body, her buttocks flaring, her full breasts, her rhythmic movements that aroused her, Leena nodded, the understanding therapist, to each of the girls' no longer secret inhibitions.

"Based on what we saw, I'm in no rush," she said.

Mitzy told Leena it was girls like her who end up the biggest sluts. Joanie headed to her parents in Queens, Susan to her family in the Bronx. Sia toured New York's sights, and Leena meandered along the city's crowded streets toward Penn Station.

Of course THEY could do THAT. For THEM it would be easy, she decided. But could she, or would she want to get that intimate with anyone, even with someone her own sex? If becoming like her girlfriends was her goal, how difficult could it be to replace her affinity for women with the same for men? Turn one off, turn the other on? Psychological drives, mere textbook print, could surely be overridden by her determination to become normal. All she had to do was take control of her needs, vary her tastes. What if it were that simple, switching off what turned her on? What if one man grinding into her like that janitor had done to that woman would cure her in one evening? It would violate the no-sex-before-marriage taboo, but why should society dictate what she could or couldn't do with her body?

Defying the status quo was suddenly as exciting as it was tempting, and difficult to ignore. She was more rebellious than she realized. She slid into a seat on the Penn-Central in the practically empty late-morning car. The University-State Mixer flew into her mind. Didn't Joanie tell her the time was right?

The clique outfitted her in a flowery, tight-wasted balloon skirt, a clinging peach waist-high scoop-necked sweater, and ivory pumps. Joanie fashioned her shoulder-length hair in soft waves, and highlighted her blue eyes and flawless skin with an impressive array of makeup. Upon entering Joanie and Mitzy's room, the Chiffons "He's so Fine" blasted from Susan's portable pink 45 r.p.m. record player backed by all the girls singing that it was "She" who was so fine. How embarrassing. She hated to be the center of attention, but when she ran back into her room for a coat, a furtive glance in the full-length mirror behind the closet door gave her pause. She *was* pretty. Really pretty. Hadn't her family always said so?

Hallowed ground. No matter how often she caught a glimpse of it on a ride into town, the college green at Bracknell University of Science and Technology, built during the early 1800s, was impressive. Lined by fifty-foot oak trees, on the north was Wizener Library, the south by a bronze statue of the university's founding fathers, the west by a single-spired Methodist Church, and the east by the new Museum of Science, all designed to match the style of the already proven edifices.

She stepped out of the old green Ford driven by a Bracknell freshman who volunteered to chauffeur State's women to the Mixer, a requirement of Sig Tau's Fraternity hazing. Walking toward the fraternity house, marked by hand-drawn signs taped to trees, sides of buildings, and plaques stuck into the earth, felt like a journey of the weaker sex towards the strong. Too late to turn back. She had given her word to her clique, girls determined to offer her untold happiness in the form of a Bracknell University male.

People would instantly know she didn't belong, that her being there was a scam, she was a fake, not willfully but out of desperation. She was reminded of herself as a teenager, going with her mother to the synagogue for services and privately conferring with the Rabbi for personal advice while her mother prepared the Oneg in the kitchen. Who else could she talk to about her situation? Could she even be honest with him? Barely, so nothing came of it. She hoped if she made it to college, her sexuality would somehow level off, morph into what she needed it to be. Yet here she was a frightened neophyte ready for everyone to stare and point.

But what if this guy was cute, even handsome, sensitive, and giving? What if he thought she was divine, both of them a perfect match? What if the seesaw of her life, the unpredictable ups and downs, would level off during her first real date with a man? What would she do then?

Through a dimly-lit corridor in Sig Tau's Fraternity house, Leena walked onto a threadbare rug inside the wood-paneled room where anxious-looking coeds waited silently on chairs or sofas, a few anxiously standing. The stink of cigarettes was appalling. She chose a high-backed wing chair in a corner, perfect cover for spying on a young man who appeared, glanced around the room with as much trepidation as she had upon entering. He was wearing dark slacks, a blue blazer, gray shirt, no tie. He had a welcoming voice, and a certain nonchalance, as he approached her. "Hello. I may be wrong, but if your name's Leena, I'm Teddy Goldman. Your date for the mixer."

"Well then, consider yourself lucky." She rose, and without a word, followed him outside, but be it her lack of grace, her inexperience with high heeled-shoes, or her sudden desire to be elsewhere, as she descended Sig Tau fraternity's eight stone steps, the ankle of her right foot twisted beneath her, propelling her to land on the cement walkway with a loud ouch!

He leaped down the steps. "Here. Take my hand. You okay?"

The feel of his hand, warm and strong, signified nothing more than a stranger coming to the aid of a clumsy college senior, green as they come to the world of dating.

"It's these stupid shoes." Leena examined her scraped knee. "I guess we won't be doing much dancing tonight."

"I'm ok with that. Fraternities make me nervous anyway."

She let go of his hand, wondering if he meant what he said. Maybe, like her, he was laying the groundwork to be counted out. They entered the gymnasium side-by-side and sat at one of the small round tables that lined the walls. The DJ was blasting Chubby Checker. She didn't care if the question she was about to ask was imprudent, or what he might think of her.

"Did you really want to do this?"

"Really? No. I wanted to do my laundry, but here we are."

"Your laundry? No kidding? And what did your roommate Ritchie say to get you to leave your laundry and come here?"

"Well, if you want to know, I was running out of clean underwear, so he told me to do what Italians do. 'They wear their briefs inside out.'"

"And you said?"

"You're sure want to go into this?"

"Sure. I'm a psyche major. The reason may be fascinating."

"I told him Jews don't wear dirty underwear. It's against our religion. We favor cleanliness. We pluck, we wash, we sterilize meat with salt, we circumcise, so Ritchie asked if I can ever answer a question like a normal person, he wasn't interested in my cultural history and he had promised Joanie that I would meet her friend, you, and if I didn't that would leave him with zero sexual activity for the weekend and that you don't go out much so I asked what was wrong with you, and he said nothing was wrong with you, and that I don't go out much either. So I said when I do go out, women overlook my flaws because of my good looks and winning personality, and he said maybe this girl will be like me: A smart ass."

When Leena finished laughing out of embarrassment and surprise, she told him she didn't think the evening would be this amusing.

"We're both Jewish. What did you expect? If we can't laugh at our dysfunctionality, who can we laugh at?"

She smiled thinking about all the laughs she could conjure up about her family. The DJ had started "In the Still of the Night." He reached out to dance.

"My knees, remember?"

"Oh yeah. Sorry."

He told her he was a chemical engineering major, geology minor. She told him she applied to college because it got her away from home. In his family, education was as vital to life as breathing. She told him her graduation was iffy because she had to redo a math class. He said he was on the dean's list. She lived in a large old house, an hour away, with her mother, for whom she could do nothing right; her father a soft-spoken sensible man; her uncle a bothersome pain; and her grandmother, who kept the peace. He said that he and his parents and two younger sisters lived in a three-bedroom apartment on Manhattan's Upper West Side.

When couples began to leave at "Good Night Sweetheart," Leena panicked. What was the protocol? No one in the clique had prepped her.

"How about we visit a friend of mine?" she tossed out like a misplaced tennis ball. "She shacks up with her boyfriend off campus. Does that shock you?"

"It's after 1 a.m. They're probably asleep. Aren't you going to call first?"

"No. We'll just go. It's a short drive."

"How can you make a decision based on that? Anyway, I have to be up early for a test."

She had a sudden urge to make a mockery of his good-boy upbringing combined with a touch of revenge at her group for placing her in this situation.

"It's called spontaneity. Sometimes you have to ignore the rules and let go."

They parked in front of a small house with a purple door. Leena knocked loudly. Tamara, in a silky robe, and her boyfriend, Tom, in boxer shorts and a t-shirt, welcomed them. They sat on a dilapidated couch and beach chairs discussing music, art, politics, and psychology with competitive displays of intelligence until past 3 a.m., when Leena casually mentioned that the girls' dorms were locked at midnight so she'd have to walk in nonchalantly as soon as they opened the doors around 5:30 a.m. "They'll think I was studying with a friend all night."

"But those are the rules of your university? How can you be so nonchalant about that?"

The others laughed. Somewhat perturbed, Teddy turned to Leena hoping for an explanation. "Have you ever considered the injustice of shutting women out of their dorm based on some arbitrary hour when you, as a male, are free to come and go as you please, even though my parents are probably paying tuition not that different from yours? It's female injustice."

"You may be right, but I still have to get back," Teddy said without missing a beat.

"You're both welcome to stay. We're going beddy-bye." Tamara pushed Tom down a short hallway and they disappeared.

Left alone with the curt remarks she had thrown at him, not that he seemed at a loss, if she truly wanted to know what it was like to date a male, this wasn't how to go about it. She had to control her prejudices, give him room to flounder or succeed in whatever ways the male animal chose to behave in these circumstances.

"I've made you angry and I didn't mean to. I'm sorry. It's just that . . . I'm vehement about certain injustices. I don't expect you to understand. Look, if you stay here, you can leave as early as you like, go straight to your books or your lab or whatever. You on the couch. Me in the bedroom. I won't attack you."

"I appreciate your apology, but three people laughing at one is uncalled for. It's manipulative and childish. Am I expected to apologize for not being part of your in-group?"

"No. In fact, I'm impressed."

"And I'm not concerned about you attacking. Handling women who attack me is my forte." He smiled. She laughed. "I'll drive you back so you don't get caught."

"An accessory to my crime!"

Early the next morning, the clique showed up en masse at her door.

"You stayed out all night."

"Nothing happened."

"No way!" "A little something?" "A kiss, a hug?" "Not even a smooch?" "Making out?"

"I slept in the bedroom. He was on the couch."

"Did you at least like him?" Joanie asked.

"He's very straight laced. Bookish. That was probably our first and last."

The following day she heard from her mother.

"*Your Teddy* called. He thought you were still on Homecoming break. We had a nice chat. He's quite a young man. Perfect manners, polite, and such a beautiful speaking voice."

"How did all this happen? And he's not 'my' Teddy."

"He wanted your dorm number."

"You know better than to do that. I told you never to—"

"I had to be polite. He offered his number. He wants you to call. It would be rude not to, and when you do, invite him for Thanksgiving."

"Inviting someone I barely know for Thanksgiving? It's two months away."

"You're not inviting someone. You're inviting Teddy Goldman. You don't turn your back on a boy like that. Listen to your mother for a change. Just give him a call."

Through no fault of her own and despite the absurdity of where it might lead, the news of Teddy's call anointed her as the latest source of dating intrigue.

"You have to see him again," Susan said. "What have you got to lose?"

"Go with him to Schroder's coffee house. Listen to some Dylan, Baez," Sia said.

"Give the guy a chance before you dump him. I thought you cut out that man-hating shit after all we did for you?" Mitzy warned. "Get to know the guy. There's September and October."

"Mitzy's right," Joanie said. "So what if he comes to your house for Thanksgiving?"

The clique couldn't possibly imagine it. A date in Amory Lane, that combat zone of hidden agendas and shifting power forces. Her family would take him apart piecemeal, each in their own way, and why would she allow a man into her life after staying true to herself since junior high school and Margie McGlochlin? She analyzed and debated having him a guest in her home, until it hit her like a finger in a wall socket: *Teddy Goldman was the most effective testament to her heterosexuality. The perfect cover for who she really was!*

The next evening Leena heard from her Uncle Solomon who rattled off what had occurred the night of Teddy's phone call.

"Your mother prepared a sumptuous dinner: roast chicken with chestnut stuffing, baked apples, herb-roasted new potatoes, and a blueberry tart for dessert. Your grandmother asked why the flutes were lined up on the dining room table beside a bottle of Piper Heidsieck. Your mother spit over her shoulder three times, poo, poo, poo, for good luck. 'Our Leena has found a husband,' she said. 'His name is Teddy Goldman.' 'It was only one call,' you father said. 'It's a chance,' your mother told him. 'You don't give up on a chance.' So let me be the first to congratulate you: Mrs. Teddy Goldman."

He laughed so loud Leena took hold of the receiver and smashed it against the brick wall that housed the dorm pay phone cracking it in several places.

Chapter Twenty-Six

An Invitation. An Assassination. A Gathering.

"Leena Rothschild. Phone!" one of the girls yelled from the hallway.

No, Leena thought. *Please, no*.

"I know we only met once but just give me a chance. Let me tell you the whole story. The Gestalt." He paused.

"I know. You can't get me out of your mind." It was the most ridiculous thing she could think of.

"Actually, it's true. You're different from the few women I've dated. And you're very different from me. My world is about method and deliberation"

Leena held out the phone and looked at it to make sure she was really hearing this stuff.

"But you're spontaneous."

"You mean carefree?"

"Edgy, actually. I prefer that."

"Okay. So?"

"So I'd like to see you again. I looked up 'Rothschild' in the Pittsmill phone book. I dialed, but hung up. Too chicken. When I tried again, your mother answered. She said you weren't back from Homecoming. She insisted on giving me your dorm number. I knew you'd be furious if I called at the dorm. Everyone would know I did, and you'd hate that, but here I am. I gave it a shot."

Leena felt a rush, the possibility of leading him on mingled with a chance to wreak revenge at her mother for giving him the dorm phone number.

"So what now?" she asked.

"*The Birds*, Hitchcock's latest thriller, it's at the Rialto. Want to go?"

It would fulfill her obligation to her clique and a movie, any movie, was preferable to revising her Abnormal Psychology paper.

Two weeks later it was *Hiroshima, Mon Amour*, then *Yojimbo* at the University's Film Club, then back in town for the Beatles' *A Hard Day's Night*. After *Woman in the Dunes*. she ended up with a terrible headache, slinking deeper into her seat each time that woman tried to dig out of her subterranean sand home. He suggested the town diner for a late night snack.

She was attracted to his thick dark springy curls. She told him to let his hair grow. He said he would. And it wasn't that school work had gotten easier. Or that she enjoyed studying, or that her grades improved. There was a distinct change she felt about herself, a change that granted her some freedom, a sense of relief from being different from the other girls, because maybe she wasn't. She didn't feel more confident about her sexuality, or more trusting that others wouldn't judge her if they somehow found out who she truly was. It was how being seen with Teddy on evening or weekend dates, or walking across campus with him, meeting smiles, approvals, a nod that brought her recognition for having entered the world of social acceptability solely because of one singular action: her association with a male. How astounding, she thought. At times she felt—dare she allow it?—normal. She was pleased for having decided, was it two or three semesters ago, to leave room for what she had labelled, 'The Male Thing.'

Leena and Mitzy joked when they heard the rumor. They had just finished midterms and were heading across campus starved for lunch. When they walked beyond the student union's heavy double doors, along the marble hallway toward the cavernous main room, instead of the usual boisterous din and clamor they were met with a silence so astounding it frightened them.

The usual hundred or so students were standing, packed together staring at a spot high on the wall where a voice, the words broken and halting, came from the loudspeaker.

"President Kennedy in Dallas, Texas, in his motorcade, beside his wife, Jackie, has been shot. In the head. He is being given last rites, but he's still alive."

Leena trailed Mitzy who was burrowing slowly, carefully through the crowd until she stopped because nothing seemed to make sense. They had congregated in Comanche Dorm's basement, the recreation room, to watch John Glenn orbit the Earth, Martin Luther King's "I have a dream" speech, Medgar Evers' shooting death. But the biggest event for the class of '64 was the swearing in of President John Fitzgerald Kennedy, in sub-freezing temperatures, January 20th, 1961 in Washington, D.C.

"American presidents are so handsome," Sia had said. Mitzy had said, "Kennedy is the only one." Joanie said she'd go out with him. "Who wouldn't you go out with?" Susan asked. Marian Anderson sang. Robert Frost recited from "The Gift Outright," Chief Justice Warren administered the oath, and the new President, who took off his overcoat and silk topper despite icy weather, inspired the country with words that made history as he spoke them. That was less than three years ago. Now college students eager to enter the world, standing together in silence and disbelief, inside their student union with its 20-foot-high ceilings, waited.

As soon as the President was out of danger, everyone would inhale, file out, Leena with them. Relieved. He would return to his duties, be back to himself. This unreality in the Student Union would fade.

"President Kennedy is dead." The words stopped time. Cries, tears, loud gasps.

"No. Wait. This is an unconfirmed report." The voice was abrupt, awkward, shaky. "He's still alive. They're attempting a blood transfusion. We're unable to confirm the information. Everything is happening so fast." There was a sigh in the room. A moment. Maybe two. Then, "John Fitzgerald Kennedy, President of the United States, is dead. November 22, 1963. Twelve thirty p.m. Let us pray."

Leena pushed her way through the crowd down the double flight of stairs toward the ladies' restroom desperate to find refuge. Every stall was shut, echoing her own sobs. The middle-aged Negro attendant, her white ruffled apron tied over her navy blue skirt and blouse, stood at her usual place, the row of white porcelain sinks. She looked without seeing as she folded and refolded her grayish-white wash cloth.

"Oh no, Lord Jesus. No. Don't take him from us. Don't take him, Lord, please," she pleaded as more female students, broken and tearful, fleeing the news upstairs, piled inside.

No longer caring if she had a place to hide, Leena buried her face in her hands and sobbed with the rest of them that afternoon in the Student Union Ladies' Room filled from its high ceiling and rising up from its tiled floor with all it could hold of devastation.

Funeral services were shown repeatedly: Jackie, her two young children, Carolyn and John, world dignitaries attending, the lengthy silent procession.

A week later, it was Thanksgiving. The holiday was a saving grace in a country that needed one.

Sunday, the last day of Thanksgiving, peeking from behind the parlor's green velvet drapes, Leena saw Teddy pull up in his gray Ford Falcon. Her heart raced. Her jaw clenched. Sweat dripped down the back of her neck as he moved slowly along the curlicue walkway. The door chimes rang. She took the smile on Teddy's face as approving of her white blouse and bell bottom jeans, tight through her hips.

Throughout the meal she hoped Teddy would remember her father's compliments; her mother's delicious cooking; her grandmother's soft-spoken kindness. Solomon's advice, "You had best suck up, young man, so they'll permit you to marry my niece," Leena countered with a laugh. She wanted to kick her uncle under the table but if she had, he would have asked, "Why did you kick me?" Her family's behavior among the presence of a male she had managed to snag into Amory Lane, she graded as remarkably normal.

On the drive back to school, feeling as if she had vanquished her enemies, Leena rested her head on Teddy's shoulder and fell asleep.

With winter's holiday season approaching, Leena entertained the possibility that dating a man wasn't so outrageous as she once believed. As the budding psychologist studying personality development, she was increasingly curious about how far the relationship with Teddy might go, and what she, in turn, could discover about herself within it. Beyond joining him for movies, dinners, parties, and making out in his car, which she limited to tongue kissing, if only there was some mathematical formula to gauge how fully she was inhabiting a heterosexual woman, she would feel more secure knowing where she placed on a scale of normal. As it was, she was left guessing, but with Christmas break looming, her clique taunted her to invite Teddy for a second overnight stay, certain something sexual would occur. She wouldn't plan every move. Spontaneity, playing it by ear, would free her to be more attuned to whatever sexual inclinations might arise. If any.

Her mother prepared dinner early so "you children," as she called them, could catch a movie at the Odeon.

"Let's drive around," Leena said once they were inside his Ford Falcon.

"What about the movie?"

"Not my idea," she said definitively. "Turn here. Follow the road."

"I'll get my map."

"Forget the map. Let's see where this takes us."

Teddy drove cautiously through a rapidly gathering fog, dropping temperatures and patches of black ice forcing the car into an occasional shimmy.

"Have you ever had sex?" Leena blurted out.

"Sex? You mean, real sex? I've made out with girls, but real sex. . . ."

His embarrassment gave her the upper hand.

"I bet you're the only guy in your dorm who hasn't done it yet."

"Most of the guys in my dorm don't know shit about sex."

"How do you know?"

"By the size of their genitals. We measure them periodically, post the results on the bathroom doors." He was focused on switching the headlights from bright to dim, dim to bright, ensuring their safety.

Leena laughed. "You have my dad's sense of humor. I like that." She snuggled into him. There was something welcoming about a man's protection. "Do you think you have to be in love to do it?" she asked.

"It? You mean the real thing? Not really, but I think that makes it better."

"But if two people aren't in love and do it anyway, they would feel emotionally unencumbered, not obligated by vows or promises."

"Marriage vows are serious. I like the way you laugh."

Surprised at the compliment, she nudged his shoulder. "What else do you like about me?"

"You're beautiful, but you don't realize it. You're not into yourself like some girls. Then there's your breasts."

Such a bold statement from him. Should she be the aggressor, or the uninitiated damsel? How much pretense would be required after dating for three months? She opened her coat, and placed Teddy's right hand precisely where he had obviously dreamed of placing it.

"Permission to feel."

His foot fell off the pedal and the car stalled. He restarted the engine, pulled to the side of the road, turned the engine off, unzipped his jacket, leaned over and kissed her. The urgency inside the car caused the windows to steam.

"I'm aroused," he said.

"I can tell," she said proud for understanding as she placed her hand over what Joanie had referred to as a pole. "I never saw a man… naked."

"I wouldn't think you had."

"Take it out."

"You're kidding. You're not ready for this. I mean....are you?"

Into the dark cold night, a full moon reflected silver white through the windshield where a single lone car was parked on the side of a rarely-travelled country road.

"Go on," Leena said, sounding bold, brash, failing to completely understand exactly what he meant by 'this.' She watched him prop up his middle, unzip, and dig into the opened space.

Seeing it, bare and exposed, Leena drew back, initially shocked and bewildered at its pinkish brownish sturdy uprightness. So unlike a woman's breasts or buttocks, covered yet visible in their own right compared to this secretive, hidden oddity, abiding in unknowing positions, dangling or stiff inside clothes, now before her, this private thing—Teddy's device.

She reached out, determined yet reluctant, repelled, mostly curious, fascination and disgust combining somewhere around her middle. She tried to urge it left, right, but it was unbendable, as if it would burst through the encasement of her hand. She didn't dare show her inexperience. She couldn't bear the embarrassment, having led him on motivated purely by self-interest, surprised at how smooth it felt.

Teddy moaned and closed his eyes.

"Should I do more?"

"Yes," he barely got the word out. "No. Wait. Stop. Better stop. Stop!"

Teddy dove downward, pushing her out of the way, grabbing himself in a vice-like grip. His head sank back against the seat, breathy moans from his throat. A long silence.

"I'm sorry. I couldn't help it. It happened so fast." He took out his handkerchief. "What you did, it felt so amazing." He returned everything from where he had unveiled it.

"You didn't give me a chance to say good-bye," she joked.

"I'll make it up to you. Whenever you want more."

Leena succumbed to the warmth of his neck, the breadth of his chest, the length and strength of his leg pressing against hers. She didn't ask, "make up what?" When he took her face in his hands, she returned his long, slow kisses.

Back in her dorm, the intimacies shared between herself and Teddy left her emotionally drained and astonished that people participated in such private activities, exposing parts of their body. Despite four years of the cliques' endless penis jokes, and her guessing or imagining what the girls knew about sex versus what she didn't, Leena fought to organize her thoughts into meaningful categories, desperate to label unrecognizable sensations that ransomed her body. Teddy, so readily exposing himself, his spontaneous climax, and she touching that part of him, witnessing all of it was so unforgettably dramatic and shocking. Beyond his wanting her, irrespective of what she thought or how she looked or what she knew or didn't, she felt astonishingly cared for. And what he felt, she could only guess: confirmation of what guys take for granted; astonishment because it was so sudden and physically out of his control?

During their last college semester, five months of it dating Teddy, what Leena used to refer to as her "true self" had undergone a sexual awakening. Her relationship with him was *really happening*. Together, or apart, Leena treasured a quiet assurance of being adored. Despite occasionally considering that this lifestyle might be temporarily on loan, Leena willingly offered herself to a boyfriend, a word that no longer felt weird or uncomfortable, except when she smiled to herself at the reality of it.

For the concluding segment in Leena's World Literature class, the teacher assigned readings from *Earthly Paradise,* an autobiography by the French writer Colette. The adoring relationship between Colette and her mother, Sidonie, enthralled Leena for how deeply it contrasted with that of her own mother. She completed the assigned readings then delved into the book which led to an unexpected, discovery—Colette had female lovers. Not only did she have lovers, she paraded them before her husband, her friends and family. That such a thing could exist, did exist with Colette, and who knew how many other women? To be so acceptable in France? And where else? The possibility made Leena feel very Humpty Dumptyish, as if her outer shell was cracking.

Teddy Goldman had become the safety net that satisfied her longing for a male-female relationship, but her acquaintance with Colette tempted her to explore what her true destiny might be compared with how far she had strayed from it. Normal had its benefits, but she needed to understand what *not* normal was like. Unless she balanced out the underdeveloped side of her personality, the side that had never been with a woman, with what she shared with Teddy, how could she be fair to herself, and to him? The truth was as tempting and enticing as it was revealing and burdensome. Had she been waiting for something like this to happen? Discovering that one of France's most prized female writers was a lesbian!

Scribbling in her private notebook unearthed a course of action. *When a date with him feels like having to do laundry, or clean my room. When I'm pressured to keep up with his brainy self. When he makes all rules. If he knew how often I imagine a woman when we make out....*

She had taken the Male Thing to a reasonable resolution, but she had to be fair to herself. Fair was the crux of it. Unlike her mother who had given up her singing years ago, who had learned or convinced herself to live with *not* singing, this male business weighted Leena down. It was there wherever she went, whatever she did, whoever she spoke to. But because she considered herself sufficiently different from her mother, her destiny would be her own. As she chose it. She would make of her life whatever she wanted.

One evening, after a performance at Schroder's coffee house, they paused for him to drop her off, as usual, at the entrance to Comanche Dorm. Lights from the windows, warm and consoling, beckoned Leena. It was time. She didn't need convincing, a scenario, or a case study with reasons and retorts. It had to be quick. One sharp, painful cut.

He tried to change her mind. Why now? Her decision didn't make sense. He would miss being with her. They were good together. He had his books, his studies, his career, but not being with her would hurt. She watched him walk away. Time to have sex with a woman.

Chapter Twenty-Seven

Default to Normal

Leena didn't plan what happened next much less expect that the one female who consistently caught her eye around campus would be standing behind her on the student union cafeteria line. They exchanged a "hello," and because it seemed uncomfortable not to, they had lunch together after which Ursula invited Leena to her sorority house. Sigma Tau Epsilon.

Throughout the following day, she threw herself into her usual compulsive analyzing. Did Ursula recognize in her a look, an intention, a yearning that signified her readiness to explore what two women did together sexually? Was this her chance to liberate the part of herself that had never been with a woman? Would whatever occurred between them convince her of her true sexual preference? She was excited by the possibility except for imagining what would happen if they were discovered. What sort of penalties were in place for girls like them? The finality of knowing was chilling. Leena decided there was no turning back.

Colorful flowering plants lined the windowsill in Ursula's room. "Like the tulips? They remind me of Holland, my home," Ursula said. "Like my posters?" Taped on the walls Leena recognized Babe Didrickson, Florence Chadwick, Althea Gibson, champion female athletes.

"Wilma Rudolph won the Olympics in Rome. Track and field, 1960, 100 meter, 200 meter, four by 100 meter relay....I told you I'm a phys-ed major."

"I know who they are. Psych majors know stuff like that." Leena was pleased at how exceptionally neat and clean the place was, this place that would confirm her sexuality.

Ursula rose from her desk chair and sat on the bed beside Leena. "I guess we both know why you're here."

"Yes," Leena said, trying to sound self-assured despite the tremor in her voice.

Ursula reached out, placed her hand behind Leena's head and drew her in. At the touch of a woman's lips upon her own, a flash of heat seared through her. Deep prolonged kisses, unlike Teddy's kinder, softer ones, made it clear: this girl knew exactly what she was doing.

"How about you stretch out? Go ahead. Lie down." Leena did as she was told. They removed each other's clothes down to bras and panties. From her dresser drawer Ursula withdrew what looked like a plastic penis. With a twist, she started it buzzing, and placed it on Leena's middle, aiming it downward as she sat on the edge of the bed.

"Do you have as sweet a love triangle as I think?"

"Love triangle? Oh, you mean. . . ."

Ursula silenced the device. "Don't tell me. You're not a virgin?"

"No, no." Leena didn't want this stranger, this girl, to conclude she was an ignorant neophyte, or worse, pitifully submissive. "Just go easy with that."

"Oh, I will. I'll take great care. You know why? Because it's an honor, you letting me be your first." Ursula caressed Leena's breasts, not the way Teddy felt her up, as he called it, but with cupped fingers, easing lightly across each nipple. Ursula's musky rapturous scent, favored by female athletic students at State, was transforming. Leena sank inches into the bed, her body acting on its own. She would go all the way, no longer due to her private manipulations but because the pleasure would be derived from a woman, like herself. They would take turns pleasuring each other, exchange female words of love-making through repeated orgasms, as soon as Ursula abandoned that plastic thing. But the tingling in her groin at Ursula's perfect timing drowned all hope of thought. Leena heard herself moan over the buzzing. Loud on the surface of her skin, muffled when Ursula pressed it into the flesh between her legs. Loud then soft, clear then buffered, she felt herself giving way, sinking, ready to crash then explode, but that sound.

While Ursula's know how had brought her seconds to what she longed for, their interactions seemed forced, artificial, distancing her from Ursula's expertise. Inside this room, where she had anticipated unknown ecstasies, Leena felt suddenly exposed. Unmasked. That intrusive, overbearing buzzing evidence of her flaw.

No longer able to dismiss the obvious, she and this girl had become queers of a certain kind. Isn't that what everyone called people like them? People like her? Queers. They might just as well be in a circus sideshow. The girls in her clique would agree.

"Turn that thing off," Leena shouted.

"Okay. Okay. If it bothers you. I have lots of other toys."

Ursula let the plastic device drop to the floor, then she positioned herself on top of Leena, gripped her arms and positioned, more like forced them, into a "t." "Is this better?"

It didn't take four years of college psychology classes for Leena to recognize Ursula's craving to dominate. The girl's ability to hold Leena against her will, pressure her to respond, invade places that had never before been touched felt suddenly alarming.

Leena began to squirm and kick which encouraged Ursula to press harder, tighten her hold. She laughed out loud, misinterpreting Leena's action as a game, mistaking Leena's fear and helplessness for pleasure.

With her legs astride Leena's body, their crotches tight together, Ursula bent forward and kissed Leena, her tongue invading her mouth. It wasn't until she sat up, released her hold and glared down triumphantly, that Leena could breathe, free from Ursula's subjugation.

"If this is how you treat virgins, it stinks," she said.

"You know I'm not a femme, like you. Why would a pretty-face like you come after me anyway? For a tease? What did you think it would be like?"

"Not like an attack."

"Let me at least finish you off. How long have you been dreaming about having it nice and rough? Huh?"

"I have no idea." Leena sat up, visibly shaken. Ursula slid off Leena onto the bed.

"What the hell do you want anyway? Do you even know?" Ursula ran her fingers through her short, straight hair in a gesture of anger and frustration.

Leena didn't know, and if this was how it was with a woman, she didn't want any of it.

"Okay look, if I read you wrong, I'm sorry. Don't go. I'll be gentle as a lamb. We'll do everything natural. I'll tone it down. I'll start over. You guide me."

"No." Leena reached out slowly and took hold of her sweater, ready to pull it over her head. Her jeans were within reach.

"Come on. Give me another chance. Don't leave like this. How about I get you whoever you want, a pretty one, like you? They're all over campus. I'll do it as a peace offering. As long as I can watch."

Leena never imagined such a proposition. Is this what Colette, her so-called heroine, experienced? Sex without sensitivity or beauty? Battery-operated romance?

"I don't think so." Leena yanked on her jeans and grabbed her navy blue pea coat.

"How far do you think you'll get without connecting?"

"As far as I want." Leena twisted the door knob and ran across campus until Comanche Dorm came into sight. At the bathroom sink, she hand-washed her bra, panties, sweater, even her jeans with a cake of Ivory soap. She wrung them out, and smoothed them over one of the curtain rods. In the shower stall, she scrubbed her body with what her mother had insisted was a necessity for personal hygiene—a wash cloth that sat in a dresser drawer for her almost four years at school and was never used.

The next morning Leena awoke feeling estranged from herself. She was someone she used to know but no longer did. She had avoided sex, intercourse, the real thing, with a man, and her experience with a woman, even if it might have been a run of bad luck, or a bad choice, filled her with a familiar word: weirdo. She had to escape from herself, alter her geography, find some place that would allow her space to think.

Her room at Amory Lane. With the door closed, she had quiet, solitude, privacy. Her mother would berate and pry until she had a satisfactory answer for why her daughter had so unexpectedly ventured home. After her session with Ursula, it wouldn't be anything she couldn't handle.

Meat loaf with gravy, cheddar mashed potatoes, glazed carrots, and pineapple cheese cake, her favorites waiting on the dining room table. Her mother always knew how to win her over, to get what *she* wanted. Her father insisted she sit beside him, took her hand each time he spoke to her. Uncle Solomon avoided one snide remark, and Charlotte repeatedly interjected "you need to come home more often." After dinner, Charlotte and her father headed upstairs "to rest after the evening meal, especially on weekends," Bayla explained. Her uncle headed to his room to smoke.

"Come, we'll sit in the parlor and talk like we used to." Her mother, so solicitous.

"We never talked."

"I'll tell you what's on my mind."

"Why do I want to know that?"

Bayla smiled and looked down. Leena remained standing.

"What decided you to come home? Was it something at school? You and Teddy?"

"Why ask?"

"I like Teddy. Those few times he was here, we were comfortable with him."

"He wasn't comfortable with us. We made him tense."

"He would never say that." Bayla laughed.

"He didn't. I just knew it. I'm sorry, but I've had a long day. I need to rest."

"Sleep well."

Leena raised her eyebrows, and walked out of the dining room.

Oh, she was good. Oh, she was smooth, and so patient. Her mother.

The next morning, before breakfast, "How about we get you some new clothes?"

She wants to spend money, Leena thought. "Sure, I'm game."

They dressed for March's chilly winds, roamed in and out of boutiques in small fashionable towns, Baldwin, Brentwood, West View. They ate lunch in Longines, the fanciest restaurant in McKeesport. Once they returned home, Bayla reconnoitered.

"The outfits you chose were perfect. The pants suit. The long skirt with the draped top. That blue dress."

"Perfect for what?"

Bayla placed two brimming mugs on the French bistro table in the kitchen. Leena took a sip of the warm sweet liquid. "For going out, with your Teddy."

"Hot chocolate in winter. You never forget, do you? My favorite each day after high school. And he's not *my* Teddy, so stop saying that. "

"Women your age don't realize how fragile men are. You're all so focused on how you look."

"I hardly ever care about how I look. How could you not know that about me?"

"Men," her mother said with a smile, as if the entire species was something of a joke. "Tough on the outside. Fragile on the inside."

"Teddy's not fragile. He's aware. Of my feelings."

"Well, that's a prize in a man. What woman wouldn't want that? He'll be some provider. His wife will never have to lift a finger." Her mother spoke slowly, purposefully, emphasizing words designed to linger, like prayers. "Six months already together. You must have gotten pretty close."

"You're wrong. I broke it off and that hurt him." The way she said it, with a modicum of hope, as if a possibility of getting back together had entered the room leaving something akin to a calling card.

"Go rest," Bayla said. "You'll tell me more tomorrow."

The Sunday, before she left for school, Leena took a walk with her mother around the neighborhood. Rather than allow the subject of Teddy to be managed by her mother's inquisition, she raised it.

"I'm in no rush, you know. I've plenty of time for dating. And he's almost two years younger than me, only twenty. He skipped a grade, completed a five-year degree in four, while genius me, I have to do an extra year to catch up on two statistics classes as part of my psychology degree to graduate. So embarrassing that he knows."

"So you'll graduate a year later. Girls your age, they're getting married one after the other. Joanie is expecting a ring."

"How do you know?"

"Wasn't I there two weeks ago with homemade brownies? It's all she talks about."

"Mitzy says she's next."

"I'm sure he wants to hear from you, no matter what you think."

"You have a crystal ball? I can be with a man or not be with a man, but I don't *need* a man. It's different then when you were married. A woman today can make it on her own. I can do what I want, live where I choose."

"A single woman, Leena? Some things don't change. A boy like him, some girl will snap him up fast. With him, if you want to work, you'll work. If not, what's a career next to marriage and family?"

Her mother, so polite, twisting her daughter's goals, making mincemeat of her thinking. What did marriage do for her mother except provide her with excuses that prevented her from pursuing what she wanted most in the world?

"There's something I'd like to tell you." Her mother's voice grew softer, almost gentle. "A few weeks ago. I awoke in a panic. What had happened to my music? My singing? Where had it gone in all these years? I left my morning chores, got into the sedan and drove. I had no idea to where. I parked, turned off the engine and looked around. I was in town, across the street from Cafe Genteel. Men carrying instrument cases, and young smiling girls were heading inside. I crossed the street, walked up to a man, tall and handsome, gold epaulets on his shoulders, like the uniforms I used to sew at

Goldmacher's for ushers at New York City's Loews on East 96th Street. I was so unconcerned about being recognized, even if he somehow knew I was from Amory Lane. I looked beyond the store-front window, beyond the Café Genteel letters outlined in gold. Dancers were taking their places on stage. A band, maybe twenty pieces, was setting up.

"If you're here for an audition, you'd best go inside," he said. So polite. I was wearing a flowery cotton housecoat, slippers on my feet. An overweight mother and full-time housekeeper. My legs naked. No makeup. Strands of hair flying in my face. I looked up into his eyes and saw a world so distant and foreign, I couldn't think of a word to say."

"What did you do, Mother?"

"My hands, so red and rough from housework, I hid them, slid them down the front of my housecoat, into my pockets, walked back across the street, and drove home."

"I'm sorry. I'm so sorry, but maybe...."

"What I'm saying is sometimes a chance comes along, and you should take it. You shouldn't miss out, like I did."

Leena, a psychology major, recognized that her mother's behavior was such an uncharacteristic departure from who she knew her to be, she suspected something more was beneath the surface, that something more was coming. Her mother wasn't yet finished.

The next day, before she rode the bus back to school, there it was: Her mother had saved the best for last.

"Your father and I will make you a lovely wedding. With your grandmother's contacts, a full page in *The Pittsburgh Gazette* society section. You and Teddy will be a couple people will admire."

Leena stepped into her mother's embrace, and for the first time in a long while, she felt something close to maternal love.

While studying for her last midterm, statistics, in a flurry of abandon Leena suddenly dug out her private notebook and wrote in capital letters: *A WEDDING, MARRIAGE, LIFE WITH A MAN. DEFAULT TO NORMAL.* Her academic pursuits would become a thing of the past; the imposition of a career and earning her keep would be dissolved at the altar; she and Teddy a couple, perhaps parents one day. Was it too much to expect, too much to bargain for?

Marriage would resolve a great deal, offer a life clearly marked, properly defined. How bad could it be? As men went Teddy was attractive, comfortable to be with. They enjoyed one another's company. Being heterosexual wasn't so untenable a part to play, but was marriage as inevitable a part of her life as it was difficult to dismiss?

The girls in her clique, probably every female in State, was headed for marriage. Why couldn't she have the life they were destined to follow? What was the worst thing that could happen if she defied her true sexual orientation? It wasn't as if she were losing a limb that could never be replaced. Regulating her libido, that's what would be required versus years of wretched uncertainty and indecision over and done with.

Days later Leena telephoned Teddy Goldman and asked if he had it in him to forgive her. He did. They had been apart from early February to early March. To Leena, it felt much longer.

She and Teddy spoke daily, unconcerned about who called who first. They discussed weekend plans, upcoming graduation, and what each had done when they were apart: Leena went with the clique on a Saturday night. "We drank pitchers of beer. The next morning, I was comatose." Teddy and his pals commandeered a classroom in the engineering building over a weekend to complete their final project. "We fell asleep there Sunday night. When the Monday class took one look at us guys and the room, they decided to relocate."

Leena felt returned to settled territory, built on sturdy footing. His choosing her to participate in what she referred to as his "braininess," deepened her confidence and left her giddy in a buy-one-get-one-free sort of way. By accepting his place beside her, she felt elevated as a woman who gained a great deal of what she couldn't accomplish on her own, as an ordinary coed.

It was after 1 a.m. when she and Teddy closed down Schroders, the place where Leena never considered going alone, every eye on her, an obvious loser, a singular female unable to get a date while college students, couples or groups, lined up on weekends for what Teddy called kumbaya stuff, performers doing Baez, Dylan, Kingston Trio, Peter, Paul and Mary.

Amid a gentle March breeze, she and Teddy were leaning side-by-side on the wooden porch rails of the hand-hewn log cabin built on the outskirts of Schoharie. There was an ease, a comfort she felt from the sturdy sense of a male, his body touching hers. They watched other couples, stragglers like themselves, drive off, one-by-one. Beneath the darkened sky and the sudden snap of Schroder's lights turning off, leaving the world around them darker still, Leena felt a kind of lift off. With the scent of fresh ground coffee in the air, their breath hovering, and Teddy's own fading after shave, he reached for her hand. At the touch of his fingers, she watched him raise her hand to his mouth offering his lips upon her upturned palm as if nothing else existed for her, and believing nothing but his caring for her existed for him, she stood momentarily transfixed without thought, judgment or reasoning.

After a long silence, "Do you think we're in love?" she whispered.

"Could be," he said, and while they sensed what was at once new and foreign to each of them, Leena would return many times to his lips upon her upturned palm as the most intimate expression of devotion she could have ever imagined.

Chapter Twenty-Eight

Gift

As May approached, Leena agreed to her mother's invitation for lunch at Amory Lane. It would be a break from finals and studying, and 'bring Teddy,' her mother had said. Now that she and Teddy were once again an official couple, her mother wouldn't dare jeopardize how she had successfully finessed bringing them together two months earlier. And lunch was such an innocuous occasion.

After grilled cheese on croissants, ratatouille and a green salad, "my own dressing," her mother detailed the recipe, Leena headed upstairs 'to powder her nose,' her mother said laughingly, a pompous formality that made Leena do a double take. When she returned to the parlor, an ominous silence had replaced the previous camaraderie.

"What's going on?" Leena looked questioningly at her mother, her father. Teddy was uncharacteristically pale, his expression a blank stare.

"Why so serious? What have you got there?" she joked, but he backed away. She elbowed her right arm towards his pants pocket, where he had buried his hand, and tried to tug his hand free, but again, he resisted.

"I couldn't stop her," Izzy said, shaken and baleful. "I tried."

"Teddy knows his own mind. If he wants to, let him," Bayla said as if the scene were commonplace, almost business-like.

"Let him what?" Leena was immediately beyond suspicious. "Should I point to the troublemaker or does someone want to confess?"

"I had nothing to do with it," Teddy said, looking like a rodeo animal, roped and tied which made Leena want to rescue him. "I have to talk this over with my parents. I mean, it's only right. I haven't told them much about ... us. This isn't how they do things. With them there are rules so everything turns out just so."

"I understand perfectly," Bayla said.

"Suddenly so understanding," Leena said snidely.

"That's enough," Izzy raised his hand for silence. "It's up to you, Teddy. You decide, and if Leena agrees, the two of you take it from there. A relationship, it's between two people. Sometimes my wife forgets. It's one of my jobs, to remind her, when she lets me."

Leena swallowed hard. She had to control herself. As she grew older, her mother had become increasingly intrusive and controlling. Her father, he dealt with her in his way, but why say another word, expose so readily the wretched family flaws Teddy would be marrying into?

"Why, Mother? Tell me. Why?"

"With all the talk among your girlfriends, one already engaged, another on the way, your mother was anxious." Her father tried to explain.

Begrudgingly Teddy withdrew his hand from his pants pocket allowing his fist to drift to his side. Leena reached out and placed Teddy's fist into her upturned palm. One by one she unclenched his fingers.

"Your mother handed it to me when you left the room. If I want to make you happy, she said I should surprise you."

"Were Grandmother and Solomon in on this?" Leena asked.

"Your mother told me not to say a word," Izzy said. "Your grandmother would tell Solomon, and with his yenta mouth, he'd tell the world."

"What's the rush?" Leena raised her voice and threw up her hands.

Bayla shrugged. "You're dating eight months already."

"That's not it. Try again."

"You never trust me. Why don't you trust me?" Bayla asked.

"You taught me not to."

"I'm sorry," Izzy tried again. "This isn't how things are supposed to work."

"Not in front of the boy," Bayla demanded.

"He's not a boy," Izzy shouted. "He's a man. And it's their life. Certain protocols should be followed."

"I have to talk this over with my parents." Teddy's voice was strained, sporadic.

"Do I have a say in this," Leena interrupted, "or am I some sort of commodity to be bought and sold?" The manipulating, authoritative mother who had temporarily disappeared weeks earlier was back triple force.

"Getting good grades are what's important in my family," Teddy said as if he hadn't heard. "With them, there are rules so everything turns out just so. This isn't how they do things. My parents haven't even been introduced to you. I have to finish my education. Get a job. That's how I was raised."

"Son, you don't have to do this. My wife's pushing you like a kamikaze on a mission."

"When you're a success in business, you'll pay us back," Bayla said with a smile.

"Don't you two realize how embarrassing this is?" Leena shouted. She wanted to snap her fingers, make everything disappear, fade to black. And that thing in his hand drawing her in, urging her on, tempting her to grasp the significance of its impact. The entire scene felt like a circus side show, pitiful, freakish and shameful, each of them, including herself, playing a part.

"It's awfully premature," Teddy said. "

"What will your parents say? Your mother?" Leena asked.

"You don't what to know what they'll say. What *she'll* say."

"But it's wonderful news," Bayla chimed in. "For two young people to find one another. Your parents will be thrilled. We'll have a big celebration, both families together."

"Enough!" Leena stamped her foot.

"I'm sorry. I'm sorry, " Bayla said raising her voice, her lips tight, her eyes downcast.

In the silence that followed, Leena and Teddy, each wounded and confused, looked to one another for answers. Leena lifted the box from his hand, and without a sound, placed it in the palm of her right hand. She glanced at it momentarily, withholding a smile at its weightlessness as she considered the consequences if she satisfied her curiosity. The pear-shaped diamond engagement ring was the exact style Joanie had received, the one for which Leena had expressed a preference to her mother.

"We've plenty of time," her voice was soft, steady and low. "We can discuss this, privately. You don't have to give in. They can return it, if that's what we decide."

Teddy took a breath. The color had returned to his face, and as Leena had done moments ago, he too paused to acquaint himself with the object benighted with such significance. "If we think about this, we both know it's going to happen. It formalizes what you and I have talked about."

"Look how happy she is. Look at her face—"

"That's it! We're leaving." Leena closed the box, and grabbed Teddy's arm.

"Leena, wait," Teddy shouted. "In a way they've done us a favor."

"You don't have to be so nice in front of them. What do *you* want? What do you think of all this? Forget your manners. Forget courtesy. Talk to me."

Teddy took the box, opened it, and lifted the ring from its black satin surroundings. He held it gently but firmly between his thumb and index fingers for what seemed like forever, but was barely a few milliseconds. Leena felt herself drifting toward him. Or was he somehow drawing her in so as to embrace all of who she was? The sense of herself in that room, inside the parlor at Amory Lane, the exact positions where each of them stood, the feeling that the entire house and everything within it would align with whatever she would do next was so strong, details of it would remain in her memory for years.

Leena slowly extended her left hand. Teddy reached for it, held it in his own and just as slowly, chose the finger where the ring belonged, and eased it into place.

As her eyes met his smile, deferring to what seemed to be his wishes, Leena felt an overwhelming sense of relief, like a flush of warmth upon entering a perfectly heated room during the coldest of winter days.

Amid the scurry and running water, showers turning on and off, and toilets flushing inside Comanche Dorm's double-sided bathroom, Sia saw it first through the haze of steam during the third floor girls' morning rituals.

"You're engaged!" she said out loud.

"I can hardly believe it," Leena said. She had stayed awake most of the night pondering how years of analyzing and conjecture was done with because she would follow the same path as the rest of them, as a married woman.

"Pear-shaped, like mine." Joanie peered over Leena's finger.

"Maazol tov," Susan said, wrapping her hair in a towel.

"I'm next," Mitzy said with a sleepy yawn. "Now you can fuck your brains out."

Other girls from the third floor offered good wishes, a touch of envy, impressing Leena that a ring could garner such attention, adoration, praise and respect.

"Did you set the date?" Joanie asked.

"Teddy's parents want him to wait another two years, until he completes his Master's, but Teddy said being a married man in grad school would give him a certain status. My mother says timing is encroaching for a 'wedding no one will ever forget.'"

Joanie suggested Labor Day, the first of September, before the semester began. "Everyone will always remember to send cards and presents."

One brutal realty loomed: The Goldmans face to face for dinner at Amory Lane, next Saturday. They lived on Manhattan's Upper West Side. Teddy's father, Max, a lawyer. Fanny Goldman, his mother, undoubtedly like all the rest of them. His two sisters, much younger. But what had Teddy told his family about her? What words did he choose to describe who he thought her to be; her looks, her personality; the nature of their relationship? Perhaps his family didn't care who he dated, or maybe, as she did, he kept that part of himself secret from them.

"All homemade," Bayla said of the carrot-ginger soup, roasted stuffed veal, zucchini-potato kugel, and lemon sorbet that cleansed the palate before her white chocolate mousse. Seated across the table from one another, Bayla's seating plan, she and Teddy exchanged eye rolls, winks, and smirks in concert with whatever was being said. Her father was gracious and endearing. Charlotte was sprightly and charming. Solomon excused himself before he got too drunk. Fanny was a compact affable woman with dark wavy hair like Teddy's. Max, a stout man with a hearty appetite, barely spoke two sentences. Teddy's younger sisters remained back home.

"With a five-hour journey, we let them stay in Brooklyn with their eight cousins from my husband's Orthodox side," Fanny announced. "We took a room for one night in a motel. We'll visit the cultural sights, Carnegie Mellon. The Frick Museum. The trip shouldn't be a complete waste." She folded her napkin into a perfect rectangle, and placed it neatly beside her dinner plate now that dessert was over. She thanked Bayla for the delicious food, then raised up her small frame in an attempt to appear taller, or stately, Leena thought.

"Our Teddy had been accepted to Harvard Business School for his Masters," Fanny said.

"Mazel tov," Bayla said, pretending Leena hadn't already told her.

"Since we're going to be family, maybe you'd like to hear a little about my son." She didn't wait for a response. "He was born before my husband went to war —THE War, that's what our generation called it, right, Mrs. Rothschild?"

"That's what we called it," Bayla agreed. "I told you already. Please call me Bayla." Fanny continued as if she hadn't heard. Leena grimaced.

"They sent my Max to the Pacific, and I went to live with my mother, the grandmother, who held Teddy, didn't put him down for a minute. Despite the painful delivery he put me through, I'd do it again because of the person he is."

"Mom, please," Teddy said.

Leena knew he had heard the story a thousand times. It made her feel more connected to him because of these mothers who embarrass you at every turn.

"Before he entered kindergarten he could read, write, and tell time. How did he learn?" Fanny asked, raising her eyebrows to mitigate pride with modesty. "Somehow. When Max came home, Teddy was almost four years old, a *menchlikite,* his head already in books. As Jewish people, you understand the importance of education for a solid future, to make the world a better place—the foundation of Judaism. But a wedding now? What's the rush?"

"Because they are so in love," Bayla said as if their marriage would guarantee peace on Earth. "It's a beautiful thing when two people want to share a future. School can wait. Why should they? Look how they shine from happiness."

Leena wanted to reach across the table and choke her mother. Izzy lowered his head and stared into his lap. Charlotte glanced at Teddy. Teddy looked to Leena. Fanny bit her lip, and Max rose, ready to leave. He didn't need to say, "I've heard enough!"

Chapter Twenty-Nine

Ceremonies

When Leena opened her eyes, each day closer to becoming a wife, she was brought face-to-face with having made the worst decision of her life: allowing her mother free reign.

With barely two months to organize a wedding "no one would ever forget," her mother's incessant guarantee, there was always more to resolve: food and music choices; flower arrangements; guest lists; table settings. Who from each side should walk down the aisle with whom, in what order? Should the hors d'oeuvres be eaten before or after the ceremony? Should the bride and groom's names be printed on cocktail napkins, match boxes, or *yarmulkes?* What favors should the wedding party receive? What colors should the bridesmaid's dresses be? Since the bride's family was assuming the major expenses, shouldn't the Goldmans pay for more than a klezmer trio which performed only Yiddish songs which most of the Rothschilds wouldn't understand? Who should determine the seating arrangements, each family independently, or, God forbid, in concert with the Goldmans who made arguments about everything?

Leena told her mother if she failed one final exam, she'd have to repeat a class and be unable to graduate the same time as Teddy who would head to Massachusetts causing their future plans to unravel.

If she could only rid herself of the overwhelming urge to short-circuit what accepting that ring on her finger had necessitated.

How difficult could it be, she asked herself, play acting the bride, mingling with guests, exchanging polite, superficial nothings, reciting after the Rabbi's "Repeat after me"?

"What bride doesn't want to be involved in her own wedding?" Bayla frequently asked and pulled her daughter into the fray like an unforgiving rip tide. "I suggested to Fanny Goldman how nice it would be to offer shrimp cocktail on ice in one of those stemmed glasses as an appetizer and the woman screamed: 'What's wrong with you? The Orthodox are *glatt kosher*.'"

"You suggested serving shrimp?" Leena practically jumped into the receiver. "Teddy's father's Orthodox people abide by the strictest rules concerning what is forbidden to eat like shellfish that swim at the bottom of the ocean and eat garbage."

"You think in the tenements my mother and I knew from shrimp? We were lucky to afford the food that we had." Then it was the wedding invitations. Fanny Goldman insisted it should include the groom's mother and father. I told her our head librarian showed me how a wedding invitation should read: 'Mr. and Mrs. I. Rothschild request the honor of your presence at the wedding of their daughter, Leena to Teddy Goldman.' No mention of the groom's parents. That's how it's done, and that's how it will stay, I told her. Goldman trouble, that's what I call them. Goldman trouble."

"Now it's the catering hall. It has to be strictly kosher. They assigned one of their Orthodox scholars to approve my decision. How do you like that? If it's not approved, the four Orthodox sisters, with their husbands, and children and grandchildren, won't come, won't eat, won't participate."

Leena tried to convince her mother to let her father lend a hand. He would be good at explaining the sensitivities on both sides, and her grandmother, who's worked with all sorts of people, she would enjoy pitching in. But her Uncle Solomon had to be kept out of it no matter what. Bayla said Charlotte would be choosing table linens, flowers, and china, but Izzy, he didn't need another heart attack. As for Solomon, "he would put those people in their places, " she laughed, at Leena's wide-eyes disbelief. "I'm thinking out loud."

With the wedding only three weeks away, the Rothschilds declined an invitation to Teddy's graduation party, a full-blown *simcha*, "like a Bar Mitzvah," he told her. "Food throughout the apartment." Leena refused a graduation celebration. Her gifts would begin at the altar: a career and earning her keep no longer an imposition, the freedom to do as she pleased, she and Teddy in their own apartment.

Leena was grateful for Teddy's daily phone call. He missed seeing her. He had studied enough. After Richie completed his last exam, he told her he took off with Joanie for the weekend.

"They did? We should do the same. This wedding, it's for my mother to let everyone know someone wants to marry her daughter."

"Leena, we found each other."

"Between being pushed, neglected and studying, you need to save me."

"How? My last final is this Wednesday."

"That sleazy place off the highway near State —Night's Inn? How about we go there Thursday night?"

"That's a pretty daring proposition, even for you."

"I need to be daring to survive."

"What will you tell your mother?"

"I'm at college. Who has to know?"

She and Teddy together, before their wedding, in a grunge motel was perfect If they had sex, did the dirty deed in secret, then went through their wedding paces, what better mutiny toward her mother, her family, the wedding guests, even her clique? If they didn't have sex, she could at least preview what it felt like to sleep beside a man. A way to ease into all that.

Teddy had let his hair grow longer to please her. Beneath a non-descript sweater that fit snugly against his taut body, his shoulders were broad, his wrists, "the sexiest parts," she'd often tell him. "Square. So manly."

To hide her self-consciousness, Leena bounced on the end of the bed, such a stupid, clumsy move. "It's not bad," she said, whatever that meant.

"Look. A new watch, a graduation present from my parents."

She laughed to herself at the absurdity of his self-consciousness and the oddity of the two of them surrounded by unrelenting freedom.

They removed their clothes, tossing them wherever. Naked and embarrassed, they ducked under the bedcovers where the heat between them was more of a turn-on than Leena could have ever imagined.

"I have condoms," Teddy said.

She ran her hands along his back, his buttocks, across his chest. She needed to become familiar with the feel of a man so the soft flesh of a woman, the kind she imagined and used to dream about as much as she fought against it, would be closed to her.

"How do you want to do it?" he asked softly.

"I thought you'd know."

He rose, and straddled her, pulling the blanket around his shoulders, shrouding both of them as if to hide what was about to take place. He took her hand and gently guided her, until, working together, she moved to his rhythm. With him inside her, she was drawn to his expressions, pursed lips, eyes shut tight, teeth gritted as if he were being tortured. Sounds of cars in the parking lot just beyond the door to number eighteen merged with his breath, his baring down on her, their bodies wet, each an intimate part of the other. Moments later he grunted, followed by a long-held "ohhhh-hhh," then he rolled off her.

"I never knew it could be that way."

"What way?"

"Better than I ever fantasized, or read about. It was like my entire body was inside you. Like every sensation I felt belonged to you."

Was she that far removed from him, from her own body, for how excluded she felt from what he claimed she had given him?

"What did you feel?" he asked.

"Stretched. Puffed up, like I was stuffed . . . .down there."

"Did you have . . . ?"

"An orgasm? How could I? I don't know how to do it." She expected him to know better.

"You will. We'll have plenty of time to practice. Uh, there's blood."

Leena removed spots on the bed sheet with a wet washcloth.

They put on sleeping clothes and retreated under the covers. Teddy slept soundly, his breathing barely perceptible. Leena stayed awake, unable to sleep. After all, sex with a man, a genuine penis. The word "penetration" popped into her mind. What would she tell her clique: "He penetrated me?" They'd laugh at that. When she tried to understand what it meant to her, there was his caring, gentle ways, his strong, muscular body, rocking and rolling on top of her.

At daybreak light seared through a rip in the window shade.

"How about we do it again?"

"We'll be married soon enough," she said, and fell asleep.

On the day of the wedding, a dense cloud cover persisted and by late afternoon light from the window barely reached her bed. Darkness where her mother had impeccably arranged everything: Wedding gown and veil on a white velvet padded hanger, ivory pantyhose, ivory silk pumps, new face makeup and lipstick beside a fresh bottle of L'Air du Temps, Charlotte's favorite perfume, a keepsake box filled with embossed stationery: Mrs. Leena Goldman.

Leena ran her fingers along the peau de soie train as if it belonged to someone else and she might, by imposition, spoil it, so delicately attached by endless pearl buttons. She put on the matching lace bra and panties, the hose, the full-length slip, and lifted the gown over her head. How weighty it felt with decisiveness and obligation, as it slithered down her body, and touched her toes, like a shroud.

She remembered the nuns milling around St. Raymond's Church on the East side of town; women, all ages, peering beneath their wimples. How similar she was to them, taking her final vow, resigning herself to a male.

"Rejoice," she declared sardonically at her dearth of choices.

"You didn't wait for my help? You dressed yourself. You look.... beautiful." Bayla's voice was filled with awe.

"You approve?"

"Approve? You're set for life."

Oceans apart, Leena thought. Not a patch of common ground between us. How could a mother know so little about her only child?

The family moved crisp as royalty into a white limousine. "Pomp and circumstance for the benefit of the townsfolk," Bayla insisted.

Inside the Aura of Vineyards, the finest Kosher catering hall in Pittsburgh, 250 guests, 125 each from bride and groom *fressed* during the cocktail hour on carved meats, hot casseroles, finger foods and a wine bar, while a pianist from Carnegie Mellon played Broadway show tunes on the baby grand. The *ketuba* already witnessed and signed in a private room with the Rabbi when her parents escorted her down the aisle to a harpist performing Handel's *Water Music.* "Stunning," Leena heard someone whisper, meaning her. Under the *huppah*, the groom smashed the wine glass, followed by Teddy's passionate kiss among *simitov* and *mazel tov* from two distinct camps—Orthodox women in long dark dresses seated beside bearded husbands in black jackets and hats separated by an aisle from heavily made up women in alluring dresses, their boyfriends or husbands in fashionable suits.

In the Grand Ballroom, ten musicians broke into Gershwin's "Strike Up the Band," a perfect background for Joanie's dick advice: "Feel it, hold it, suck it." Teddy's Orthodox cousin, Schmulie, performed the *kazatsk,* joined by a her inebriated and surprisingly entertaining Uncle Solomon; the bride and groom lifted above the crowd on chairs, and a procession of Viennese tables featured dazzling mouth-watering pastries surrounding a five-tiered wedding cake.

As soft phrases from the band created a soothing calm over the raucous goings on, Teddy was as unaware as everyone else that the bride's mother had drifted up the five red-carpeted stairs onto the stage, reached for the microphone, and gazed at her audience as the sequins on her rose-colored off the shoulder gown glistened in the spotlight.

"For our children."

"No," Leena gasped. The fire door was only a few feet away. "Let's go," she grabbed Teddy's hand, but smoky, bluesy tones were already drifting gently across the Grand Ballroom, mingling with the singer's voice.

"I took one look at you, that's all I meant to do, and then my heart stood still."

At the far end of the dais, Leena saw Fanny take hold of Max.

"Your parents are going to leave."

"Shhhh. It's not our decision. You told me she was a singer. She's good."

"My feet could step and walk, my lips could move and talk and yet my heart stood still."

Teddy eased behind his wife, circled her in his arms, and drew her close.

"See, my parents are staying. She's captivated them."

Though not a single word was spoken I could tell you knew,
That unfelt clasp of hands told me so well you knew.

"My Orthodox aunts will say she sings with a talent that could only come from Hashem."

"I never lived at all until the thrill of that moment when my heart stood still."

When the song ended, in the room's still lingering romance, Bayla bowed to heart-felt applause, walked back down the red-carpeted steps, her gown too showy, too tight, too revealing, but a woman, Leena decided, who had returned to where she was destined to be. A woman who should never again let go of performing.

Teddy looked lovingly at his wife, took her face in his hands, kissed her cheeks, her nose, her lips.

Near to 3 a.m., a waiting limousine drove the couple to the Four Seasons Hotel. At noon, they made love again, the taste of sweet raspberry ganache between the layers of chocolate mousse in their five-tiered wedding cake still lingering on Leena's tongue.

Her life was set except for one question that refused to let her be: How long would it take, weeks, months, or years until she would bear witness to the damage she was certain to inflict by disavowing her deepest, driving desires by attempting to live a heterosexual life?

JUNE 1969 – DECEMBER 1971

Chapter Thirty
Shipwrecks

The newlyweds rented a three-room, four-story walkup on Boylston Street with a view of heating units and roof vents that extruded waste odors. Leena was pleased at how appalled her mother would be, if she knew. During a two-week honeymoon, she and Teddy strolled the waterfront and the cobblestone streets of Beacon Hill, took a mid-morning "T" into Harvard Yard, browsed head shops and ate cheap lunches, Middle Eastern kebabs at an outdoor stand, potato knishes and hot dogs at a Kosher deli. They saw the latest foreign films of Bergman, Antonioni, Fellini, and Truffaut at the Brattle Street Cinema, Leena in miniskirts, her eyes rimmed in black pencil, Teddy in button-down shirts and jeans.

Money from wedding presents and Teddy's scholarship barely covered living expenses so Leena found a job at the checkout counter of a local grocery store. For Teddy, earning a business degree, attending class, doing library research then coming home to his wife, was idyllic. They were set until graduation in two years. But one night, his books splayed across the kitchen table, preparing for an onerous exam and a paper due on Coaching Paradigms —"Don't even bother to explain it," Leena told him—she knew there was no right time to bring it up.

"I'm pregnant."

"That's not funny. Don't even joke."

"Don't make me repeat it."

He raised his head from his books and put his pencil down. "Really? How? We take every precaution."

"I ran out of pills. Who gets pregnant without two days of birth control?"

"Obviously, you."

"That's unfair." Leena banged her fist on the table.

"Unfair? Why didn't you tell me you ran out? We would have stopped."

"Don't imply that I'm not as smart as you."

"This isn't about smarts. It's bad timing. We're barely married five months. I'm not even half way through my degree. How are we going to manage?"

"I'm not telling anyone. It's too embarrassing. What are *you* going to do?

"I'm going to be a father at twenty-two. The sole support of my family. That wasn't the plan. My parents will go nuts. They'll think it's the end of my career."

"My mother will be thrilled."

After three months of going up and down the stairs to their apartment, and feeling unbearably exhausted, Leena quit her job.

"We need to tell them something," Teddy said.

"Not yet. We won't be seeing them anytime soon and the doctor said I won't be showing for at least another month. *Showing*. As if I'm on exhibition."

"Leena, we're making a baby."

"You did the dirty deed."

"You were the one I deeded it to."

She didn't laugh. "Six more months, for God's sake, what am I going to do in all that time?"

"Do whatever you want. It's a problem I wouldn't mind having."

Leena slept until 11 a.m. She skimmed *Psychology Today* magazines, ate leisurely breakfasts. Bombarded by endless free time led her, somewhat habitually, to follow her father's penchant for world news, not from his beloved newspapers but on TV. If it wasn't the

Viet Nam war, it was the Warren Commission Report investigating JFK's assassination, or apartheid in South Africa, or the battle for civil rights: anti-segregationists in Arkansas and Alabama, fighting those who would protect the status quo, each side determined to annihilate the other's beliefs, if not the believers themselves. The conviction and vehemence between those who wanted the system changed, and those who didn't, led her to the place where a child was growing. A child, planted by a man's seed. A man. Of all things. The airwaves pared down news events to infinitesimal trivia, but who would report her side? Who would highlight her battle between the life she was living versus the life she always wanted—to love a woman? Who would explore the tangled chronology that turned her into the person she pretended to be? If the life she had chosen was the one she needed to inhabit, why did she feel as if she had sold her soul?

"It's hormones." Charlotte tried to soothe Leena during their telephone conversations. "Your mother was the same, happy one minute, crying the next. When they put the baby in your arms, it will all make sense. I promise."

Charlotte, Leena's biggest fan, the diplomatic buffer between herself and Bayla. If only she had confided in her grandmother, admitted the truth about herself years ago, her growing up might have been filled with less angst. Less pain. "I'll always be there for you," Charlotte had promised, but days before her great grandchild was due, Charlotte, fragile and unsteady, had a stroke. As streaks of pink dawn surged through Pittsmill's skyline, she took her last breaths. Her father gave her the news.

"Your mother was barely consolable. 'How will I go on without her? Who will explain things to me? Who will stand by me when I don't know how to act? Without Charlotte, who will save me from myself?' Don't worry, Leena, she's my concern. The doctor gave her something. You're going to have a child. You must think about yourself.

"Zolinsky's Funeral Parlor was packed. Everyone was there: your grandmother's remaining relatives, friends from across the country, business associates from the old days, fabric store owners, refinishers, upholsterers, decorators, even the boys who used to drive the delivery truck. Townsfolk congregated outside, waiting for news, any word.

"In his eulogy, the Rabbi described her, a smart-looking, feisty woman who worked hard with her husband, moved to Beleaguered Hill with her family, and stayed. If she thought she could put something right, help people in need, or speak up to support a worthy cause, she did. Her respect for people was magnanimous, no matter their beliefs or what they looked like, or how full or empty their pocketbooks were. I think your mother should tell you the rest."

"Why? Go ahead."

"Well, you know she had some very beautiful pieces of jewelry. Some she gave to her three best friends, a few for you, money to charities, her stocks, bonds, cash divided between me, Solomon and you. And Amory Lane, Amory Lane she deeded to your mother."

"What? What do you mean?"

"She left your mother a note. *You have become like my child, devoted over thirty years to the family, and to the home I cherished. Amory Lane is yours, Bayla. May you run our home with the same dedication and love you showed our Roseamond.*"

"Roseamond? She was my aunt. Died very young?"

"Yes, your mother loved her dearly. They were very close. My angelic sister."

"Not so close that my mother rarely mentioned a word about it. Why wouldn't she? Roseamond," she said out loud. "Pretty name."

In Boston, the grief that accompanied Leena was unimaginable. No matter what she did or where she went, the place inside her previously occupied by her grandmother's love and devotion felt like a gash that hurt from the inside out and the outside in. Time washed over her like ocean waves, endless and repetitive, leaving her drained. Silent and still. More than ever, Leena wanted to share doubts and uncertainties about herself and her upcoming motherhood with the woman who promised that everything would turn out fine.

One week later, September 25, 1965, Jacqueline Carlotta was born. Leena named her after John F. Kennedy's wife, for her strength and fortitude, and for Carlotta after her grandmother. That same week, having completed his MBA, Teddy was hired by AT&T's fiber optics division. A training seminar in New York City caused him to miss his graduation which infuriated the Goldman family, especially Fanny. "Who misses a graduation from Harvard," she chastised. "What are you doing with your life, my son?"

"I'm living it, that's what I told her," he told Leena.

"Good for you." Leena was pleased that her husband was sticking up for the three of them. His family.

The realms of power available as a parent left Leena heady. There were daily surprises, a sense of direction, a newfound stability. The child gave her a focus, a place to be. For the first time, maybe ever, Leena wanted to do her best. Her life as a wife and mother felt settled like the layers of sedimentary rock she had learned about in geology, the one three-credit college science class she was required to take. But it was her psychology background that would allow her to create the person she wanted her daughter to be. She would have a strong ego, speak her mind, be an independent thinker, socially adept. Unlike her mother, nosing into every aspect of her life, she would allow her daughter to choose whatever she wanted out of life.

She never counted on, much less imagine the increasing acrimony and competition between the respective families; the push and pull of each side wrangling for what they thought was best for the new baby—what she should eat, what she should wear, when she should be bathed, or put to sleep, or taken outside for fresh air and sunshine. Inscrutable trivia, unknowable after effects of a delivery, made worse by her mother, Bayla.

"I'll pack a suitcase. Stay. Indefinitely. Why pay for a nanny? I'll clean, make the baby's formula, read to her, bathe her, you know I know how to do such things."

Separated by over six hundred miles from Pennsylvania was an insignificant barrier to Bayla. The few times Leena allowed her parents to visit, sleep on the pull-out couch in the living room, or schlep back and forth from a nearby hotel, the effort to plan and cook meals, and acclimate the child to strangers called grandparents, Leena found disruptive and overwhelming.

When Teddy insisted his parents receive equal time, Leena insisted they stay at the Holiday Inn. Each morning, after their complimentary breakfast, once they arrived at the door to their home, Leena would hand over Jackie's stroller with suggestions for walks around the neighborhood, the playground and take-out dinners with recommendations on a hand-written list.

Teddy promised his family could visit without the Rothschilds. Leena promised her family could visit without the Goldmans. Together they dispelled the possibility of visiting New York, or Pennsylvania, and eventually congratulated themselves for having successfully minimized the influence of overly concerned, unnecessarily worried, neurotically interfering first time grandparents.

After three months with AT&T, Leena, Teddy and Jackie moved into a two-bedroom colonial with red shutters, an eat-in kitchen, and a small backyard on a quiet street in Brookline.

For the next three years, Leena appropriated a life for herself that had clear edges and boundaries. Her friends were married woman with children, like herself. When someone at the supermarket, drug store, or library stopped to chat, she felt accomplished, part of a community. On a Saturday night, she and Teddy would join other couples for a movie or dinner in a restaurant over conversations about childhood behavior and comparing babysitters. She was one of multitudes, self-assured, unquestionably accepted.

Living as Mrs. Teddy Goldman, with a young child in tow, offered Leena peace of mind. The effort to deny the size and shape and impact of her true sexuality had faded. The possibility that someone might look at her askance, question her lifestyle, learn the truth and shamefully expose her no longer invaded her thoughts. As a wife and mother, she had attained social acceptability. In Boston she slept each night comforted by being at peace with herself. In Boston, she woke up each morning knowing she fit in.

"This isn't easy for me, but if you're the caretaker, I'm the provider."

"What are you talking about? Is this a guessing game?" It was evening. They were in the living room, Leena on the couch, Teddy in the club chair.

"A prestigious placement firm in Philadelphia that specializes in metallurgical engineering has had their eye on me for Manager of Research at a major steel company."

"How exciting, a brain like you." She laughed.

"I had two interviews over several months, but there was nothing tangible so I didn't mention it. But today I received the letter, an offer for a staff of fifteen at a U.S. Steel plant."

"Marvelous. Where and when?"

He took a deep breath, as if it would help him prepare more than he already had. His eyes landed on the center medallion of the Delhi hand-woven rug in maroons and turquoises on the living room floor, a gift from Charlotte. After a moment, he raised his head.

"Pittsmill," he said softly. "It's in Pittsmill." He threw the second one out like a dirty pitch, the kind he had taught her to spot at Red Sox games when they were first married.

She grabbed the pillow behind her head and threw it at him. "You're joking."

"No. It's for real, and I'm sorry. I'm truly sorry."

Leena saw no point in staying silent. "How could you? For God's sakes!"

"I know how you feel about going back there."

"No you *don't*. You'll never know. The soot, the grey skies."

"The Clean Air Act will change that in a year or two. The mills will be required to do their part."

"You're spouting legislation to me?"

"Leena, I've been with AT&T three years already. Nothing will happen in telecommunications until there's increased competition. We can buy a big house. You want a maid, a housekeeper, we'll be able to afford one, and it's not for three months. We can plan, settle in. It's perfect for Jackie. She's only four. She'll barely notice."

"You have to refuse. You have a degree from Harvard. You can get a job anywhere."

"I'll make it okay for you. I'll do whatever I can."

"It's not that. We're fine *here.* The house, the neighbors, the schools. Going back there, it will be like returning to a war that was fought but never won. Hurt feelings. Bad memories in every corner. Please don't insist we do this." She buried her face in her hands.

"It's an excellent career move. I'm sorry. I'll say it as many times as you want."

"I don't care how many times you say it. I can't go back there."

"You're different than when you left. It's been five years. You're a parent. Confident. motivated. We're older, and your mother's been the head of Amory Lane. Her life has changed too."

"Sure! She was crazy then and she's crazier now." He sat down beside her and encircled her in his arms. She fell sideways into them knowing it wasn't about giving up or giving in.

"Why now? Maybe I am different in the ways you said, but why rock the boat?"

"What boat?" Teddy laughed. "We're a family. We're all in the same boat."

How thoroughly blameless he was for what he couldn't know. It had nothing to with his job. Or Jackie, or the soot. It wasn't even her mother. Boston was a multi-faceted shield, her safety net, protection from who she truly was. Why head full force into the unknown? If the family were uprooted, what limits could she reestablish for herself? She had withstood temptations, a woman's walk, or appearance; an urge to reach out. Explore that kind of friendship. She refused to allow room for what she dared not name, relying instead on marriage to forestall indefinitely who she truly was. To explain to her husband what she meant by not rocking the boat, she would have had to admit that the ground upon which that façade was built was more tenuous than he could have possibly fathomed.

That night Leena dreamed about a shipwreck. The deck, the rudder, the hull smashed and scattered, chaos and destruction everywhere.

Chapter Thirty-One

Women's Movement

"Cedar Grove. Mallary Landing. Bentley Park." Leena voiced the names of the new communities, tastefully displayed every few miles on signposts among the unrecognizable landscape that brought her close to a smile for the changes she hadn't counted on, much less foreseen. Pittsmill's new suburbia led them in early June to Delwood Gardens where streets were named after U.S. Supreme Court Justices—Brandeis, Holmes, Warren, Marshall.

Their two-story, sienna-colored brick with rectangular floor-to-ceiling windows, on 23 Cardoza Place, a twenty-minute drive from Amory Lane, made it easy for Bayla to appear, unannounced, "to make up for lost time taking care of your father and uncle, whose needs I alone can fulfill," she explained. In the eat-in-kitchen with its butcher-block center island, her mother would wait to be served from the new Mr. Coffee while seated at the antique pine breakfast table, recommended by an interior designer Leena had hired.

"You have no idea how your father's changed," Bayla would begin after a few sips. "He picks at his ears, digs his teeth with a toothpick, in and out of his mouth, sucking and hissing. Awful sounds. Turns my stomach. He's become an old man. Sixty-one. Six years older than me."

"And what do you do, Mother?" She had unpacked the kitchen, arranged the family's clothes in closets, and sorted bathroom sundries. Cartons marked "living room" still lined the hallway.

"Didn't I tell you? I get nauseous."

Five years of living apart and how little her mother had changed. The same fierceness in her voice, the fire in her eyes, the conversation, centered on her. But the way she peered over the top of her coffee cup waiting to pounce where Leena had failed: a dirty spot, a misplaced item, an empty space where something should have filled it. And unseen, beneath the visible, something was missing in her mother that used to exist and no longer did. Leena wouldn't bother to ask questions, locate the culprit. Tolerance is what she needed to withstand her mother's visits in this place she didn't consider home. Not yet. Maybe never.

"You're making a big deal out of nothing, Mother." Leena sliced an English muffin, and placed both halves in the toaster. "Why don't you let your husband have some peace after all these years?"

"Didn't you even hear what I said? He rattles the newspaper, folds the pages this way, that way, smooths the wrinkles. It's an obsession. Folding, smoothing. Folding, smoothing. Endless noise. I can't think straight."

Leena buttered the muffin and passed the plate to her mother. "Did you ever think maybe it's *you* who has a problem?" Teddy was right. She *had* returned to Pittsmill a different person. As a married woman with a child, she had the confidence to confront her mother's complaints, soap-opera sob stories, as if anyone's life was, or ever could be, perfect.

"Me? Oh, no, no. Not me," Bayla said, tears filling her eyes as if something she was neither aware of, nor understood, had taken hold.

"Uncalled-for emotion mixed with unfounded anxiety," Leena concluded, her mother's latest attention-getting technique.

"You're too involved, Mother. You need to find something to do. Why don't you go back to singing?"

"How dare you joke about that. You know nothing about my career."

"I'm not joking and I —"

"Who'll stay with your father and take care of that bastard Solomon?"

How quickly her mother reverted from sorrow to anger, Leena

noted, the way a therapist is attentive to such things.

"He writes me notes, that Solomon, what he wants me to cook, writes instructions on how to fold his t-shirts the way your grandmother used to so they line up perfectly in his armoire. Demands breakfast and dinner in his room off a tray I leave outside his bedroom door. He lives like a monk. Sold the business four years after your grandmother died. She put the business in his name. What could your father do? " Bayla took a breath and smoothed the wrinkles on the front of her blouse, her palms in a repetitive downward direction. "Do I look like any performer you've seen?" There was a touch of embarrassment in her laughter. "Remember at your wedding? I stopped the show. Brought the house down. You saw for yourself. Timing is everything. Now I'm a grandmother. My time for singing is finished. To want something so badly, then one day….."

"But, mother . . ."

"Yes? You think the time will come again? What are you trying to tell me?"

Leena wanted to say singing used to be her mother's life. Yes, a hit at her wedding almost six years ago. One song, a captive audience, but what chance did she have, out of touch and out of practice with whatever it took to get back up on a stage and entertain? "Maybe you shouldn't give up so soon. Maybe you will perform again."

"What do you know about dreams?"

"I know about wanting things."

"What could you want?" Bayla laughed disparagingly as she waved her arm indicating what surrounded her. "A big fancy home. A wonderful husband. Beautiful daughter. Come tomorrow. I'll cook a meal. Amory Lane is mine. I snuck it from under their noses, signed my name to the papers. You think it was easy? You think they would give Amory Lane to me, a nobody from nowhere with a mother I couldn't please?"

"Grandma signed the house over to you in her will." Leena spoke slowly, emphasizing the truth, hoping to nudge her mother toward reality. "She said you ran Amory Lane like no one ever could. Don't you remember?"

"I remember Bessie Smith. Blues were her kingdom. I got Amory Lane. Wrong kingdom." She lowered her voice. "What you don't know about me would surprise you." She lifted the coffee cup, allowing the last drop to fall into her mouth.

Leena submerged a smirk and rolled her eyes. What secrets could that woman have? Women of that generation? Her mother was an open book. Occasional signs of mental illness that she had previously witnessed in her mother, appeared to be more evident.

"Where's your daughter? I came to visit her."

"She's there in the living room."

"All I see is a tent of blankets."

"She's inside it. She has a cold. I kept her home from school. She's playing with her dolls. She talks to them, makes up stories. When she's not play acting with them, she bosses me around. Wonder where she got that from?"

"I know about a child alone, and only four years old. She's hiding. That child knows her mind. Nothing wrong with that." Bayla glared at Leena. In the living room, she crouched down, speaking softly, prompting the child to emerge from her tent.

"She's coming with me. She'll stay the weekend. I'll get rid of her cold."

"Great. I'd love some free time." She'd had enough of crossing items off lists, things that needed to get done. Bayla taking Jackie to Amory Lane meant freedom from her mother, time to ponder the irony playing out in plain sight: Bayla, as a grandmother, was a better mother to Jackie than she had ever been to Leena, her own child. The patience and affection her mother had for Jackie bore such little resemblance to the woman who allegedly raised her, that women might just as well have been a stranger.

Jackie's weekend stayovers became a habit during Pittsmill's long hot summer, accompanied by Bayla's detailed reports, which Leena could have done without.

"The child creates the most gorgeous jewelry, bracelets, earrings, necklaces from beads we string, and such an artist, her watercolor paintings of flowers, fruits and vegetables arranged by your father. We bake cakes and cookies, and on a rainy day, it's the Odeon Cinema. Walt Disney's *Bambi*, and the new musical, *Oliver*. Jackie loved it.

"And you each take turns reading her picture books recommended by the librarian at Strobe."

"Yes," Bayla said beaming, "she told you. I teach her the titles and the authors, a sign of intelligence, and Sunday mornings your father makes what Jackie calls 'the deliciousest pancakes,' served with warm maple syrup. She mixes the batter."

Leena had to admit that Jackie flourished from the care and attention she received, but despite the levity the child kindled in Amory Lane's three inhabitants, it was clear that her mother received no respite from the forces that compelled her behavior. From her usual place in Leena's kitchen there were new laments.

"He picks his feet. Dead skin surrounds the bed like sand, on the sheets, the blankets, the floor. Every day I have to vacuum. And the constipation. He swallows laxatives constantly, little things that look like Hershey's Kisses. Chews them like gum. Keeps a record of his bowel movements. Gives me reports. I tell him a thousand times . . ."

"What do you want me to do, Mother?"

"Do? What's to do?" Bayla shrugged, and in the midst of nothing in particular, she rose and let herself out.

"It's my mother. She's severely agitated," Leena told Teddy after dinner that night as he relaxed in his club chair, his feet on the ottoman across from Leena on the couch. "You have no idea how much time I spend counseling her. She's getting worse. Confused. Can't remember a thing. Complains non-stop. I can't take much more."

"Who says you have to?" Teddy said barely looking up from *The New York Times* crossword puzzle which he did in ink at breakneck speed every night after dinner, and weekend mornings, his head bent forward, his eyes bearing down, chin into his throat. Her husband's escapes into the puzzle were further proof of the ruthless sameness of parenting and housework and her mother's tireless visits. Exhaustion plagued her. Time drained out of her days as easily as the water that had evaporated from the glass tea kettle whose burner she had forgotten to turn off causing its black plastic top to melt into a thick, gooey blob leaving the house stinking of unnamed chemicals, no doubt carcinogenic. "I'm leading a life of diminishing returns," she blurted out. "In my dreams, I'm on the edge of a precipice ready to leap into I don't know what or where. I'm surrounded by road blocks. Dead ends."

Having completed the crossword puzzle, Teddy folded the paper.

"Take your mother to a doctor. Get her therapy. Encourage her to sing again. I don't know what else to tell you. Why doesn't she get back to it? What does your father say?"

"Please, he couldn't manage her when they first met and now he hasn't the strength. She's worn him down over the years. Everything is always about her. Always has been. And I do tell her to sing. I tell her repeatedly. She changes the subject. Her mind goes elsewhere like she's in a daze. She's totally self-absorbed. That's my diagnosis."

"You're a psychology major. You want to diagnose your mother? Go back to school. Get a graduate degree. You don't have to be home every day for Jackie. We'll get a babysitter, a nanny. I can't understand you not wanting to pursue anything. Your mother's neglected her music and what do you do? Complain, like she does."

Leena rose from her chair. "You're comparing me to my mother! Five mornings every week your extraordinary talents are admired and respected by people twice your age. Who validates me? Huh? For years my mother has pushed aside her singing for everything else. She's ignored what she wants to do most in the world because life keeps getting in the way so now she's lost control over any of it. She sang at our wedding, then she gave up the fight."

"And you are free to do whatever you want, but you don't. Get out of the house. Do something!"

Rattled by his harsh tone, his cutting words, Leena took a breath. "Jackie's upstairs. You put her to bed. I'm taking a bath. She prefers you, anyway."

"Mea culpa. Please, that wasn't necessary."

It was necessary, she told herself. Living with her had changed him, and not for the better. He had become withdrawn, barely communicative. Angry. Carping.

"Leena, wait." She paused on the staircase. "I know you're frustrated. A housewife, a mother. It's hard work and your mother is no picnic. I'm only suggesting —"

"I know what you're suggesting." Leena kicked apart a cluster of dirt on the wooden stair that Jackie had no doubt dragged in from outside. "I never cared for school. I never liked studying, or taking tests. I'm not like you that way." She sounded almost conciliatory. "And I don't like living here. I said I wouldn't and I've made it tough on you."

"You're right about my job. It welcomes me every day. It validates me, but it leaves you with. . . ."

"Thanks," she cut him short and disappeared up the stairs. She had warned him about not rocking the boat. She had capitulated to his decision to leave Boston, as if she had any choice, accepting, without question, how her warning to him had materialized: Clothes scattered helter-skelter; laundry waiting to be put away; newspapers and magazines everywhere; toys underfoot; the pantry devoid of necessities—bread, cold cereals, basic condiments. Family dinners, when she had the energy or inclination, were Betty Crocker's chicken or Hamburger Helper, Chef Boyardee's Ravioli, White Castle hamburgers. More than once, behind Teddy's silent acceptance, she saw him wince at what she had placed on the dinner table.

Each morning she awoke to the same monotony that lulled her to sleep the night before. She had become someone her husband could no longer tolerate, someone folded up inside herself like her father's well-read newspapers.

To certify her complaint, hadn't her father called that hot July day to invite her to Amory Lane to show her the slate walkway he had designed in the back garden, while her mother napped, to explain in his gentle, fatherly way that Bayla had become completely bonkers.

"She talks to herself, nonsense, I can't make it out. Other times angry words at no one special. And she's always planning, scheming, or she's miles away, in her mind. It's gotten worse since Charlotte's funeral, but I blame myself, taking her out of New York, away from her singing —"

"If mother really wanted to sing, she would have."

"And Uncle Solomon, who always called your mother terrible names, now settled on nut case. He bought himself one of those big TVs for his room and sometimes, like two old men buddies, the two of us sit together and watch whatever. We're not fussy."

Leena knew that her father was desperate in his uncritical, diplomatic way to encourage his daughter to use her psychology knowhow to help his wife.

When fall arrived, barely acknowledging her disdain for Pittsmill's gray skies, Leena was pushing a shopping cart up and down the aisles of Kroger's supermarket selecting this or that from the shelves, the freezer counter, the produce section, unaware that Jackie had disappeared. She searched around a corner and saw her talking to a boy about the same age standing beside a woman. The boy's mother, she supposed.

"Hello. I'm Myrna." She was shorter than Leena, her makeup carefully applied, her dusty-blonde hair beautifully coifed. "Our children are in the same kindergarten class. Seems we're neighbors. I live on the other side of Cardoza, on the cul-de-sac." She wore a navy skirt to her calf, a peach-colored blouse with a loose red belt, navy shoes with a small heel. The outfit gave Leena a twinge of embarrassment for her black leather jacket, loose jeans and Teddy's t-shirt, the closest at hand that morning. They chatted, eyeing one another, waiting for what they had ordered at the deli counter. When Myrna suggested in a neighborly kind-of-way that they have lunch sometime at her favorite Italian place outside of town, Leena agreed.

Through scrubbing burnt pots, sorting laundry, and heating leftovers, the "existential grist" of her life, Leena called it, thoughts of her lunch date brought what she hadn't experienced in a long while—something to look forward to. Teddy told her he was pleased about her excursion, but Bayla still acted like a petulant child at her morning arrival.

"You're always out when I need you."

"What are you talking about? I'm always here," Leena said indignantly.

"I came to give you important news. Come here. Stand beside me. I don't want you to miss a word." Bayla put her arm around Leena's shoulders.

Leena pulled away. "What?"

"Men don't clean like women," Bayla lowered her voice. "They over-spray, over-soap, miss crumbs, put glasses, filled ones, on top of antique tables, without a coaster. Never leave tell-tale signs. That's what I came to tell you."

The concerns Leena might have had about her mother's bizarre behavior were tempered by her jitters about her upcoming outing. What would she talk about and how would she act and worst of all, what would she wear since she rarely cared about her looks and barely left the house? After trying several outfits, she chose a turquoise cashmere sweater, tan cotton slacks and small gold hoop earrings.

In Ricardo's, a small Italian family-run restaurant where everything looked delicious and homemade, the hostess sat her in a booth for two, her eyes on the front door. Leena waved the moment Myrna walked in looking lovely in a skirt, a loose scooped neck blouse and low-heeled sandals. She felt nervous, hoping to at least make a good impression the way she had in Boston.

Both women had moved into the area because of their husband's jobs. Myrna had an older daughter and a son. She married young. Never completed college. Her parents previously lived in Manhattan close to her grandparents, immigrants from Romania.

Leena was excited by their similarities. "My mother grew up in Manhattan. My grandparents emigrated from Hungary." She was surprised at how animated she sounded.

"The difficult part of leaving New York was missing my grandmother," Myrna said.

"I was close to my grandmother too. She knew my secrets." Leena knew that was something of a lie. Charlotte never really knew Leena's "secret" but she figured Myrna would assume her secrets referred to crushes on boys. The broken hearts they gave her.

By the time the waiter brought dessert, apple pie with coconut ice cream for Myrna and cream puffs with chocolate syrup for Leena, both had agreed to plan regular luncheon dates in restaurants as far away as McKeesport. Myrna offered her eldest daughter Stacy, a high school freshman, to baby-sit for her younger brother and Jackie until they the mothers returned, late afternoon.

"You've made my day," Leena wanted to say, but judged it too obnoxiously trite after what had been accomplished: new restaurant, new food, and new friend. A woman.

Weeks later, while thumbing through the local paper, Leena noticed Fellini's *Eight and A Half* showing at the art cinema in Pittsburgh.

"I love Fellini, love foreign films," Myrna said as she sipped her Pinot Grigio at another luncheon in another new restaurant "The auteur theory," they said simultaneously, and laughed.

"My husband despises subtitles," Myrna said, shaking her head at the absurdity of it.

Leena broke into the cannoli dripping raspberry syrup, and held out her fork full for Myrna to try. "My husband doesn't mind them one bit."

"You got a good one. You're lucky." Myrna's tone was somber.

Leena thought it best not to probe into her friend's marriage, most likely peppered with difficulties. Whose marriage wasn't? Something else they had in common.

Surrounded by the jovial Neapolitan atmosphere in Center City's Umberto's, its walls covered in immaturely rendered scenes of Italy's coastline, Leena took a breath to compose herself.

"Stacy was my first, not that I favor her but she was such a good student. Now her grades are falling. She's hanging out with the wrong crowd, older boys, townies, with tattoos up and down their arms."

Why did Myrna suddenly choose to delve into difficulties with her eldest daughter? Was it a closeness she felt from their three months of palling around, or was Myrna encouraged because Leena had unburdened herself about growing up in Amory Lane, among townsfolk's' gossip, and the exigencies of being raised in a house full of adults. Best to remain calm, use her skills: listen, stay interested, ask meaningful questions:

"Stacy's behavior reminds me of how I rebelled against my mother because she was so controlling. Still is," Leena said. "If I had to guess, that's not you."

"No, it's not me. My husband is the controlling one. He gives Stacy curfews that make her furious and I think are unreasonable. Home on weekends at 10 p.m. when her friends are at the movies. Before she's allowed to a house party, we have to check with the parents. He's not a bad guy, just bossy. 'Dinner at six. Light's out at ten.' He prefers that I obey."

"Obey. That's a strong word. What if you don't? Obey, I mean? I don't mean to pry and you needn't answer but... Perhaps he's the source of Stacy's rebelling, in addition to normal teenage stuff. Teenagers aren't very practiced in discerning specific emotions much less expressing them."

"Stacy's a good kid. I guess she'll pull out of it, but lately no matter what I say to her, she hears as criticism."

"Pent-up emotions are very stressful. For you and her. Have you ever tried to sit with her in a calm moment and talk about some of this?"

"Good suggestions. I guess that's common knowledge. How do you know —"

"I'm a psychologist," Leena said, nodding, smiling slightly so as not to assume too much pride for who she wasn't. "Well, not officially."

"Oh yes, I remember. Your college work. So if I need your advice....?"

"Anytime."

That evening, after an early dinner, the summer skies still light, Leena and Teddy walked the neighborhood's quiet sidewalks with Jackie in her stroller.

"You're smiling," he said.

"Yes."

"So much time has gone by without any indication that the corners of your mouth were still capable of turning up." Leena pursed lips and rolled her eyes. "I'm not being critical," he added. "I'm glad to see the change. It's a compliment. Must be your new friend."

She barely heard. She was intent on how best to encourage

Myrna to reveal more about her marital situation. Who else would listen to Myrna's concerns? She couldn't count on her husband who labelled such things as puerile and immature. Complaining to her immediate family was verboten. Turning to her other girlfriends would bring harsh judgments, a sense of failure, unwanted pressure that she be as perfect as they appeared to her. But for Leena, this was the perfect opportunity to practice her métier. She would interpret behaviors, uncover blame, suggest solutions. She would become an expert on Myrna's married life. Myrna's flesh and blood savior.

"How enticing," Leena said after lunch, pointing to the bookshop in Waverly, Pennsylvania, as she and Myrna strolled toward the storefront window and door framed in old wood painted dark green. "It's neighborhood places like these that offer the best picks."

Inside the store, in a basket of for sale items, Leena spotted campaign buttons with the sign *For the Women's Strike for Peace and Equality, August 26, 1970.*

"That was less than a month ago, wasn't it?" she said. *"A woman without a man is like a fish without a bicycle."* She read aloud the feminist slogan in green words on the button's white background.

"It was the largest rally for women's rights. The fiftieth anniversary of the 19th Amendment granting women the right to vote," Myrna said.

"Feminism. The women's movement, all that '60s stuff," Leena said. "I was pregnant in '64 with my daughter, married only a few months. I was looking forward to being a mother." She didn't say she was trying her damnedest to play a heterosexual, counting on motherhood and being a wife to convince herself and everyone else that was who she was.

"I appreciated the feminists for letting us know we weren't doomed to domesticity, but so what?" Myrna said. "My husband wouldn't have approved if he found me reading about the dregs of my life as a housewife, which was and still is exactly where he wants me. Betty Friedan's *The Feminine Mystique* in our house? I don't think so."

"For me, it was more about my mother. So devoted and caring to the family she married into, but her singing, her wonderful voice stilled. She couldn't manage how to get what she wanted beyond home and family. At times I felt sorry for her."

"Consciousness raising is what appealed to me," Myrna said. "Women gathering in each other's homes, opening up about how they were living their lives in a male-dominated society, suspecting, believing something wasn't right about that, but what?"

How am *I living my life?* Leena wondered. Far from what was being promoted back then, with herself as a priority. Did she even know anymore what her priorities were? They had become so mashed and bent and scuttled over the years. After constructing a life of pretense, could she even name them?

"Imagine it," Leena said. "Equal rights for women in a world run by men! Freedom to create the life you want, to be yourself without needing or asking permission from anybody."

"All this women's movement stuff, it's about us, isn't it?" Myrna said as if she were awakening to the reality of it in her life.

"Envisioning our lives revolutionized for the better, is how the feminists described it," Leena said and purchased the green and white campaign button. "My gift to you." And as she secured it to the front of Myrna's jacket, words not entirely unfamiliar, bombarded her thoughts. Perfect in its simplicity, the words delineated what seemed to have formed between them: a bond built on dissatisfaction with their lives, and shared feminist hoopla which they had once observed from a distance, but now felt necessary to reconsider.

Two months later, amid the crunch of fall leaves underfoot, the Equal Rights Amendment, designed to prohibit sexual discrimination, was being debated in congress. Leena and Myrna chose to replace their restaurant escapades with meeting in each other's homes to witness frenzied television coverage where thousands of women across the country disrupted Senate hearings, held marches, lobbied for the legislation, and protested universities, corporations, and organizations that ostracized women. In trying to bolster momentum for happy-to-stay-at-home housewives, women's groups opposed to the effort fought back with hysterical cries of, "Don't draft us!" Or "we'll have to share public bathrooms with men."

"Can that happen?" Myrna asked Leena who was always more certain of such things.

"So we'll pee in urinals." They laughed.

A blustery rain storm made it too treacherous to venture out the afternoon Myrna telephoned Leena to say she was getting a divorce. As if the news were infused with something portentous, and having known Myrna only some 15 months, Leena decided there was no harm to indulge herself. If she had inherited anything from her mother, it was a strong will. That afternoon, she eased onto their queen-sized bed and proceeded to masturbate imagining all the while that she was making love to Myrna. With that place between her legs still throbbing, she cleared her mind of whatever possessed her.

At dinnertime, she was surprised at Teddy's response. "I know Myrna's husband's a workaholic but … they have two kids. Have they tried everything? You say the word divorce like it's nothing."

"Her husband moving out is exactly what she needs and wants. I've told you how she's suffered. I've been a great help to her."

"A marriage vow is forever, and I'm not talking about your counseling abilities, though I'd like to know what makes you think you are one. She and her husband will scatter to who knows where and the children will be left wanting. We all have disagreements. Marriage is never perfect. How bad could it have been between them? A family is worth fighting for. *To him that is given much, much is expected.* I learned that in Hebrew school."

"I have no idea what you're talking about. Is this a test? Referring to our diminishing sex life?" Ungenerous, rote, purposeless mechanical gyrations, damned embarrassing. She fought against saying the words as she rose and cleared the table, slamming dishes one on top of the other as if each clang could shatter how close he had come to the truth.

The next morning Bayla waited at Leena's kitchen table. "All dressed up, I see. No coffee today? Leaving Jackie again with that woman's daughter, a high school kid? What kind of mother are you? Babysitters! All the time babysitters. I couldn't wait till you were born."

"Really?" Leena smiled broadly. "That's not what Uncle Solomon said." She and Myrna were heading to a restaurant in Youngstown for sushi.

"What did that bastard tell you?"

"He said when anyone mentioned you giving birth, you walked out of the room. You didn't let them buy a crib, a high chair, a rattle, not even a bib or booties. Grandma worried you didn't *want* a child. He said you felt like Lon Chaney playing a hunchback because your breasts weighed you down. You made a spectacle of yourself."

"I took advantage of being pregnant. So what?"

"Believe what you want, Mother. I have a date. It's January. A new year."

"A date? A date with that Myrna woman?"

As Leena eased beyond the driveway, where she had left the car for a clean get-away, she glimpsed her mother without a coat, her shoes planted on the iced-over front lawn.

"A date! It isn't right. Do you hear me? I'll put a stop to it. A stop," Bayla continued to shout, her head bent slightly toward her right shoulder, her left hand on her lips, as if anyone where streets were named after Supreme Court Justices cared.

Chapter Thirty-Two
Personality Disorder

College reminiscences, bittersweet and mellowed over time, allowed Leena the luxury to think kindly of the years she struggled to blend into her clique at Comanche dorm. Through almost seven years of married life, budding sexual fantasies about herself and Myrna during this second spring of their friendship, that had previously languished in her mind's eye, slowly, stubbornly began to escape their habitat, and peck at her resolve. The comparison was inevitable: She and Myrna, married women, not college age students, not two out of five. Just two of them. Two. Two women. *Together.*

Having learned to replace her true self with the person she thought she should be, or whom she thought others wanted her to be, Leena was brought to a dead stop. Was it possible that her life wasn't a throwaway?

All of that isn't coming back? Is it?

Don't dare think beyond the friendship of two married women, she told herself, but she knew she was beyond heeding her own advice. She could no longer deny that a relationship with Myrna was teeming with rich sexual possibilities. But precautionary measures were needed to prevent her mother from curtailing the pittances that fulfilled her fantasies if they were ever to develop, one day, into real life physical exchanges. With the path before her clearly defined, the pursuit of Myrna within arm's reach, the next morning her mother sat down to a breakfast of scrambled eggs, coffee and buttered toast.

"They call it a test," Leena explained in her most convincing counselor style, "but it's more like a game, interpreting pictures, telling stories, answering questions. It will make it easier for you to manage Daddy and Uncle Solomon."

"Not something to ignore," Bayla said somewhat hopeful.

"You do so much for both of them. You need some time for yourself."

"You'll take me? Stay with me?"

"Of course. I'll make the appointment. We'll have a nice afternoon. Now that the weather's warmer, we'll spend the day outside. Have lunch. Just the two of us."

It was difficult to say who was more pleased by the visit: Bayla, lured by the promise of time away from what she called 'my nursing duties.' Or Leena, who attributed her mother's cooperation to her therapist's skills.

"We have a solid diagnosis," Dr. Charles Abrams, Chief of Psychiatry at Pittsmill Hospital, a tall, youngish man with dark wavy hair, a white coat over a suit and tie, told Leena one week later. "Without getting too complex, your mother has a narcissistic personality disorder combined with deep-seated feelings of inadequacy and a strong need for approval."

"I knew it," Leena practically shouted. "She's been self-absorbed for years. I was a psychology major, did clinical work here in the Hospital."

"I'm aware of the attention your mother craved when she was performing, before she was married, but the findings also indicated a mild paranoia, perhaps from a childhood trauma. Guilt. Things for which she blames herself. As her daughter, you might have some idea." Dr. Abrams paused. "I don't usually share this, but since you have some background, there were indications of dissociative behavior and a period of significant depression 25 years ago, she was in her thirties. You find this amusing?"

Leena stifled a laugh. "How little you know about my mother's game playing."

"It's in her records signed by a Dr. Javitts: *A deep depression, overwhelming feelings of hopelessness, and loss of self – esteem despite having run an entire household and, according to her mother-in-law, having run it exceptionally well.* In those days, the shame and guilt resulting from some form of mental illness could easily darken the lives of a family in a small town like ours."

"When I was maybe five, every day after school my grandmother would take me upstairs to visit my mother in bed. They told me she was recovering. I didn't know what that meant, but she didn't seem sick."

"There wasn't much they could explain to a child."

"My grandmother took care of me. My father and uncle got me ready for school. Babysat. My mother hardly spoke. She never came to school like other parents. My classmates said I was adopted, that my mother didn't want me. I believed it."

"Of course the tests require a degree of professional interpretation, and without the benefit of one-on-one therapy. I'm not sure she would..."

"She won't."

"Symptoms like these don't disappear. They may worsen, triggered by one, maybe more events." His phone rang, startling them.

"There's an emergency downstairs. I'm sorry. I'm prescribing medication to normalize your mother's behavior. Her normal. You'll find her calmer, more manageable, but don't expect miracles. The medication takes a few weeks to kick in. If you wish to see me for yourself...." he looked directly at her for a moment, raised his eyebrows, and was out the door.

That summer, Myrna's son moved to Pittsburgh to live with his father, and her daughter Stacy took a job in a sleep-away camp. Was it a sign, Leena thought? An opening. Time for her to risk their friendship with the truth about herself?

"Myrna needs comforting," she explained to Teddy, "someone to fill her empty evenings alone." It was a late night and they were channel surfing in the living room. "Jackie is her own person, almost six, managing school, friends, responsibilities at home. It's just for a few hours, occasionally. My mother's always willing to help if you need it."

"And everything else is perfect. Like, for example, our relationship? I keep asking you what can I do and you keep telling me nothing's wrong. For the life of me, Leena, I'd like to know what's going on." He turned from his chair, *searching for what?* she wondered. A reaction. A word. An emotion. Seeing him that way, so unexpectedly transparent, almost fragile, she was determined to be nothing less than diplomatic.

"Look, times have changed, and so have I. I'm allowing myself to be more than a housewife. You can appreciate that."

"You're alluding to the Woman's Movement?"

"In a way, yes. Fulfilling my own pursuits like you're always telling me."

"Myrna is a pursuit?"

She had done it, driven him to defending himself against her unyielding behavior and his hopeless attempts to uncover the source of their problems which was impossible because he had no knowledge of what she was determined to never reveal.

Aside from all that, there were struggles where there never used to be. An innocent word would flare into a fight leading them to find refuge in a silence as devastating as their conflicting emotions. The worst, most embarrassing part was when they had sex. It had become a self – conscious waiting game. Lying there at night, ready for her "wifely duties." Wasn't that how Mitzy in the clique referred to it years ago? None of them knew enough then to realize that so much about sex was comprised of supposition. How women were *supposed* to anticipate when their husbands wanted to make love, supposed to give in to his cozying up, accept his abundant need, his craving, his body, his breath, his thrusting into her. If this is what it had become for her over time, she was failing her heterosexual game playing. On a night when she was no longer able to accept any of it, it all spilled out.

"You don't say the right things. You don't have the right approach. Your timing is off." The words flew out of her the moment she felt his hand on her leg, under the covers, moving her nightgown out of his way as one would discard a felled branch in a windstorm.

"You have no idea where to start or how to attend to me when it's over. You don't make me feel included. There's no pleasure in it."

He turned away from her, edged to his side of the bed and in wrapping himself in their comforter, it became a twisted bulky mound, an impassable bunker separating them.

Now most evenings, after dinner, Leena left the house to spend hours with Myrna. Walking home those late hours, dressed in a light outfit, linen slacks and a loose, buttoned-down blouse, as warm puffs of air embraced her bare arms and face, she succumbed to being led toward the possibility of loving a woman.

Inside Myrna's meticulous designer-decorated home, they sat across from one another in the family room on matching chintz couches. They watched old movies on TV, talked about their children, neighbors and the latest news. They splurged on Cokes, coffee or wine. Munched on Mallowmars, Snickers, or Oreos splayed in their boxes, willy-nilly, on the coffee table. Leena fantasized about how her visits best served Myrna, but rather than the push-pull of asking or digging for specifics—compliments, an indication of affection that might lead to love—patience was best.

"These hours we share are a treasure to me," Myrna said. "I'm so relaxed with you. Practically meditative. How does that happen?" she asked with a laugh.

"With me, you've nothing to prove," Leena said cognizant of playing this just right. "There's no special way you have to be, no one you have to satisfy, the way it was with your husband. With me you're yourself, however that is, however you want to be." Her words, which she had considered, indeed practiced, for some time, were perfect.

"But leaving your family to come here? What does Teddy say? Your daughter? Don't you feel guilty? Is he that generous with you?"

"There's no guilt. I put Jackie to bed, and we've already eaten. I told him you need company. Basically he's a nice guy, a great Dad."

"Hard for me to imagine a husband like that. Mine never was. But what do you get from me? From you being here?"

"I feel…liberated. I don't have to straighten up the room or think about stocking the refrigerator. Or what to cook for dinner. Just talking, reading aloud, or listening to music with you. The silence. The peace. Your company. That's everything."

She didn't mention the image that unexpectedly filled her mind's eye of Teddy in bed, in her absence, reading so many trashy paperback thrillers until he fell asleep, the books piled so high on his nightstand, he began a second pile on the floor.

On a hot August day, Bayla barged into Leena's kitchen waving an envelope. "It's summer-stock time. Tickets for Saturday matinees at Pittsburgh's Warner Theatre—*South Pacific*, *Oklahoma*, *My Fair Lady*, *The Music Man*. Jackie's almost six. Perfect for live theatre. It's only right that she comes with me. I'm a performer. I can point out things. Teach her appreciation. Anyway you're never home on Saturdays."

"She's hardly home ever," Jackie said.

"Take some time away from you-know-who," Bayla said.

"Please stay out of my business," Leena chastised, her voice low.

"You stay out of mine," Jackie said to her mother.

"Don't copy my words. It's rude," Leena scolded, but her mother was so alive and motivated, she was relieved that she had done right with the psychology tests and the meds.

That winter when Jackie turned six, she had the lead in her first grade holiday play, *Father Christmas Meets Mrs. Chanukah*. The title was originally Mr. Chanukah, Jackie explained, but when Marcus Smithfield got strep throat, she volunteered, having already memorized his lines. In rehearsal, the teacher announced that Jackie had played the part so beautifully, she made the necessary title and script revisions, giving Marcus, once he recovered, the role of

Joseph, of Arimathea, which had not yet been cast.

"I'm going to coach her," Bayla told Leena. "I'll follow the teacher's staging and work with her on her solo —'Rudolf the Red-Nose Reindeer.'"

Now two afternoons a week, until opening night, Bayla picked up Jackie after school and took her for 'rehearsals' at Amory Lane.

"Grandma set up the portable record player in the sunroom. The tiled floor is our pretend stage. She uses white chalk to mark off where I have to stand. 'Gesture like this,' Grandma tells me. 'Arms. Fingers. Find your balance. Feel the ground beneath your feet. Put feeling in those words. Breath deep.' But I can't do my song for you until the show. Grandma says it's bad luck."

"You should appreciate the genes I've passed down to her," Bayla said, patting Leena's back as if they were old chums.

"I do," Leena said, fully aware of the impact of Jackie's summer-stock experiences with Bayla: the live music, singing, dancing, and musical show-stoppers from *South Pacific* and the *King and I* had so captured Jackie that Bayla gifted her LP sound tracks. Jackie played them repeatedly until she knew the words to every song, so Bayla expanded her record collection to Rogers and Hart, Irving Berlin, E.Y. Harburg, Rogers and Hammerstein, Lerner and Lowe. Even Gilbert and Sullivan.

With Izzy, Bayla, Uncle Solomon, Teddy, and Leena anxiously seated in the second row of Pittsmill's packed Elementary School's auditorium, the children played their parts well. Adorable and cute was the consensus, but Jackie's song, followed by her solo tap dance, initially received with silent awe, barely concluded before exuberant applause filled the room, then a standing ovation for Jackie, which closed the show.

The following day at their morning coffee, Bayla explained that the child's talent had to be handled properly. "I'll find the best people, take her for singing, dancing, and acting lessons. My treat. What do you say?"

"Fine. Do it."

If Bayla's mental state had coalesced in a healthy way around what she labelled "Jackie's career," so be it. It would give Leena more time to fine tune her relationship with Myrna who was coincidentally freed from her own wifely duties.

At first it was poetry readings at the Pittsburgh library, art history lectures at the university, and concerts in Pittsburgh's music hall. The overnights excursions to D.C.'s National Portrait Museum, and New York City's Lincoln Center, Itzhak Perlman playing Mendelssohn. Leena garnered Teddy's approval for these excursions, and weeks passed without a word from her mother. Though she suspected there would be a reckoning, when it occurred, it was a surprise: her mother at the front door, barely able to stand, her arms filled to bursting with shopping bags, returned to the car for two more trips of the same.

"Leena, come see what I've done."

Dust mops, pails, brooms, cleansers for toilets, sinks, floors, containers of wax and spray polishes, boxes filled with soap powder, steel wool soap pads, sponges, packages of paper towels and a new electric dust mop with a bevy of attachments, covered the floor, counter tops, kitchen chairs, the pine table.

"Time to clean up your act," Bayla reprimanded. "I've held it in long enough these past weeks. Your husband is too soft on you. He told me what's going on."

"What's going on?"

"He waited 45 minutes at the pumps last Saturday to fill up his car because the industry is hoarding thousands of barrels of oil. And our President is being investigated in a cover up. 'And so what if my wife spends all her time with Myrna?' he said. 'Jackie is learning to be self-sufficient, straightening up her room and eating warmed up leftovers.'"

"Something wrong with that, Mother?"

"It's that Myrna woman," Bayla shouted. "I've outsmarted every one of my enemies, and I'll outsmart you, too."

"What are you blaming me for?" By remaining calm Leena piqued her mother's anger. "I returned to Pittsmill to please my husband, exactly like he wanted."

"Don't interrupt. What was I saying? I forget. Was it about your father?"

"You told me you don't sleep with him. Everything he does disgusts you. And you think something I'm doing isn't normal?"

"You don't know the half of it. His latest peccadillo are enemas, laxatives wrapped up in silver paper like Hershey's chocolate kisses. He runs to the toilet in the middle of the night. I've tried to keep it from you, but it's pushing me over the edge."

Leena refused to believe she was witnessing a return of her mother's paranoia. Not now. Not when everything she had planned for her and Myrna was progressing so smoothly. "Are you taking your pills? I'm heading past the pharmacy today. I'll refill your prescription."

"Those things? I ran out of them. Gave me indigestion. I came here to tell you clean up. Stop doing what's not normal." She let herself out the front door.

When Teddy came home from work that night, he was brought to a standstill at the bizarre kitchen scene.

"It's my mother," Leena said off-handedly.

"What set her off?" Shocked by the display, he looked for some indication that Leena had prepared dinner, but the stove's burners were empty, the house devoid of cooking smells.

"You're the brilliant one. You tell me. What did you expect, bringing us back here? You thought she had changed. You were right. She was crazy then, and she's crazier now. Didn't I say that?"

"We're here almost three years. We have a good life. Tell me what I can do. What do you want?"

"Not this." Leena gestured with her arm to the ludicrous array, and as she did, her hand glided across something she grabbed on to, and in a desperate, frustrated, spontaneous gesture, she threw it at him. As a plastic bottle filled with something green flew over his head, he ducked.

"And I don't want this." He stormed across the room and wrenched open the refrigerator door. Leena avoided looking into what she already knew he would find. A container of juice and milk, a dozen eggs, a package of white bread, a jar of peanut butter, strawberry jam and stale odds and ends wrapped in foil.

He slammed the door shut with such force it shook the wall

cabinets. "And I don't want an absent wife. And I don't want my daughter to have to fend for herself because you're on the phone with Myrna or never around. I want our marriage back. I want us to function as a family again. I want you to face what's happening. Why won't you let me in? I'm tired of asking and I'm tired of fighting. I can't fix our marriage by myself. We talk *at* each other, not *to* each other. Nothing gets accomplished."

"Why should I feel responsible for what you won't do?"

"What won't I do?"

"You've taken total control of my life."

"How? I work all day. I go on every business trip I can to get out of your way and when I'm here, you're with Myrna. You might as well divorce me and marry her."

"Stop! Enough."

A fault line as startling and raw as their emotions stood between them. When he stared at her across the divide, she knew he was searching for the woman he had married, the one who had gradually disappeared, leaving behind remains that bore little resemblance to the original.

In Pennsylvania, she had put on considerable weight. For her hair to be less of a bother, she had it cut short. She stopped wearing makeup, dressed in dungarees and comfortable, oversized sweatshirts. Cowboy boots made her steps heavy, her movements awkward. She appeared to her husband like a stranger on foreign terrain who understood that any attempt to rely on his superior mapping skills, that had long ago brought him to Amory Lane, would prove to be a futile escape for his wife, their daughter, and himself.

Chapter Thirty-Three

Her Only Choice Was To Risk Everything

From the built-in speaker system, Stevie Wonder sang his latest hit, "You Are the Sunshine of My Life," courtesy of WFAS, the gentle music station.

As she sat on one of the pine stools at the center aisle of the butcher block counter in Myrna's country kitchen, Leena smiled. The loosening of boundaries in her marriage had occurred so gradually, over time, Teddy and Jackie had moved beyond needing explanations. "It's a special evening," or "I have to be there," were no longer required.

"This will be my best birthday cake ever. Pecan carrot and cream cheese," Myrna promised as she sliced into a thick carrot, then suddenly cried out. Leena grabbed a paper towel and wrapped it tightly around Myrna's finger to stop the bleeding.

"Hold it like this."

"Tonight of all nights! I wanted everything to be perfect." They eased side-by-side into the cushions on the couch. "How could I be so clumsy?"

"You're not clumsy," Leena said. "You're graceful and beautiful. I thought so from the moment I first saw you in the supermarket."

Leena had taken a long, slow bath that morning and lingered over her choice of clothes. For the first time in a long while she put on makeup, scrutinized every touch, line, and smear. She dressed slowly, buttoning her blouse, zippering her slacks over newly-purchased under garments, no longer worn and outdated. She stood before the freestanding full-length mirror in the master bedroom to examine the person she would allow herself to be, the person she had never fully accepted—a woman on the edge, a poseur portraying an inexperienced lover anticipating a tryst.

Like Leena, Myrna had gained weight from their restaurant indulgences, but unlike Leena, she had lost it, toned her body with the latest craze: Jazzercise, which left her more beautiful and tempting than ever—a real knockout. Myrna's close-lipped, hard-working family had schooled her to never discuss finances accrued to her grandparents who had migrated from Romania at the turn of the century with a few antique jewelry pieces which they parlayed into a successful business on New York City's Madison Avenue. It took two years and three months for Myrna to divulge that her children had their own trust account, that her divorce agreement covered her living expenses and child support through graduate school. Once Leena assessed the depth of Myrna's pocketbook, she translated Bayla's pithy maxim: "It's as easy to fall in love with a rich man as a poor one," substituting *woman* for *man*. Oh, her mother would love that!

"Go on. Embarrass me some more," Myrna laughed. "I'm glad you're here, on my birthday. And thank you for your help." She raised her injured finger. "There were times, I don't know what I would have done without your advice about the divorce."

Leena's head sped. Outright exposure was never anything she considered, not since college and that episode with Ursula. Myrna would never jeer or punish, not after the intimate details they had shared about their personal lives. But if more than friendship were to occur reaching out could bring rejection. Shame. Disgrace. She could lose her best friend. Lose everything. Was it worth living with the consequences? Risking it was the only way. She held herself back, afraid to turn to Myrna, to experience close-up her face, her eyes, the touch of her skin; their shoulders, thighs, knees already touching.

Controlling herself, yet wanting; fearful yet determined, she felt walled in. "It's my choice to feel complete once and for all." Leena's silent declaration, expressed after years of indecisiveness, felt dangerously potent, and damned explosive as if its manifestation was no longer her doing, but a force on its own.

As the sound of cushions beneath her gave way to the squish of down feathers shifting, she eased closer to Myrna, barely moving. A touch forward, a slight turn, Myrna's sigh, as if acquiescing, looking into her eyes, a smile, so close to that one place until she touched, with her mouth, Myrna's warm lips with her own.

"I'm sorry. I hope I didn't. . . ." Overcome with the need to apologize, Leena backed away from Myrna's scent, her delicate perfume. Guerlain. Gardenia Royale.

"I've never been kissed by a woman," Myrna said whispering, out of embarrassment or disbelief? Not a word of reproach, or disdain.

Her face already red, her clothes damp from sweat, despite how difficult it was to breathe, "It's who I am," Leena said.

"What do you mean?"

"I'm a woman attracted to women." There was a long silence. They glanced briefly at one another. "A woman who cares deeply about you." Leena's voice was soft, breathy.

She had no idea about what to do or say next. Her confession labeled her queer, declared her evil-minded and unfit. The news would reverberate throughout town. Her family, her daughter, her husband would be regarded with pity and scorn, jokes and sneers, but Myrna hadn't moved. Leena had kissed her on the lips, and Myrna hadn't moved.

Leena pictured herself reaching out, drawing her beloved's taut body into the fullness of her own, allowing whatever to follow, but for months, whenever she moved too deeply into her fantasies, she accustomed herself to stop. Gradual was the way forward. Gradual worked.

"What do we do now?" Myrna asked.

"When I kissed you, how did you feel?"

"In my wildest dreams, I never thought. . . ." Myrna paused. "Our poetry for Lovers Seminar at the University of Pittsburgh."

"Mr. Pushkin held the class outdoor. Remember? You dangled

your bare feet in that stream, and he sat next to you. I was jealous."

"Jealous of old Mr. Pushkin the midst of Keats?" Myrna laughed. *"Bold Lover, never, never canst thou kiss, Though winning near the goal – yet, do not grieve.* That's how I felt when you kissed me. Suspended on that urn, their love never to be consummated."

"Do we love one another?" Leena asked, seeking answers to the most important questions that needed to be asked, trying to control the quiver in her voice.

"I trust you with everything—my feelings, my hopes, my pain. You're the dearest person to me. I don't know what else to say."

In the stillness of the hour, the neighborhood shuttered, families sound asleep, Leena considered it was premature for Myrna to comment on what had just occurred. Reasonable emotions hadn't yet formed. Everything for her was too new.

"What do you think it's like, what women do?" Leena asked.

"Have you ever…?"

"No, only thoughts, dreams about us, for some time. Growing up, I always thought the way I felt toward women was a mistake. I felt like … a weirdo. A misfit."

"A misfit?" A flash of sympathy crossed Myrna's face for the tough-minded, clear-headed, always sure-of-herself Leena. "I can't imagine it, the burden you've had to carry around."

"As a child, I knew I was different. All the girls wanted boyfriends but I was attracted to girls. Who could I ask? I was afraid to tell, so I imitated what my girlfriends did. If I wanted to survive, I had to act like them. Be like them. Grow up like them, become a wife. A mother. As far as I could tell, the world I wanted to live in didn't exist."

"The person you knew you were, was the person you tried so hard to avoid. I'm so sorry. All those years, not being able to be yourself."

"I feel . . . I'm sorry, but I have to say it. I feel my life began when I kissed you." Like the lens of a camera, Leena wanted to encompass everything that a second later would be memory, to preserve in exact word-for-word, picture-for-picture, sound-on-sound detail. Everything had to be captured, each second more precisely than the last. She could barely compose herself. And Myrna, fascinated, uncertain, waiting.

"We can give each other so much more."

"More than what?"

"More than we've had in our marriages, more as mothers, more as women."

"How do you know such things if you never—"

"I know because you've given me the courage to be honest. You're the most understanding person I've ever met. You've allowed me to be who I am."

"But I haven't done a thing. You are who you are. I don't know enough about women —"

"There's nothing to know."

"There has to be." Slowly, gracefully Myrna extended one hand, as if she were granting her willingness to follow where Leena wanted to lead. Encouraged by the unexpected offering, Leena placed Myrna's hand in her palm, raised it to her mouth and slowly kissed each finger. Myrna took a long slow breath and exhaled. Was the sensuality of Leena kissing her fingers so moving? Did Myrna dare to long for more?

"We don't have to rush," Leena said. "What's most important is for you to be happy."

"I want to understand what's happening, what I'm feeling. What you just did, I had this overwhelming urge to give myself to this person who, more than anything, wants to please me."

Leena lifted both of her hands, placed them ever so gently on each side of Myrna's face, feeling the delicately smooth well-cared for skin. She shaped her kiss to Myrna's mouth, found her tongue, heard her moan. When they drew apart, Myrna was shivering.

"How do you feel?" Leena asked.

"Shy and shaky, but most of all...different. It's not like it hasn't crossed my mind. You and me sexually."

"Really?"

"I had this dream about you. Like a man and woman, we were dating, walking down an empty street, hand in hand. We turned a corner and found ourselves in an alley. You swept me into yourself and kissed me and I, I had an orgasm, just like that. I was ashamed to tell you."

"You're afraid to feel a certain way about me. I know those feelings, and those fears." Leena drew Myrna towards her so that her head rested on her shoulder. "We'll go one step at a time. Think how it can be between the two of us."

"Illicit thoughts?" Myrna laughed.

"Why not? Outlandish fantasies. Outstanding indulgences." Their laughter produced a release of something awkward, raw and unknown.

Leena rose, and without a word, she walked behind the couch. Slowly she massaged Myrna's neck, her back, her upper arms, allowing her palms to ease across Myrna's breasts. Myrna closed her eyes, her head slowly drifting back.

"I'll make you feel more loved than any man ever has," Leena said.

"What do we tell our children?" Myrna whispered.

"How we feel about each other is what matters. No one else has to know."

"Isn't that dishonest?"

"It's our secret." No one would stand in their way, not her mother, or Teddy, or her daughter, not Myrna's children, or anyone in Myrna's family. Not even townsfolk's gossip.

As the sun rose inside Myrna's newly-decorated bedroom, Leena made love to Myrna, delving easily, freely, guided by passion and a yearning that seemed to exist since before she was born.

DECEMBER 1972 – MARCH 1973

Chapter Thirty-Four

Double Vision

Bayla turned the knob, surprised when the front door opened. She rang the bell anyway, keeping the door ajar with her foot, but there was no sign of her daughter. Since it wasn't quite lunch time, thinking Leena might be preparing coffee, she eased her way in. Dirty dishes in the sink, crumbs on the floor, smudges on the kitchen cabinets. She walked along the hallway that led to the master bedroom, and hearing the sound of the shower, she shouted: "Don't you instruct your cleaning girl to....?" when Myrna, naked underneath a partly-opened white terry robe, suddenly appeared.

"What was that, my pet?" Leena appeared in a similar state of undress, looking puzzled for the briefest moment at what sparked Myrna's gasp. She turned, and saw her mother, her face the color of agony.

"Oh, you're here. I must have left the front door unlocked in our rush to cool off. We came from playing tennis. Myrna's teaching me."

Confronted by her daughter's brazen nonchalance, Bayla trembled at what she surmised.

"She can take a shower in her own house."

"I invited her. What's the big deal?" Leena retied her bathrobe more tightly around her middle. Myrna did the same.

"You are fresh and rude. What if your father finds out?"

"About what?"

"About this." Bayla thrust her index finger from one semi-naked woman to the other. Myrna edged closer to Leena. "And what if your husband came home from work early and saw the two of you like this?"

"You're accusing me of inviting Myrna to take a shower? You'll be in the psychiatrist's office in no time." She turned to Myrna. "You left your clothes in the guest room. Why don't you —"

"You're the one who should be in a psychiatrist's office," Bayla said as Myrna walked quickly past her.

"For playing tennis? We have to get ready, Mother. We're going out."

"Don't think I don't know what's going on. All anyone has to do is look. Using Teddy and your children to hide behind. People see, Leena. They'll talk. The whole town will belittle me. Laugh at me because of you."

"People laughing at you is not something I can control." Leena said, casually searching through her closet, intent on choosing an outfit. "You have no idea what you're saying. That's why you take medication, that's why you *have* a psychiatrist."

Conscious now of holding her breath, Bayla inhaled in the face of Leena's implications. Leena who made everything sound so reasonable, two young women guilty of what was shameful and unnatural. Bayla wrung her hands together as if she were squeezing water out of a washcloth. In her day women like that, fearing a tell-tale life, a ruined reputation, their family dishonored, knew to hide their feelings. Women like that understood the importance of keeping their secrets secret. She knew about such things precisely as if she had been there herself.

"At least try to be discreet."

"Don't threaten me when you have no idea what you're talking about."

"I know perfectly well what I'm talking about. You can't fool me. It's all over the news, on television. Feminists marching for equality, books pushing women to work outside the home, to fulfill their dreams for a career. Turning a housewife into a nothing. There were no such things in my day. And you who can do whatever you like. Look what you're choosing! "

"Lecturing me on the women's movement? Good for you. I

didn't think you were even aware it existed. Now I have to get ready, and you have to leave."

Bayla inched closer to her daughter: "The front door open, dirty dishes in the sink, a filthy kitchen floor, smudges on the cabinets. I'm telling Teddy."

"Go ahead. Tell him. Tell my husband whatever you want!"

The next morning, Bayla let herself in.

"Is she still here?" her voice was refreshed, lively.

"Who, Mother? Is who still here? My friend Myrna?" Leena sneered, her voice brazen.

"Don't play smart with me," Bayla said. *Not one word about my new lipstick, baby blue eye shadow, pink cashmere sweater and ankle-length wool skirt instead of my usual housedress,* Bayla thought. She marched into the kitchen and sat in her usual chair. Leena cleared the breakfast dishes from the table.

"You're embarrassing our family. And how you look. The weight you've gained. It isn't healthy. And how you dress. You're an executive's wife."

"How I look is who I am."

"What is that supposed to mean? Now you've done it. I got up this morning, put myself together, a new outfit, makeup, I had a reason. Now it's gone because of you."

"Haven't you had enough, Mother? I mean, really. If you're so embarrassed because of me, your only child, it's because you're only thinking of yourself."

"I gave up my career because of you."

"You never gave up anything for anybody."

"I was a great singer. My teacher, Milhady, said so. They never let me speak of her. She was a colored woman from the Nutmeg. I drove there in secret, on dirt roads, past shanties where public housing is now. I was younger than you. She was famous. She took me as her pupil because I had talent. I told her I was pregnant and...."

"I supposed she helped you try to get rid of me," Leena said jokingly.

"I begged her to, I did, but she refused."

Leena paused. Her eyes narrowed. "You never wanted me. You never wanted a child. I knew it. I always knew it. I wasn't wanted, not for a moment!"

"'Have your baby and sing too,' Milhady told me," Bayla said oblivious to Leena's words, her pained expression. "How could I, living in Amory Lane, your grandmother's position and the townsfolk watching our every step? I gave up my debut to be your mother before the gossip-mongers could destroy us. A pregnant woman on stage. Our heads would spin." Bayla took several breaths. "Why aren't you sitting? Come," she smiled. "We'll have coffee."

"Coffee? I don't think so." Leena grabbed hold of her mother's shoulder wrinkling a handful of her pink cashmere sweater.

"What are you doing? Don't pull me. I don't need help. I can walk by myself."

"In there. Move." Leena pushed Bayla beyond the open door and into the living room. "Now you can sit."

Bayla fell backwards into the couch.

"What are you going to....?"

"I've put this off long enough, Mother. We are going to have this out. All my life you talked about how having a child stood in the way of the one thing you wanted most. I've been your perfect excuse for years. Not father, not our family, not living here or *me* are the reasons you gave up singing. Only one person is responsible for that, and that person is you. You're the reason you never fulfilled your dream. You're the one who gave up your wonderful talent. No one but you."

Bayla's hands rushed to her mouth to suppress an inhuman cry. The top part of her body folded forward as if her insides were crumbling, and loose pieces of herself were breaking off, detaching from what was once a whole human being.

"No more threats, no more plying me with guilt because you want me to live a life that makes you look good. I know who I am. Do you hear me, Mother? I know who I am, and not you or anyone else is going to change that. You want me to be your perfect little Leena?

Well, I'm going to be. You know why? Because of Myrna, Myrna, my beloved, yes, 'that woman.' Do you have any idea what it means to be fully accepted for who you are by someone who loves you?"

Bayla gazed at the floor and reached into her dress pocket, frantic for one of Charlotte's handkerchiefs, which she still painstakingly laundered, a fresh one each morning.

"Yes. I knew that. A long time ago," Bayla whispered, the handkerchief at her mouth.

A long silence followed. Leena paced back and forth, finally easing into a chair, seemingly calm as if she had been set free from some lengthy injustice.

"When Myrna and I enter the world as a couple, I'm going to be as beautiful as I've always been but never knew it. Despite what you see, despite who I am, I'm your child. Maybe one day, you'll accept that person."

How strange, Bayla thought, the way the light from the morning sun had landed in her open hands as they rested in her lap. She watched intently as she curled her fingers into her palms, grasping the light in her fists. Feeling the need to stand, she pushed down hard on either side of her, taking deep breaths, struggling to raise her body which was stooped and hunched over from helplessness and humiliation. Her eyes searched the room, chairs, floor, walls. Everything so very meaningless, along with her pink sweater, and ruby-red lipstick that she had so carefully applied.

Everything Bayla had trusted, everything she had counted on to make her a somebody, the fates had usurped. Despite her mother's warnings, her teachings all those years, she failed to take the fates seriously. For disregarding her mother, the punishment would be hers alone to bear. More cruel than she had ever known them to be, the fates had led her through a life of pointless self-sacrifice and turned her into what she had become—a mother who had forsaken a talent that had set her apart and made life worth living, rejected by a daughter she had failed to keep normal.

Chapter Thirty-Five
Everybody Change Partners

Leena realized she had no choice except to plan her next move encouraged, as she was, by the final entry, written the day before her wedding, in the notebook she discovered inside the zippered pouch of an old suitcase containing Comanche dorm memorabilia.

> *Tomorrow my journey of denying my sexuality will be sealed forever. I must bury thoughts of who I might have been to avoid shame, ridicule, being exposed as someone deficient. Survival resides in staying hidden minute by minute. Will I ever meet the person who will fulfill what is right and true for me?*

She laughed at her melodramatic pangs, but Myrna commended her determination, the courage it took to cut ties she no longer believed were viable. That was exactly what Leena needed before she put on her coat and drove into the night.

"What are we discussing now?" Teddy asked as soon as he let her in. "The movie we're going to see this weekend? Vacation plans? How to celebrate my birthday? Must be something life threatening that brought you here after Jackie's fast asleep. Calling me at work to let me know ahead of time."

"Don't be obnoxious," Leena replied.

In the living room, she sat in the armchair, he on the beige couch across from her. Beige. She never liked that color, or the fabric. Corduroy.

"We need time to cool down, at least for a trial period. I'll continue to stay with Myrna until you and I decide our next steps. Jackie's life should be disturbed as little as possible. Just because we're having problems, she shouldn't suffer. I know you agree. She'll live here with you. I'll be close enough to take care of her whenever she needs me, when you're on a business trip or are come home late. And given my mother's unstable behavior, you might want to consider hiring someone. My father can help but he's going to have to get used to his wife going through some kind of therapy."

"That's it? That easy? You there, us here, as if no one will notice, as if none of us will feel the difference? And describing your mother that way. And your father perhaps alone? You, the alleged therapist? Your empathy astounds me."

"People talk. That's nothing new. Myrna and I have been seen around town. People know we're friends. What I'm proposing is only temporary. My father will continue as usual. I'll see that my mother gets proper care."

"What about Jackie? The hurt. The disruption. I watch her at bedtime walking up the stairs, her head bowed, her feet dragging. Childhood innocence on the battlefield of her parents' marriage. You don't see it. You're out with Myrna. Jackie's attached to your mother no matter what you say or think, I have to rely on her. She fosters Jackie's talent. She knows how to deal with who she is: a precocious, talented child, or haven't you noticed? They're a lot alike, you know. Jackie's determined to be a star. I'm sure she will be. Nothing's going to stop her. I'm sorry. I won't cover your tracks. Don't expect me to."

"You won't have to." Leena had thought it all out. The best way to get through to him was to stay calm and reasonable. He was diplomatic. He respected negotiation. The give and take of a discussion. "I know she'll miss having a mother in the house, but I'll be around to explain things to her. To work out problems she has at school. Or socially. I'm not irresponsible."

"And what about us?" The words shot out of his mouth. "Can I bring that up or is that against your rules?" His anger startled her.

"Of course. Say what you want." She laughed somewhat

haphazardly to appear magnanimous, to make light of where they were at that point, or what she expected would follow.

"If I had to guess, I'd say you're copping out. It's obvious you've been working up to this, delivering what should I call it? A lecture? An ultimatum? We've barely tried to fix what's broken between us. Can you even tell me what that is? Do you even know?"

"Okay. Look." Her voice was strong, steady. "Those first few years were great, but we're not right for each other. We never were. I suspected it from the start, but I gave in. To you. To my mother. To the world. I thought I could be a good wife. I made a mistake. I was wrong. I admit it. But there is one thing."

He turned to walk away. "Should I bother asking?"

"You should consider seeing an endocrinologist." She spoke authoritatively, her expression devoid of any indication of where she was headed.

"What?" Teddy laughed. He swirled to face her. "Where'd you get that from?"

"I think you're missing hormones."

"For God's sakes, Leena, this isn't the time to play analyst. I thought we were going to discuss a trial separation, like adults."

"You might as well benefit from my expertise while you can. I'm only trying to help."

"Is that what you call it?" He shook his head from side-to-side. "I've always marveled how you parse things into pieces, suitable for you to analyze, but don't try it with me. I will not get suckered into your diagnosis, or that crack about your expertise."

"You were always one for truth. Don't you want to hear it?"

"Do you even know what the truth is?"

She was prepared for a backlash. She fully expected one, she believed he was clueless, but somehow he had struck at what she had tried so hard to bury—that place within herself that convinced her to make a life with a man because she didn't think she had any other choice.

"You want explanations? Okay. There was so little about me you got right. You never held my hand properly, or knew how to turn me on. When you approached me, you were clumsy and awkward.

You never touched me in the right places, at the right time, and when we made love, you were selfish and uncaring."

She watched him wince at believing that everything was his fault. She had more to say, but his body stiffened.

In the long silence that followed, she believed she had achieved an unquestionable win, until he looked directly into her, gathering steam for a comeback.

"I've been a good husband, a loving father, and you're blaming me, for what?" He suddenly banged his fist on the coffee table positioned between them. "For taking a job in Pittsmill? For not confiding in you beforehand? For failing to find one damn inroad to our problems after nine years of marriage? What part do you play in this? Never a word of appreciation. No recognition of how hard I worked, the freedom you have—a wife who could do whatever she pleased. You broke the rules, changed the formula, stopped being domestic, neglected Jackie, shunned any attempt at sex. You weren't there, for God's sakes. And how ironic. Tonight you've paid me more attention than you've shown in years. Missing hormones!"

Leena bit her lip to prevent herself from striking back. "I'd better go," she said, almost apologetically. The pressure to fit in that hounded her, that lived inside her, characterized her life from childhood, was about to disappear. Loving and living with a woman who felt the same way towards her was already taking effect. It wasn't right to draw blood. In a perverse kind of way, her return to Pittsmill proved justifiable. It brought her Myrna.

The following day, after Jackie came home from school, Leena spoke to her in the master bedroom, that place where all three of them used to snuggle in bed and watch cartoons Sunday mornings.

"Your Dad and I are having problems. I don't have to tell you that. You know we haven't been getting along. We disagree. Argue. So we've made a decision that will work for all of us. I'm going to move in with Myrna, my best friend. It's only temporary. I'll be here most days when you come home from school, and you can call me whenever you want."

Jackie listened intensely, trying her best to withhold her tears, until she couldn't.

"Why are you going? We need you. What will Dad do without you? You're always with Myrna. When her family got divorced, her children went to live in different places. Will that happen to us? I don't want to live away from Grandma, and does Dad have to go to Viet Nam?"

"Jackie, you're already seven years old. You're a big girl. I'll just be in a different house. Close by. And no, your father isn't going to Viet Nam. Where did you hear that? You'll still have Grandma and Grandpa and you've been to Myrna's many times. You know where she lives."

"Dad told me he wants our family to stay together. He's ready to go to a marriage doctor with you. Why don't you go with him? Grandma says you don't listen."

"I'm pleased your father has spoken to you about this and I'm proud of how you're trying to understand. Come here."

When Jackie took a tentative step toward her mother's open arms, Leena had no idea that her embrace, such a rare occurrence, would forever mark her departure in Jackie's memory.

At first Leena felt responsible, in a triumphant way, for the cessation of Bayla's daily visits and phone calls. It was all that truth-telling, she decided, confessing who she was, bringing her relationship with Myrna out of the dark into the light. But weeks, then a month passed without her mother appearing for a single coffee morning. When she called Amory Lane, her father didn't hold back: "Your mother hardly speaks. Not to me, not to anyone. Not even phone calls. Some days she sits for hours in the parlor staring into space. I do most of the cooking. She needs help, Leena, and I don't know how to reach her."

Teddy confirmed what her father had already stated. "I can't count on your mother anymore. I had to leave work early to take Jackie to her after-school activities. Jackie told me her grandmother says things that don't make sense, and her clothes don't match. I've hired a woman to help with Jackie after school. I can't count on Bayla. You must be concerned."

"Tell Jackie the word for her grandmother is eccentric."

"Is that a joke? If that's your diagnosis, it's insufficient. Your mother needs to see a doctor. And your dad can't manage her by himself anymore, poor guy."

When Leena shopped in the supermarket, dropped off clothes at the cleaners, or bought toiletries at Reads Drugs, her feigned smiles and greetings did little to deter townsfolk gossip.

"The missus has vanished." "No sign of her anywhere." "Maybe she's ill? "Sent away?" "Front porch knee-deep in leaves." "Lights left on all night." "Something's a miss."

The Queen-Anne Victorian mansion at the top of Beleaguered Hill had become cloaked in mystery.

Dr. Abrams, her mother's psychiatrist, had recently been named Chief of Psychiatry at newly-built, ultra-modern hospital just outside of Pittsmill in Greensburg, Pennsylvania. Leena secured an appointment with him for mid-August.

"It's been over two years, since 1971, when I saw your mother. How is she doing?"

"Not well. My father does his best with her and I refill her prescriptions but we don't know if she takes them. We're all rather worried."

"I've reread her file. She had a breakdown after the war, you were almost five, the doctor at the time diagnosed her as having a depressive episode. I remember telling you that the behaviors she was beginning to display weren't going to disappear. Is it possible for a 57-year-old woman to unearth everything she's buried inside her so she can spend her remaining years a psychologically healthy person?"

"It's worth a try," Leena tried to sound hopeful.

"Your mother always wanted a singing career. She deserves that chance. Would she be willing to come in for an evaluation? I'm not dismissing the possibility of a short hospital stay."

"My father and I, we'll make it work. I'll be forever grateful." But how to convince her mother to agree? Leena told her Uncle

Solomon what Dr. Abrams had said.

"I have no idea what she might say to a hospital. I'm concerned as much as you and my dear brother. She feels like dead weight to me. I try to rile her up, but she no longer wants to play. I know we're older but I think she's gone a little cuckoo. You're the psychology maven, do something."

When Leena entered Amory Lane that morning, her mother was already up and dressed, having coffee with her father at the bistro table in the kitchen.

"Mother, I have something to tell you."

"Yes, dear, what now?"

"Dr. Abrams thinks it's time to reevaluate your meds."

"You mean I no longer need them? Sign me up."

It can't be this easy, Leena told herself. Life doesn't happen that way, but her mother rose from the table, collected the dishes and placed them in the sink. Her father gave her the high sign, rolling his eyes, and raising his eye brows, wisely refusing to say another word. He knew as well as Leena did, one wrong turn, a misplace intention, and the entire scheme could fall apart.

How peculiar the way her mother could appear unhinged and then, for whatever reason, return to some semblance of normalcy. Perhaps she suffered from an on and off mood disorder like manic depression, the text book name, but she wasn't going to guess or offer it as a diagnosis for what had built up over the years as her mother's mental condition worsened.

The reality of it was frightening, mental illness seizing control of someone she knew, much less her mother. Even if her mother could be made whole, then return to Amory Lane where she had lived for almost 40 years, the immediate family, even Jackie would have to relearn how to reconnect with her. Leena suspected that not even Sigmund Freud could grant sanity to someone who probably never had it to begin with.

Jackie would have to be told.

"I have something important to tell you about why your mother brought you here today," Bayla said to Jackie on a Saturday afternoon after lunch of grilled cheese sandwiches. "Seems your mother has spoken to Dr. Abrams about me." Cotton slacks, and a blue cotton pullover, pearl earrings and a touch of lipstick made Bayla seem younger. "He thinks I should sing again. I'll be going to his new facility to rehearse with the musical director. It's a sleep-away place, and I don't have to audition."

Bayla and Jackie were snuggled on the settee. Leena sat across from them, stunned by her mother's reasoning, her complete lunacy. She wondered if Jackie believed her grandmother's explanation presented with such genuine excitement, if she didn't know any better, she would have almost believed it herself.

"Is it far away? When can I come see you?"

"Jackie dear, rehearsals take time. They want to make sure I'm good enough. And it's not far, maybe an hour's drive. Or two."

Jackie put her arms around Bayla's middle and began to cry.

"Why can't you perform here? Who will coach me and help me with dance routines and take me to my classes?"

"No tears, Jackie, dear. I'm sure your father will find all the best people."

"But no one else can do what you do."

"I'll call you every day and you'll tell me everything you're learning."

"But what will happen to Grandpa? He'll be alone."

"You forget your Uncle Solomon. They play cards, bet plastic chips like two little boys. They both love to cook. Those two can eat me out of house and home."

"Come on, kiddo," Leena interrupted, concerned about her mother's loss of reality. When did those two ever cook a meal?

In the car on the way home Leena felt compelled to bring some measure of realism to the situation. "The truth is Grandma's having problems. She doesn't always make the best decisions or behave properly. You're almost eight years old so you already know that. She's going to a place where she'll be cared for. You don't want people making fun of her, do you? If you're upset by any of this, we'll talk it out together. Okay? She's going to be fine. Nothing stops either of you. You both have that in common."

Leena considered it inevitable that she would awaken most mornings with thoughts of indulging her lover given the unexpected turn her life had taken. When Myrna complained about living in a house filled with constant reminders of her ex-husband, who had moved to California, and was engaged to a lovely dance teacher, so her son explained, Leena intervened.

"Not to worry. I'll find us a place of our own, miles away. We'll head north. Explore. He has his life. You'll have yours. With me."

At the start of November, with her mother safe in Greensburg Hospital during the past six weeks, Myrna drove her black Mercedes, with Leena beside her, through Vermont's picturesque countryside. Down a private dirt road, they stopped in front of a gray farmhouse with a red roof situated beside a small red barn. Thick cedar beams made for a low ceiling in a cozy front room that led to a country kitchen, two bedrooms, and one bathroom on two acres of farmland in Mt. Holly. *Fodor's Pocket Guide* described classes in Middlebury and Bennington colleges, and highly-rated restaurants in Weston and Londonderry.

"The isolated surroundings, perfect inspiration for my poetry. How did you know?" Myrna asked as she peered out the kitchen window. She bought the property outright. "But what about your Jackie?"

"Teddy will manage. He'll arrange everything. Nothing's too much for him and his compulsive tendencies. Everything will work as it should. I've raised Jackie to be independent, to speak her mind. If something's going on, my daughter will tell me. She knows I'm there for her. Our lives, yours and mine, will be ideal, and people in Vermont mind their own business."

Awed by the novelty of herself with a woman, Leena rewarded herself by feeling complete. With Myrna at her side, she tiptoed into a world shielded by her own volition to allow enough time to sufficiently inhabit it. The more she moved in that direction, she no longer cared what others might say, or how she might appear to them. When she journeyed into town, alone or with Myrna, she chatted with other women, a teacher, doctor, lawyer, lesbians like herself. The joy she felt sharing her life with a woman she loved became a habit that flavored the passing of time, freeing her from moment-to-moment choices to forestall unwanted scrutiny.

"I'm not sick, Mrs. McGlochlin," she pictured herself saying to the mother of her first love. Margie. Those years when she was unable to understand or embrace her attraction to girls, as if she were the only one on the planet who felt that way, now seemed amusing. She hoped Margie would one day forgive her.

The tentative steps of living with Myrna after their three-year affair left Leena feeling giddy. She helped outfit their home: art to hang, linens to buy, a pantry to fill, paint colors to choose. Myrna paid for authentic New England furnishings purchased in local stores. Leena covered their daily upkeep.

As spring semester approached, they applied to Bennington College. Myrna for a degree in fine arts; Leena for a masters in social work. Throughout their first winter, while their home was warmed day and night by a log fire set into their enormous brick hearth, followed by their first summer when they dozed in white Adirondack chairs surrounded by flourishing green countryside, Leena discovered what it was like to live as a sexual person.

"I have never experienced anything like it," Myrna whispered to Leena one night after they marveled at the heat and longing of their lovemaking.

"Neither have I," Leena confessed. "It's like nothing I could have ever imagined."

AUGUST 1973 – DECEMBER 1973

Chapter Thirty-Six

Talent

Jackie was almost eight years old when her mother moved to Vermont with Myrna. The abrupt change in her family life made Jackie feel as if she were wearing shoes that didn't fit. She was the only kid in school who didn't have a mother living at home and that made her stand out. Jackie never minded standing out. In fact she preferred it, but it had to be on *her* terms, not because someone else made it happen, even if it was her own mother.

The first time a group of girls at school pointed fingers and taunted, "Where's your mom? Where's your mom?" Jackie told them how she could do whatever she wanted like playing her favorite Broadway musicals instead of doing her homework because her mother had moved away. After that those pesky girls left her alone.

The hurt that Jackie felt when her mother moved to Vermont was much less than the hurt she felt from missing her grandmother Bayla who also went away.

When she was four years old and her family moved from Boston to Pittsmill, Pennsylvania, the love she felt from her grandmother Bayla flowed so freely that no matter how much of it Jackie received, she was certain more would follow. This certainty, for which she didn't yet have the words, gave her a sense of entitlement.

In her tap dancing class, her grandmother got permission to

sit in the back of the studio and write down the steps in a little notebook. Then she instructed her shoemaker to put taps on a pair of green pumps that had fat heels and a strap across the front. She and Jackie practiced routines together on Amory Lane's marble floor, which made their tapping sound absolutely stupendous, her grandmother said.

"That child is something," Bayla would tell others so that Jackie overheard. "She will accomplish what others say they will, but don't."

"Why don't they?" Jackie would ask.

"Because life gets in their way, but that's not going to happen to you. You're going to be a success. I'm sure of it."

Then there was the bond. "You were born connected to me, and I to you." That convinced Jackie she'd never be alone in the world. "Nothing can ever change that," her grandmother emphasized.

Jackie never told anyone how her mother used to count on her fingertips: Disobedient. Short-tempered. Wise guy. Talking back. Fresh. Maybe it was those reasons that sent her mother away, but she hardly ever displayed those behaviors to Bayla, and she went away too.

Jackie's impression of grandmothers was that they were and always would be special. Mothers, not so much. Even when her mother was with her, Jackie felt she wasn't really there, or didn't want to be.

With her mother there wasn't much she could do right. With her grandmother there wasn't anything she couldn't do if she decided to do it.

It was early fall and Bayla had been away about a week when Jackie heard her father whisper two strange-sounding words into the telephone: *Mental illness.* She had no idea who he was speaking to and she didn't much care but those two words repeated themselves like a whisper, over and again, inside her head without providing the tiniest clue as to what they meant. She understood illness: colds, sore throats, bronchitis. But mental? She looked it up in Webster's. "Relating to the mind," it said but nothing about if her grandmother would die from it, or was it catching? And because no one in her family mentioned a word, she was afraid to ask.

Then one day, quite unexpectedly, while glancing through TV Guide, she noticed a movie called *The Snake Pit* with Olivia De Havilland who played a woman with 'mental illness,' the description said. There it was: her chance to find out what those words meant. So at 2 a.m. on the night the movie was to be shown, Jackie snuck out of bed, tiptoed downstairs and turned on the TV. Everything began calmly enough until Olivia loses her way in this institution where her family sent her to get well just like Bayla's family sent her.

Olivia wanders outside her room and gets lost at the end of a hallway facing a door. With no other way out, she opens the door, and finds herself on a platform above a kind of dungeon filled with crazy-looking men. One of them spots her, and lets out a terrible shriek. Now other men, bedraggled, bent over, with no teeth, eyes popping out of their heads, slowly, step by step, move toward her. When they get close enough, they reach up, pull at her skirt, grab her feet, her legs. Olivia screams and tires to back away but there's no place for her to go. She's no longer a movie star but a woman in danger and Jackie, so immersed in what was going on, felt the same exact thing happening to her. So before Olivia's screams became her own, Jackie ran back upstairs, leaped into bed and hid under her blanket crying and shaking until morning, wishing she'd never think about "mental illness" ever again.

After Jackie's mother and Myrna had been living in Vermont about a month, Jackie's father told her that he'd accepted a new job, with a big promotion which meant the two of them would be moving to New York City, closer to her father's parents, Grandmother Fanny and Grandfather Max.

"New York City?" Jackie exclaimed jumping off the couch. "You mean Broadway?"

"No. Broadway is on the West Side. My job is on the East Side.

We'll be living in the suburbs, Westchester County. In a two-story townhouse. I'll have a short commuter train ride into the city, and you'll have your own room and the schools are supposed to be excellent. You'll be starting third grade September, 1973, and at the end of the month you'll turn eight years old, so we'll have a birthday party with your new friends, and Grandma and Grandpa."

"How far is that Westchester place from the theatre district?"

"It's 24.8 miles. How did I know you would ask?"

"So I can continue my lessons with New York professionals, and maybe my New York grandma will pay for them like my real grandma, Bayla, from Pennsylvania does."

"Like she *did*. I've been paying since Bayla went away, and my mother, Fanny, is your real grandmother too. And you'll still have to telephone your mother once a week, and visit her on certain holidays."

"Why, Dad? It's such a pain."

"All parents are pains, that's why we're called parents."

Her father hired a high school senior to stay in their house until he returned from work each night. Unfortunately, the person she referred to as a "gum-chewing, pimply-faced, overweight babysitter with a boring name—Marion," was, for Jackie, no cause for celebration.

At eight years old, Jackie was tall for her age. Her dark brown hair was long, straight and flowing, her eyes hazel, sometimes green depending on the light. Bayla would be forever telling her she'd grow up to be a beauty, and though her looks rarely concerned her, what Jackie desperately wanted was to prove to her new third grade class just exactly *who* among them had arrived.

Each day, two third-grade classes were combined at recess, freeing teachers to chat while students meandered on and off playground equipment or participated in games on the tarmac. While sitting on a cement stanchion at the edge of the chain link fence, taking a break from dodge ball, Jackie happened to overhear one of the girls say her parents were taking her to see a revival of *Hair* at the Minskoff Theatre. Living this close to the city meant the kids in her school would be familiar with Broadway musicals. Maybe they had seen *Funny Girl* or *Oliver* or *Peter Pan* or *Godspell*, or *Chorus Line*. If not the originals, at least the movies or travelling productions. She knew the words to every song in every one of those shows but rather than brag, it was one girl's mention of *Hair* that gave her the greatest idea ever.

The next few nights before she fell asleep, as if she were visualizing moves on a chessboard—Uncle Solomon had taught her years ago how to play—Jackie devised a plan. First, she had to find out which of her classmates were familiar with what songs from which Broadway musicals. Why did they want to know, they would ask? Once they did, Jackie knew she had them.

"It's only for a select few of us," she said, acting coy. "There's going to be a big surprise so you have to sign a pledge of secrecy."

By day three of her plan, Jackie had secured an impromptu performance group of ten plus two back-ups, set in motion during outdoor recess. Due to inclement weather, for the next two days there was no going outside, and she couldn't conduct her planning meetings in the gym because the walls echoed every word. So rather than risk being overheard, she remained patient. When the skies cleared the following Monday, she returned to action.

"It's an outdoor entertainment for family and friends. We'll perform on the tarmac, rehearse after school before school buses arrive to take us home, but since that won't give us enough times, we'll meet here again on Saturdays so I can teach you the choreography. You'll each have to contribute $1.00 for a costume. Something like a crepe paper flower will visually tie us together so we resemble a real performing troupe," she explained. "When the words, the timing, the moves are perfect, we'll invite our parents, and as the director, I get to take the last bow as a solo, after all of you."

Unfortunately, once the lyrics were memorized and the choreography was down pat, Felicity Ann Weinstein complained to her mother because Jackie wouldn't let her sing "What I Did for Love" from *Chorus Line* "because Jackie wanted to hog that song for herself." Soon after, Teddy received a phone call from Mrs. Wolfarth, the principal.

After dinner that night he told Jackie to take a seat at the kitchen table. She knew she was in trouble. "Mrs. Wolfarth told me what's been going on."

"What do you mean what's been going on?"

"Don't play smart with me. Your little show."

"We rehearsed the songs and the dance steps and I collected money for crepe paper flowers. So?"

"So Mrs. Wolfarth showed me your homework folder. Not a speck of work was in there after all these weeks and I hadn't the slightest idea about *Broadway in the Burbs* because you kept it a secret, on purpose."

"Great title, right, Dad?" Jackie smiled. She rose from her chair, her nostrils flaring, her arms akimbo, and mounted her defense. "Dad, having an empty homework folder is nothing compared to what I accomplished. Didn't Mrs. Boneynose Principal tell you that I'm in the Drama Club? This Thursday, on Open School Night, talk to Mrs. Fineman. She's my teacher AND the head of the Drama Club. She knows me better than that dumb, skinny-necked, know-nothing...."

"No name calling. The Principal seemed very taken at how determined you were to carry it off, but you need to keep up your school work. Even your favorite Broadway and Hollywood movie idols are educated."

"Not really. Barbra Streisand barely finished high school when she got a part in *I Can Get It For You Wholesale*. And Liz Taylor and Judy Garland, and Gwen Verdon and Bob Fosse and Audrey Hepburn," Jackie took a breath, "all schooled on movie lots. The Beatles and Rolling Stones never finished high school either, and....Mrs. Fineman will tell you everything. She's a big fan of mine."

"You've got fans?" Teddy ran his fingers through his hair. He told her that his new job and scrambling to compete in the field of energy was far less taxing than dealing with his daughter's ambitious plans for her future.

When he arrived home the Thursday of open school night, before he got his coat off, Jackie accosted him.

"What did Mrs. Fineman say?"

"Why aren't you asleep? It's past your bedtime."

"Well?" Jackie said. "Well!" He escorted babysitter Marion out the door.

"Mrs Fineman confessed to your weak academics but she said that organizing the kids the way you did at recess was a noble effort. She said she encouraged you but someone snitched on her, told Mrs. Wolfarth. Killing your show was her reprimand. Seems the Principal has been trying to cut drama and music to use the money for new urinals in the boys' bathrooms."

"Why can't the boys pee in what's already there?"

"The point is, when your little group did a run-through for her after school during Drama Club, Mrs. Fineman was quite impressed. She thought it was very professional." He paused a moment to prepare. "She said you don't belong in that school."

"What?"

"She said I need to take you to a professional children's school. Now please stay calm before you start bouncing off the walls. Okay?"

"Yes. Fine. Sure." Jackie tightened her lips and turned her hands into fists to contain her excitement.

"She said once you get a part, and you will, you'll be assigned a tutor. She said you have real talent, in her opinion, but you have to keep a perspective."

Jackie wanted to shout, "I did it," out of every window in the house, but if she was going to be an actress, how would it look getting hysterical over the best news in the world, when controlling one's emotions as an actress was critical?

Two weeks later on a Friday after work, Jackie followed her father's directions. Instead of changing into her usual after school play clothes, she put on a dress and shoes, not sneakers, for the drive into Manhattan for what he called, "Shabbos dinner" at his parents' apartment. "We never did much of this at home because you mother didn't think it necessary, but I think it is. It's about traditions. Our tradition."

"You mean like in *Fiddler on the Roof*? Tradition." Jackie shouted out the first word of the song, her arms over head, prepared to sing the rest of it. Her father restrained her because traffic on the East River Drive was killing and they had to reach Manhattan before sundown.

Jackie characterized her Grandmother Fanny as more kooky than her Grandmother Bayla but in a different way. Fanny interjected Jewish words into her sentences, which made Jackie laugh. "Not Jewish, Yiddish," her father said." And she liked her Grandfather Max who hardly spoke but when he did, everyone listened. Concerning her two aunts, her father's two younger married sisters, one in New Jersey and one in Connecticut, "they're having Shabbat dinner with their families, exactly like we are," Granny Fanny explained. "That's what Jewish people do."

"It begins at sundown," Max announced. "Fanny," he pointed out the window. "It's time. Light the candles."

"Only a woman lights candles," Fanny explained with pride.

"No men?"

"Oi, Gotteniu. No, never a man. Lighting candles on Shabbat, it's only for a woman."

In the silence, everyone turned to Fanny, who gently covered her head with a lace cap, struck a match and lit two white candles, each one set into a beautiful silver candlestick placed on a silver tray. She waved her hands over the light once, twice, three times, placed her hands gently upon her closed eyes, and recited a short Hebrew prayer. When she was done everyone said "amen" and "Good Shabbos" and exchanged hugs and kisses. Then Fanny served the meal.

"It's good," Jackie said of the roast chicken and what her father called potato kugel.

Fanny gave her a kiss. When the meal ended, everyone gathered in the living room. Jackie spoke first, while holding up a sheet of paper.

"Mrs. Fineman, my drama teacher, gave my dad instructions. She made a list. You all have a chance to volunteer."

"We know from Cornell, MIT, Harvard, taking college entrance exams, but the theatre?" Fanny's voice trailed off.

"Who are we to question the teacher?" Max said. "Rabbis are teachers. Do what the teacher advises. Everything should fall into place."

By asking a colleague in his company's Public Relations

Department, Teddy located a seasoned photographer who did head shots for TV's child stars: Patty Duke, Ron Howard, Jerry Mathers. His studio was in Washington Heights.

The parents of Kerry-Ann Mulligan, the Drama Club's star tap dancer, Jackie's best friend, helped Fanny locate a voice teacher. She was a tall, stocky, middle-aged woman, a belter, she bragged, who had appeared in Broadway shows years ago and "only accepted exceptionally talented students in her West Side apartment," she said.

Max's pinochle friend, Meier Zolman, whose sister came from Jerusalem to visit a friend whose aunt was the head of the Theatre Department at New York University, recommended an acting teacher, a stylish Hungarian woman who lived in Soho.

The dance teacher came from Mrs. Fineman's nephew, a member of the Joffrey Ballet, trained in ballet, jazz and tap. He offered small classes in a studio near Lincoln Center.

Over buying brisket one Friday morning, Fanny mentioned to Moishe Kalb, their butcher, that she needed a theatre agent for her granddaughter's career. Only the most experienced. And wouldn't you know, his daughter, the beautiful one, in med school to become a hematologist, something to do with blood, used to work as a casting agent for movies filmed in Manhattan. "I'll give you the best," Moishe vowed. "So I'll have a small part in making her famous."

"From your lips to God's ears," Fanny told him.

After a day of school tutoring, Teddy dropped Jackie off at Granny Fanny's for a sleepover. The next day the two of them rode the downtown bus to the theatre district, off West 48th Street. Side-by-side they watched a smiling elderly man, a glove on the hand he used to open and close the manual metal grate that made the elevator run. On the fifth floor they walked along a dimly-lit hallway and paused at a glass paneled door that read *Charlie Engle's Broadway Children* in peeling gold letters.

Jackie glanced at the metal chairs with worn red plastic-covered seats, the threadbare rug, the framed posters of Broadway shows—*Gypsy, South Pacific, You Can't Take it With You, Our Town.*

"Grandma, everything is so old, so dingy. Are you sure....?"

"Jackie, we have to have patience. Moishe Kalb insisted five days a week, from ten in the morning till all hours, Mr. Engle interviews hundreds of talented children who sit where we are now. They come with their mothers, stage mothers, they're called. Women who know what's what in this business."

When Mr. Engle opened the door to his office and invited them inside, Jackie immediately noticed how everything about him was rumpled: his loosely knotted tie, light blue long-sleeved shirt, brown blazer hanging off the back of his wooden desk chair, even strands of greying curly hair atop his chubby rumpled face.

"Your portfolio," Charlie Engle said, and glanced through the pages, with practiced indifference.

"So you're a singer. Okay. Go ahead. On your feet. Sing."

Unfazed by his brash approach, forgetting the condition of the place and Moishe Kalb who Fanny said wouldn't steer them wrong, Jackie took a breath for what she and her voice teacher had prepared: "As Long as He Needs Me," from *Oliver,* and "Look to the Rainbow," from *Finian's Rainbow*. The first song demonstrated her mature sensibilities. The second incorporated a playfulness, a perfect combination to impress an agent. She got halfway through the first song when Charlie Engle put his hand up for Jackie to stop.

"You go to a professional school?"

"Yes."

"What else do you do?"

"I take voice, dance, and acting lessons."

"Tell me why you wanna do this work."

"It's what I want. It's all I want."

He opened a drawer and dug out some papers.

"Here's my standard contract. Take it home. Review the information, talk with your parents." He spoke to Jackie as if she were an entertainment lawyer. "One of them has to sign here, on this line."

Then he leaned forward and peered into Jackie's face as if

embedded in her talent, her spunk, no-nonsense will to succeed, he could assess her future. Jackie stood her ground and stared back undeterred, certain, self-confident. With a slight smile on his lips, he leaned back in his worn brown leather chair, where puffs of white stuffing protruded from arm rests.

"You'll be one of Charlie Engle's Broadway Children. I'm pleased to have you as a client, and I don't say that often."

After her father picked her up from his parents' apartment and she was at home in her room in Westchester, Jackie wrote to Bayla who had been away in that sleep-away place for two weeks already. Jackie knew how long she was away because she checked off each passing day on her wall calendar until she would see Bayla again, even though her father said no one knew when that would be. Her mother told her that the place was a kind-of hospital where people had to stay until they understood why they had to go there in the first place, and though the words *mental illness* never completely left Jackie's thoughts, she was still afraid to ask if that was the reason. Besides, she had promised her drama teacher, Mrs. Fineman, that she would focus on her career.

October 20, 1973. Mature 9 to 15-year-old female for lead role in a new musical. Trained in ballet and tap, alto-soprano, boyish figure. As she stretched out on her bed, and read through the open auditions in *Backstage Magazine*, Jackie thought the part of Frankie Adams, a precocious twelve-year-old tomboy, and her passage to adolescence in a Southern town during World War II in *Member of the Wedding —The Musical* was perfect. For her. The story was based on the novel by Carson McCullers. The original Broadway production had starred Julie Harris. Lyricist and composer, Julie and Richard Mosher, favorably compared to Richard Rogers and Oscar Hammerstein, would complete the libretto and musical numbers by that summer.

Jackie examined her profile in the full-length mirror in her father's bedroom. Mature? Absolutely. Dance trained. Her voice the proper range. Boyish figure? She was thin with short dirty blonde hair. "No tits, not yet," she said out loud. "That part is mine."

Charlie Engle said she was a little youngish for the lead, but once the producers started their nationwide search on the West Coast, it could take up to a year until they started auditions in New York. "Maybe more," he said. "Jackie should be in the running." He advised Teddy and his talent daughter to "sit tight."

It was too much too soon at her age, her father said, what with steady rehearsals and the pressure of auditioning; and if she were chosen, the stress of performances six nights a week, and two matinees. Jackie crossed her heart and hoped to die, she could do her school work with her State Education tutor, and keep up with rehearsals.

Over the fall, accompanied by Grandma Fanny, Jackie was hired to deliver lines in a TV toothpaste commercial, sing in a chorus for an Off-Broadway musical, and do a walk-on at a West Side dinner theatre. She never missed a lesson, kept up with her school work, and still had plenty of time to audition for the lead in the McCullers Broadway production.

Meanwhile, Charlie Engle worked behind the scenes to convince the Moshers that Jackie should try out at the first New York City audition on November 25th, one month after her eighth birthday. But Jackie had already dug through the Yellow Pages for the phone number of the Drama Book Shop in lower Manhattan and asked her father to order the *Member of the Wedding* script. Once it arrived, as she was taught in her acting class, she analyzed similarities between herself and Frankie Adams, the role she needed to inhabit.

Frankie felt as disconnected from her world as Jackie did when the kids in Pittsmill made fun of her for having an absent mother. Frankie's mother who died in childbirth was reminiscent of her mother Leena who she rarely saw and most of the time didn't want to. Frankie loved her brother, who was about to be taken from her in marriage, just as Bayla was taken from her for something she still didn't understand but was determined she would one day find out.

Jackie perfected a Southern drawl with her acting teacher, and got to work memorizing Frankie's lines, but for the first time in her life she realized how little control she had to make happen what she desperately wanted to have happen.

Fearful and panicked, she began to do things that she believed would help. She learned much later on that the things she was doing had a special name —obsessive compulsive —and since she kept what she was doing a secret, her family had no idea that she needed to be saved from what became, for her, a new way to be.

Her Grandma Fanny was the first to notice certain of these new things about Jackie when they sat together in the plush red velvet orchestra seats inside the Ziegfeld Theatre on Seventh Avenue and 54th Street, waiting with at least 100 other girls to audition.

"What are you doing with your hands?" Fanny asked. She meant how Jackie placed each fingertip precisely on one hand to the corresponding fingertip on the other hand, and pressed them together so hard her fingers turned a bright bluish-red. Then she'd released them, shake her hands out, and repeat the process again and again.

"It brings me luck," Jackie said, and although she had already witnessed girls who couldn't act, forgot lines, had awful voices, were too old, too large or too way wrong for the part, she repeated that activity with her hands because it boosted her confidence.

"Does it work?"

"Always."

"Okay, if you believe it," Fanny said," who's to say it doesn't?"

"No more talking, Grandma. I have to concentrate."

When her name was called, Jackie walked down the red-carpeted aisle and up the stage steps. She performed one song and followed it up with one of Frankie's monologues. At the cordial "thank you's" from the producers, the music director, and the choreographer, she nodded, smiled and returned decisively to her seat, terribly out of breath but absolutely certain no one could tell. That's how well she controlled herself.

She was certain that the buzzing in her head and the whirring in her stomach, which she had never experienced after an audition, were signs that she had made it to the next round. But to play it safe, before she went to bed, and every morning after she opened her eyes, she preceded with several rounds of her hands-to-fingers good luck configurations. After three weeks the call came for a second audition to be held end of December at a rehearsal studio near Lincoln Center. She made it through that and was gearing herself up for the third and final audition.

Two weeks later, Richard Mosher told Charlie Engle that the final audition for the lead was set for January 10, 1974. They had narrowed it down to Jackie, and a 14-year-old from Oregon, who had stage experience.

"I need Bayla," Jackie commanded her father. "She's the only one who can teach me what I need to know to win this."

"Your grandmother is still in the hospital. We have no idea if she's capable of doing anything on her own. It's not like a movie where you buy a ticket and when the show's over you leave."

"Call her, Dad. Please. I know she'll want to do this for me." One call and her father would know if Bayla were normal, the way she used to be, the way she had to be to teach Jackie. "She's already been gone almost three months. Maybe she's all done with what she had to do to get out of there. Please, Dad. Only adults can call. Please. It's my life."

"Jackie, I know she'll want to coach you but she's been through an ordeal. She needs time to recoup. Your grandfather was planning to take her to Florida for a vacation."

"If she gets out by the end of December, she can rest in Florida and then come here. It will all work out. You'll see."

It was the start of a new year, January, 1974. A sign of good luck. New beginnings.

Jackie imagined her grandmother's arrival: Bayla would fly to New York. Her father would pick her up at La Guardia Airport and after a one-hour drive they would arrive in Westchester. She had done it, gotten her grandmother to come here. The coaching she would receive would be the start of her dream: To be a star.

In the solace of her room, surrounded by silence and the freedom to do as she pleased, Jackie proceeded to do what guaranteed her peace of mind:

She smoothed out the daisy border on her top bed sheet, aligned her two daisy pillows upright against her white iron headboard, and placed her stuffed wooly lamb equidistant between them, smoothing folds, straightening corners, forbidding a wrinkle.

At her desk she sharpened three pencils, lined them up according to size, a pink pad to their right, angled slightly because she was left-handed.

In her closet she made sure that her blouses, sweaters, skirts, and pants were arranged in categories, then in size places according to how they hung when suspended from their pink satin hangers which all faced the same direction.

On her knees, she aligned the white cotton fringe on both sides of the rug so that it lay uniformly, then she adjusted the bedspread so it was equidistant to the floor all the way around.

She refolded the bathroom towels into thirds because her father had folded them in half and she didn't consider that perfection.

She fluffed the drapes until each fell exactly into place, and pulled the window shades halfway down to create a uniform appearance from the street, the view her grandmother would see when she arrived.

When she closed the door to her room, she knocked lightly on it three times, the way she always did when she entered. Now everything would work out exactly as she wanted it.

Her grandmother always told her she knew how to make things happen.

JANUARY 1974

Chapter Thirty-Seven

Teachers

"Me a teacher!" Bayla exclaimed. To think that she could she teach anybody anything when she was only beginning to learn about herself, who she was; no, who she had become, now that she considered herself remade.

After being a patient in a psychiatric hospital for three months, then two weeks of sun and warmth in St. Augustine, Teddy's call felt like an invasion. It was a rainy Florida lunch time, and Izzy, who had assumed the role of chef while Bayla was away, had just prepared a nutritious salad of greens with a side of bagels and cream cheese. He handed her the phone.

"You've no idea what I've been through," Bayla said fingers at her mouth as if to prevent what would come out because she was uncertain how to respond to her son-in-law. "Medication. Pills. Liquids Shock treatments that made me forget. Are my mother's curses are on or off? I still don't know. She would curse me in Hungarian and Yiddish, languages that flew out of my head, just like that, but for the first time in my life my spirit belongs to me. I'm free in here." She placed her hand over her heart as if Teddy could see. "And I'm not controlled by how my daughter lives her life. That's something, isn't it?"

She didn't need or want her son-in-law's sympathy. She thought her mind was in the best working order it had ever been, but she still wondered if she was making sense. She didn't doubt that Jackie was the culprit behind the call so her father could assess her grandmother's state of mind.

Izzy, as usual, encouraged his wife. Their granddaughter deserved a chance at winning the lead in a Broadway production. Who better than she could accomplish such a thing? "You can do it, my dear. I know you. Your spirits, your energy, you've got plenty to go around. I'll be fine here. You know I've fallen in love with golf."

"But the hospital, my room, the people I've left behind, and Dr. Abrams. It's all so fresh in my mind."

"There's something you need to know." The doctor's remarks replayed inside her head like an LP. "The closer our patients come to leaving here, the more they teach us. Patients have an inherent motivation to be healthy. When they arrive, it's basically unavailable, buried, hidden inside them. It takes time for them to get in touch with it, if ever, but you already have. Everything you've learned and absorbed here, you'll take with you."

Despite Izzzy's pep talk, and Dr. Abrams' confidence, Bayla continued to doubt the progress he claimed she had made. Her fears and guilt, the fates, her distorted childhood beliefs, everything that had taken months to dig out of wherever she had hidden those feelings, and stories, and memories and misperceptions. What if she made the journey and her anxieties, all of that, reasserted themselves? What then?

"Challenges, frustrations, tempers distilled into about ten days for a theatrical competition will be good for you. You don't have to go if you don't want to." Dr. Abrams always gave her choices.

"That child has inherited my musical genes," she reminded him.

"So you've told me," he had said. "Perfection in treatment is not as important as gaining insight into your life, using your talent, managing your will to no one's satisfaction but your own."

Bayla considered the audacity of such a thought — as if it were something she actually deserved. She a teacher! A teacher was someone who could get a person to live her dreams, if such a thing were possible.

Days later, she made up her mind. Her husband's confidence had buoyed her determination. She would make the trip alone because what would Izzy do in the midst of what she imagined would be concentrated work over long days and nights?

"I've decided to enter what the staff in Greensburg Hospital refers to as 'the real world,'" she told him.

"A good place to be," Izzy said with a kiss and a warm embrace.

When she spotted Teddy, his arms outstretched, the uncommonness of hugging her son-in-law in the midst of a crowded airport made her laugh out loud.

"I know, I know," she said. "I look wonderful."

"You do. You look better than ever. Tanned and rested."

When they were settled in his car, heading North to Westchester, her promise to Dr. Abrams involving the truth about her part in Leena's marriage to Teddy pecked at her resolve. Given the weight of that secret, the effort to withhold it, while there was so much that she had already shed, she knew it was time to confess.

"I'm so glad to have courted you all those years ago. Why are you laughing?"

"You courting me? Is that how you think it worked?"

"It's the truth. Time you knew."

"I find that interesting, you bringing up the topic of truth."

"Why? Have you been keeping secrets?"

"No, no, but for the longest time, I've held onto something, I guess I'd call it unfinished between us. If I'm overstepping your tolerance —"

"Teddy, my dear son-in-law, these past four months have prepared me for anything. Whatever you want to say, my tolerance knows no bounds."

"Well," he said hesitantly, "two women falling in love wasn't an easy thing for me. I had no answers for how long my wife knew she was .... that way. Why did she marry me, make everyone believe she was someone she wasn't, and me always after her, trying to fix what I never knew existed? I wanted to ask you, but I couldn't.

Maybe I didn't try hard enough. Then this last Passover, I took Jackie to my parents and during the Seder, something happened."

"So tell me."

"The portion from the Haggudah that my father asked me to read was about how men can be enslaved by poverty and inequality. *"When the work men do enriches others, but leaves them in want of strong houses for shelter, nourishing food for themselves and for their children, and warm clothes to keep out the cold, they're slaves."* I've read those words countless times over the years, but this time they reached me in a way they never did. They made me realize that everything I enjoyed about marriage made Leena feel captive. Marriage curtailed her freedom, and for me, fighting to make our marriage work, I felt boundaries everywhere I turned. Myrna, a woman, was my wife's freedom. Leena chose her, and in the process, I was granted freedom from myself for not realizing what she couldn't admit to me."

"And I'm telling you, I have to accept blame. I pushed the two of you together."

"No. No. Leena took the ring. She wanted the wedding. We were intimate."

"Teddy," Bayla lowered her voice. "I knew what you didn't. I was obsessed with making her," she paused, "what I considered 'normal.'"

There was a long silence. Teddy spoke first.

"I always believed if there was something Leena hid about herself, sooner or later you would find out. I thought the two of you were in cahoots hiding what I didn't know."

"I'm sorry. I'm so sorry. I never would have done anything to hurt you or Jackie."

"I know that, but I had to tell you my side, to hear your response. Whatever price Jackie and I are paying for my marriage not working, or for whatever part you did or didn't play, everything is on the way to being healed. And now you're back in our lives."

"You're here. You're here. It's really you."

Jackie flew out the front door of the two-story wood and stone townhouse that cold January afternoon. Dressed in a brown puffy winter coat, Bayla stepped laughingly into her granddaughter's outstretched arms beneath an overcast sky and streets dotted with bare-limbed trees.

"This way, this way," Jackie commanded Bayla into the house for a 'this-is-the-kitchen-this-is-the-dining room – these-are-the-bedrooms tour.' "You unpack. I'll come get you in ten minutes."

Left alone in the guest room of a strange house, Bayla glanced around her. In the full-length mirror on the closet door, she appeared stark and out of place. "Who's gonna know you're pregnant? Get up on that stage and sing." Milhady had said. *But instead of honoring her with the success she knew I could achieve, I handed my teacher defeat.* "I made my teacher fail," Bayla said aloud, "and in so doing, I failed. Now there's only me to prevent the same with Jackie."

Jackie's final audition required one song of her choosing, and one from the show. Bayla suggested "Nothing Can Stop Me Now" from *The Roar of the Greasepaint, The Smell of the Crowd* which proved Jackie's range, her sense of timing, and "The Me of You is Getting Married" from the show. It expressed how Frankie imagined she'd feel at her brother's wedding while she played cards and drank lemonade with her six-year-old cousin, John Henry, and their Black housekeeper, Berenice Sadie Brown. Bayla knew this intricate, syncopated number was the key to winning the audition. She knew too that harmonies of voice and feelings, not played or acted, but felt and sensed, as if Jackie alone had lived them, would get her the part. The family room fitted with a music stand, ballet bar, an upright Spinet, LP collection, and a record player, "arranged by me," Jackie explained.

Jackie remembered her lines and interpreted Frankie Adams using a variety of motivations. Her portrayal was accurate, but too self-conscious.

"Breathe. In from the pubis, up through the diaphragm. Fill your body, exhale the stale air. Good, now again."

Twice Jackie forgot the lyrics. Her monologue was pretentious, awkward. She was playing a part, instead of embodying it. Her disappointment with the child reminded Bayla of her own failings during those early weeks as a psychiatric patient when her singing voice faltered, even at a hum. When she breathed into a note, it stuck, refusing to release. Air displaced phrases. She had hidden so much inside herself, secrets, fears, confessions, all ganged up on her, stifling her voice. Her will.

To build on the healthiest parts of her personality, Dr. Abrams agreed to let her work with Mr. Schoenfeld, the music director.

"We'll start with major and minor scales," Mr. Schoenfeld had said. Acappella, arpeggio, soto voce, vibrato, a language she once spoke. Twice a week, at half hour sessions, she began to once again experience the joy of expressing herself through her talent. She loved the music therapy room, her stance upon the wood floor, surrounded by walls that echoed her voice, her focus beyond two tall rectangular windows that looked into a lush forest. As a teacher, she was back there. Again.

"Think of your motivation," Bayla instructed. "Are you listening to yourself? What's your face doing? What's happening on stage? Wear those words like they're your life. Are you nervous with me here?"

"No, I want you here. I'm trying to do what you're telling me but it's no good." Jackie glared at the pages on the music stand. They had been at it all day and it was already past ten o'clock. "I want to know about the hospital? You didn't have to go."

"Is that where you're stuck? Is that what's blocking you?" Bayla paused. She took a long deep breath. "I did have to go, Jackie. When I arrived, I thought I was in a sleep-away school with classrooms and a student cafeteria and teachers, and study sessions. I promised Dr Abrams, my psychiatrist, to be a good student."

"You were in a hospital and you thought it was a school? You were pretty far gone, Grandma."

"Yes, I was. I always loved school, but I had to leave to work.

That was a long time ago so enough. Now it's bedtime."

They slogged up the stairs, and went their separate ways. The next morning, they continued as if night had never intruded.

"Feel the music. Sustain that sound. Don't embellish. Now let it go with control." They took breaks. They stretched. They focused on breathing. They role-played.

Teddy occasionally walked past the open door, curious about Bayla's teachings and his daughter's progress. Strange sounds filled the house—elocution exercises; atonal repetition of scales, monotonous recitations of the alphabet. Jackie remembered her lines and interpreted Frankie Adams using a variety of motivations, but her portrayal was still self-conscious.

"Grandma, why don't you just tell me what's wrong? We only have five days left. I know you know. Think!" Jackie tapped her forehead with her index finger.

"That is fresh and disrespectful. I know you've grown up since I saw you last, and maybe I'm not as good at this as I should be, but you may not speak to me that way."

Bayla turned her back, ready to flee from this room to a safer, more familiar one papered with a delicate pattern of daisies on an off-white background, her room in the hospital. Mentally ill grandmother seeks to resurrect her squandered talent to coach granddaughter to success sounded like cheap radio soap opera.

This entire escapade was misguided. Reentering the real world with unstructured, unsupervised—dare she say it —freedom? Nothing was how it should be. All her granddaughter yearned for was the smallest clue that would release the prodigious talent meant to make her shine.

What was Bayla holding back? She thought she was done with all that.

Acccch. Accch. Ch.Ch. Ch. Rurrh. Rurrh. Gu. Gu. Gu. Grrrr. Grrrr. Argh. Argh. Uneven growls, deep, gritty, and muffled, interspersed with breathy, guttural, voiceless fragments, sounds that would make someone flee before aiding a creature in such desperate straits. Staff on Bayla's floor knew the sounds oozed from her throat as she tried to free herself from fingers that gripped tighter around her neck, forbidding her any chance to breathe, narrowing her voice, plugging her airways.

No need to lie awake, waiting for the sky to brighten beyond the rows of wire hexagons, forty-eight horizontal, fifty vertical, buried inside her window's double panes that protected her from the outside world, the place that led her to Greensburg Hospital. Afraid to close her eyes to forces that brought cold sweats, the white cotton blanket, issued to all patients, twisted, as if by itself, into a thick rope around her neck from nightmares that left her shaken, and filled with fear as she tried to free herself from fingers that gripped tighter around her throat, forbidding her voice and any chance to breathe. The more she struggled, the more the fingers plugged her airways.

How much longer would it take to rid herself of shapeless fears and imaginary enemies lurking in darkness to strike her unawares?

She would untangle the blanket, put on a dry nightgown, gather the bed sheet, wet and clammy from her fruitless nighttime treachery, create a pile on the floor.

Back in bed, with no sirens, no nurses shouting emergency, no doctors scurrying, no medication carts careening along polished linoleum floors, she recalled a small child asleep on a cot beside her mother's bed in a tight room in a city tenement.

Who came to that child's aid, calming her fears of being without food and proper clothes, of not finding work or knowing the right things to say, of walking alone on city streets, a child unfamiliar with an understanding nod, a kind word, a child who waited in silence for imaginary rescuers? Never her mother who filled the child with Old Country superstitions about fates who controlled their lives as if such teachings were substitutes for love and care.

"She taught me to be afraid so I left her alone."

How that daughter tormented her mother, coming home from work to prepare a measly dinner, only to leave again to perform, making her mother's nights more dreaded and senseless than her days. That voice, still critical and threatening, forbidding happiness born of her mother's rage over her pathetic life.

"She hated me for being my father's favorite, so I put her away."

Unable to face what she knew, she ignored her husband's behavior behind a closed door, allowing him to steal a child's' innocence, forcing himself in silence and darkness, as if she were a woman instead of rescuing the child who was victim to it. And if the child failed him, she was the guilty one worthy of nothing more than her mother's scorn and curses.

"She left me no choice, so I killed her."

Her palms tight around the icy bar of the wheelchair, the rickety-rick of the wheels over ruts, the staff marching towards them from that decrepit, run-down place where her mother ended her life. And who was in charge? *Me. Only me. I was in charge. Who else? A child guilty of her mother's demise.*

"Mother. Mother. Mother." Bayla's voice was painful and gripping. "You were as frightened as I was. Both of us desperate for love and comfort. Unfamiliar with words of need and care, we didn't know how to ask. We built walls around us. We built walls between us. We turned our backs. We blamed one another. Guilty, both of us, for wanting to survive.

"Forgive me for putting you out of my life, so I could have a life. Forgive me for not easing your fears, for never holding you so you could sleep in peace, for understanding too late that you could have ended your days with me at Amory Lane so that I might have had a mother who came when I cried for help.

"And Leena, my own dear child. What have I done?"

When Bayla awoke to morning light through the clear glass windows in the guest room, inside her head the words were already waiting.

"Rely on the truth," Dr. Abrams always said, "if and when it surfaces."

"With the entire day ahead of us, I just remembered something wonderful. I'll tell you if you'll listen."

"I'll listen. I'll listen."

"You don't have a clean slate."

"What? What are you talking about? " Overnight her grandma had lost part of her mind.

"Emotions. Anger. Jealousy. Hurts. They need to be released, so you can use them in your performance. Until you find the truth in here," Bayla tapped Jackie's middle, "what comes out will be mediocre. Bad acting at worst."

A long silence followed.

"How did you do it when you were 19?"

"I was voluptuous and sexy," Bayla smiled. "Men were crazy for me."

"I don't even need a bra." Jackie flung her shoulders back emphasizing her flat chest.

Bayla laughed. "My voice teacher told me it's not about your body, or what you wear —"

"You had a voice teacher?"

"Yes. She's the one who taught me about a clean slate. She was …." Bayla's voice softened. "She was a famous blues singer who lived in the poor section of town. Milhady was her name. I had to sneak out of the house for lessons. If they found out —my mother-in-law, Charlotte, Uncle Solomon, even Grandpa Izzy —I'd be in big trouble. I wanted to surprise them with my debut."

"You told me you never had a debut."

"I never did, but Milhady taught me that I could recreate anywhere the inspiration she brought me—in the Nutmeg, or here, in your home."

Bayla reached out and embraced her granddaughter. "Jackie, so much is happening for you. To get this part, you have to let go of some things, make room so your talent will take you where you want it to go. I have a feeling your mother —"

"She's not a part of my life." Jackie backed out of Bayla's embrace. "You told me you would listen."

"My mother's a creep. I only call her and visit cause Dad says we have to. She left us, and we have to rehearse! You're here for a reason and it's not this." Jackie stomped one foot on the floor.

"When you were little, I'd say that you're going to accomplish what others say they will, but don't, and you would ask why."

"And you would say because life gets in their way, but that's not going to happen to me. I'm going to be a success."

"That's right. If you get this role, can you forgive your mother?"

"Why should I? She doesn't care about me."

"I had a mother who I also thought was mean to me," Bayla began slowly, as if she were reading a story. "She crossed the ocean, fourteen days, sick to her stomach, to come to America to make a good life. Her second child died of tuberculosis. Her husband ran off, and she was bound to a wheelchair, worked at home, sewing hats for pennies. I had to leave school. Support us."

"You never told me, Grandma."

"I'm telling you now. We can complain forever about who did this or that to us, or why we never got what we wanted because things didn't turn out right. But complaining doesn't change a thing. So you get angry, so angry you let go of your hope and dreams."

"Not me. I want to be famous."

"Then believe you can get there, no matter who did or said what. No matter if you didn't get treated the way you wanted to. You can't control your mother's life, but you are in charge of your own. Make peace with her. Write to her. Tell her if you get the part, you'd like her to come see you perform."

Jackie grabbed the sheet of writing paper out of Bayla's hand. "I'll do it because I want to be the star."

"Good, and when you get the part, and you will, and when you perform on that Broadway stage, everyone in the audience will know you're Frankie Adams."

Two grandmothers, former combatants, sat side-by-side on one of the wooden benches in a hallway outside a rehearsal studio at the Shubert Theatre, West 45th Street. Drawn by their love, and devotion to their uniquely talented granddaughter they admired, amused and complimented her without question, determined to get her through this final challenge for a Broadway debut.

Jackie's audition lasted sixteen minutes, ten seconds. Fanny timed it. The three of them left without a word. Bayla warned it was bad luck to mention it.

Fanny stayed on pins and needles. Grandpa Max prayed, his tallis around his shoulders, a yarmulke on his head. In Westchester, Jackie delved into school work, Teddy completed an important business presentation, Bayla cooked wonderful meals.

Three weeks later, Grandpa Max came home one afternoon for a client's file when the phone rang. He wrote down the message, leaned it against the sugar bowl on the kitchen table, stabilized by an empty glass: MR. ENGLE CALLED. TEDDY COULDN'T BE REACHED. JACKIE GOT THE PART!

"I did it, I did it. I did it," Jackie screamed over the rush of congratulations that night when the family gathered at Teddy's invitation for the official announcement.

"Your Grandmother Bayla helped," Fanny said. "Give credit where credit is due."

Jackie ran to Bayla and reached up for a hug. "You helped, Grandma, you helped a lot, but I went out there and did everything I needed to do, and did it just right."

"It's true. I helped, but you won the role. No one can take that from you."

Alone in the quiet of the room, the one she was soon to depart from, flushed from her coaching triumph, Bayla felt strangely bereft, empty, useless unconnected to anything she had imparted as a teacher. She spent the night awakened by familiar pangs of anxiety. Where was *her* career, the one she had yearned for, the one she was determined to have from the time she was a child?

"One more chance, that's all I ask," she whispered into the darkness as if it were a prayer, as if she were being heard.

"Looks like you're working up to something," Bayla remembered saying to Dr. Abrams as she released her grip on the sides of her chair wondering if she could escape what she knew was coming.

"Will there be times when you struggle with life on its own terms? Of course, but that's true for everyone. The big difference is you are now prepared." He gave Bayla one of his penetrating looks.

"And my singing?" she asked ruefully.

"Give yourself permission. It's what you've always wanted."

When Bayla walked out of Greensburg Psychiatric Center after three months at 59 years old, she left behind her ruinous childhood, fears born there, guilt that accompanied them, and misconceptions harbored for years. She left the seamstress with a useless life, the deceiving wife, the unfit mother. She left doctors and therapists who helped her, people who got well, and those who never would.

She took with her forgiveness for those who hurt her, insight into her parents' behavior towards one another, especially towards herself, the realization that she was worthy, and the freedom to cherish Roseamond free of shame. She felt blessed for having cared for others, been cared for by them, thankful for family, and for her husband's love.

APRIL 1974

Chapter Thirty-Eight

Opening Night

With Jackie's round-the-clock rehearsals and barely three months before an April 20th opening for *Member of the Wedding—the Musical*, Teddy rented a room at the Parker Meridian Hotel in the theatre district so Grandmothers Fanny and Bayla could alternate staying with the future star. Grandpa Izzy and Uncle Solomon waited at Amory until opening night.

"*Fiddler on the Roof*, with Mostel, *Chicago*, Bob Fosse's triumph. *The Wiz, Godspell, Chorus Line*, heavy competition, but if you get good reviews, your show could make it." In the hotel room with its double bed, dresser, and window onto Shubert Alley, Bayla read to Jackie from the latest *Variety*.

"Grandma, you're not helping. With three days left, I can't remember Act One, Scene One, center stage, what's my first line? Nothing. Blank. I can't do it. Why did I think I could? I've wanted this my whole life, but I'm a wreck."

"Come with me. We're going out."

"Grandma, it's one a.m."

Manhattan's theatre district transcended the boundaries of time. Wide-eyed tourists, homeless people searching for empty doorways, and neighborhood regulars bumped shoulders under bright marquees with well-known actors and newbies, subjected to all night rehearsals while theatre-goers meandered in and out of the Algonquin Hotel, Lindy's Restaurant, and night clubs open until early morning packed with cabaret performers and die-hard fans.

In an open-all-night coffee shop on Eighth Avenue, an anxious, fatigued, very sleepy Jackie admired her Grandmother Bayla who quite determinedly at this ungodly hour pointed a finger at a booth in the back. They eased into it, side-by-side, and through cherry pie a la mode and vanilla egg creams, Bayla spoke determinedly to an almost nine-year-old Jackie who listened mesmerized.

"Every word and move, every musical note and stage marking, they're all in your head. When you're on stage, it's all going to flow like water. And when you begin your first number, sing it for me like there's no one else around. Sing as if it's a gift, because that's what it will be. The greatest gift of my life."

Making her way through the crowds under the marquee, the packed lobby, lines at the "will call" window, Jackie walked beyond the stage door to the dressing room with the star on the door. Backstage conversation, the buzz of the audience, a C-major piano chord, the strings, the winds, the brass tuning up was all as it should be. Costumed, her makeup perfect, the five-minute bell sounded.

"Places, everyone. Places," the stage manager announced.

"Come on, child. Who are you looking so hard for?" It was the middle-aged Black actress who played Berenice Sadie Brown, the housekeeper.

"No one special," Jackie said as she peered at the audience from behind the maroon velvet proscenium curtain. "It doesn't matter. Okay, let's break some legs."

With the right amount of seriousness and a touch of comedy, the last line of the play, spoken by Frankie, had to encompass the character's growth from childhood insouciance to a mature acceptance of the circumstances that had altered her life. Jackie had practiced it repeatedly with Bayla—"Mary and I will most likely pass through

Luxembourg when we decide to travel around the world together."

The curtain started down. The audience that had applauded politely after the overture and again when the first act curtain went up, broke loose. There were five curtain calls for the leads—Frankie, Berenice, and little Jarvis—three more for the director, musical conductor and composers.

Not one missed line. Perfect pitch. Great chemistry between the leads. The laughter, applause, standing ovation, everything she had hoped for.

"Wonderful show, Ms. Goldman." The director stuck his head inside her dressing room and dashed off. Another knock. "Special delivery. Miss Goldman."

Jackie placed the dozen red roses beside one of the vases on the makeup counter sprawling with foundation, eye shadows, facial sponges, powders, lipsticks, colored pencils. Rather than read the card, she was replaying fantasies: With an exquisite bouquet in one hand, her mother would embrace her the only way a loving mother can. "You were terrific. You amazed me. I've missed you."

She stared into the mirrored wall ringed with light bulbs. At the clothes rack along the wall, she evened out the costumes on their hangars. She sat in one of the makeup chairs and tissued off her makeup, but after revising the ending yet again—Leena would apologize for running off with Myrna, promise to leave Vermont and come home to her family —her mother still hadn't shown up. Though Jackie told Bayla she wouldn't forgive her, she did, in secret when she mailed the handwritten invitation before the final audition. Fanny, Max, Teddy and Grandpa Izzy dashed in for hugs and kisses. Friends and well-wishers had piled up outside the door. Bayla, in conversation with the director, would walk in any minute. Another knock.

"Come in," she said, more nervous than at the opening curtain.

Leena was dressed in gray tweed pants, a gray turtleneck sweater, and a dark brown jacket. There were no flowers.

"I got your invitation. Thought I'd surprise you. So," Leena said in what Jackie remembered was her mother's off-handed way, "how does it feel to be famous?"

"Okay," Jackie said uncertain what answer her mother would consider correct.

"Okay? That's it? That's all you can say?"

Jackie shrugged at the admonishment. "Grandma says I'll be here for a while, if the reviews are good."

"The reviews will be wonderful. I was very proud watching from out there."

"Proud? Of me?"

"I don't know another mother who can brag that her almost nine-year-old daughter is a Broadway star."

Leena tossed her jacket on the couch, plopped down in a makeup chair. "Come. Sit." She patted the chair next to her. Jackie moved cautiously toward her mother.

"What happened to your monthly visits to us?"

"I had rehearsals. Do you have any idea how hard I had to work to get this part?"

The door opened and Bayla rushed in.

"Look at these lilies. Magnificent. From the producers, for you, because you're the star!"

"Grandma!" Jackie ran to Bayla and hugged her with such exuberance several petals scattered.

"I can't take you anywhere." Bayla laughed. Then she saw her. "Leena," she said softly. Leena held on to the makeup counter with both hands as if to brace herself. "I see you have a visitor," Bayla said to the child still snuggled into her grandmother's middle.

Feeling confident with the addition of a personal protector, Jackie eased away from Bayla and swaggered past her mother. Bayla gently set the flowers down. With her arms outstretched, she turned to Leena.

"How about a hug?"

"Won't a hello do?"

Bayla lowered her arms to her sides. "I can accept that."

Jackie put her head in her hands and moaned at her mother's refusal. Her grandmother remained calm, a slight smile about her lips at Leena's somewhat shocked expression.

"I don't need to be center stage anymore," Bayla said. "We're all important. We all count. Right?" She turned to Jackie for confirmation.

"I count the most because I've got the lead."

Bayla placed one hand under Jackie's chin and raised her head so that their eyes locked. "I'd like to have your mother to myself for a few minutes. You get dressed."

Jackie inhaled the stale scent of makeup from age-old theatre productions, a frivolous, almost corny backdrop to the intensity in the room. She moseyed to the clothes rack for her street clothes, pants and a loose blouse, similar to what Frankie wore on stage.

"Might as well sit," Bayla said. She eased into the makeup chair beside Leena. "How's Vermont?"

"Why do you ask? You want to show me a better way? Your way?"

"A parent is never as powerful as a child believes," Bayla said softly. "Did you ever think through the years that you've given me too much power?"

"I never gave you power. You took it."

"You're right, but I've learned to relinquish it. Now you take it. Do what you want with it, and don't let anyone have that kind of power over you again."

Leena tugged at her turtleneck as if it was restricting her breathing. "You're kidding, right? All this reasonableness. Is this really you? I can't tell anymore."

"You want to have a life with Myrna? I have no intention to pry."

"Myrna is an ugly name," Jackie interrupted. "I've always wanted to tell you that."

"Thanks." Leena stood up and reached for her jacket.

"She's a child, Leena." Bayla gently placed her hand on Leena's arm. "She misses her mother."

"I don't miss her!" Jackie shouted.

"Your mother misses you, too," Bayla said to Jackie.

"Still speaking for me?" Leena said. "At least I raised my child with the freedom to do what she wants. When she's ready to see me, she will."

Jackie walked up to her mother, hands on her hips, dressed in her street clothes. "Once you met Myrna, you were never home. You left me and Dad."

"What is this? A set-up?" Leena's eyes darted from Bayla to Jackie. "You have your father and two grandmothers, and a grandfather, and you still feel abandoned. There's no way you two are going to let me win, is there? Why did I drive all the way down here?"

"Wait, Leena." Bayla reached out but seeing Leena's expression, she withdrew. "I want to apologize for not letting you be yourself. For what I did knowingly or unknowingly, for what you would have wanted me to do but didn't. You, me, Jackie, we can all win. As a family."

Jackie sat down on the couch. Leena waited before she spoke.

"I appreciate that," she said.

"Good, and who knows? I may still be somebody, one day."

"They taught you to believe in fairy tales when you were away?"

"Fairy tales aren't just for a child." Jackie interrupted. She swung her backpack in her mother's direction with a lip-smacking grin.

"Besides being a star, is that also your job too? So protective of your grandma. She can take care of herself."

"Jackie, please," Bayla said. "And Leena, give me another minute."

Leena sat beside Bayla again.

"Are you happy?"

"What's not to be happy? I'm loved. I have someone who cares for me. I know who I am, and it's all wrapped up in a beautiful setting."

"I'm glad, I'm not attached to the outcome anymore."

"Thanks for your permission. I never had your ambition, Mother. I never cared about being noticed. I only wanted to get by."

"I know that. I suppose I always did."

"I want to be noticed," Jackie shouted. "I want to be noticed by the whole world."

"I'm sure you will be," Leena said relieved the focus had shifted from her mother's new self. "You're talented and you're special."

Jackie grinned. She pumped her fist in the air.

"There's one thing, Leena, if I may," Bayla said. "You once told me that I brought you and Teddy together for my benefit, to look good. I would have done anything to protect you, to keep you from, well, a difficult life."

"The way you pushed me to be with him. You barely knew anything about me."

"I knew."

Leena searched her mother's face. Bayla stared back.

"Teddy's a good father. You found a good man. He's figured it all out. He's okay."

"I don't know what to say. I'm overwhelmed."

"Live your life, Leena. Live it beautifully for all those who never had the choices you have and remember you have a mother. Call me sometime."

Jackie sidled up to her mother and held out her jacket. "Here, Mom."

"What service." Leena took the jacket, then turned to Bayla. "Dad and Solomon?"

"Two grey-haired old guy buddies. As for Amory Lane," Bayla smiled. "Pittsmill's Women's Historical Society designated it as a 19th century historical site."

"Grandmother Charlotte would have been thrilled."

"Yes. One Sunday a month we open the house to visitors. People line up along the walkway, welcomed by tour guides. Seeing it for the first time as I did, a new bride, the marble entranceway, paintings in gold frames, palm trees in terra-cotta pots, Victorian furnishings, our family photographs. People know: this house has seen life. Your father and I are considering moving to New York, where we first met."

"Really. Well, that sound exciting. And Uncle Solomon?"

Bayla laughed. "He's in all his glory. He's usurped the role of royalty. Your father and I, we let him. During the tour days, he answers the personal questions. He loves embellishing. Need I say more?"

"All these changes in you. And tour guides at Amory Lane."

"It's all planned, Leena, that's what I think. Everything that has happened was supposed to, even the tough parts."

The dressing room door suddenly swung open. "Frankie Adams?" It was the young boy who played Jarvis. "It's opening night party time. Come on. We're waiting."

"Frankie is coming," Leena said, "and I'm going." Leena gave Jackie a hug.

"Grandma, say good-bye to your only child," Jackie instructed.

"Good-bye, my only child," Bayla said.

"Move, move," Jackie pushed through the crowd outside her dressing room to catch a glimpse of Leena before she disappeared down the hallway that led to Seventh Avenue where she would be greeted by theatre marquees—the mother of a Broadway star. That night Jackie walked out of her dressing room forgetting to knock lightly three times the way she always did whenever she closed a door so that when she returned she would feel safe behind it.

APRIL 20 – JUNE, 1974

Chapter Thirty-Nine

With the Band

The best of Broadway were jammed into Rosoff's 1899 theatre restaurant on West 43rd Street: groups of singers around the baby grand, solo dancers or couples improvising across the parquet floor, up and coming newbies dazzled by the spontaneity, all of them, Izzy and Solomon, Teddy, Fanny and Max, who took off early from work to arrive "when the curtain goes up, not down," Fannie had warned, anxiously awaiting the reviews of *Member of the Wedding—the Musical*.

Maybe it was her blue silk suit, her auburn hair pulled back in a French knot, gold hoop earrings and choker, or maybe it was the crowd's infectious spontaneity or perhaps there was no reason whatsoever for why Jackie turned and said, "Sing something, Grandma."

Bayla couldn't grasp what Jackie was saying.

"Go on. Sing."

If this was Jackie's idea of a game, Bayla didn't want to play.

"Sing something, Grandma," someone beside Jackie repeated.

"Jackie, I'm not prepared. These are professionals. I'll make a fool of myself."

"Sing something! Grandma!" others coaxed, smirking and laughing as if the attractive, mature woman's singing would be so much camp.

"No. Not here. I can't."

"Sing. Something. Grandma." More joined in, clapping in unison, each beat louder, as if at a sporting event.

"Grandma," Jackie yelled, "take my hand."

As Bayla's large, sturdy fingers gripped the hand of a child who had just captivated a Broadway audience, something inside her gave way. Or perhaps it wasn't her, but someone she used to know, long forgotten, someone who willingly followed her granddaughter through a crowd of people laughing, applauding, making room for the odd couple, a tall mature woman and a child, every part of her beaming, as they headed toward the dance floor.

The lights dimmed. Everything quieted down.

"Now what?" Bayla asked as a few ceiling spots turned the red leather upholstered top of the baby grand to raspberry syrup.

"Sing as if it's a gift, because that's what it will be," Jackie replied. "The greatest gift of my life." She lifted the microphone off its stand. "This is my grandma," she said. "Miss B," and she handed it to Bayla.

If she glanced into their faces, would eye contact warm her tones or tighten her throat? Would they be welcoming or unforgiving, Bayla wondered, as she bent slightly and whispered to the attractive young man at the piano.

At the bluesy syncopated introduction, she took one long, steady breath displacing all that she was, all that she knew except for herself, a performer.

Oh listen sister, I love my mister man and I can't tell you why
There ain't no reason, that I should love that man.
It must be something that the angels done plan.
Fish gotta swim, birds gotta fly, I gotta love one man till I die
Can't help loving that man of mine.

When it was over, and she was no longer Julie from *Showboat*, her style, the colors in her voice, her polished phrasing—the talent none of them expected—whistles and bravos soared above applause.

With her gaze turned upward, her lips barely moving, "Thank you," Bayla said.

They clamored for her to sing it again. The third time everyone joined in until one of the stage hands, his arms filled with a stack of newspapers, burst into the scene.

"Reviews. Reviews." A few shouts, some screams, then a roar. *Member of the Wedding—The Musical* was a hit.

"I like what you did up there. You're no newcomer." He was a stocky, middle-aged man, handsomely dressed, with stylishly long graying hair. His Brooklyn accent made her smile. "Your voice, the way you handle your audience. You can't fool me. Ever sing with a band?"

"No. I ...."

"How about you put some material together. Blues, pop, swing, jazz, whatever ya like. Even Lady Day sang Gershwin. I'd like to hear you with my buddy Frank Borelli. What do ya say?"

"Tell me where and when," she said, wondering if she had actually said those words.

He pulled out a small notebook from his breast and ready with a pen, she offered her phone number. "I'll call ya." He slapped his card into her hand, and disappeared.

Robert Della Fiore. Theatrical Promoter. Bayla threw her head back and laughed. Mario, the butcher, who kept the family in sirloin no grizzle, veal roasts tied crossways during the war, he had recommended Della Fiore way back when. If her escapade at Rossoff's turned into "This Could Be the Start of Something Big," like Steve Allen's song predicted, why did it feel so stagey? Almost planned?

She would have to remain at Teddy's for the next few days practicing fifteen, twenty minute sets while Izzy drove home with Solomon. How long should she wait for Della Fiore? What was reasonable? She hoped it wouldn't be long. If she was as good as he said, he would call her within two weeks. Her mother would have said it was up to the fates, but no whims of fate would ever again pilfer her happiness. He called three days later.

"Be at 531 Broadway and 48th Street, 11 a.m. next Wednesday. It's a rehearsal studio from Tin Pan Alley days."

Borelli's band evoked Glenn Miller's sound, Louis Armstrong's beat and Artie Shaw's creamy sway. The guitarist knew Delta blues.

They rehearsed with an arranger for the next two months, some blues, swing, up beat rhythms and ballads to build an act.

At the end of June, the start of New York's tourist season, Mr. Della Fiore handed Bayla a six-month contract. "New York will be jammed with tourists. They'll pack the clubs. All those faces expecting you to be fabulous. Aw, come on, don't get teary on me."

She needed a moment to step out of herself, not in the way she'd done when she was ill, but to savor the phenomenon—New York audiences. Herself on stage. The spotlight. The banter. The musicians. The life where she belonged. Was it possible?

He billed her as "Miss B," the name Jackie used to introduce her at the cast party. Her show was *Sweets and Blues for Lovers*. The venue Friday night was Eddie Condon's, an intimate dinner theatre on West 54th Street. And yet, when the time came, she hesitated. She considered not appearing. The change in her life would be too dramatic. Was she up for it? The work, the appearances, the pressure to be her best, to become the blues singer who people would come and pay money to see. Performing on stage in a club in New York City. Fiori's public relations person had achieved a sell-out weeks before the opening. All those people expecting her to be fabulous.

Everything she had or hadn't done in her life had brought her to this. As the edges of her dream moved close enough for her to step into it, time became more of a gift, less of a dare she had to win. She was relaxed, confident and blessed to have the luxury to consider only herself. She told her family they would have to wait for the next performance. She would arrive alone, a seasoned professional carrying her hard-won independence with a modesty that would belie the years it took for her to achieve it. Izzy didn't even blink. It had all come to pass, his wife's gift to herself. She had earned it.

Poised under a single spotlight on a modest semi-circular stage, leaning slightly on a wooden stool in front of a burgundy curtain, she was dressed in a long-sleeved silk turquoise blouse draped over a slightly flared black velvet skirt, her hair waved softly around her face, pearl drop earrings, and a 32-inch pearl necklace on her still enticing bosom. The audience murmured their approval as she reached for the microphone.

"I've waited for this my entire life," she said as if she were intimately connected to each person in the audience. "This is for you."

> Embrace me, my sweet embraceable you, embrace me, you irreplaceable you. Just one look at you, my heart goes tipsy in me.
>
> You and you alone bring out the gypsy in me.

Her rich soulful tones drifted across the room, caressing the crowd like cigarette smoke. With a chuckle, a tear, sultry or modest, taunting or anguished, her performance was about making dreams come true, and wanting; she never learned how, she just always did.

After three months, the booking agent requested her for Reno Sweeney, New York City famous cabaret revival, its walls covered with photos of Barbara Cook, Odetta, Jane Olivor, Patti Smith, Cab Calloway, Peter Allen and Karen Akers.

One Saturday night, after 1:30 a.m., her last set over, her fans drifting out the door, "Miss Rothschild?" It was barely a whisper. Who would know her real name at Reno's? Two people stepped into the light.

"Travis? And Christine." That terrible night. Milhady frantic. Her son beaten up; his girlfriend, a young white woman. Seeing her emotions well up, to give her a moment, Travis spoke first: "We came tonight for your performance, but mostly to let you know you saved our lives. Risking what you did back then —"

"Happily married, I see. Your mother wrote to me a while back. Your boys?"

"Nineteen and 14. I'm with the *New York Times*. Assistant press supervisor."

"And I'm at Mount Sinai, earned my nursing degree. New York has been good to us."

"We're only as good as what we do to make the world a better place, if you call Reno's the real world." She laughed. "I studied with your mother only three months and look where it got me. Is she...?"

"Passed a year ago. Peacefully," Travis said. "She was forever telling me to check the papers. She read the reviews. She knew you'd be famous."

Like a shift in rhythm or a drop in an octave, the burden of living the rest of her life without her teacher knowing what she had achieved had vanished. Bayla would share the rest of her dream with the person who showed her the way.

Summer 1975

Pesky, demanding and unforgiving, one street in Manhattan refused to let her be. It made her feel as if something had been left undone, a coat without sleeves.

"We're here," Izzy announced. "Two-thirty-six East Eighty-Ninth Street.

"Are demons at the door?"

"Come on, you may be surprised."

"Surprise is what I'm dreading." She was breathless, hesitant. Shaky. Out of place and out of step. Izzy had never seen her like that.

Early that morning she and Izzy had left their three-bedroom apartment in a pre-World War II brick and stone Tudor building in the same suburban town where Teddy and Jackie lived. They drove down the Major Deegan, across the Third Avenue Bridge, along the East Side Highway.

"Security. We can't get in," Bayla said more relieved than disappointed at the buzzer on the front door except it suddenly swung open revealing a young woman with a baby in a stroller.

Izzy helped lower the stroller down the cement stoop while Bayla peeked inside. The floor was the same, black and white tiles, but the walls were peach. A brass chandelier replaced a naked light bulb, and an elevator offered a slow, creaky ride to third floor.

"There's two apartments where five used to be, and no bathroom down the hall. Renovated, like my life."

Bayla stepped haltingly to where the door to her apartment probably would have been. She reached out and leaned against the wall as if to encompass in her arms pieces of her past.

"What do you think, Mamma? I've come back to ask forgiveness for leaving you all those nights, for putting you in that place, for not doing enough. I'm here so you can forgive me."

The slow whine of the elevator door sliding open from its trip to the third floor was her reply. An elderly woman with a Gristedes supermarket bag inside a shopping cart stepped into the hallway and gazed at the two strangers.

"Excuse me. Pardon me. I don't want to disturb, but if you don't mind, I must ask, young woman.... Excuse me, but you remind me. Are you, maybe you're Bayeleh?"

"My name is Bayla. Do you know me?"

"You're Lillian Szabo's child. I'm Rakel Silverman from across the hall."

"Mrs. Silverman! I never thought.... How are you?"

"How am I? I'm already eighty-one, eight years younger than your dear mother. *Guttenu.* So many years." From her coat pocket she withdrew a tissue, wiped her tears.

Bayla gave her a gentle hug. "This is my husband."

"Hello young man, and thanks be to God on a day I thought would never come. I tried to find you. But no one knew where you went. And now, a miracle. Months ago, a letter came from some institution, but with a different name on the mail box, it sat on the radiator. Someone opened the envelope and left it, so I knew about your mother. I'm so sorry."

A letter of her mother's passing lying for who knew how long on the hallway radiator?

"If you don't mind," Mrs. Silverman glanced respectfully at Izzy. "Can I speak with your wife. I've waited so long."

"Go ahead. Take your time. I'll go to Zabars. Pick up a few things. Meet you out front." Bayla raised her eyebrows indicating she had no other choice.

"I live in a palace now. Two apartments from five. The rent from forty to eighty-five a month." She focused on her key until the lock gave way. "Come in. You'll have some ruggeluch, a cup of tea.

Your mother loved ruggelach. I used to sneak her a few from the Hungarian bakery down the street. She didn't want you to know. Ah, what your mother didn't want you to know. She liked secrets, your mother."

While Mrs. Silverman made her preparations, Bayla glimpsed the heavy tapestries and cut velvets in faded browns, golds and greens inside the living-room-dining room, the bronze clock on the dark wood mantel, lace curtains and tasseled tie backs that allowed light from 89th Street. Such a contrast to the dim, bare-bones rooms where she and her mother had lived.

At a small round table draped with a worn ivory-colored cloth embroidered with leaves and vines, Mrs. Silverman took a few sips of tea and with a steady hand returned her cup to the saucer. "You know your mother had a sweet tooth?"

"When I had a few pennies, I'd buy her a Hershey's chocolate."

"She told me."

"She did?" Bayla was surprised at her mother's praise for a candy bar.

"And why not? A child good to a mother is something to be proud." With slow moving fingers, she gathered into a small pile scattered ruggelach crumbs. "So you'll listen to what I have to say on a day I thought would never come?"

"Yes, of course." Bayla tried not to laugh imagining how she would describe to Izzy whatever mystery would follow.

"I loved the Yiddish theatre," Mrs. Silverman began. "The Windsor. Kessler's. On Second Avenue. My husband would watch our two boys on a Saturday, give me money for a matinee. I'd wait at the stage door for Molly Picon. Joseph Adler. Fannie Bryce. There was one singer, a good actress, not always the star, I took her autograph, so she gave my name to the backstage man, told him to let me in after *The Century Girl*, with Marie Dressler.

"In the dressing room with chorus girls, next to her is an infant in a bassinet. The girls adored the child, took turns caring for it, but it wasn't right. You understand. She had to go on the road with the show, asked if I'd take the child for a few weeks. What did it matter another in our home? So I did. When she returned, she had an offer for a silent movie. In California. Now she wants for me to keep the child."

Mrs. Silverman sipped her tea, and reached for another ruggeluch. Bayla wondered why she was her telling this story and in such detail.

"Did you know, your mother, when she was a young girl had trouble conceiving, and married already three years. And the chorus girl pleading if I knew someone. I told your mother. A six-month-old girl. 'Bring her to me,' she said."

"I don't understand."

"I'm here to tell you, that child…" Mrs. Silverman lowered her voice, and looked directly into Bayla's face before she spoke again. "I'm saying that child was you."

The story was made up, an old woman's fading memory.

"Everyone in the tenements knew your business, and my mother wasn't pregnant."

"Darling girl, she never wanted you to know. You were hers just like that. The child she couldn't have. It was summertime, July. You know, you were born January 10th. We wore such loose dresses then. And when I saw you today in the hallway…. You were brought here for this." She exhaled what seemed to Bayla an exceedingly long-held burden.

"But my sister?"

"Once your mother had you, she conceived. These things happen. Who knows why? Catch your breath. Finish the cake. Have another sip of tea. You must have questions. Ask. Ask."

Bayla's checks felt hot, her face bright red.

"My mother, my real mother was a performer? An actress and singer?"

"A fine singer. Bayeleh, it wasn't so unusual then, what the girl did. She had a chance for a life, a career. She did the best what she knew how."

"What about her family? Who were they? Where were they from?"

"Like the rest of us, in those days there wasn't enough money for family so she came alone from Poland. She sent money back for more to arrive, but the Great War came. She spoke good English. Her town was Nowy Sacz, beautiful mountain country."

Bayla had returned to the tenements to ask her mother for forgiveness, not to listen to stories that threatened her existence, turned her into someone she no longer knew.

"The baby's father? What did she tell you about him?"

"He was one of her lovers. With chorus girls, Back Stage Johnnies they called them, always waiting after a show. It was a romance."

"What was she like?"

"At nineteen or twenty, she could pick and choose what to sample from life like Hungarian pastries in Moisha's Deli. When she knew you would be cared for, she went to California. She wrote, asked about her baby, did some silent movies, sang on a record."

A life Bayla had never known had been laid before her over a worn embroidered tablecloth. How to find her place within a secret, unspoken for 60 years? The sound of traffic along 89th Street deepened — automobile horns, the scream of an ambulance tearing across town.

"I could never explain where my singing voice came from."

"Now you know. Maybe you'll come on a Shabbat mornings to Tikvah Shalom on East 91st Street where your mother used to take you. Sing for the congregation." Mrs. Silverman swallowed the last drop of tea. "Your real mother, I saw how she loved you. I don't want you to think different. She had to give life to the talent she was born with, and to have two mothers who loved you, it's not so bad."

Bayla rode the elevator to the ground floor, and held on to the glass-enclosed wrought iron door so it wouldn't slam the way it used to. How much of what Mrs. Silverman had explained was a gift? How much a curse? After more than a year of taking apart the person she thought she knew, and rebuilding herself one clear memory at a time, it all had to be retrofitted. Was it something of a miracle to discover the person she called 'Mamma' had chosen her without question to love and cherish? And her real mother, with no ties, close family, or husband and so young, to have given up her child was neither shameful or reckless, but courageous for having summoned the strength and determination to live the life she wanted. Though Bayla pondered the same when she was pregnant, it took her forty years beyond her birth mother's twenty to initiate her own career, a need, so powerful in her mother, it persevered until it reached the child she gave away.

The gray skies had cleared and the warmth of the sun felt welcoming on her face. Izzy looked up from his newspaper and stepped out of the car.

From across the street a young man called out.

"Miss B. Miss B. See you next Friday at Reno's."

Music critics praised Miss B's unique mix of mother earth and divine inspiration, her nuanced moods and ethereal tones, as well as her finessed ballads, and deeply-felt blues that reflected the grace of her inheritance.

Acknowledgments

When Mrs. Rosenberg, who taught the Creative Writing class in Christopher Columbus High School in the Bronx, admitted me to her sophomore class, I was convinced I would be a writer. Of course, when I was five years old, and I gave me mother my first and last science fiction story, I had already decided that writing would be my profession.

On the way to achieving that goal, I have many people to thank. The most long-standing, from The Writer's Center, Bethesda, is Barbara Esstman, my editor, her books made into TV films, who punched back when I needed her to, and never gave up even when I did. Bill O'Sullivan, who instinctively knows what needs to be on the page and what doesn't, opened for me the world of essays. Extremely helpful were developmental editors Wendy Besel Hahn, Christine Koubek, Ross Feeler, and Melissa Scholes Young, teacher, editor and fierce promoter of women writers through her Grace and Gravity series, founded by Richard Peabody.

I especially wish to thank the extraordinary community of women writers in the DC, MD and VA areas brought together by prodigious writer Mary Kay Zuravlev, who gave my novel its head start; early readers Cherie Jacobs, Morgan Brown and the group from the Writer's Center who have continued to work together: Kay Drew, Kate Lemery, Robin Tricoles, Celia Wexler, Mary Ann Roberts, Dina Adler, and those who left us too soon, Sydney Frymire, Yvonne Brown, Myrna Seidman and the distinguished and forever encouraging Dr. Joel Breman.

I am grateful for Sheilah Kaufman, esteemed cookbook writer, for introducing me to The National Press Club where I was able to present on the public stage some of today's most exciting writers, for friends from the Iowa Writer's Center, the Women's National Book Association, especially Sarah Birnbach, for Susan Coll, Politics and Prose, and the Maryland Writer's Association.

Forever ready to read and offer wise critiques throughout the years, my loving husband, Bill Halpern, selflessly devoted himself to my work.

I am especially grateful to publishers Kelly Huddleston, and David Ross, for selecting this book as one of their prestigious Open-Books offerings, and I remain most appreciative for Kelly's patience and diligence as my first editor.

And to my family, thank you for always believing.

www.ingramcontent.com/pod-product-compliance
Lightning Source LLC
LaVergne TN
LVHW041107080826
845145LV00007B/1717